Ms. Patricia A. Berkey
10481 Prouty Rd.
Painesville, OH 44077-2204

 Ms. Patricia A. Berkey
10481 Prouty Rd.
Painesville, OH 44077-2204

continued . . .

"Jodi Thomas is a masterful storyteller. She grabs your attention on the first page, captures your heart, and then makes you sad when it is time to bid her wonderful characters farewell."

—Catherine Anderson

"Fantastic . . . A keeper! . . . A beautiful story about unexpected love. An exceptional storyteller, Thomas has found the perfect venue for her talent, which is as big—and as awe-inspiring—as Texas. Her emotionally moving stories are the kind you want to go on forever." **—RT Book Reviews**

"Jodi Thomas's Whispering Mountain Series is the perfect blend of rough and tumble cowboys, and women who command their respect and love. . . . I am ready to saddle up and take a ride!"
—Coffee Time Romance

"A fun read." **—Fresh Fiction**

Titles by Jodi Thomas

CAN'T STOP BELIEVING
CHANCE OF A LIFETIME
JUST DOWN THE ROAD
THE COMFORTS OF HOME
SOMEWHERE ALONG THE WAY
WELCOME TO HARMONY
REWRITING MONDAY
TWISTED CREEK

***

PROMISE ME TEXAS
WILD TEXAS ROSE
TEXAS BLUE
THE LONE TEXAN
TALL, DARK, AND TEXAN
TEXAS PRINCESS
TEXAS RAIN
THE TEXAN'S REWARD
A TEXAN'S LUCK
WHEN A TEXAN GAMBLES
THE TEXAN'S WAGER
TO WED IN TEXAS

TO KISS A TEXAN
THE TENDER TEXAN
PRAIRIE SONG
THE TEXAN AND THE LADY
TO TAME A TEXAN'S HEART
FOREVER IN TEXAS
TEXAS LOVE SONG
TWO TEXAS HEARTS
THE TEXAN'S TOUCH
TWILIGHT IN TEXAS
THE TEXAN'S DREAM

Specials

EASY ON THE HEART
HEART ON HIS SLEEVE
IN A HEARTBEAT
A HUSBAND FOR HOLLY

$\mathcal{P}$ROMISE $\mathcal{M}$E TEXAS

JODI THOMAS

**Doubleday Large Print
Home Library Edition**

BERKLEY BOOKS, NEW YORK

THE BERKLEY PUBLISHING GROUP
Published by the Penguin Group
Penguin Group (USA) LLC
375 Hudson Street, New York, New York 10014

USA • Canada • UK • Ireland • Australia • New Zealand • India • South Africa • China

A Penguin Random House Company

PROMISE ME TEXAS

A Berkley Book / published by arrangement with the author

ISBN: 978-1-62490-980-1

CHAPTER 1

January 1879
North Texas

THE MIDNIGHT TRAIN RATTLED THROUGH WINter's darkness, ignoring the howling January wind. Sliding low on the dusty last passenger bench, Beth McMurray tried to control her breathing. Anger and fear blended in her blood, freezing any movement. Evil traveled with her tonight, an evil she'd been about to marry.

"One harebrained scheme too many." She almost said her old housekeeper's warning aloud. "One too many and you'll be trapped, Bethie, and there will be no one to get you out of the trouble you go running toward."

The old woman had been right.

Only now wasn't the time for regrets: Beth had to think. She had to plan. But first, she needed to make herself as invisible as possible to the men at the other end of the passenger car. Her future depended on it. In her black slouch hat and weathered rain duster, she'd hoped to pass for a man sleeping his way to Dallas. If no one came too near, or looked too closely, she might get away with it.

Her plan had seemed simple when she'd read Lamont's telegram asking her to sneak away from the ranch and meet him for a secret wedding in Dallas before they went to Whispering Mountain for a big wedding in the spring.

The getting away proved no problem. Everyone on the ranch was busy. Beth simply left a note saying she was meeting Lamont and friends in Dallas for a week. She explained that she was taking Brandy Blue, her favorite horse, so she and her fiancé, Senator Lamont LaCroix, and his friends could ride back home with her for a winter visit on a Texas ranch. At twenty-four, no one would question her or expect her to do anything improper.

One of the old Texas Rangers who'd retired on the ranch offered to ride along with her for a while.

Only, a harebrained idea worked its way into her mind as she packed. She thought it would be fun to ride northeast and meet Lamont's train at the station stop before Dallas. Then, as they traveled together toward their secret wedding, they would have time to talk about their future.

But from the journey's beginning, not all went smoothly. She hadn't fooled the conductor when she'd boarded at the train's last stop before reaching Dallas. He'd known she was a woman even in her trousers and slicker. When she'd handed him her ticket, she explained and he agreed to go along with her plan to surprise her bridegroom, who she said was on the train.

The train was moving by the time she found Lamont surrounded by army officers. Beth had decided to sit back and listen for a while. In a way, she got her wish; she learned a great deal about Lamont as the train traveled through the night. Only, it was all bad. She'd promised herself to a fool.

Four hours ago she'd expected to be planning her wedding tonight, but not now.

As she stared at the tall man drinking at the other end of the car, Beth wondered why she'd ever thought of him as handsome. From a distance, he looked striking in his tailored black suit and gray wool coat. She could almost see him coffin-boxed and her wearing black instead of the white dress she'd carried with her to change into.

Lamont LaCroix, the man she'd fallen in love with when she was seventeen and wide-eyed, was holding court in the middle of a half dozen young army officers. Since sunset she'd learned more than she ever wanted to know about her fiancé. More than he'd told her in the twenty letters he'd written over the past seven years. She'd learned that he was worse than the carpetbaggers who'd invaded Texas after the war. The northern accent she'd barely noticed when they'd met now grated on her nerves.

At first, his letters had been friendly, as though keeping his young acquaintance up on Washington politics. As the years passed, he talked of his dreams of power and she encouraged him. Two years ago he spoke of needing her, of wanting her by his side. She hadn't bothered to think of all he didn't say. He'd fooled her completely, reeling her in.

No, she corrected. She'd fallen for his lies because she wanted them to be true. She'd wanted to be the important wife of a senator, to live in Washington, D.C., all winter and go to parties. Now, listening to him brag, Beth knew that she was an idiot. No man in Texas had ever measured up to this congressman and his letters. She'd wanted him to be real so desperately that she hadn't even heeded her father's warning. She'd jumped when she should have hesitated.

The rattle of the train couldn't block out Lamont's voice as he bragged that "the McMurray woman," as he called her, would fatten his bank account and warm his bed. She heard him tell the men around him that it was all he could do to keep from bedding her when he'd met her all those years ago in Washington. She was ripe and ready, he'd laughed. It would have been easy enough, he'd claimed, but he realized she was a gold mine. If he handled her correctly, he'd control not only her body, but her mind as well as her wealth.

When one of the young men drinking with him suggested the senator keep her pregnant to ensure control, Lamont had bragged that he'd allow her one child, maybe two, and then see that there were no other pregnancies. "I want her by my side, not home raising brats. Wait till you see her. She may be dumb as a stump, but she's built tall and beautiful with ginger-colored hair that hangs in curls past her waist. The perfect woman to stand with me all the way to the White House."

Beth bit her bottom lip until she tasted blood. If she hadn't caught an earlier train to meet her groom-to-be, she never would have seen him like this until it was too late. Now she saw the truth and mourned her dream. Lamont had lost his reelection, but with a McMurray on his arm, he thought he'd take the seat from Texas without any trouble.

"I've got two years to meet all the right people," he said. "Then once I'm elected, I'll never have to return to the state."

She slowly raised her head just enough to see him. His words were starting to slur and he'd opened his coat, revealing extra pounds around his middle that hadn't been there years ago. His brown hair and eyes made him handsome, but she saw flaws now. Frown lines marked his forehead, and silver at his temples showed the signs of aging. She knew he was more than fifteen years older than she was. It hadn't mattered before tonight, but now she saw middle age weighting his shoulders. He wasn't a young man, and by the time she bore and raised his children, she'd be nursing an old man.

Rain tapped on the windows and one of the lanterns blinked out, throwing the back of the car into shadow. Beth didn't care. At the next stop, she'd rush off this train and vanish. No one would look for her. No one knew she was here except the conductor who'd punched her ticket. From the sound of the storm brewing outside, he'd have more to worry about than one passenger riding away on the horse she'd loaded onboard.

Part of her wished she were brave enough to confront Lamont. He'd lied to her. He'd stolen years of her life as she'd waited for him. Part of her wanted to run to the front of the car and knock his bloated head off. Then instead of being almost a bride, she'd be almost a widow, which sounded far better to her right now.

The rain pounded harder and lightning flashed, pulling Beth from her anger and making her think. It would not be wise to confront Lamont here. The train would arrive before dawn in Dallas. No one would be there to meet her. She'd be alone with Lamont.

The men up front were now telling stories of her family and how spoiled they'd heard the youngest daughter of Teagan McMurray was. Everyone commented that any man lucky enough to meet her bragged of her beauty and her wealth, but none said anything about her character. **Spoiled, temperamental, headstrong** were words tossed around about her.

"Great beauty does that to a woman," Lamont shouted above the storm. "She'll need a strong hand to keep her in line. With her in Washington, D.C., and all her family in Texas, I'll have no problem. Women are like children; they need the hand of discipline lowered frequently. That's one of the reasons I want to meet her in Dallas. We'll get a few things straight from the beginning."

The others laughed, but their laughter didn't ring true. Beth wondered if they weren't simply playing along with Lamont. If so, they were far more dangerous to him than to her. She studied them closely and noticed the way they glanced at one another when Lamont wasn't looking. The army officers weren't Lamont's friends and the drunk didn't even know it.

Beth waited for her chance to escape the car. Even if the next stop was for water or wood, she'd climb off and ride in the car with her horse before she'd spend another moment with the senator and the men who were baiting him.

They talked of the tricks they'd played on people and the women they'd slept with. Two of the men even got in a playful fight when they both claimed to have slept with the same socialite in the capital. None of the soldiers drank as much as Lamont did, and all fell silent when he shared something he'd gotten away with in Washington. They were digging his political grave, and Lamont was handing them the shovels.

Finally, the train began to slow. She saw the single lantern swinging beside the water tank. Salvation awaited.

With her head low, Beth slipped from the car and melted into the rain on the dark side of the train. She had to feel her way back to the first freight car. Her horse was the only animal inside the car. Much as she wanted to pull Brandy Blue off the train and ride open land, it was too dangerous in the mud and storm. In a few hours they'd be at a proper platform in Dallas and she'd have a road to follow at daylight.

Rain soaked all the way to her skin by the time she slipped into Brandy Blue's makeshift stall. She stood beside him, patting his neck, whispering to keep him calm. He was restless, but she couldn't help telling him how much better company he was than what she'd left behind. She'd grown up around horses at Whispering Mountain Ranch. She couldn't remember not being able to ride. The McMurray horses were the best in the state and like family to all the clan.

Beth checked her saddlebags, thankful she'd worn trousers. Pulling her gun belt and Colt from the leather, she strapped them around her waist. Another lesson her papa had insisted on. When a McMurray travels alone, he or she always travels armed. If anyone did see her ride away at the platform, they'd think she was a man.

She'd be out of Dallas and heading home by full light.

Pulling a small towel from her bag, she wiped her face, thinking of all the names Lamont had called her over the last few hours. **Headstrong, beautiful, spoiled, simple.** She grinned. He'd left out one. **Determined.** She wasn't a girl anymore, but a strong woman. Her papa had raised his daughters to be independent. It was time she took charge of her life and stopped waiting for a husband.

Nothing would keep her in the same town with him. She'd wait until Lamont and the army officers left the station, and then she'd saddle up and ride. As long as she headed south, she knew she'd be going home. She wanted no one seeing her in the same town with her almost-husband. In fact, she never planned to see him again for as long as she lived. As soon as she got home, she'd burn his letters and marry the first man who asked her before the ashes were cold. Any man, anywhere, would be better than the braggart she'd seen in the passenger car.

Beth set her mind. If no one asked her again, she'd never marry. Being alone had to be better than being with the wrong person. Her papa had made sure she had her own money, so she didn't need Lamont.

She patted Brandy Blue. "Let's go home, boy. I need to ride the hills of Whispering Mountain and forget what a fool I've been." Smiling, she wondered if her wish and the horse's weren't the same, as he didn't like the train, or the night, or the storm.

Between the drafty slats, she saw men climbing onto the back of the train as it pulled away from the circle of lantern light. Not passengers, she thought; invaders. They moved like rats in the dark, slipping in between the cars and crawling up ladders to the roof.

One broad-shouldered man in a long, black leather coat tried to pull another off the step, but the first jerked away and climbed aboard. They seemed to be arguing about something, but she couldn't hear their words. A moment later the man in black reluctantly followed. The flash of a red bandanna tied around his throat seemed somehow out of place in the night.

Holding her breath, Beth realized that they had to be robbers. They'd probably stop the train miles from anywhere and rob, or maybe kill, everyone. She'd seen an army guard loading something in the mail car that looked like a strongbox. It must be a huge payroll, or gold, to be worth the risk of a midnight robbery. The officers with Lamont could be part of the guard, but they'd been drinking, thinking themselves safe tonight.

Beth pulled her senses about her like a cloak. Her survival depended on her being totally aware of everything and everyone around her. She'd grown up on a ranch when Texas was wild. She had to be ready to run or to fight. Without taking her eyes off the entrance to the car, she checked the gun belt around her waist.

She had to warn the others on the train. But how? Even if she could cross between the cars to the mail car, they wouldn't let her in. The door was bolted solid. Behind her, only cattle cars followed. No one would hear a shot in the storm, and she didn't know if she was strong enough to hang on if she tried to cross over the top of the mail car.

In the last flash of light from the water tower's lantern, she saw the broad-shouldered man in black take a few steps up to the roof of the mail car. He and his friend had made it over the freight car's roof without her even hearing them. He pulled on the arm of what seemed the younger of the two robbers as if trying to pull him down but was ignored. He tried once more to draw the other man back against a course already set. The younger one shook his head and jerked away, vanishing into the night.

She thought she heard the one left behind yell, "Ryan, no!" but his cry was lost in the wind.

The one called Ryan would be moving to the engine, she reasoned. He'd stop the train at gunpoint, and then the others would move from car to car, robbing and killing anyone who tried to stop them.

As the train picked up speed, Beth noticed several horses being held by a shadow rider fifty yards from the track. They looked half-wild and in poor condition, except for a pinto with front stockings that almost bolted from the others, giving the handler fits. The horses finally galloped in the same direction as the train. They wouldn't be able to keep up for long, but all they had to do was follow the tracks to find where the robbers had stopped the train.

Holding Brandy Blue's neck, Beth tried to think of what to do. She closed her eyes, remembering who she'd seen on the train when she'd walked through looking for Lamont. Three passenger coaches. The first had four or five salesmen with their wares and a couple of gamblers passing the time with card tricks.

The second coach held families. One couple with a tiny baby. Another with two boys small enough to use a bench as a bed. She thought there was a third couple, but she couldn't remember how many children. Sprawled near the doors, cowhands slept, probably heading to Dallas to work the trains going east.

The third car housed Lamont and the army officers.

Assuming all the men were armed, the passengers outnumbered the robbers, but the bandits had surprise on their side.

They might never make it to her. Surely even the drunk soldiers around Lamont would fight. But if the robbers made it to the mail car and broke in, one of the gang was bound to notice her position. Any light would show her outline next to the horse.

The old conductor had complained that this run wasn't making any money hauling folks or stock, so they had to be after whatever was in the strongbox.

Beth moved, feeling her way in the darkness. She checked the railing against her horse. She wanted him boxed in if the train came to a quick stop. She'd known even as a child that the horses had to be taken care of first. Her father was a powerful rancher who'd never raised his voice to his daughters, but one lift of his eyebrow would send all three back into the barn to finish brushing down their mounts or make sure they'd stored everything correctly. Now, his attention to detail might save her life.

The train was traveling slower than usual because of the storm. Even without robbers onboard, they were all in danger. She might be able to jump and roll free from the train at this speed, but she couldn't risk Brandy Blue and she wouldn't leave him. Lamont had wanted them to ride back to her ranch together after they'd married and spent a few days in Dallas. As soon as he got to know her family better, he'd hinted that they might settle in Austin.

She knew now that he ultimately meant to take her away from Texas. Away from her home. Away from all she'd ever known and loved.

Closing her eyes, Beth fought down fear. Lamont and his men were right. She was an idiot. If the robbers thought she was a man, they'd probably shoot her on sight. If they discovered she was a woman traveling alone or that her last name was Mc-Murray, they might hold her for ransom, or worse.

Slowly, she straightened. Whatever happened, she wouldn't go down without a fight. Moving to the front of the car, Beth tried to guess how far they were away from town. Halfway. More. It was hard to tell.

Silently, she slipped onto the platform between the cars and struggled to see around the mail car without getting soaked. Knowing the six bandits were somewhere up front, maybe already in the passenger coaches, maybe riding between or above, waiting, made Beth's blood cold.

Carefully, she leaned around the edge one more time, hoping to see the lights of a town. Wind and rain splattered against her face and knocked her hat backward. Beth closed her eyes and smiled, remembering something her papa had told her about facing trouble head-on no matter the storm. He'd said buffalo face the storm, and McMurrays were every bit as stubborn as buffalo.

Just as she pulled back into the blackness, the train seemed to buck in the wind, like a toy being tossed. Brakes squealed in a panicked cry and the cars shook violently.

Beth fought to keep her balance as the train left the tracks. Car after car slammed into one another.

Like the wing of a giant bird, something flew over her, turning the night another layer of midnight as strong arms circled her from behind. A moment later she was airborne, as if flying away from danger.

She heard boards splintering like twigs as whoever held her twisted so that his body hit the ground first. The jar of impact knocked her against the hard wall of his chest. Her scream blended with Brandy Blue's cry. Something hit her head as the man holding her rolled across the rocky ground with her tucked into his arms.

A moment before she blacked out, Beth realized that she wasn't facing a train robbery, but a train wreck. The broad-shouldered man she'd thought she might have to kill may have just saved her life.

CHAPTER 2

THE FIRST HINT OF DAWN TURNED THE EASTERN sky a dusty pink as Beth awoke. Soft rain brushed her cheek, blending with warm blood. The man was still lying next to her, his black leather coat wrapped around them both, but he was no longer holding her. He didn't move.

Stretching, she twisted until she saw his face. A strong unshaven jaw, brown hair, and blood. It poured in tiny rivers from his head and neck. Rain smeared the stranger's blood over his face like a mask.

Tugging her hand free of the coat, she brushed away the hair covering his eyes and saw several cuts. One zigzagged across his forehead and into his hair. Another, just below his eye, pumped blood out with each heartbeat, and another slashed from the corner of his ear to his collarbone. All looked troublesome, maybe deadly.

He'd risked his life for hers, and she had no idea who he was or why he'd done such a brave thing.

The hit to the ground must have knocked him out cold, but she had to push hard to break free. Something primal, beyond thought, made him hold to her.

"I'll get you help," she whispered, even though she knew he couldn't hear her. "I promise, I'll be back. I won't leave you here."

As she stood, she moved the coat over him. It would do little good in the rain, but even wet, the leather would keep away the wind. Brushing her hair back, she felt the thin cut above her ear. The slouch hat was gone and most of her hair had come loose from her braid, but Beth barely noticed as dawn crawled across the clearing, revealing the chaos before her.

Twenty feet away, the stock car had

shattered like a flimsy box being dropped. Two sides lay on the ground and Brandy Blue stood, all four feet planted wide in the buffalo grass. Beth ignored the pain in her limbs as she ran toward her horse. He seemed content to nibble on the grass as she ran her hands along his body.

"Not a scratch," she whispered as she hugged him. "We survived."

He nudged her away as if bothered by her show of affection.

Beth smiled, gave him one last pat, and ran toward the wreckage.

Her car and the two hauling cattle were scattered on one side of the tracks; the others had tumbled on the opposite side. Steam still belched in gray smoke from the engine like dying breaths from a huge beast.

She felt like she was walking through a dream. A misty rain cloaked it all in a foggy reality as if trying to buffer the shock. Bleeding and crying people moved among broken pieces of the train and luggage scattered all around.

The mail car was on its side with army officers circling it. None looked badly hurt. A few had bruises. One stood guard with

his arm in a sling. All seemed to have sobered to their duty.

Lamont was nowhere in sight. She
crossed on through the wreckage, checking on all she passed. Somehow, in one
moment, these strangers had become her
tribe, her people. All, like her, battered but
moving.

One of the gamblers in the front car
was dead. His body lay in a twisted angle
that unbroken bones would not have allowed. Everyone was busy with those still
living, but Beth took a moment to kneel and
close the gambler's eyes. "Go in peace,"
she whispered, almost reading his life in
the wrinkles of his face. He'd survived the
battles of war like most men his age had,
but he'd lost his family or maybe aban-
doned them for the adventure out west.
From his worn boots and tattered suit, she
guessed his life as a gambler hadn't been
easy.

Five feet away, the conductor knelt with
a man who looked like a salesman. They
were working on the other gambler, but
Beth saw death in his stare. They were
wasting their time. The man's flashy silk
vest seemed to be dripping blood.

When the conductor rocked back on his heels in defeat, the salesman began to pray over the dead man.

Without being asked any question, the conductor looked up at Beth and said as calmly as if they were just passing time, "The engineer and two other men are dead, still trapped in the engine's cab. I'll deal with the living first, then get them out. You all right, miss?"

She nodded, trying to take in everything she saw at once. A thin, twisted shadow inside the blackened engine reminded her of the robber who'd insisted on climbing.

The conductor stood, trying to wipe away blood from his hands. "We've telegraphed up the line for help." He shook his head. "I don't understand it. By my count we've got more bodies than passengers. Did you see your man on the train before the wreck?"

She nodded, fighting the urge to tell him that Lamont wasn't her man.

"That's good. The army has accounted for all their people, even the one in the mail car. I think we've got the gamblers and salesmen in the count, but I'm not sure how many cowpokes were on the train sleeping.

Now that I know you and your husband made it, that's two less to worry about."

"I found him." She lied so easily, the words took her breath for a moment. "We were tossed on the other side of the tracks. He's hurt bad."

The conductor nodded. "We'll get to him as soon as we can. This fellow knows a little about medicine." He patted the salesman on the shoulder. "If your man is hurt, we'll make sure he's in the first group to head for town."

The salesman moved on to the next man crying for help while the old conductor leaned back, looking lost. "The extras we got must have boarded the train illegally; I figure that makes them robbers. I asked the station to send a sheriff. We'll let him sort them." He motioned with his head. "Four are over there. They're all hurt bad or already dead like the one trapped in the engine. They must have been caught between the cars or on top. One of the army officers is guarding them while a few passengers try to save them for hanging."

Beth moved toward the engine. In the stillness, she thought she heard horses a hundred yards away in the trees. Standing still, she watched the lone rider pulling saddled horses away. He was leaving his comrades to face their fate. By the time anyone else noticed, he would be too far away to arrest even if they had men on horseback willing to chase. Most of the mounts vanishing into the fog were little more than shadows moving in the trees, but she thought she saw the stocking legs of the pinto she'd seen earlier when the train stopped for water.

Beth crossed to the men scattered near the engine. Every part of her wanted to turn and run. In three minutes she could be back with Brandy Blue and riding. No one would catch her, and no one knew her name to tell the sheriff.

Once he came, she'd have to give all her information, including why she was on the train. The story would make the news. Wild, rich Beth McMurray was acting a fool. Those who knew her would shake their heads. Those who knew Lamont would probably feel sorry for her even if she was a fool. But all would believe any story written about her.

She saw Lamont's gray greatcoat, now splattered with blood, tossed into the burned grass beside the wreck. Lamont was sitting up, trying to stop blood from dripping down his face. He swore and complained to the couple trying to help him.

Beth held her breath as she walked behind him. His cut looked to be no more than a scratch. Lamont would live, but without her. She wanted no part of him, and he was too absorbed in his aches to notice anyone else.

A baby's hungry cry caught her attention as she walked around the couple offering Lamont water. They both looked battered, but alive, unlike the four men lying near a worthless fire someone had tried to build with wet wood.

These were the robbers, she thought, noticing that each still wore a red bandanna. A soldier stood guard, but none looked in any shape to try to escape. Maybe he'd built the fire, but he hadn't offered care. All were too far gone to even cry out for help.

If there was one more in the cab, then the last of the outlaws lay across the track where she'd left him. He'd saved her life. She couldn't let him be hauled into town to hang.

Walking back toward the stranger, Beth found her saddlebags lying amid the rubble. By the time she reached the man in black who'd rescued her, she'd already begun to tear her wedding dress into bandages.

He hadn't budged and she wondered if there were wounds she hadn't noticed. Kneeling, she moved her hands along his body, feeling for the warmth of blood or a broken bone. Nothing. His body was lean and powerful. Strong enough to take the blow when they jumped from the train, she guessed. He was dressed in black except for the bandanna.

Carefully, she began to wrap his forehead, trying to pull the wound together as best as she could.

The cut below his eye still bled, but there was no way to close it without stitches. Beth had seen her aunt stitch men up, but she'd never attempted such a thing. There was always someone else around who knew more or would be better at the task of doctoring.

Removing the red bandanna from her broad-shouldered savior, she tossed it aside and wrapped the silk of her expensive wedding dress around the stranger's throat. She knew little of doctoring. Her simple plan was to slow the bleeding until they could get him to town.

The rain had stopped by the time she'd finished, but the stranger still hadn't moved. He looked pale as if already half gone to the grave. Most of his face was covered with a bandage below his eye, but she saw strong features.

When she straightened to move away, his hand locked around her arm. "Stay with me, Hannah," he whispered. "Lie with me for a while. Don't leave me yet."

His voice was deep, dreamlike, but his hold on her was iron.

Beth knew she should pull away. He'd lost a great deal of blood and she'd done all she could for him.

But she didn't. She owed this man. Who or what he was didn't matter. In the split second before the train crashed, he'd chosen to save her. If he hadn't, she might be smashed between the cars like some of the others.

Edging in beside him, she felt his arm circle her and pull her close. Then he stilled, as if all he'd wanted was her near.

She pulled the coat over them both as

the rain started again. Two days without sleep and the rush of adrenaline from the wreck all worked together. Bethie Mc-Murray, proper young lady and heiress to the McMurray fortune, slept next to a total stranger.

CHAPTER 3

ANDREW MCLAUGHLIN STRUGGLED IN AND OUT of consciousness. If it hadn't been for the pain below his eye, he would have thought he was dreaming or living inside one of the stories he sometimes jotted down in his journal.

A band of robbers. A train wreck. A beautiful lady curled up beside him.

He'd been alone for so long, the nearness of her was well worth the pain. He could feel her breathing as her body rose and fell softly against his side.

"Are you awake?" she whispered.

He felt the brush of her words near his ear but didn't move.

"Yes," he managed. He didn't want to open his eyes and find he'd only been dreaming. He wanted her near so he could memorize how she felt and smelled and moved. One more memory, one more to save.

"Thank you for saving my life."

"You're welcome." He hadn't given it much thought. He'd been leaning on the corner of the platform preparing to jump before the robbery started when she'd almost bumped into him coming out of a freight car. A moment later the accident occurred, and grabbing her had all been instinct.

His confused mind wanted to ask her whether, if he'd saved her, he could keep her, but she'd only think he was out of his head, and she wouldn't be wrong.

"I have to know your name." She nudged him lightly on the shoulder. "They'll ask me."

"Andrew," he answered. "Andrew McLaughlin." He was floating, feeling like his mind might go underwater and disappear any moment. He wasn't sure if he was talking to her or simply hallucinating. "What's your name?"

"Beth McMurray." Laughter filtered through her words. "And, if you've no objection, Andrew, I've told people you and I are engaged."

Hallucinating, he thought, **definitely hallucinating.** She might be a dream, but the pain in his muscles told him the wreck and the fall from a moving train had been real. "I had a friend with me. He may still be on the train."

"I'm sorry, Andrew. I saw the body of the man you climbed on the train with." She touched his chest as if to offer comfort. "He's dead, along with most of the others. Was he a good friend?"

"No," Andrew answered, "but he was the only friend I had left."

Without moving away, she told him of the wreck on the other side of the tracks. He finally looked at her, wondering how long it would be before she left. She had pretty eyes, though, and a voice he could get used to hearing.

Only, she'd leave. Everyone did.

Maybe that was why he'd given her his real name, a name he hadn't used in years. Not that it mattered. No one knew him by any name. He'd changed it so often he wasn't even sure sometimes what had been his family name.

His earliest memory was of his mother dancing with a man as he watched from the stairs. She'd stopped when she saw him and laughed saying, "Andrew, this is your new father. We're changing last names." And so it went throughout his childhood. Every year or so, she'd change names and he was expected to go along. It really didn't matter because the names, like the men, were only temporary. They were always older, sometimes double in years to his mother, and all favored the idea of sending him away to school. So he went, studying first one thing and then another. One insisted on banking, another law, one said he had to be a doctor, and the last wanted him to study languages.

Between husbands his mother always went back to McLaughlin, so when she died, he went back to it as he packed his bag and left one of a long list of houses that weren't home.

"Beth," he said when she finally stopped talking about all she'd seen, "how long have we been engaged?"

"Since we were children, dear. I've always loved you."

He could hear others moving closer, so he played along. "Oh, yes, I remember."

Her hand moved along his arm. "Just rest, Andrew. The doctor from town is here to check your wounds."

Andrew put his fingers over hers. "Don't leave me too soon," he whispered as two men knelt down beside him. One, stout in build, wore a badge. The other, older with hard eyes, carried a black bag. Andrew had no doubt who they were.

"I won't leave," she promised as she moved behind the men.

Andrew felt the cold air where she'd been pressed against him as the doctor turned him on his back in the wet grass.

"He's lost a lot of blood, Harris," the older one said as he checked the bandages Beth had tried to put on. "We need to get him on the wagon fast. I can't do much for these cuts out here. They're deep, but once they're stitched he'll live."

"Look, Doc," the sheriff grumbled. "If he's not wearing a red bandanna, I don't much care one way or the other about him. You save the passengers, I'll round up the gang of train robbers. Only one is still breathing, and he probably won't make the ride home. If I'm right, this is Chesty Peterson's gang out of Waco, or what's left of it. Chesty's too smart to be among the bodies; he always rides in after the shooting's over. He's close, though. I swear I can smell him."

The doctor opened his bag as the sheriff walked away still complaining about train robbers.

Andrew heard the woman called Beth telling the doctor his name and that they were headed to Dallas to marry. He brushed his thumb over the two rings he wore on his left hand. One ring to remind him he'd once known a real love and a smaller one next to it on his little finger so he'd remember to never fall again.

Watching people in his life leave or die was tolerable, but losing a true love wasn't something his heart would take a second time. Even the tall woman who'd curled up beside him was just someone passing through.

He could hear her talking to the doc as men loaded him in the wagon, and then she swung up easily on a powerful blue roan. Andrew couldn't make himself stay awake long enough to know if she was riding along with the wagon. His last thought was that only a crazy woman would pick up an injured stranger and claim him for a fiancé. If she'd seen him and his friend climb onto the train, she must know they were planning to rob it.

When he woke, the day had aged into dusk and she was gone. He didn't even bother to be surprised that he was lying in a hospital bed.

For the first time since the train wreck, his mind seemed to be clear. He opened his eyes, trying to remember what town he might be in. When he and a young man he'd met on the road decided to travel together, they'd never thought they'd have much more than a few boring hours to share.

At the first trading post, Ryan, his new friend, met up with the gang traveling in the same direction. It didn't take Andrew long to figure out that the gang was about to rob a train. They'd been somewhere near the Red River that first day. Too far from any town to worry about Andrew or Ryan turning them in to any law.

Andrew found them interesting, but Ryan was fascinated.

When the leader, a big man named Peterson, asked if they'd like to join the gang, Ryan was all out for adventure. He thought talking to the gang of outlaws was exciting. He was only seventeen and everything was new to him. He'd finished his first cattle drive and had no ties to anyone—he claimed.

Andrew agreed to the company and even played along. He thought Ryan knew he was never seriously considering joining up, but all Ryan saw was an easy way to make fast money.

Andrew thought meeting them might be interesting to write about in his journal. He never dreamed that two days later he'd follow Ryan onto the train. The game turned far too real in that moment.

Now he looked around the small hospital ward made up of a dozen beds. He wished the cowboy he'd met were still with him. Sometimes Andrew had the feeling he was cursed. Anyone standing too close to him wasn't long for this earth.

The ward was empty, except for him and a man bandaged and tied to the bed half the room away. The place looked like it was probably a private ward, which doctors often ran in small towns. Patients were housed here more so the doc wouldn't have to make daily house calls all over the county than to improve patient care. If Andrew were betting, he'd say the doc's office was across the hall and his apartment on the second floor.

After a few minutes, Andrew made out a boy about ten sleeping beyond the open ward door on the hallway floor.

Andrew knew why the boy was there. His job was to clean the place and call the doctor if needed, in exchange for a bed and maybe one meal a day.

He knew the kid's job, because it had been his first employment after he left home. He'd been eighteen and the war had ended. Men were coming home wounded and crippled. Some were half dead from being in prison camps. Andrew had worked in a hospital outside D.C., sleeping in the corner or in a hallway, cleaning up during the day. The smell of that place still lingered in his nose sometimes. The smell of death. But the worst of his memories were the sounds at night.

Men crying in pain, sometimes begging to die. Men without limbs or eyes. Men without anyone to take them home and care for them. In the daytime there would be doctors and nurses, but at night they were given drugs and expected to sleep.

He'd told himself he was lucky. If the war had lasted a few more months he would have been in the fight. He'd heard rebel boys were fighting at fifteen, but his last stepfather had sent him to Europe to study and ordered him not to return until he was of age. Only he'd returned in time to bury his mother a week before the end of the war.

His mother, who always danced, and laughed, and loved men with money, had at least been lucky enough to die at home.

Closing his eyes, Andrew remembered his wife. Hannah had suffered her last days in a Boston hospital. The same smell of death was there also, but he'd ignored it to stay by her side.

As he watched her die, he'd sworn that he would never care enough about anyone in his life to cry again. He'd kept his promise. Though he liked people, no one would ever matter to him. He didn't want to live, he simply wanted to observe and write about it. If he lived a long time, when he was old and too crippled to travel, he planned to read over the journals of where he'd been and all those he'd met. The memories would keep him company.

When he died he wanted no one mourning his passing and no headstone over his grave. Let others live and hurt and want and need. He'd go through alone so that no one felt the hell of being left behind when he passed.

Relaxing, he let the image of Hannah drift in his thoughts. Like a painting left in the sun, she was beginning to fade. He couldn't remember her voice or the exact color of her eyes. It had been seven years . . . seven years of running from memories.

He heard a woman's skirts moving toward him and for a moment let his mind pretend that she'd come back to him.

"Andrew." The woman called Beth pulled him from his thoughts. "Andrew, are you awake?"

He thought of not answering. What difference did it make? He should end this make-believe relationship now since he'd regained his good sense.

But curiosity won out, and he opened his good eye. Thanks to the doc's stitches just below his left eye, it was almost swollen closed. "Evening, Beth," he managed, feeling like his mouth had been washed with sand. "We still engaged?" He'd thought her pretty in buckskin and chaps, but in a dress she was stunning. The kind of woman men stop to watch walk down the street.

"No, we're no longer engaged," she snapped as if he wasn't keeping up with the program. "I told the nurse we got married about noon." She brushed her hair back and he saw the cut over her ear. It had already scabbed over, but the imperfection somehow made her even more beautiful.

When he frowned, she pouted, and he wondered if a man had ever said no to her in her life.

"Well, Andrew, I had to tell her something, and you wouldn't wake up to offer me advice. I wanted to leave, but I thought I should stay around until you revived. After all, you did save my life. However, I didn't think it would be all day. Now I'll have to wait until tomorrow morning to ride out."

He frowned. Somehow he'd made her mad even while unconscious. "So saving your life amounts to one day of company."

She was pouting again, and he decided she had to be the most kissable woman he'd ever seen. Being around a woman like her would probably kill the average man within a week, but he told himself he only found her interesting. He had no desire to get involved, even if he was curious about the taste of those lips. One kiss would only make him hunger for more, and he'd promised himself never again.

"Well, Beth, thanks for staying around. It was nice being married to you."

She waited a few heartbeats, then added, "I do wish there were something I could do to repay you, but the doctor says in a few weeks you'll be fine. Maybe a few bruises and scars that you didn't have before, but compared to the others, I'd say you were lucky. You're not dead or in jail."

"And you really do have to go," he said, finishing her thought.

She put her hand on top of his. "It was nice meeting you, Andrew. You seemed an easy man to be almost married to, but I must get out of this town as fast as possible. I have troubles I haven't had time to burden you with."

Before she could say more, the door to the ward snapped open, and three men stormed in as if invading hostile shores. Beth's hand closed around his, silently asking for his protection, but there was nothing he could do to help her. Andrew wasn't sure he could stand, much less fight off trouble.

He closed his eye when he saw the doctor on one side of a tall man and the sheriff on the other side. This couldn't be good news. Not at this time of night.

The well-dressed man in a gray wool coat bellowed as they neared, "I told you she was here, gentlemen. This is Bethie McMurray, my bride-to-be. I recognized her hair from across the street when she left the hotel an hour ago, but it took me a while to find where she'd gone."

With the bandages covering half his face, Andrew continued to act like he was asleep, but his grip on Beth's hand remained strong. Whoever this tall man was, he frightened his almost-wife to near panic.

"Miss." The sheriff's rough voice sounded

next. "This is Senator Lamont LaCroix, and he claims you're his fiancée. He thinks you got mixed up, maybe hit in the head and—" The sheriff couldn't seem to find the right words. Finally, he rushed on, "—and married the wrong fellow."

"Of course she's mixed up, Sheriff. We were going to meet here in town this morning, but the train delayed me. Who knows, maybe she thinks that's me beneath all the bandages. The man's hair is lighter, but he is my height. Maybe the thought that I might have been killed sent her over the edge of sanity. It often happens to the weaker sex, I've heard." The senator lowered his voice, but Andrew heard, just as he was sure Beth did, "The youngest McMurray woman might be beautiful, but she's not too bright. She's gone off in the wrong direction, that's all. I'm sure this can be straightened out."

"Miss." The sheriff tried again. "Are you or are you not Beth McMurray? The senator feels an obligation to take over your care if you are. I can see you have taken a blow to the head recently. Is there a chance you're confused right now? Or maybe you're in shock?"

When Beth didn't answer, the sheriff continued, "You needn't be afraid; he assures me he'll see you safely back to your family, and the doctor is willing to prescribe something that will calm your nerves. You've been through a terrible ordeal."

Andrew risked a glance at Beth, knowing no one in the room would be watching him. What he saw in her beautiful green eyes was pure fear. He had no idea if she was crazy, or dumb as a rock, but she was in trouble.

"I'm not Beth McMurray. This senator is mistaken. I'm Mrs. Andrew McLaughlin, and I'm not going anywhere with this man no matter who he thinks he is."

"Now, don't be absurd, Bethie." Lamont's voice took on a tone he might use with a child. "You know you're not married to this man. You came here to meet me. We were to be married at dawn when my train arrived. I know I shouldn't have asked you to come along, but I wanted you to myself for a few days. Now look at the mess you've gotten yourself into."

"I'm Mrs. Andrew McLaughlin." Her voice was steady, but her grip was tight.

The group pulled back a few feet, mumbling about whether a future husband had the right to take charge of an unstable woman.

Andrew knew the law. Beth, without family, would have very few rights. A senator might talk the doctor into declaring her unstable. If so, the sheriff would be on La-Croix's side.

He told himself he'd only known the woman a matter of hours, and most of them he'd been asleep. For all he knew she was batty as they come. After all, she had been traveling alone in a freight car with her horse when he met her. She'd claimed they were engaged even though she knew he'd been with the robbers. That outlandish claim was the reason he wasn't in jail right now, so he did owe her something.

He'd saved her and she'd helped him and now, damn it all, he'd save her again if for no other reason than he didn't like the way LaCroix talked to her. It seemed to Andrew that a man who loved a woman, even a nutty one, would try being kind first and not ordering her around with a sheriff and an opium-offering doctor at his side.

As Beth trembled beside him, Andrew

pulled her hand into both of his. With movements not even she noticed, he slipped the ring from his little finger and moved it onto the third finger of her left hand. The ring fit perfectly.

When the three men moved forward again, LaCroix offered his hand. "Come along, dear. This game is over. I'll wire your father and tell him you suffered an accident and that I'll look after you. Teagan McMurray will be forever beholden to me, his new son-in-law. I'll insist we take our time traveling to give you an opportunity to recover and get used to being married."

"My papa will kill you for trying to order me around," she whispered.

He laughed. "Death threats won't work. You belong to me. We agreed to marry. You came to meet me alone. No one forced you. I have a room for us at the hotel where you can rest. You'll see, in a few days everything will be as it should be. You got mixed up, that's all."

Andrew had had enough. He opened his good eye and cleared his throat. "I don't know what your game is, mister, but I'm guessing there's not a court in the country that'll find me guilty of shooting a man trying to force my wife to leave my side. Get this straight. She isn't going anywhere with you."

Everyone, including Beth, stared at him as Andrew pulled himself up. Every muscle in his body was sore, but they all worked. He circled his arm around Beth's waist and was relieved to find her Colt still strapped to her side. Smart girl.

"I didn't put a ring on her finger to give her away to the first man who wants her. If you're interested in marrying my wife, you'll have to bury me first." He leveled Beth's gun at the senator's middle.

"Now hold on a minute." The sheriff took a step backward and looked at LaCroix. "Senator, I thought you were saying that this woman claimed she was engaged to a dying unconscious man. You didn't say she **was** married." He pointed at the ring on her left hand. "I want no part of taking a man's wife away."

Lamont no longer looked sure of himself. He stretched his neck like a huge turtle and examined Beth's face. "There couldn't be two women who look like her.

She's a liar, Sheriff, and obviously, so is he. The two of them are trying to pull something over on me."

"Yeah, and I'm starting to think I'm joining their ranks, 'cause damned if I don't see matching gold bands on their hands. Seems to me like a man playing a joke wouldn't have time to leave his deathbed to go with his crazy bride to pick out rings."

"I tell you it's a trick. She's not married to him. Just ask anyone who knows her. She's spoiled and probably figured out she couldn't get everything she wanted if she married me, so she's made up this story. I've heard tell a hundred men have proposed to her and she's said no to them all."

The sheriff nodded as if trying to follow along. "I'm starting to see the light here. It seems to me, Senator, that any man determined to marry a woman he thinks is a babbling liar and spoiled to boot—**and** doesn't want to marry him—might have a few spokes missing from his wheel as well."

He turned to Andrew. "Put down that gun, son. No one is going to take your wife away from you. In fact, I'm real sorry about this whole mess. You look like you two have enough problems with your injuries without having to worry about someone trying to separate you."

"I tried to tell you both that the woman's been with him since the train wreck." The doctor chimed in as if he'd finally been proven right. "She wasn't waiting for Lamont LaCroix in Dallas; she was by this man when I got to the wreck. She'd been trying to stop his bleeding. If she hadn't, he might have been dead by the time I got out there."

The doctor moved around Lamont as if the senator had grown roots. "Except for when she went to take care of her horse, she's been right here by this man's side. Seems a strange thing to do if she wasn't his wife."

"You got anyone in town who knows you, Mrs. McLaughlin?"

"Only my husband." She smiled at Andrew. "He knows me quite well."

Lamont obviously wasn't a man who ever thought he was wrong. He glared at Andrew as if he knew that somehow they were cheating him.

For a moment Andrew thought of shooting him for simply trying to take his wife, but then he remembered that Beth wasn't his and this was all some kind of make-believe that she'd invented. If she stayed around after the sheriff left, he planned to ask her a few questions, like **Why?** and **Why him?**

He tugged her closer and she leaned her face into him as if no longer even willing to look at Lamont LaCroix.

When the men finally left the ward, he felt her tears on his shoulder. "It's all right," Andrew managed. "He's gone. I don't blame you for not wanting to marry him. I don't even know him and I hate his guts."

"You saved my life again," she whispered. "I was about to start screaming at him, and if I had, that would have only proven that I needed a caretaker. I've never been so angry, or lost. I've never had someone try to control me. It's like he thinks I'm a thing he lost, not a person."

Andrew moved his hand along her back. "You did fine. He's nothing but a bully. Some men, once they get a little power, think they run the world."

She pulled away. "He couldn't have forced me to marry him, could he?"

Andrew had spent a year studying law once, then hadn't bothered to take the exam. "I don't think so."

She frowned. "If he had, I'd have made every day of his life hell."

"I have no doubt," he said, grinning, "but I can't blame him for trying. You are one beautiful woman."

She shook her head, telling him she didn't care for the compliment.

"You were also smart to keep quiet and let me make the threats. I have no doubt you wouldn't be wearing that Colt if you couldn't use it, but you showed a great deal of courage to stand silent. No one, not even the sheriff, blamed me for pulling a gun, but if you had, that might have worked against you."

She nodded. "Are you telling me you're the better liar?"

"Without a doubt." Andrew leaned over and kissed her lightly on the mouth. "And don't you ever forget it, wife."

The kiss had been playful, meant to help her relax, but the ease of it reminded him to be careful. Don't get involved. Don't care, or, more important, don't allow her to care for him. She was just a person passing through his life. In a few days all she'd be was an entry in his journal, and all he'd be to her was a stranger who'd once helped her.

She mistook the worry in his stare as pretend. "Be careful, sir. I have a derringer tucked away that I also know how to use."

"I believe you completely, dear." He leaned back, suddenly exhausted. "I think I'd better lie down before I pass out. I've lost so much blood I think my body has given up trying to pump any to my head."

When she tucked him in, he caught her hand once more. "Promise you won't leave me yet. I'd like to talk to you some more."

"I promise I'll be here when you wake up." She brushed his hair back. "Only once you're asleep, I have to go check on my horse."

"The roan?" he said with his eyes closed.

"Yes, Brandy Blue. I've had him for years."

"I have a horse I need to find as soon as I get out of here," Andrew whispered almost asleep. "A pinto with front stockings. Everything I care about in the world is packed away in saddlebags tied to that horse's saddle."

He closed his eyes, hoping she wasn't lying about being there when he woke. She was the kind of woman he wanted to know better, not only so he could log her traits into his journal, but also so he could let her slip into his dreams.

As he drifted into sleep, he heard her tell the man in the other bed that she'd get him some water. It crossed Andrew's mind that she might be married to that fellow by the time he woke again.

CHAPTER 4

As Beth McMurray walked out of the ward after making sure Lamont was gone and Andrew slept solid, she almost stepped on a little boy sleeping in the hallway. He jumped up, wide-eyed and afraid.

"What are you still doing here?" She reached to touch his shoulder, but he pulled away. "It's far too late to visit. Are you lost?" He had a ragged, unkempt look about him.

He gathered his blanket and shoes. "The doc lets me sleep here if I stay out of the way. I go get him if there's any trouble, and he pays me for sweeping up."

"It's after dark. Shouldn't you be home?" From the look of him, no one ever worried about him.

"My kin knows where I am. If nobody is staying in the ward, I sleep in the barn loft a block away. It's warmer in here, but sometimes it's quieter in the loft."

"What's your name?" She'd seen children who managed to live in town on their own. The war and illness had left many families shattered.

"Levi Hawthorne, miss." He straightened. "I can write my name real proper and can read most of the words in the Bible. My father taught me."

Beth smiled down at him. "That's wonderful, Levi. I was wondering if you could do me a favor. I'd pay you, of course."

"I'll try, miss." He tilted his head sideways as if measuring trust out by the ounce.

"Did you see that tall man who came in here yelling at me about an hour ago?"

He nodded. "The one with Sheriff Harris and the doc? Dressed all fancy-like but huffing and puffing like a steam engine."

"That's him."

Levi shook his head. "I don't trust him any more than I do the doc. He's got cold eyes, like something's already dead inside him."

She decided to let the boy's judgment of Lamont pass for now. "Why don't you trust the doc?"

He looked around and whispered. "He don't doctor to help people, he just does it for the money. If he thought your man couldn't pay, he'd have him moved down to the nuns' charity ward."

"Oh." Beth didn't doubt the boy's words, but tonight she had all the trouble she could handle. "Between me and you, Levi, I'm kind of scared of the big man who huffs and puffs. I was wondering if you'd walk with me to a place where I could eat in peace and stay with me while I have some supper. I'd buy you a meal and pay you two bits for being my bodyguard. If trouble does come, all you have to do is run for the sheriff. You do trust the sheriff, don't you?"

"I sure do, miss. He's a hard man, but not cruel."

"Good, then you'll come with me?"

"I reckon I could." He sat down to put on shoes several sizes too big. Then he stored his bedding under a vacant cot, checked on the man tied to the bed half a room away from Andrew, and followed her out. "I know a little place where nobody will bother you. It's run by a nice girl after dark who gives me and my brother free soup sometimes. Her name's Madeline, but she hates it so we call her Madie."

They went to a little café near a run-down livery so badly in need of repair that Beth had walked another two blocks to stable Brandy Blue. The roads were muddy and the boardwalks in need of repair.

Levi offered his arm as if he were a man escorting a proper lady. His kindness made her proud to be by his side. He might be only half-grown, but sometime, some-one had taught him manners.

The menu choices in the café were lim-ited, but the place looked clean. Beth didn't talk to the kid while he ate, so she learned a great deal watching him. It had been a few days since he'd had a regular meal, so he tried to eat slowly and use his napkin each time before he drank his milk. His clothes might be those of a street kid, but he'd had someone who cared about him once.

When she noticed him squirreling away

rolls with a bite of meat inside, she motioned for the waitress to bring more rolls. The young, well-rounded girl smiled down and winked at the kid, then set a full basket of rolls on the table.

"Thank you, Madie," Beth said. It crossed Beth's mind that the girl might be pregnant, but she didn't look to be older than fifteen. Surely not. Maybe she ate far too many of her boss's hot rolls at night while she watched over the customers.

Finally, when Levi sat back to rub his stomach, he said, "You know that pinto your man was talking about losing?"

Beth leaned forward. "The one with front markings like white stockings?"

"Yeah. I know where a horse like that is. I was next door at the livery before dark and I saw a man ride in with several ponies he wanted to sell. When I told him the owner wouldn't be back for a while, he said he'd wait and put the horses in the corral like he owned the place."

"How many horses?"

"Six besides the one he was riding. Most looked all broken down, but the pinto was fine stock."

"Were they all saddled?"

The kid nodded. "Yeah, come to think of it they were. I thought that was strange. Never seen anyone sell a string of saddled horses. My father used to trade horses now and then. He taught me to tell the good ones from the bad."

"Where are your parents?" Beth knew she was prying, just as she knew they were probably dead. The boy hadn't answered when she'd asked about them earlier.

"My mom's buried somewhere near New Orleans, but my father, Theodore B. Hawthorne, is off wandering the great and massive world. Our mother always said if something ever happened to her, finding our father would be a grand quest, and it's proving to be. Sheriff Harris said he could have been here in town for a while last spring. Thought he heard some drunk say that a gambler with a fancy name moved on to Fort Worth for some big poker game going on in Hell's Half Acre."

Levi Hawthorne began to play with the dozen peas left on his plate. "After Mother died, he left us in Jefferson with his half brother. Our uncle was a mean little man who liked nothing better than to swing his cane across our backsides. We stood it for as long as we could, but my mother always said our uncle had mean baked in him to the core.

"When our father didn't come back after three months, Leonard and me decided to leave and go find him. The day he left he was heading west, so we did too." He propped his chin on his fist. "We're on a quest, miss, plain and simple. Like the knights in stories my father read us, except there's no riches involved. Our father is a good man, he just forgets about us from time to time. With no money for a train, we're doing odd jobs until we can afford to move on."

Beth didn't miss the grown-up way the child talked. When he'd said his family knew where he was, she'd thought the boy meant his parents. Now she realized he'd meant his brother. "Is there anything I can do to help you on your quest?"

"I'll let you know if an idea comes up." For a moment Levi looked very old for his ten years. Sometime along his quest, he'd lost the little boy in him. Too small to be a man, too worried to be a kid. Even the way he talked hinted that he wanted to be older than his years, or maybe he thought he needed to be.

"We're doing all right, miss, but that guy in the bed down from your husband, he could use some help. Would you check on him? But don't tell anyone I asked you to."

"What's wrong with him?"

"Nothing but a snakebite when he came in, but every morning before dawn the nurse gives him a treatment and he gets weaker. He asked me for water a few days after they tied him to the bed. Even said thanks when I helped him. But the next day he was all mumbles that didn't make sense. After the next treatment he quit making any sounds."

"Who is he?"

"Don't know, and I've never seen him have a visitor. Someone said he got bit at the hotel, but I've never known a snake that could climb to the third floor, and any cowhand would know the sound of a rattler before it strikes. He looked all beat up. I never heard of a snake beating a man up before he bites him. Nothing makes sense about him. The doc comes in every morning and asks him to sign some papers, but lately they have trouble getting him to listen. I get the feeling that if he could sign they'd leave him alone, but I don't know if that would be good or bad."

She remembered how fast the doctor had been to offer something to calm her when Lamont said she was in shock. He'd also known she was with Andrew at the wreck, yet he hadn't come to her defense until the sheriff questioned Lamont. "I'll check on the man. I promise."

Gunfire rattled the night like a line of firecrackers popping in the street. Everyone in the café jumped. A woman screamed. Levi melted under the table, and Beth ran to the window with several others.

They couldn't see much. A few men running. Gunfire. Shouting. People who'd been on the street hurrying into the café for cover.

"What's going on?" someone yelled.

"Sheriff's got the last of the outlaws from the train robbery cornered in the livery," a man answered as he ducked for cover. "Bet it's Chesty Peterson. Old coyote finally got himself caught."

Everyone started mumbling as more gunfire came, along with shouts for the outlaw to come out with his hands up or be shot. Beth moved back to the table and knelt to see the kid and the waitress huddled low. Even in the shadows she could see he was fighting back tears as Madie tried to comfort him.

"It's all right. We're safe in here." Beth knew her words were little help.

He shook his head. "My brother's in the barn. He's not safe, and I made him swear he'd stay put until I came back. I tried to make him come sleep at the hospital with me, but he preferred horse smell to blood smell."

Beth didn't argue. "He'll know to stay down. This will all be over soon."

The boy didn't look like he believed her. His round eyes stared up at her as someone in the growing crowd shouted that the sheriff should burn the barn and take no chance of the train robber getting away. Then someone else agreed that the livery was a pile of rotting board anyway, and fire would only improve the value of the lot.

Another yelled that they should shoot the horses in the corral, cutting off any attempt at escape.

"We got to do something." The kid closed

his hand around Beth's wrist. "I got to do something fast."

"You're right." All the stories her uncles used to tell her of the Texas Rangers floated in her mind. There was no time to be a coward. Sometimes acting and maybe being wrong is better than waiting and doing nothing to try and help. "If I can create a distraction, can you get in the barn and get your brother out?"

"I think so. There's a few boards loose on one side. I could slip through, but I'd have to go in the corral to get there." Neither pointed out that if the sheriff's men shot the horses, the boy would be right in the line of fire.

"Get as close as you can and wait until you hear my voice before you run for the opening. Then, get in and get your brother out as fast as you can. I'll meet you both back at the hospital."

The boy nodded, looking like he didn't believe her plan would work, but he was willing to give it a try.

A moment later he ran for the back door of the café, and she marched to the front.

An hour ago she'd been too frightened to face Lamont and fight, but now Beth knew what she had to do. The kids' lives depended on her, and marching into trouble seemed to be her one talent.

She grabbed a lantern from the porch and stepped into the cold night. As she walked down the center of the street, she swung the lantern just beyond her skirts so that no one would mistake her for a man.

Before she reached the barn, the sheriff shouted at her. "Get out of the way, lady. We're in the middle of a gunfight here."

Beth kept walking toward the barn, holding the lantern high so that anyone could see her plainly. "Hold your fire!" she yelled. "I have to talk to the man in the barn."

All gunfire stopped, but the cussing continued like a loose pot lid rattling over boiling water.

When she was within twenty feet of the barn, she shouted, "Mr. Peterson, are you in there? I need to talk to you about something that can't wait."

"What do you want, pretty lady?" A man's voice came through the darkness, sounding almost friendly. "I ain't seen nothing as pretty as you in years."

The sheriff yelled for her to get back,

but Beth ignored him. She stood dead center between the barn and the sheriff.

"I was wondering if you'd sell me that pinto you got? I saw it in the corral and would love to have a fine horse like that."

The sheriff's cussing could be heard for half a block away, and Chesty Peterson yelled back, swearing he'd double-kill any man who fired near the lady.

When all was silent, the outlaw said, "I'm kind of busy right now, lady. Don't have time for horse trading."

"I've got a twenty-dollar gold piece I could pitch you. If this fight doesn't go your way it'll pay for a real nice funeral."

Laughter rattled from inside the barn. "Twenty-five and any horse you want is yours."

"Twenty and I'll take the pinto."

The outlaw swore. "You got yourself a deal, pretty lady. I ain't got time to bargain. Toss the money in the opening and take your horse. I'll even throw in the saddle. Don't look like I'll be using it."

"Thank you kindly, mister." She curtsied politely. "It was a pleasure doing business with you."

Beth tossed the gold piece in and

opened the corral door. To her surprise the outlaw walked the horse out of the darkened corral, careful to keep behind the animal. He stopped, checking the saddle before slapping the horse on the rump hard enough to head her toward the gate.

When Beth reached the pinto, she could barely make out the outlaw in the shadows. He tipped his hat to her. "I'll be seeing you, pretty lady," he said, loud enough for her to hear.

"Who knows? Life does take strange turns now and then," she replied, though she doubted their paths would ever cross again. Beth wouldn't take a bet that Chesty Peterson would live the night.

A few minutes later, when she brought the pinto out into the lamplight, all the men on the street were silent as she walked first past the sheriff and then his deputies.

"You really are crazy, lady," the sheriff said. "LaCroix was right."

"I simply wanted to buy a horse." She smiled. "Now, I suggest you get back to your business, Sheriff, and I'll get back to watching over my husband."

The gunfire didn't resume. Evidently the sheriff figured if she could talk to the outlaw, so could he. Within ten minutes Chesty Peterson surrendered without another shot being fired.

When Beth got back to the hospital, she tied the pinto out front and found two small boys curled up in old blankets in the hallway, sound asleep. She pulled a new blanket from the supply shelf and covered them both before checking on Andrew.

He was sleeping, so she didn't wake him. His color was better, but he'd need days to heal. The bandage around his neck almost looked like a fancy tie, but the one across his forehead was spotted with blood that had dripped around the stitches.

She was surprised how much it bothered her that most of his wounds probably happened because he'd been protecting her when they'd jumped from the train. He might have been about to rob the train, but in that moment he'd been a hero. **He'd almost been a man worth the loving**, she thought. Someone she'd been looking for all her life. No man ever measured up, and this one didn't either. But for a moment he almost had.

She brushed his chestnut hair away

from his bandaged forehead. The memory of the way he'd kissed her lightly, like he'd done it a thousand times, crossed her mind. On impulse, she leaned down and gave him back his light kiss. "I told you I'd be back," she whispered. "I'm staying here with you all night." She didn't add that it was the only place she'd feel safe.

As he slept, she pulled a chair near and searched the room for another blanket and something to use as a step stool. The room, though it looked like a small ward across from a doctor's office, didn't seem to be used much. Maybe the doctor was slowing down, but he didn't even keep the ward staffed or properly stocked.

In the shadows she walked to the other man several feet away from Andrew. No one had checked on him since she'd arrived. She lit a small lamp, wanting to make sure he was still alive.

His skin was so pale he matched the sheet pulled to his chin. Knowing she shouldn't, Beth pulled the sheet away slowly. His arm was bandaged below the elbow, and red streaks ran up and down his arm. **Snakebite**, she thought, having heard how one bite could poison the blood in an arm or leg so badly the victim could lose a limb.

But bites didn't cause a man to go mad, she thought, so why strap the patient to his bed? She looked closer. His wrists and ankles were tied beneath the covers. If he'd been a prisoner brought in for care, wouldn't the sheriff have at least looked in his direction when he'd been here earlier?

Maybe the sheriff didn't know the man was so near death. He'd have no reason to inspect other patients. The doctor would know, though, as would the nurses who worked during the day.

She turned his face to the light and was shocked to see a young man, maybe not out of his teens. One eye was black, and the imprint of a fist was bruised along his jaw. She remembered what the boy had said about snakes not usually beating up folks before they bite them.

Levi suddenly appeared at her side, startling her. It took a moment for her nerves to settle. "Has this ever happened before to someone in the hospital?" she whispered.

"I've been helping out for two months. Women come in to have babies sometimes. Old people already half dead come in so the doc can make their last days not so painful. Town folks drop by to be patched up across the hall. One other time a stranger came in who had no one with him and no visitors. The doc said he fell off a horse. That night, I saw the midnight nurse start what she called treatments, and they buried him two days later. I figure this guy's got maybe two more treatments before they start digging his grave."

"The midnight nurse?"

"Yeah, that's what me and my brother call her. She comes before dawn. She usually gives a shot, checks to make sure her patient is still tied up, and leaves. Don't try to talk to him or nothing like the day nurse does."

Beth felt a chill. She patted the young man's cheek, harder, harder. On the third slap, he came to, but his eyes were blurry and couldn't seem to focus.

"Do you need help?" she asked. "Is there someone I can contact? Family? A friend?"

He whispered something, but she couldn't hear.

She leaned closer.

He whispered again. Two words. "Murdering me."

Beth needed to be sure. "Someone is murdering you?"

He nodded very slightly, and Beth shook with frost crawling over her body even though the temperature in the room hadn't changed.

She took the hand of the stranger and said, "Don't worry. I'm staying close."

CHAPTER 5

AN HOUR BEFORE DAWN, ANDREW SLOWLY stood and moved silently to the window. He felt kitten weak, but he needed to push himself. Every minute he lay in bed put him in more danger. With Chesty Peterson in town, Dallas was not a place he wanted to be. The outlaw wouldn't be happy to know Andrew had survived when all his men died. Andrew wouldn't be surprised if the man came gunning for him if he escaped, and knowing Peterson, he'd escape.

Andrew had watched Beth tie his horse to the railing out front last night, and the animal was still waiting for him now. It seemed unlike her to leave the animal out, but maybe she figured the horse wasn't her problem anymore. She'd gotten the pinto for him, and that was where her duty ended. He wished he'd asked her to at least bring in his saddlebags. Two weeks of his writing was tucked away in his journal amid his dirty clothes.

She drifted through his thoughts like she belonged there. Dressed in her leather trousers and duster she looked well seasoned to this western way of life, but dressed in skirts she was every inch a lady. When he wrote about her, and he would definitely write about Beth McMurray, she wouldn't be easy to describe. So beautiful she took his breath away. He'd never met a woman like her. In fact, he doubted there was another like Beth. She seemed to run toward life while he spent most of his time running away.

He saw her move from the shadows now and realized she'd been with him all night.

"Morning, husband." She smiled, still playing their make-believe game. Tiny curls had pulled free from her braid and now framed her face. Her reddish-brown hair looked darker. He wished he had the right to touch it, but he was no more than an imaginary lover, and that was about as close as he'd risk.

"What are you still doing here?" he asked as his eyes drank her in. "I figured you'd be off for parts unknown by now."

"I'm watching over you and the guy in the other bed. He's been restless the past few hours, mumbling in his sleep, fighting the straps. I believe he thinks he's about to be murdered."

Andrew watched her closely. "Of course he is." The woman's entire life must read like a novel with a villain behind every corner.

"No, I'm serious. He thinks the nurse is slowly poisoning him."

Andrew decided he'd play along. "All right, if you say so. What can I do to help?"

"We have to keep the nurse from giving him a shot. Levi says she comes in before dawn to give him medicine that she pushes into his arm. When she's finished, he doesn't move for hours."

"Who is Levi?" For all he knew Beth had an imaginary friend.

"The boy sleeping in the hallway." She

looked bothered that he wasn't keeping up. "He said the man came in with a snake-bite and he's getting worse every time the nurse gives him a shot. He says the man is tied down so he won't fight."

Andrew looked toward the door and saw the wide eyes of a child staring at him.

"She's coming," the boy whispered.

A few moments later, the chubby little gray-haired nurse opened the main door and clomped down the hall. She told the boy to go back to sleep and hurried into the ward, not even noticing Andrew and Beth standing in the shadows by the window.

She went straight to the young man's bed and opened her case. There was something hard and uncaring about her manner, as if this were simply a chore she had to do. She tossed the sheet back and tugged his arm toward her as far as the strap would allow. "Time for your treatment." She laughed. "This should settle you down, cowboy."

As she lifted the needle, Beth rushed into the light. "What are you doing, Nurse? Can't the shot wait until the doctor shows up?"

The gray-haired woman turned to Beth and frowned as if bothered. "It's only an elixir to make him sleep. He missed his shot last night because of all the racket you caused. The doctor told me to hurry over early before he wakes up and starts complaining. By the time the day nurse comes in he'll be causing no problems around here."

"But he's getting weaker with each shot. He told me so."

The old woman's face hardened. "You're not a doctor, miss. You don't know. The doctor says this shot may not help him, but it will block the pain from his brain. He has to take it twice a day until he gets better." Her voice shook slightly. The nurse obviously didn't believe her lie and added in a whisper, "If he gets better."

The young man in the bed woke and began to shake his head. Beth saw panic in his drugged stare. This time his eyes were less foggy. Missing a shot may have cleared his mind. He glanced at the huge glass-and-metal needle, then back at Beth as if begging her to stop the nurse.

"Now see what you've done," the nurse complained. "Your questions woke him before I could get the shot into him. I hate it when they're watching me do this." She leaned closer to the man's face. "Now you keep quiet or I'll gag you again. This ain't no place to be yelling."

"No," he managed to whisper through chapped lips. "Oh God, no."

Beth moved to the same side of the bed as the nurse. "Why are his hands tied?" She said the first thing she could think of to stall what was about to happen.

"He fights me, I already told you. This young cowboy doesn't know what's good for him. The first day they brought him in he knocked me down with one blow, but since the doctor prescribed these shots he's been pretty quiet."

Beth was several inches taller than the nurse and had no trouble reaching around her quickly and covering the hand that held the shot with her own. "If it's nothing but an elixir, why don't you take the shot instead?"

The nurse panicked. "No. I'm only doing what the doctor told me. The patient is dying and we're just helping him rest easy till the end comes." She tried to pull her hand away, but Beth was half her age and held tight. "It'll mean my job if I don't do this, miss."

"If the shot doesn't hurt him, it won't hurt you." Beth began forcing the nurse's hand down so that the needle pointed toward the nurse's middle.

The nurse jerked hard, sending the glass cylinder flying across the room and shattering. Dark liquid spilled across the floor in fat little pools.

Beth let go of the nurse.

"You don't know what you've done." She stormed toward Beth. "It will take the doctor hours to make another, and this man will be awake and in pain the whole time. I'll be fired. At my age it won't be easy to find another job."

Beth almost felt sorry for the nurse. Her reasoning had been such a circle of lies Beth wasn't sure what the woman believed to be true. "Then how about we don't tell the doctor you broke this one. He'll never know. I'll be here when the cowboy comes around and I'll keep him quiet."

The nurse must have feared more for her job than she cared what happened to the patient. "You won't say anything? After all, this was your fault, not mine."

"No, but if you do I'll tell everyone what is happening here. If this man dies, you'll be the one who goes to prison because you were the one who gave the shots that killed him. The doc's not helping him, don't you understand? For some reason, he's killing this young man."

The nurse shook her head, not wanting to believe such an outrageous claim. "Tell the cowboy to act like he's asleep when the doctor checks on him at noon, and don't untie him no matter what. He's a man in his last days, the doctor told me for a fact. You've only prolonged his suffering by not letting me give him the shot he needed."

She wanted to believe the doctor, but Beth could see her fighting with the truth. "I'm not killing him with the shots, miss. They make him sleep. Doc told me it was better than him dying screaming."

Beth could see how the nurse had been pulled into this crime, but young men don't just die. "Has the bite been treated?"

The nurse shook her head. "Only bandaged." She held her head up. "Doc said it was fatal, so there was no need. I don't know what else is wrong with him. Doc said his number was up."

"It's all right. I'll see to him from here on out." Beth tried to look like she knew what she was talking about. "I've been trained in these matters."

The nurse gave a jerky nod and ran.

For a moment the room was silent, and then Beth heard Andrew whisper as he neared, "You were right. They were trying to kill him, and that woman knows the truth even if she won't admit it."

Beth smiled at her make-believe husband. "As long as we've been married, and you haven't learned that I'm always right, dear?"

They both moved to the young man, who was shaking like a newborn calf. "Thanks. About the time my mind would start to come back, she'd poke me with another shot. Each one sent me further under," he whispered in a voice that sounded like he hadn't used it for a while.

"Who are you? Why are they doing this to you?"

"Name's Colby Dixon, and I have no idea why anyone would want to kill me. Three days ago I was on my way farther south to my ranch. I thought I'd spend a night here before I headed on. Biggest mistake I ever made."

She wiped the sweat from his forehead. "Are you in pain?"

"Yeah, but it's better than being in that dark hole of nothing." He swallowed a little water and drifted back off talking. "Watch over me, lady, until I come back around. I thought you were an angel. Glad to know you turned out to be real."

"I'll do that, Colby," she said, knowing he hadn't heard her.

Andrew pressed his finger along the side of the boy's throat. "His breathing is regular and his pulse seems solid."

"Do you think he'll live?" she asked, not sure she wanted to be told the truth.

"He's at least got a chance now. I noticed a nurse giving him shots yesterday every time he made a sound. The doctor only checked him once, and I didn't miss how frustrated he looked. I thought it was because the fellow wasn't getting any better, but maybe it was because he wasn't getting any worse. Now, if the drug in his system can work its way out, he should start to improve."

"You a doctor **and** a train robber?"

"Neither. I did take a semester or two of medical school when I was nineteen but I didn't go back for the second year." He thought about telling her he'd tried every profession. Nothing fit. How can a man be good at nothing in this world?

"You found my horse." He changed the subject.

"I thought you might need her when you're able to ride. Levi told me where the pinto was." She looked out the window. "I should have taken her to the barn last night and brushed her down, but it was so late and I don't like walking these back streets alone. As soon as I can, I'll go feed her this morning."

"How'd you know that pinto was mine?"

"I know horses, Andrew. I noticed her the night of the robbery. Some people notice color and markings first. I remember the way the pinto moved that night. Head high. Front legs dancing in the mud as if she wanted no part of traveling with the other robbers' horses. Your outlaw boss

must have needed money bad to risk selling off the dead gang's mounts so close to
where the robbery happened."

"He's not my boss," Andrew said, wondering if he'd ever have time to tell her the
whole story of what had happened. "I'd be
willing to bet that no one saw the horses
that night except you. You were at the back
of the train." He raised an eyebrow. "By
the way, why were you riding in the stock
car with your horse? The train was almost
empty. It couldn't have been comfortable
standing in the smelly car." He studied her
and said his thoughts out loud. "You were
hiding."

Before she could answer, they heard
footsteps in the hallway. Beth moved to his
side and circled his neck. "I'm glad you're
standing this morning. I didn't realize until
now how tall you are," she whispered as
she kissed him on the mouth.

Without a doubt, he had to add **dangerous** to the list of her traits. Probably more
so than all the outlaws put together, but
he couldn't resist. He kissed her back. The
taste of her was a hundred times better
than he imagined. They weren't two young
lovers learning and he didn't kiss her

lightly, but with the seasoned passion of a man who'd known love once.

To his surprise, she kissed him back the same way.

When someone cleared his throat from a few feet away, Andrew remembered why she'd kissed him in the first place. For show. Just as well. He could have lost a good measure of willpower if that kiss got any better. He could handle "for show." He wasn't sure he would ever be able to handle "for real" with a woman like her.

He straightened and looked over her head at the sheriff and two of his deputies. "What is it today, Sheriff? Someone else want to marry my wife?" He tightened his arm about her waist. "I'm still not giving her up." **Hell**, he thought, if she kissed him again he'd probably forget that they weren't really married.

The sheriff shook his head. "I doubt anyone wants to take her away today, except for that outlaw in my jail who's crazy about her after she walked through a gunfight last night to buy that pinto tied up out front." He barked a laugh. "I told him she was married and her husband seemed downright partial to her, but Peterson says he'd gladly kill you and take her for his sixth wife. Course, by the time he gets out of jail he'll be too old to remember what to do with a woman, so I doubt you have much to worry about."

"I think I'll keep her if it's all the same to you, Sheriff. She bought me that fine horse last night." Andrew wasn't sure he wanted to know more of the details about how she found the animal.

The sheriff shrugged. "She sure did. Walked right up to the outlaw and bargained with him. Folks will be talking about that for years in this town." He moved a few feet closer and frowned at Andrew. "Looks like you're feeling better, McLaughlin. Any chance you'll be leaving soon?"

"Ready to get rid of us?"

"Look, I don't care that you married a wild woman who interrupts gunfights, but that senator is still over at the saloon drinking and telling everyone she really belongs to him. I figure it's just a matter of time before he downs enough courage and comes back for another try, and I don't much like the idea of having to break up a fight."

Andrew decided not to push his luck. He wasn't so worried about Lamont La-

Croix bothering him again as he was about Chesty learning that he was still alive. The outlaw had lost not only his freedom but most of his gang as well, and he'd be looking for someone to blame. "Sheriff, if you'll help my wife load a wagon, we could be on the road in an hour. I'm not sure I could stay on a horse, but I could sleep in the back of a wagon till we get back home to Fort Worth."

The sheriff looked downright tickled. "I'll do that."

Andrew reached for his coat. "I got money for the wagon."

"Don't worry about it, dear," Beth said, "I have enough for what we'll need. You rest, I'll be back in an hour."

He added **wealthy** and **independent** to his list of her traits. Frowning, he decided that when they were alone, they could split the cost. After all, she needed to get away as much as he did, but he didn't like the idea of her paying for everything now.

After she left with the sheriff, Andrew washed up. The day nurse, a duplicate of the first nurse, changed the bandages around his throat and across his forehead. The stitches along his hairline were healing, but the dozen around his neck were dark and puffy. He grinned, remembering an old professor telling the class once that a man without scars by the time he's thirty hasn't done much living.

As the day nurse tied off the fresh bandage, Andrew said, "The doctor dropped by last night and said the man over there is doing better."

This second nurse didn't seem as bright as the first, but she was friendlier. "Oh, really? I figured he was a goner for sure."

"Doc told me to tell you to go clean the guy up as best you could and give him water whenever he asks."

She nodded. "I might even try a little broth. He reminds me of my boy who died at Shiloh. He's Rachael's charge, but I got the time this morning and who knows where Rachael is. That woman wanders off more than a hungry squirrel living next to a nut forest."

Andrew kept an eye on the nurse to make sure she did no harm. The cowboy let out low sounds of pain as she cleaned him up as best she could without untying him, but he didn't protest. Maybe he'd tried too many times before and it hadn't worked.

Andrew planned to tell the sheriff to watch over the guy. The doctor rarely made it in before noon, and then the smell of last night's whiskey always lingered on his breath. When Andrew wrote about the doctor in his journal, he'd write about a broken man who sold death to support his habit.

It was his suspicion that if he took the time to investigate, he'd find someone paying the doctor to make sure the cowboy didn't recover.

CHAPTER 6

ANDREW LEANED AGAINST THE WINDOWSILL FOR balance as he studied the street. Dallas wasn't as wild a town as Fort Worth, but it held its secrets. He'd be happy when he left. So much had happened in the past two days. He felt like he'd fallen through a trapdoor into a life he had no control over.

About ten o'clock Beth pulled up with the wagon, and Andrew let out a long breath he hadn't been aware he'd been holding. The old buckboard was wide with the sides painted red. She'd put her horse in the harness and tied his, still saddled, to the back.

She rushed in wearing another western outfit that had to be new. This one had a long, split skirt that covered the top of her boots and a soft, white blouse with a blue scarf looped beneath the collar. The day was warmer and she wore a leather vest, fringed with Indian beads. Her hair was pulled back in a long braid, her hat worn low like she was ready to face whatever storm blew her way. It crossed his mind that if she modeled for posters, men would flock to Texas.

"I'm back," she said, stating the obvious. "Did you get the clothes I had sent over for you?"

He turned to face her wearing the western-cut shirt, vest, and jeans. "Thanks, they're not my style, but at least they're clean and you did a good job of guessing my size."

"Between uncles, cousins, and nephews, I know sizes." She studied him. "I thought you'd be a cowboy or a live-off-the-land outlaw. It never occurred to me you'd wear any other style of clothing."

"No, sorry. Except for the times I ride out to camp and study the land, I usually wear a proper suit." At her blank look he added, "You know, with a vest and a pocket watch."

"Really." She frowned. "What about wearing a gun? Don't you have your holster in your bags?"

"I'm afraid not. Only a rifle in case of trouble or the fishing is so bad I decide to eat rabbit. I've never worn a gun strapped around my waist. It wouldn't be comfortable."

He could almost see her mind working as she stared at him. "You jumped on a train, planning a robbery, and you weren't wearing a gun?" She laughed. "And Lamont called **me** dumb."

"I told you I wasn't in on the robbery. I guess you could say I was only an observer."

"An observer who almost got himself killed. If I hadn't taken off that red bandanna you wore, the sheriff would have you in jail right now."

"I know; thanks for that. It was Chesty's idea that we wear them so we wouldn't accidentally shoot each other. His group wasn't made up of the smartest outlaws. I got the feeling he picked most of them up along the trail. I went along to see what would happen and to keep Ryan out of trouble. That plan didn't turn out so well."

She stared at him as if he were half mule. "You're not a coward. You saved me during the crash and stood up to Lamont, but only a fool wouldn't wear a gun in this country."

"Lots of men don't, Beth." He knew very little about her, but he had no doubt they were from separate worlds. He'd never lived even on the edge of town, and she obviously knew nothing of life in the city. It occurred to him that she thought less of him simply because he wasn't armed.

"We'd better go, Beth." There was no use arguing the point.

"Yes," she agreed, but there was a coldness about the way she looked at him. With his arm around her shoulder, they began to move slowly out of the ward. "I told the sheriff about Colby Dixon," she said without looking up at him. "He says he'll check on him, but I don't think he believed me about Doc trying to murder someone in his hospital."

"At least he knows to watch. That's all we can do for Dixon. The guy will wake up a little clearer in the head. Another day and

he should be able to take care of himself."
Andrew didn't miss Beth's frown. They'd
reached the hallway. The doctor's offices
across from the ward were still closed.

"I'm going to go back and untie him as
soon as I get you settled in the wagon."
She wasn't asking permission, so Andrew
just nodded, mentally adding a few words
to his list of adjectives that described her.

At the main door, she said, "How about
we head west? I got family in Fort Worth."

"Fort Worth would be the closest town;
besides, it'd be the direction I'm heading
anyway." He thought of telling her that Fort
Worth really was where he lived, but he
guessed that would only disappoint her
too. It made no sense, but she seemed
less interested in him now that she knew
he wasn't a train robber.

"Anywhere sounds good to me. I need
to put some miles between me and Lamont
LaCroix. After that I'll worry about getting
home. He'll figure I'm heading south toward the ranch, not west. After listening to
him talk to the soldiers on the train about
what his marriage would be like to me, I
got so frightened I thought I'd be in much
better company riding with my horse."

He noticed she touched the butt of her Colt. No doubt it gave her comfort.

"So you were afraid?"

She didn't answer as they moved toward the wagon, and he guessed she hated admitting her fear almost as badly as she hated Lamont.

"I made you a bed in the back of the buckboard." She wasn't even looking at him as she talked. "Thought you could use your saddlebags as a pillow or your saddle to lean on. It'll be more comfortable than trying to ride on the bench while we're traveling. I'm guessing with the muddy roads it'll take us two, maybe three days."

"Aren't you afraid to be alone with **me**?" Andrew asked as he leaned on her for support.

"No, you're too weak." She looked up at him. "I could take you in a fair fight."

"I will get stronger, you know." He'd have to lose the other half of his blood before he'd stop enjoying her close like this. Like it or not, he was getting used to the way she fit against his side.

"I know," she said casually. "When that happens I'll probably have to shoot you. It's been my experience that men tend to make fools of themselves around me. I've always had my family to help chase them away, but this time, when you go nuts over me, I'll have to take care of you myself. With you unarmed it shouldn't be that hard." She grinned. "Maybe I'll bring along a chaperone or two."

Andrew made a mental note. Beth didn't like being called beautiful, and she hated men falling all over her. If he wanted to stay alive, and he definitely wanted to if it meant being around her a little longer, he'd simply have to convince her he wasn't attracted to her,

As they walked down the steps, Andrew noticed two little boys sitting on the back gate of the wagon. They were ragged and thin. The bigger one looked like the kid he'd seen sleeping in the hallway of the hospital. "Let me see. I got engaged two days ago, married yesterday, and now I have a family."

"Correct," she said, as if it all made sense.

"Great," he mumbled as she helped him into the back of the wagon. "I can't wait to see my grandchildren tomorrow. Don't you think we should sleep together at some point? That's one step I was kind of hoping we wouldn't skip in our marriage."

"Hush, dear. You shouldn't talk of such things in front of the children."

Andrew looked at her closely, wondering if it was possible that she believed the lies she told so easily.

He tried to make small talk with the two boys while she ran back inside to untie the cowboy. The little boys looked afraid of him. Apparently, they hadn't noticed he was unarmed and therefore harmless. About the time he ran out of anything to say, he looked up the steps and saw his "wife" half carrying the young man from the hospital out the front door.

"Help me, Levi," she called, and both boys jumped to help.

Colby Dixon had a bandage around one arm and bruises striping his upper arms that looked like he'd been held down with strong hands. He wore a flimsy hospital gown and one sock. Though he was almost as tall as Andrew, Colby was ra thin. His hair, three months past needing cut, blew around him in a sunny mess thick curls. The young man was either t young or too sick to realize what a sight made to everyone passing.

Andrew moved sideways into the wa

until his back was behind the driver's seat. Shoving boxes and luggage around, he pulled his saddlebags forward to use as a back support and covered them with a blanket as his "wife" and the little boys reached the wagon with their load. "Beth, what are you doing with that man, trying to kill him? He's not even dressed and it's freezing."

She looked up, green eyes flashing. "I'm not leaving him in there alone. He begged me to get him out, and that is exactly what I'm doing. Hand me a blanket, Levi, and then run in and see if you can find his clothes. People are starting to stare."

"I know where they are," the boy re-ponded. "I saw the nurse store them away." darted up the stairs.

ndrew watched as she made Colby a in the back of the buckboard, then the tailgate. In the morning sun An- saw his pale face more clearly. He more than a kid. Tall and slim, he have been more than seventeen en. He curled into a ball, too weak it up. Beth covered him com- blankets.

rned with a stack of clothes, un belt. Andrew didn't know a

great deal about guns, but he knew an expensive Colt when he saw one. Colby's clothes were western down to his worn chaps and custom-made boots. Before he'd been hospitalized, he'd been a working rancher.

Beth climbed onto the bench with the little boys and looked back. "Everyone ready?" She sounded as cheery as if they were heading on a picnic.

Andrew lowered his hat over his face and slid down, using his saddle to rest on. Two or three days on the road with a half-dead cowboy and two kids. Not his idea of an outing. So much for being alone with her. "I think we're about loaded to capacity."

As the wagon picked up speed, he heard a scream and raised his hat. His first thought was that maybe the young cowboy fell out of the back of the wagon, but the pile of blankets hadn't moved.

A chubby girl of about fifteen darted out of a café and jumped up on the bench with the two boys. She carried a pillowcase pack and a basket of hot rolls. Near as Andrew could tell she couldn't talk, but she had no problem laughing and squealing.

"We have three children?" Andrew

asked, wondering if the day could get any stranger.

"Yes, dear," Beth answered. "Only, I should tell you that the boys are really little knights on a quest to find their wandering father."

"Of course they are." Andrew had spent his childhood reading fiction, but he'd never met a woman who lived it. Now, apparently, she'd found kinsmen overnight while he slept. If they didn't get out of town fast, he'd be traveling in a caravan.

The sheriff showed up to see that they made it out of town and congratulated Andrew for giving the children a ride. He said his guess was that the petty crime in his town would drop with the Hawthorne boys gone.

By the time the houses faded, Andrew had fallen asleep on his saddlebags. Tucked away inside were his journals, his life in words, the one thing that would keep him company when all the people he met left him.

Only right now his world seemed a very crowded place.

CHAPTER 7

By noon Beth's back ached, but there was no one to complain to. She loved riding and could easily stay in the saddle all day, but she'd never liked traveling in a wagon. She'd learned to drive one when she made trips back and forth to town with her older sisters. One of them usually drove, just as one of them usually carried the list of supplies they needed to pick up as well as the rifle for protection. Baby Bethie had been a grown woman before she'd ever driven alone to town, and then half the ranch seemed to worry until she was back safe and sound.

She was the little one, the pretty one, the one everybody spoiled. Maybe that was why no man was ever good enough for her. Finally, Senator Lamont LaCroix seemed to fit the bill. He was rich, powerful, and able to give her everything.

Tears blurred Beth's vision as she stared straight ahead at the road. She hated who she was . . . what she was. A woman so shallow she'd been taken in by a man like Lamont. Her mother was a strong woman. Strong enough to travel with three tiny girls to join Teagan McMurray in Texas. Her sisters were strong. Even both of her aunts stood equal with their husbands. Only Bethie, the baby of the clan, seemed to always need someone else to plan for her, someone to entertain her, someone to save her. Even her three little brothers thought they should take their turn watching over her.

"You crying, lady?" Levi asked as he stepped around a sleeping Andrew and climbed onto the bench seat. He thought it his duty every hour to make sure Colby wasn't dead.

"No," Beth lied. "How's our young cowboy in the back?"

"Breathing." Levi shrugged. "He's mumbling in his sleep, so I guess that's progress."

"It is," Beth guessed. "Madie, would you take him some water?"

"All right." She bumped into everyone on the bench turning around and moving back.

Levi took her place beside Beth. "I brought you a roll if you want it. Madie put butter in them for us. I hope you don't mind me telling her we were leaving. She says her man is in Fort Worth and she needs to find him." He passed her the roll and she handed him the reins.

"How'd you know we'd be heading to Fort Worth?" she said between bites.

He shrugged, and she knew he must have heard her talking to the man she'd bought the wagon from. He'd said that if she was going much farther than Fort Worth she might want to replace a wheel, but she didn't want to take the time. "Do you follow me everywhere, Levi?"

"Pretty much," he answered. "You mind?"

Even the little boy was trying to take care of her, Beth thought. "No. But if we're going the same direction you might as well walk with me."

"You wouldn't care?"

She grinned. "I'd be honored to have such an escort."

She looked back at the girl. "Thank you," Beth said.

"No problem. The guy asked me if I was an angel. When I told him no, he looked at me as if he didn't believe me and then went back to sleep."

"He's getting better." Beth winked at Madie. "Keep giving him water every hour, would you?"

"Sure."

Beth settled into silence, trying to plan for whatever lay around the corner. The boys had come to her with their request to ride along while she was buying supplies. They'd even offered to pay. When she'd said it was unnecessary but they were welcome to travel along, the boys must have darted over to the café and told Madie.

The girl looked too young to have a fellow, but sometimes people married young. Maybe if he was a few years older than she was, he'd help her get settled in Fort

Worth. Madie seemed to believe all her Micah told her. Beth decided she'd see for herself the cut of the man before she let Madie go with him.

She'd also check out the boys' father. Not all men were meant to raise kids, and this one had a few things against him already. He'd left his children with only a promise to return. "Levi, what are you and your little brother going to do if you don't find your father?"

"Well, miss," Levi explained, "we all figure we're no worse off in the next town than this one. If he's not there, I can get work sweeping up, and Leonard is almost old enough to pay his way. We tend to find things lying around, but I knew we were about to run out of luck with the sheriff back in Dallas. Everything that went missing seemed to be our fault."

"If you come with me," Beth held her face stern, "there will be no stealing."

Levi nodded. "I kind of figured that."

"Swear." She looked at Leonard and pointed at him. "You too. Swear."

"We swear, miss, but my brother don't talk. I told him you're a good woman. We'd rather take our chances with you than stay in Dallas. We'll help you take care of your man, and if he dies we'll bury him. Same goes for the other guy you picked up at the hospital."

How could Beth say no to that offer?

"You got kin somewhere?" Levi asked as he ate a roll.

"Yes," Beth answered, wishing she were back at the ranch with all the family around. "I've got lots of kin. I even have a brother not much older than you. All three of my brothers are away at school."

"I'll bet they are missing you." Levi took another bite.

"Probably, but my family all believes I'm visiting friends right about now, so they don't expect me back."

She thought of all the dreams she'd had riding over to meet Lamont. Now, they seemed almost childish. She'd grown and changed thanks to one midnight ride in the back of a train car. She swore she'd never be that taken in by a man again as long as she lived. Andrew might not have been exactly what she'd expected, but surprisingly, he was far more honest than Lamont.

After noon, Madie offered to take the

reins, and Beth talked the boys into riding shotgun on the bench while she climbed into the bed of the wagon next to Andrew. He hadn't said more than a few words. He was cramped, sitting sideways, with his knees bent, but he made room for her without saying a word.

To the slow clip-clop of the horses, she fell asleep with her head on his shoulder. As she drifted off, she felt his arm circle her and pull her against him. It never occurred to her to protest. His warmth felt too good.

At dusk, they made camp in a clearing. Levi built a fire and Madie helped cook beans and bacon. The boys were almost too tired to eat. They curled up inside their bedrolls without a word. Colby was awake long enough to put on his clothes, and then he spread out close to the fire and was sound asleep before supper was ready.

Madie sat down next to him and studied his face. "He's got more color to him tonight." She combed through his blond curls with her fingers.

"He's better." Beth hoped her words were true. "Let him sleep."

The girl went back to tending the fire, but Beth didn't miss that she left Colby's plate beside his bedroll.

Andrew sat on the tailgate of the wagon writing in a book by firelight as the evening stilled. The bandage on his head had fallen off before dark and he hadn't asked to have it wrapped again. With the stitches healing, the air might be good for the wound.

Beth poured the last of the coffee and sat beside him. He was good-looking with his broad shoulders and intelligent eyes. He was polite in a shy kind of way, but he wasn't the kind of man she wanted. Not that she knew who that might be, but Beth hoped when she saw him, she'd know him on sight.

"You about to turn in?" she asked, more for something to say than out of interest.

"I slept most of the day. I think I'll stay up and write a few things down while I have the fire's light."

"What are you writing?"

He smiled. "My thoughts. I've done it since I was a kid. I collect what's happened in my life and what folks tell me. I write what I find interesting about the people I meet, sometimes just stories that I make up. At the end of the day I kind of empty my mind, getting ready for what comes tomorrow."

"Really. How interesting." She tried to sound sincere, but in truth it seemed a waste of time. "Would you read some of it to me?"

"No," he said simply, and went back to work.

Beth frowned. In her family everyone loved reading. Even when her papa and his brothers were growing up alone, they valued books. They often took turns reading by the firelight, and when her papa had children he continued the practice. Beth was the only one in the family who didn't love books. She could never sit still long enough to read one all the way through. Which, among the McMurrays, made her appear dumb.

After a few minutes Andrew looked up at her. "You're used to being entertained, aren't you, Beth?"

"No," she lied. "But I like good stories. My papa and uncles sometimes sit out on the porch after supper and tell the best stories."

"Like what?"

She finally had his full attention. "Well, when they were kids their father died at Goliad fighting for Texas, and they had to take over the ranch. Outlaws came to take it away from them, but the boys fought them off while they were taking care of their sister, who was newborn. The story is often told that they carried Sage the way the Apache carry their children so they could stay in the saddle all day."

Now that they were finally talking, she told story after story, including every detail of how the boys burned the bridge, the only easy way onto their land, and didn't rebuild it until they were grown. She even told of her uncle Tobin being shot in an ambush when he was six years old. He hid beside his horse as men kept shooting at him. After that day Tobin believed that his blood had mixed with the horse's and that he understood animals better than anyone alive.

Andrew seemed lost in her stories. The night aged and the fire had grown low when she finally stopped. "We'd better get some sleep," she said, hiding a yawn.

"Thank you, Beth," he said, sounding as if he really meant it. "You've given me a great gift."

"I enjoyed sharing the stories. Don't you have family stories?"

"Not that anyone would want to hear, but your stories aren't just of family, they're of Texas. Of what it was really like. Of how the people really survived. I've never understood why anyone would want to settle in such a wild land. It never occurred to me that they'd love it so."

"I'm glad you liked them. I have a hundred more." She jumped off the end of the wagon. "I think I'll bed down by the fire. Will you be all right in the wagon?"

"I'm fine." He slid off the wagon and helped her collect her bedroll. "Feeling my strength coming back little by little."

On impulse she leaned into him and kissed him lightly. He wasn't the man for her—no man who never carried a gun would ever be—but she liked the feel of him. Andrew would probably not be flattered to learn that he was like her favorite wool blanket. Comforting.

He studied her a moment and said in a

low voice, "Don't do that, Beth, unless you want a real kiss. I'm a man who can only play at being married for so long."

She didn't know whether to be embarrassed or hurt. No man had ever told her not to come closer. By the time she was fifteen every man she met had delighted in getting to hold her hand or be rewarded with a light kiss. Andrew wanted none of that.

"I wasn't playing. I simply wanted to kiss you good night. It didn't mean anything. It was just a kiss."

"Then kiss me like a woman kisses a man." His words weren't sharp and he didn't seem open for compromise on the point.

She took two steps toward the fire before she changed her mind and whirled. He didn't raise his arms to welcome her. He stood perfectly still as she touched the side of his jaw and raised her mouth to his once more. If he wanted a real kiss or nothing at all, she'd give him the real thing.

This kiss was no light peck. After a few seconds he responded, pulling her against him as he opened her mouth for a taste.

She felt a fire go all the way to her toes. She'd never felt such raw need, and she melted against him, hoping for more.

He dug his fingers into her loose hair and held her head still as he took his time claiming her mouth. She gave willingly, loving the wild excitement of the moment, and he took like a man starving.

When she moaned against his lips she thought he'd continue, but he pulled away. His hands shook slightly as he set her a foot away from him. For a long moment they stared at each other in the firelight's last glow.

"Thanks for the good-night kiss," he said as he moved back into the wagon. "I think it may have been the best I've ever had."

"You think?" She didn't see how it could have been better, unless maybe it hadn't ended so soon.

"Yeah, we'll have to do it again some-time for me to be sure." He rolled into his bed on the wagon. "Good night, Beth," he said as he picked up his journal once more.

She walked away confused and frus-trated. She was always the one who put an end to the kissing, and she didn't like it one bit that he'd stopped before she'd been ready to pull away.

With an unladylike snort she realized that for a woman who always got her own way, she was having nothing in her life right now the way she wanted it.

In the firelight she watched Andrew trying to see the pages of his book. What she wouldn't give to know what he was jotting down at this moment.

CHAPTER 8

Long after Beth curled up in her bedroll, Andrew watched the night sky and thought of the stories she'd told him when he was finally able to get the taste of her lips out of his thoughts. The stories were the reason he came to Texas. He'd wanted to know what drove people to come to this wild land. What made them stay and love it so?

In a strange way, the stories of others made him feel alive. He was like a sixteenth-century vampire wanting to suck the blood out of the living. Nothing had mattered to him for so long that Andrew wasn't sure he still had a pulse. He rarely stayed more than a year at any one place. Growing up, there was always a new step-father, new school, new town. All his life, in school after school, he'd always been a stranger, cared for, but never loved. Some years, when he came home for the holi-days he'd find his mother gone with her husband-of-the-month. She'd always leave a note naming some housekeeper or "trusted friend" he didn't know to watch over him.

When he found Hannah, he thought he'd lucked out and discovered the one person who might love him. He was twenty-three and she nineteen. He met her at the bank where they both worked. He'd noticed her before but didn't speak until he saw she was reading the same book he was. The poems of Walt Whit-man, **Leaves of Grass.** He'd been so cocky that first conversation, telling her that the title was a play on words, with **grass** being a publishing term for "minor value" and **leaves** another name for "pages." Hannah had thought him brilliant.

Since neither had family, they were mar-ried a few weeks later by a judge at the courthouse, and she moved in with him that night. They were so happy they didn't even know they were poor. He'd had fourteen months of heaven before she died, but the pain of her loss still haunted him. Even now, his kind Hannah with her soft voice and gentle ways always seemed near, but just beyond his reach.

He'd taken her body from Boston to Washington, D.C., to be buried next to his mother in a family plot that had MCLAUGHLIN over the gate. He couldn't stand the thought of her being buried among strangers.

As he stood over Hannah's grave, he noticed a small leather pouch placed in the V of his mother's headstone. It was from a lawyer asking that if Andrew McLaughlin ever returned to this spot, he should contact someone at the firm of Smith and Adams. The letter added that all other efforts to contact him had been exhausted. Andrew hadn't thought of leaving a forwarding address. He knew no one would care.

He almost left the note there. He wanted nothing to do with his last stepfather and had no use for his mother's things. A week later, when he finally did step into the office of Smith and Adams, he found that his mother had left him a small account from money she must have skimmed for emergencies between husbands. It wasn't much, but over the years, when he'd needed money, he'd always been able to wire the lawyers.

The past few years he'd needed little, thanks to selling a few stories about his travels to magazines and articles to papers across the country. The lawyers said they'd invested the leftover money for him. Someday he'd buy a house on a cliff in Maine or on one of the little islands along Florida's inland coast. There, he'd live alone with only the memories of his travels and a kiss he'd shared with a beautiful Texas lady.

Andrew stared at the dying campfire. Beth was quickly becoming one of his favorite memories, even though she hadn't left yet. It had been a few years since he'd kissed a woman. He couldn't even remember the name of the widow who'd let him spend the night with her for a few dollars one cold night in New Orleans. She'd smelled of spices and her hair had been black. She was liquid passion in his arms, but he felt like it was a practiced recipe. At dawn he'd paid his money and left, never once looking back.

As he crawled into his bedroll in the buckboard, Andrew realized that when he left Beth McMurray in a few days, no matter what did or didn't happen between them, he'd look back for one last memory of her.

The next day, he wrote her stories in his journal as they moved along the road between Dallas and Fort Worth. The air was cold, but not bitter, and the rain had left the road more a stream at some points.

Now and then they'd pass other travelers, and Andrew was impressed with how friendly strangers were in this part of the country. Beth often stopped to talk, asking about the road up ahead and wishing them well on their journey. Once, to a family who looked down on their luck, she asked if they needed any peaches and gave away half of the fruit she'd packed for the trip. She claimed her group wouldn't eat them and they'd be doing her a favor.

It had taken him an hour last night to record everything he'd wanted to remember about the day.

By the second morning Andrew was strong enough to drive the team, and Colby had recovered enough to sit up behind him and tell him how. Andrew had been right about the kid; he hadn't seen his eighteenth birthday, but he was a hardened cowhand. He'd been raised on a ranch and he'd finished his first big cattle drive.

Andrew also noticed that Colby didn't seem able to talk when Madie was near. She was younger than he was by almost three years, but if Andrew were guessing, he'd say Colby had been around very few girls near his age. She fretted over him, and he politely pushed her away.

Two things were obvious about the cowboy. He knew his way around Texas, and he was crazy about Beth McMurray. Maybe it was because he thought she'd saved his life, but Colby couldn't stop staring at her. He saw her as Joan of Arc, and he would have followed her into any battle. He kept asking her one question after another just to hear her voice. Levi got so tired of it he declared no one could ask any more dumb questions until dark.

Andrew wasn't surprised when Beth saddled his horse and rode beside the wagon. She handled the pinto better than he ever had. He rode out of necessity; she rode for pure pleasure. With her acting as scout, they made better time and soon connected with a stage road that was far smoother.

That evening she entertained them all with stories of the McMurrays. She told how Travis McMurray had been a Texas Ranger and ridden in raids after the war to bring home children who'd been kidnapped. She told of the legend of Whispering Mountain that her Apache great-grandfather had told them about. "If a man sleeps on the summit of the mountain, he'll dream his future. My grandfather dreamed his death, and my father dreamed he'd have daughters," she told them.

Late into the night, she told them of storms and grass fires the family fought and how once her uncle had almost died in a raging river. She described the hard time during the war when her papa plowed their ranch land in long rows to plant enough food to feed the townsfolk. Madie even cried when Beth described her uncle Drummond Roak walking home after the war and how he was so thin her aunt Sage didn't recognize him.

For children raised in the West, the stories of hardship were well known, but for Andrew, who'd spent most of his life in the East, they were fascinating. He'd never owned land or cared about a part of the country. The year he'd been married, he'd worked as a teller in a bank, and his journey each day had been three blocks between their rented flat and the bank. He and Hannah had lived near the the center of town. Their exciting evenings were usually walking along the streets and watching people. He'd make up stories about all the strangers and she'd laugh.

He was twenty-four when she died of pneumonia. He'd left everything in his life behind, walking out with only one small pack and a blank journal. That day he began to wander. Always reading, always studying, hoping to find something that interested him, always writing in his journal.

Now, as he looked at Beth, he realized he might have finally found what he was looking for. **She** interested him. She'd fill an entire journal, and years from now when he read about her, she'd keep him warm with memories of her and her Texas.

That night, when she came to tell him good night, he held her, wishing she'd stay by his side a little longer. Every day was one more day he'd have to remember, but he knew they'd reach Fort Worth tomorrow. Tonight was their last night together, and her kiss had been quick, as if she'd been in a hurry to pull away.

He let her walk back to the campfire, having no idea how to stop her.

After everyone settled in around the campfire, Andrew walked into the darkness and studied the stars. Colby had said tonight that the heavens were all the roof he ever wanted. Andrew thought he might adopt that philosophy for a while. He was tired of towns and cities; maybe that was why he'd spent more nights away from his place in Fort Worth than he usually did. The past few years, every time he felt he needed to move on, he always moved west. Sometimes only a town or two, sometimes a state. He didn't want to just see new lands, he wanted to feel them around him and understand the people who called them home.

He'd change yet again. Maybe he'd start wearing western clothes and carrying a gun. He couldn't see himself joining the Rangers, but he might sign on for a cattle drive. Surely the skills needed could be learned. Who knows, he might even ask Colby to teach him.

Sometimes he felt like his life was a blank canvas, and every now and then, when he almost got a painting watercolored in, the rain would come along and wash it all away. He'd started over so many times, even starting over didn't feel new.

"It's a nice night," Beth said softly from about ten feet away.

Andrew turned, watching her move toward him. "What's wrong?"

"Nothing." She laughed. "I know you probably think I only talk to you when something's wrong, but there hasn't been much time for the two of us to have a conversation."

He had a feeling they were going to have one now, so he waited for it. She was a planner, a goal setter, a measurer of time and task. For a drifter without purpose she was a hard pill to swallow some-times, even with her beauty.

"I was wondering why you haven't even tried to kiss me again."

"I've been waiting for you to come to me if you're interested. I can't kiss you while there's an audience, and I won't come af-ter you."

"I'm interested," she said, without mov-ing closer. She'd walked all the way out here and couldn't seem to make it the last few inches. "I've always had men come after me. You seem to have become a challenge for me."

"Why do you want another kiss?" It dawned on him he had nothing to offer a woman like her. She was the kind of woman who married a powerful man with goals and ambition. He didn't even know where he'd be six months from now.

She was silent for so long he thought she might not answer. When she did, her voice was so low he barely heard. "Be-cause I'm in danger of never feeling any-thing again for the rest of my life, and you seem the only one around who might be willing to help me. Lamont killed a dream inside me. He even killed the hope I'd hung onto for too long. I feel cold and dead inside more than angry."

He knew that feeling. He'd lived with it for years.

"You're getting over a breakup with the man you loved. You'll recover and move on." Her loss was nothing like his. She was a spoiled woman who hadn't gotten what she wanted.

She shook her head. "That's just it. I'm mad about even getting engaged to Lamont. I'm more angry at myself for being so dumb to fall for a man like that than I am at him for being an ass."

Andrew laughed and wondered if she'd ever used the word before. "So, he's an ass, is he? You won't get any argument out of me."

"I'm not torn up about him. I'm more upset that I was planning to marry him and I didn't even know him." Her admission ended with a cry. "I didn't even love him and now I don't feel anything. It's like I got cheated at both ends of the rope. Maybe I'm hollow inside. Maybe I'll never feel anything the rest of my life. I'll grow old and wither like an apple left in the hot sun."

"You're not hollow, Beth. You'll feel again."

"How do you know?"

He wanted to tell her he knew because he was hollow. He'd gone seven years without caring. But, for the first time, he wasn't so sure he'd be telling the truth. He'd cared enough about Ryan to climb on that train and try to stop him from ruining his future. He'd cared enough about Beth to save her life. Maybe he was waking up from a deep sleep. Maybe it was time to feel again.

"I'll show you how I know." Taking a step behind her, he circled her waist and pulled her back against him so hard he felt her breath leave her lungs for a moment. "Relax, Beth, and feel."

When she opened her mouth to say something, he whispered against her hair, "Just relax and don't talk. I think we've had enough of a conversation tonight. If this is the last time we'll ever be alone together, we need to communicate in simpler terms."

His fingers pressed along her ribs as her breathing quickened. He lowered his head and tasted the side of her neck. "Lean into me and feel for once in your life. Don't think." He kissed the smooth flesh of her throat.

She let out a soft cry of need and relaxed against his chest.

"We're not children, Beth, but maybe we can still pretend. Maybe you need someone to care about you and, for a moment, I'd like to believe that I could be with someone who cared about me. I need to believe it, if only for a few minutes."

When she didn't answer, he moved his hand up between her breasts and began unbuttoning her blouse. On the third button, she stopped his hand by simply placing her fingers over the buttons.

He brushed his lips lightly against her ear. "I'll take away the memory of Lamont and whatever he said if you'll let me. I'll make you feel needed and desired, but if you don't want this, walk away. We can go on pretending we're not attracted to one another."

She was so still that he added, "Every time you walk near, I swear my blood warms, and when you touch me almost by accident, I want to hold you against me like this. This moment will always be one of my favorite memories, no matter how many years or miles pass."

"Will you say you love me?"

He heard the longing in her voice, but he wouldn't lie to her. Not like that. "No, but I'll show you how I feel. I want to touch you, but even more I want you to know how it feels to be touched by a man who doesn't want to own you or control you."

The nearness of her filled his senses as he waited. Slowly, she removed her hand from his and stood perfectly still, her back pressed into his chest. His heart pounded so hard he was sure she could feel it. One by one the buttons of her dress fell open, and with feather-light strokes he touched the lace beneath.

Without pushing any further, he turned her slightly and kissed her. A deep, slow kiss that warmed them both.

When he finally ended the kiss, he whispered against her open mouth, "You ready to feel a little more?"

She nodded as she pressed her lips to his once more. This time the kiss was hungry and hurried. As it deepened, he slid his hand beneath her dress and closed his fingers over her full breast, covered only by thin lace. He needed to know the woman beneath the proper lady.

Beth trembled, and he knew he'd gone

further than she'd ever allowed a man to go, but she wasn't pulling away. He found it amazing that a woman of twenty-four had never known a man's touch. The thoughts of what he'd like to do to her in the darkness would probably frighten her to death, so he kept his touch light.

She was learning and he was exploring. It was enough for them both . . . for now.

Any sounds she made were muffled by the kiss. He'd meant to teach her how to feel, but he knew he was the one coming alive. This woman affected him as none had in years, and memories flooded back of another time and another woman in his arms.

Hannah.

He broke the kiss and brushed his lips against Beth's forehead as he pulled his hand away from her breast and began buttoning her dress. "That was unbelievable, but I fear I'll die flying too close to heaven if I don't stop." Somehow, feeling too deeply for Beth was a betrayal to his wife. The soiled doves he'd slept with a few times had only satisfied a physical need. They hadn't bothered his heart. Beth was different.

Andrew wasn't playing around or acting;

he could feel alive with her if he allowed his heart to start beating again.

"You made me believe I'm not broken inside," she whispered. "Thank you for that, even if you were only pretending to care."

He wanted to tell her he wasn't pretending, but he didn't know how to explain what was happening. Self-preservation took over. "You're welcome. Now, it's time we turned in for the night, but I reserve the right to pick up our communications later if time and place ever allows."

Andrew couldn't believe his own words. If he'd had a gun he'd have shot himself for being an idiot. He had no business even saying such a thing to her, for tempting himself with more misery when they parted.

Only, part of him wanted to believe, even though he'd never knock, that the door was open to continue what he'd started.

"If the time and place ever allows, you'll be welcomed," she whispered, already moving into the shadows.

CHAPTER 9

EVERYONE ELSE IN THE CAMP WAS STILL ASLEEP as first light melted across the eastern sky. Madie Delany watched the young cowboy crawl out of his bedroll and move toward the stream. He was doing better but still wasn't steady on his feet. He hadn't said more than a few words to her, but he hadn't been mean either. She'd been on her own since she was twelve, and most of the men she'd met were mean, so she counted the snakebit cowboy on the good guy side of her life.

She wrapped the blanket around her and quietly followed him. A few feet from the water's edge, she knelt near dried brush. It wasn't full light, but she watched him take off his clothes and step knee deep into the cold water. Slowly, as if his muscles hurt, he washed his body, but the dark bruises didn't wash away. He'd been beaten badly. Kicked in the back and on his legs. Maybe even stomped on, from the size of the dark bruises along his lean muscles. More than one man must have held him down, because he was tall and built rawhide strong. She didn't really know him, but it worried her that he might have made enemies who wanted him dead.

When he walked out of the water and tugged on his trousers, she stepped in front of him.

"What are you doing here?" He looked more embarrassed than angry. "I thought everyone was still asleep."

"I figured you might like me to take off that bandage over the snakebite."

He stared at her as if he didn't trust her. The wet bandage was still tied to his arm.

"It's dirty." She pointed. "Does the bite still hurt?"

"No, not much. I tried to get it off, but I couldn't untie the knot with one hand." He held out his arm. "You can give it a try, but don't look at me. I ain't dressed properly. It wouldn't be right."

She nodded. "I already have looked at you. No need for a second viewing. Most of your skin is purple from what I see." She untied the bandage below his elbow. The area around the two punctures was red and swollen a little, but healing. "How'd this happen, anyway? You're from around here. You know about rattlers. You'd have to get close enough to dance with a snake to get this kind of bite."

He stood tall, towering over her by almost a foot. "Some men in town, rough types with whiskey on their breaths, jumped me when I stepped into my hotel room. There were four, but only three grabbed me. The fourth one held a gun on me like he planned to fire if the other three couldn't handle me. They beat me up, tied me to the bed, and rifled through my clothes and saddlebags. From the sound of their swearing, they weren't finding what they were after. I heard one say, 'The kid ain't got it on him.' But I have no idea what they were talking about.

"After everything I owned was scattered

across the room, I thought they were going to leave me, but one picked up a grain bag with a snake wiggling in it. He pushed my arm in the bag and held it closed until I yelled when the snake bit me. Then he seemed satisfied that I was on my way to the grave. The other three gave me a few final kicks and left."

Colby frowned. "One said that I'd do anything they said once the poison took hold."

He couldn't seem to stop talking to her now that he'd started. "The bite hurt, but I'll never forget feeling that snake curl around my arm with both of us sharing that bag. I couldn't move enough to get the bag off, and I was afraid if I moved too much the snake might bite me again, but he seemed to want to curl up next to me."

Madie began wrapping the wound with a clean cloth she'd had in her pocket since last night when she'd seen how dirty his bandage was. "What did you do to them that made them so mad?"

"I asked," Colby said. "I didn't have twenty dollars on me, so I know it wasn't robbery. The guy with the gun said it wasn't nothing personal. Just a job, he said, like I shouldn't be too upset."

Colby looked relieved to have finally told someone the story. "I was too afraid to tell anyone in town. Afraid the guy with the black mustache and the gun would come back and finish the job. The others were doing what they needed to do, but he looked like he was really enjoying watching. He'd come back to finish the job if the snake hadn't bit me, so I didn't even tell the doctor all that had happened."

"That was smart." Madie wasn't so sure how smart it was, but she didn't want him to feel bad because he was afraid. Fear seemed something she dealt with daily. She'd grown up afraid her father would one day beat her to death, and, when he'd kicked her out claiming she was near enough grown, she'd been afraid she'd starve.

"The maid found me the next morning and called the doctor," Colby said. "I thought I was in good hands until the doc started shooting something in me. Every shot he gave me took me one step closer to death's door. I heard him tell the nurse that strong boys like me die of snakebites all the time, but I knew that if I lived the night after being bit it wasn't the snake that was killing me."

Madie tied off the bandage that was really no longer needed. "That why you love Mrs. McLaughlin, because she saved your life?"

"She and her husband did do that, I've no doubt. If it wasn't for them I'd be six feet under by now, but I don't love her. I owe her."

"You don't love her?"

He shook his head. "She's a married lady and probably six or seven years older than me. I wouldn't mind loving a woman like that someday when I'm older and have made my way in the world. Right now, when my pa finds out what happened to me in town, I'll be lucky if he'll let me leave the ranch again before I'm thirty."

Madie grinned. "I'm glad. I was afraid you were lovesick, and that will kill you as likely as the snake."

Colby pulled on his shirt. "I do like looking at Mrs. McLaughlin. She's real pretty." He remembered his manners. "But so are you, Madie. You're pretty, too, or you will be as soon as you're grown into a woman."

"I'm grown. I don't think I'm going to get any taller." She fought to keep the indignation from her voice. "I'm a woman, though. I got a man who loves me and is waiting for me in Fort Worth. He would have come for me, but he's working real hard. He says he's going to marry me and build a little house for us to live in. I've been his girl for six months now. He takes the train down and spends the day with me every few weeks."

"That's real nice, Madie. Real nice." Colby sat on a log and pulled on his boots. "I'd like to meet him when we get to Fort Worth. If he's your man, he's bound to be fine. I've noticed you're a hard worker and a good cook, better than Mrs. McLaughlin, at least around a campfire."

She beamed at the compliment.

"My Micah is a good man. Sometimes when he comes he brings me something. Nothing big, he's saving for our house, but something little like a handkerchief, or a bottle of perfume that came all the way from New York City." She thought of adding that he was kind most of the time, but she didn't. Her Micah had never hit her except once, so that made him far more good than bad. He also hadn't written or visited in over a month, but that was because he was working hard.

She offered Colby a hand as he stood and dusted off his dirty jeans.

They walked back to the camp together, talking about how they'd get to Fort Worth soon. For Colby, it was a stop-over before heading home, but for her it would be where she found her dream. A little house, a man to take care of her. Life didn't get much better.

Beth was up and making coffee when they reached the camp. Andrew waved to them as he started the horses down toward the creek for water. The little boys were still asleep. No one seemed to find it noteworthy that Colby and Madie had become friends.

Madie started the biscuits while Colby rolled up the bedrolls.

"You make great biscuits," he said, watching her. "I never get much bread unless we buy it in town. My mom ran off when I was little, and my pa's idea of cooking is catching the first thing he sees, killing it, and then scorching it in the skillet. If it ain't fit to eat, he shakes salt on it and tries again."

She giggled. "I learned to cook at the café. Everyone is nice to me there. The owner even lets me sleep in the back."

"You like working there?" Beth asked as she handed Madie the coffeepot.

"Most times. It's hard work, getting up at five to have breakfast ready for the first rush of folks. We were usually busy until after one, then my boss had me pack up what food we had left over that would travel and take it down to the station. I'd sell sandwiches and fried pies to the people boarding the trains. He let me keep half the money." She smiled. "I've been saving my nickels and dimes to go meet my man, Micah Summerset. He works in the turnaround yard at the station, so he shouldn't be too hard to find when we get to Fort Worth. I can't wait to see his face when I walk up."

Colby nodded. "I've been to the train yard once. I'll show you where to go." He hesitated and added, "Don't you think you're a little young to have a man, Madie?"

She glared at him. "I'm fifteen and I've

had my curse more than once. I guess I'm old enough."

Colby turned beet red, like he'd stopped breathing and all the blood had gone to his head.

If Beth hadn't patted him on the back and told him to go help with the horses, he might have died on the spot.

Madie watched him almost run to the stream. "What's wrong with him?" she asked.

Beth shrugged. "Men are funny creatures. They kill game, butcher hogs, and fight until they're bloody, but most can't stand it when a lady talks about her monthly time. It's something they don't understand and can't seem to deal with."

"Oh." Now it was Madie's time to redden. "I'm always saying things I shouldn't. Now I won't be able to look him in the face again. I might as well ride in the back of the wagon and stare at the dirt we're kicking up."

"No, Madeline, you'll do no such thing," Beth said. "When he comes back, you'll offer him a biscuit and act like nothing happened. It will only embarrass him more if he thinks you noticed how embarrassed he was. I'm guessing he doesn't have any sisters or a mother who explained things to him."

"You sure? Maybe he won't want to ever talk to me again."

Beth straightened. "A lady never allows those around her to be uncomfortable. It's not polite. If you're going to start being a lady, you might as well learn the rules."

"All right." Madie didn't know if Beth knew what she was talking about, but when Colby came back she did exactly what the pretty lady told her to do. She offered Colby a biscuit and talked about how the day was warming up already.

He didn't meet her eyes, but he managed to compliment her on the meal. In return, she served him the rest of the eggs, which he promptly said were the best he'd ever tasted.

"Thank you," Madie said. "I'll pack the extra biscuits up for you and the boys. After not eating for days you must still be starving. Mr. McLaughlin says we probably won't stop again until we get to Fort Worth, so you're bound to get hungry."

He finally met her gaze. "I'm so hungry I could eat that snake that bit me."

She giggled again. "If you catch it, I'll cook it for you."

As easy as that, they were back talking. Madie spent the morning watching Beth and decided by the time she was in her twenties she'd be a lady too.

She noticed something was going on between the lady and her husband. He didn't act like most husbands; he was always offering to help her, and Beth didn't act like a wife. She was always touching him for no good reason. It was almost like they were flirting with each other.

A few hours after noon, when they drove into Fort Worth, everyone was silent. The plan to get away had seemed simple, but now the fear of what would happen next weighed heavily on them all.

The boys would have to go into the worst part of town to look for their father. Madie had talked to them many nights after the café closed and they'd sneaked into the kitchen for the last of the soup. From what she'd heard, their father was a gambler who fancied himself an actor. They knew he'd be glad to see them, but Levi had whispered once to her that he didn't know if their father could take care of them. Evidently he'd never shown any sign of it before.

Madie told the boys they could stay with her in her little house. But deep down she feared her Micah might not be as glad to see her as she hoped. Though he'd never written, when he left he'd said he'd be thinking of her every minute until he came back. For several weeks, she dressed in her one good dress and waited every Sunday for him to show. She was starting to wonder if he was thinking of her at all.

Madie looked at the others in the wagon. They were a ragged band full of dreams and fears. Mr. and Mrs. McLaughlin seemed to be running from something or someone, but problems have a way of following close behind.

Colby was recovering, but he wasn't rushing home. Surely his pa couldn't be too mad over him wanting to see some of the state before he took the train home. He talked of his ranch, but maybe he wanted adventure more. The good kind, not the kind he'd had in his hotel room with the snake.

They all seemed like migrating birds who had lost true north. Each stared wide-eyed at the dusty town built in shades of brown and gray. Fort Worth didn't look like much of a place for dreams coming true, but then neither had Dallas.

Andrew McLaughlin broke the silence as he turned the wagon down a quiet street. "I got a little place here. If you all would like to stop by, we could wash up and plan what to do first. I haven't been home in a month, so the place will be a mess, but I've got water for baths and you're welcome."

"You live here?"

Beth McLaughlin seemed the most surprised, which shocked Madie. Wouldn't a wife know where her husband lived?

Andrew winked at his bride. "Sometimes, when I'm not traveling, I like to have a base. It's not much, but you all can stay until you move on or get settled here in town. When I moved here last summer it was the devil's own brand of hot. I thought I'd stay the seasons through before traveling on."

Madie frowned. He seemed to include his wife in the "You all can stay until you move on" speech. She'd noticed the rings on their fingers and she'd heard the sheriff call Beth Andrew's wife, but Madie was starting to wonder. If the lady wasn't his wife, why was she here?

Colby made up his mind about the invitation first. "I'd like to bunk at your place if there is room. I'll need to telegraph my father in the morning. I've been gone longer than I planned. I wired most of the money from the drive to the bank last week, so he'll be wondering where I am by now."

"I've got room."

No one else voiced a plan as he pulled up to a building that had four front doors, all ten feet apart. "My town house," Andrew said, as the others looked like they'd never seen anything like it in their lives.

He climbed down and unlocked the second front door. "It's four houses stuck together. I've got a first floor with a big kitchen and my study, a second floor with two bedrooms, and an attic that I've never bothered to climb the stairs to see. You're welcome to look around and decide where you'd be most comfortable. I usually sleep on the couch in my study."

Madie climbed out next. She'd never seen houses built stuck together. "You live here all alone? You don't have to share with nobody?"

"That's right." He motioned her over the threshold. "It was all I could find that seemed near the center of town, yet on a quiet street." He glanced at Beth and added, "Of course, now I'll live here with my wife."

Beth followed Madie in and shouted back at her husband. "You don't have a parlor, dear, or sitting room?"

Madie glared at them both. Either they were acting or they'd spent no time talking before they said **I do.** Maybe Beth was one of those mail-order brides. She'd seen a few of them come through Dallas. One waited all day for her new husband in the café. When he finally came, he didn't even say he was sorry for making her wait, he just took her bag and said, "Let's go home."

No, Madie guessed, Beth wasn't a mail-order bride. They liked each other too much for that.

When Madie heard Beth asking questions about where he ate and where company sat when they came to visit, she couldn't wait to hear the husband's answer.

"I've never needed more chairs or even a table. I rented the place for a year and I've never had company. In truth, I'm gone more than I'm in Fort Worth. I thought this town, being in the middle of Texas, might be the place to set up a headquarters and have a business address for my mail. I didn't realize how wide and deep this state was. I ride out a different direction every few weeks, but it's going to take me a while to see it all."

"How do you stand living here so close to other people?" Colby asked as he slowly climbed out of the wagon, then collected his share of the supplies to carry inside. The boys followed his lead and did the same.

"The brick wall between me and the other families helps." Andrew finally looked nervous. He obviously wasn't used to defending his choices. "Why don't you settle in and I'll go find something for dinner." He reached in the wagon and handed the boys another armful of blankets, then set the box of supplies on the doorstep. "I'll stable the horses and be back in an hour."

He was gone before anyone could say a word.

Madie stared at the place, hoping Micah didn't expect her to live in one of these funny houses. She took a deep breath and wondered if her man Micah would have a house for her at all.

CHAPTER 10

BETH WALKED THROUGH ANDREW'S HOUSE AND realized she didn't know the man at all. Books and papers were piled around his study. From the looks of it he lived, slept, and worked in this one room with its bay window that faced the street. The only curtain in the entire house looked like a sheet he'd strung with wire over the study window, and it was pulled back to let the sun in.

The kitchen had one pan and a coffee-pot that had never been cleaned. No food, not even a can of peaches, stocked the shelves. A hip tub sat by the stove with clean towels folded inside it. The man didn't eat, but obviously he bathed. The smell of boiled coffee seemed baked into the very walls. He had water and gaslights, but nothing but the bare essentials. Back home they stocked enough food for the winter to feed a dozen. Here, a mouse would starve.

Upstairs she found the same. A bed. A few blankets. Two suit jackets on hooks and one drawer where trousers and shirts were folded neatly. The only real sign that someone lived in the room was an open book on the nightstand. **The Gilded Age** by Mark Twain and Charles Dudley Warner. The cover was so dusty, Twain's book obviously hadn't held Andrew's attention.

The other bedroom was empty. She thought it strange that a man who used only one, maybe two rooms would have such a big house. He would have been more comfortable in a hotel or boarding-house with a bedroom and a sitting area. It was like he wanted a home but didn't know how to make one.

The boys called down and said they'd found the attic warm and bare, but it was floored. They were already hauling their bedrolls upstairs, claiming the attic as their room tonight.

"I'll sweep up the place. It will look better then," Madie volunteered. "Get any more dirt in here and we'll have to put in a spring crop."

"I noticed wood out back. I'll chop some for a fire," Colby offered. "Come sundown it'll be cold."

Beth simply walked around thinking. They'd all been in such a hurry to leave Dallas, each with his or her own goals, but now that they were here in Fort Worth, they were in no hurry to part. She wasn't sure if they were hiding, or healing, or resting between battles. It didn't seem to matter as long as they were together.

Including herself. She knew she had at least a week before anyone in her family would worry about her. The note she'd left had been vague. Her older sister and her husband often visited Fort Worth, but Beth wasn't ready to go see if they were here. She wanted this half life for a little longer.

If she did go to stay with them, she'd have to explain what a fool she'd made of herself. They all loved her and protected her. Now they'd smother her and pamper her, and offer to fight her battles for her. For once in her life she didn't need protecting. She felt safe with Andrew, her almost-husband.

When Andrew found her an hour later in his study, she was sitting on the windowsill looking out at the street. "What's wrong?" he asked, walking up behind her.

"This make-believe marriage of ours . . ." she started. "I was wondering if we could play it awhile longer."

"You looking for a place to hide out from the world?"

"Something like that."

"Then stay, wife, for as long as you want to avoid reality."

She almost loved him in that moment. Just for a day, or maybe two, she wanted to hide away and pretend. She wanted to be safe from the people trying to hurt her as well as all the ones she loved who were trying to protect her. She wanted time to discover her true self.

Andrew sat down at his desk. "So, dear, what time is supper?"

Smiling at him, she figured maybe he needed the make-believe as much as she did. He didn't seem to be running away from life, but ignoring it completely.

The night in his funny little house became magic.

She and Madie cooked supper while the boys took baths, then chased each other around.

Andrew disappeared for a while, then returned smiling. He'd bought the boys new clothes with long sleeves and no patches. He'd also bought them thick socks so they could run down the hallway and slide across the freshly cleaned floors.

Colby helped Andrew carry in the wagonload of supplies. Food, plates, and forks went to the kitchen. Towels, sheets, and pillows went upstairs, and a checkers game disappeared to the attic.

"You bought so much," Beth whispered, knowing the others were watching.

"I set up a credit at the mercantile around the corner. If you need anything, send the boys down to pick it up. The owner said he'd be open until eight."

Beth nodded and moved to kiss him on the cheek, but he was already heading out to collect another load.

For the next hour Beth sent the boys to the store four times. By the last trip they were too tired to run up and down the stairs.

At dusk they all sat on a blanket on the floor and ate. Beth felt at home amid the chatter and laughter, but she noticed Andrew had grown quiet. Had words ever been spoken in this house of brick and dust?

After the boys went up to bed in the attic and Colby spread his bedroll in the empty bedroom, Madie curtained off the kitchen with a blanket and took her bath.

Andrew walked out of his study with a box and handed it to Beth. "I wanted to buy Madie something but feared she might be offended if I bought her clothes. After all, she thinks she's a woman and it wouldn't be proper. So"—he opened the box—"I got her an apron. The mercantile owner's wife said every young lady looks proper in a nice apron."

Beth smiled, remembering how the women in Anderson Glen near her ranch often wore aprons to church. "It's beautiful. That was very thoughtful of you."

"Just trying to help."

She took the box and slipped behind the curtain to show the apron to Madie. She squealed so loud Beth was sure the boys in the attic heard her. Tomorrow was Madie's day to go to her man, and now she had a new apron to wear.

Later, when Beth went to say good night to Andrew, she found him staring out the window into the night. "Are you all right?" she asked.

"I'm fine, just getting used to the noises in the house. I can hear the boys laughing in the attic and Colby teasing Madie as they talk across the hallway from room to room, and you walking around checking windows and doors as if you fear an invasion."

"No one knows where we are. I'm being foolish worrying, but I can't shake the feeling that trouble is coming."

"I know what you mean. When I go look for the boys' father tomorrow, will you promise me you'll stay here with them? Don't leave the house until I get back."

"Why?"

"If he's not the right kind of man, I don't want him knowing they are even in town, and the last thing I want is to take them into Hell's Half Acre with me. You don't know what it's like down there. Gunfights in the streets, whorehouses on every corner, drunks looking for a brawl. There are places like the Acre in every big town, but none quite as open to trouble as here."

"You spend a lot of time there, do you?"

"It's one of the reasons I came to Fort Worth. I heard about how wild the town was from a bartender in Kansas. Thought I'd like to see it for myself." He grinned. "Don't worry. I'm not one of the regulars, but I do go down there sometimes to hear the stories of the cowboys and drunks. Most of them would break your heart. Wasted lives. But now and then I hear an adventure. A story of heroes."

He pulled a thick folder from beside his desk. "These are a few of the stories I've heard. One of these days I'll get around to cleaning them up and sending them back east. Who knows, maybe a newspaper might publish them."

"You're a writer," Beth said. "A real writer. I thought you were writing in your journal for a hobby, but you're the real thing."

He shrugged. "I tried a dozen other jobs, but none fit. Being a writer was kind of a last resort. It doesn't make much money, but it gives me a reason to travel wherever I feel like going, and most months I make enough to pay the bills."

He laughed suddenly. "Staring at your face, I can't tell if I've gone up in your esteem or down."

"I'll have to think about it." She lifted her chin.

"Well, while you're thinking, how about kissing me good night? I wouldn't mind if you're willing."

She was almost to the door when she answered, "After I get the children to bed, dear."

Beth ran from his study. The man was a chameleon. Every time she talked to him it was like talking to another person. As a train robber he'd been dangerous but intriguing. In the hospital she'd felt sorry for him and wanted to help him. On the trail he'd been half lost and little help, but he'd kissed her like no other man had ever kissed her. Now she'd found out he was a writer. Didn't they lie for a living? She probably shouldn't believe a word this make-believe husband said.

The last thing she planned to do was go

back downstairs and kiss him good night. Beth went upstairs and checked on Colby, sleeping in the empty bedroom with his bedroll next to the window so he could see the stars. Then she crossed the hallway and climbed into bed with Madie. Everyone had agreed that the two women should have the only bed.

Beth had slept with her sisters most of her life. Even when they'd finally gotten their own rooms, they'd often crawled into bed together and talked the night away. Beth knew the rules of bed sharing. Stay on your own side, don't pull covers. If you get up in the night, don't touch your feet to the others when you return. If anyone in the bed snores, it is perfectly acceptable to poke them until they roll over.

Madie knew none of the rules. Within an hour she'd pin-wheeled around until she was cocooned in the blankets. Beth shivered for a while and then decided to go downstairs for the blanket they'd used as the dining table. It wasn't free from crumbs, but it was better than nothing.

On bare feet she tiptoed down the stairs and fumbled around in the dark looking for the blanket.

"Robbing the place, are you?" a voice from the blackness said in a stage whisper. "If you need some help, I've had experience as a robber. I could give you a few pointers."

Beth hiccupped. "Stop frightening me, Andrew. I knew you were there. I came down for an extra blanket."

"This one?"

Her eyes had adjusted enough to see his outline holding something up. She walked slowly toward him, expecting a trap, but he simply circled the blanket around her shoulders and stepped back.

"Thank you," she said politely.

"You're welcome," he shot back.

"And thank you for all you've done today. Offering your house. Probably spending your month's salary on pillows and dishes you'll never need after we leave. You've given this band a safe harbor for the night, and none of us can ever thank you enough."

"You're welcome," he shot back again.

Beth stepped on the first step of the stairs and addressed what they both were not talking about. "I'm not going to kiss you good night, Andrew." She knew she was probably hurting his feelings, but he wasn't the right man for her. Maybe no man was, but she didn't want to lead him on. They could play like they were man and wife, but at some point they'd have to step back into the real world. When she did, she wanted no regrets.

His words came cold in the darkness. "I wasn't planning on asking you to kiss me again."

"You weren't?"

"No."

She heard his footsteps leaving the hallway and heading for his study. He'd walked away. A man had actually walked away from her.

Beth stomped her way up the stairs and tried to sleep. Slowly, like a cold breeze, the knowledge that tonight might be her last chance to kiss him seeped into her thoughts. If the boys found their father and Madie went with her man, Colby would probably leave too. She couldn't stay alone with a strange man, so she'd have to check into the Grand or see if her sister was in town. Any one of her sister's friends would take her in, but she hated to drop in on someone. But she'd never survive the scandal if everyone in this house left and she stayed alone with Andrew.

He was no one important to her life, she reminded herself. He'd been an accidental meeting. They'd both needed each other, that was all. He wasn't the kind of man she wanted, and she'd never be the kind of person he needed. But as the night aged, she mourned what might have been their last kiss.

At dawn Beth dressed and went down to start the fire in the stove. She saw no sign of Andrew in his study, but when she pulled the curtain across the kitchen opening she almost screamed in surprise.

Andrew was standing buttoning his trousers. His hair was wet and a towel hung around his neck.

She couldn't help but laugh. "Sorry, husband. I didn't know you bathed at dawn."

Puffy, red skin showed along his neck between the stitches. She'd almost forgotten about the wound he'd suffered during the train wreck. Now it scarred a very nice body.

"There are many things you don't know about me, wife." He grinned back, playing her game. "Any chance you've got another strip of that silk to wrap my neck? My collar will rub against skin still raw when I'm fully dressed."

She went back upstairs and found a strip of what had once been her wedding dress. When she returned he'd pulled his undershirt on, but it hung open at his throat. Very carefully she wrapped his neck, enjoying the smell of his freshly washed skin.

He placed his hands on her waist as if to steady them both. When she finished and started to step away, he pulled her against him and lowered his mouth to hers.

The kiss was demanding, not giving her time to object as he parted her lips and made her forget all about not wanting to kiss him. His body was warm from his bath as he drew her against him. His hands moved up and down her back slowly, pressing her against his chest.

One kiss answered all the longing she'd felt during the night.

When he moved from her lips to her throat, she leaned her head back, loving the feel of his mouth against her skin. "I didn't tell you that you could kiss me," she managed to say as she tried to breathe.

"I didn't ask, and I'm not asking now." He returned to her mouth for another long kiss that left her breathless. "If you don't want to kiss me," he said against her swollen lips, "you'd better yell and kick and scream, because I'm not stopping and I'm not spending another night awake wishing I'd kissed you."

Her fingers dug into his damp hair. "I know how you feel. I couldn't sleep either."

He rained feather kisses over her face. "So for as long as you're here as my wife, there will be a good-night kiss. There will be no pretending about this one thing between us."

His hands closed around her waist, pulling her solidly against his chest. She would have kissed him again, but he lifted his head so he could look into her eyes. "Swear," he demanded. "I'll not ask for more, but you'll come to me."

"I swear." His mouth was on hers again before the words were fully in the air between them. This kiss was full of passion and need. There was nothing safe or soft about it. His big hands spread up her ribs and brushed against her breasts as he caught her moan and deepened the kiss.

She was almost lost to all thought when she heard footsteps coming down the stairs.

Andrew pulled away so fast she almost tumbled forward.

"You folks are up early." Madie's voice sounded cheery as she stepped into the room.

"We were lighting a fire before everyone else woke," Beth managed.

Andrew turned toward the study without a word, but not before she heard his chuckle.

CHAPTER 11

THE SUN HAD REACHED THE ROOFTOP OF THE huge metal barn of the train yard when Colby Dixon straightened and offered his arm to Madie Delany. "Now stand beside me and let me do all the talking. If your Micah is in here working, I'm far more likely to get past the yard boss to talk to him than some half-grown girl who thinks he's her man."

"I'm not half-grown and—"

"I don't want to get into that again, Madeline. Just let me do the asking about him. You may think you're grown, but I'm older. I know best."

"Fine." She gripped Colby's arm as they moved into the huge barn whose very walls seemed to rattle. Machinery was everywhere, and the sound of hammers ticked out an uneven beat. The floor seemed made of tracks crisscrossing. The building had been built in the round so that an engine could be completely turned inside.

Colby felt her shaking even through the thick cotton of his shirt sleeve, so he patted her hand where it rested on his arm. She reminded him of a puppy someone had mistreated, and he saw it as his duty to help her out. In a few minutes, either she'd be in her man's arms and happy, or she'd be crying on Colby's shoulder. Either path, he'd see this through to the end.

They were ten feet in when a man jumped off an engine and confronted them. "Something I can do for you folks? We're working here. This ain't no ride at the fair."

Colby straightened all the way to his six feet. "I'm here to ask about Micah Summerset. I understand he works here."

"Who wants to know?"

"His family," Colby said, figuring he was

only half lying. When she married him, she would be family. "We'll only need a minute of his time and then we'll be on our way."

"I'll go get him." The foreman didn't look too happy about it, but Colby's serious expression must have convinced him that he had bad news that couldn't wait.

"I want a little more than a minute of his time, Colby," Madie whispered. "We've got a lot to talk about now that we're starting our lives together."

"I know, but he can tell you where to meet him when he gets off. The man's working, and that has to come first, girl." Colby suddenly felt very old.

She pouted, but he acted like he didn't notice.

"I feel like I'm going to be sick," she whispered. "It's too hot and smoky in here."

"You'll be fine. This is what you wanted, isn't it, Madie? Now he won't have to come get you. You're already here in town."

They stepped a few feet closer to the open doorway, where the air was cleaner. Colby swore the girl was turning green with fear. She'd woken him early, asking if he could be ready to leave right after breakfast. She wanted to find her man, but she didn't want to go alone. Now they were here and she looked like she might bolt at any moment.

As minutes passed, Colby began to have a bad feeling about this whole thing. A man who wanted a woman usually went after her. He didn't leave her forty miles away waiting for weeks without a word. For all Colby knew, Madie had made up the whole story, probably building her hopes on a few kind words or a passing flirtation. His pa always said that if a fellow smiles at a girl too wide she starts packing her hope chest, and if he dances with her more than once, she's writing down her name tied to his.

In truth, thanks to his pa's advice, Colby was more afraid of girls than of a herd of wild longhorn. On the cattle drives he'd had a few saloon girls about his age try to cuddle up to him, but he couldn't seem to form enough words to talk to them. He could stand equal to any man, but women were another story. This one beside him wasn't full-grown and she made him nervous.

"Promise you won't leave until I'm ready for you to leave."

He frowned. "How am I going to know you're ready?"

"I'll say, 'Good-bye, Colby.'" She laughed nervously. "That'll be our secret clue for you to go."

He stared at her, deciding his father was right; women were put on this earth to drive men crazy. He barely knew this one and she was already doing a great job.

He turned when he heard footsteps and saw a man heading toward them. The worker was built short and square, with powerful arms and frown marks embedded in his dirty forehead. Colby swore he was growling as he rushed toward them

"What is it?" he yelled. "I got work to do."

Madie turned around. The smile on her face wilted as she stared at the man before her covered in grease and dirt. He wasn't young either. He had to be in his thirties, and this morning his age seemed to show itself to her for the first time.

His face didn't soften when he recognized Madie. She might be plump, but she looked small now, even next to Micah.

"What are you doing here?" The muscle in the man's jaw jerked as if he were barely controlling his anger. "I told you to stay in

Dallas. I never said you could come bother me at work."

Madie lifted her head, but her voice shook slightly as she said, "I came to be with you, Micah. I thought we could get married like we talked about doing. I don't care about the little house you're building. We can live anywhere until you get it built."

Micah turned to Colby. "Who are you and why'd you bring her here?"

Colby widened his stance. He might be ten years younger than Micah, but he'd learned on the trail never to back down from a bully. Without thinking about it, he brushed his jacket aside so he could reach the gun strapped to his leg if needed.

Micah wasn't a fool; he backed a step away and calmed. "She don't belong to me, mister, no matter what she says. She's a skirt I lifted a few times when I was working out of town."

Colby considered shooting the man, but before he could draw, Madie reacted. She flew at Micah in a rage, hitting, scratching, screaming. Colby didn't know whether to grab her or join the fight, so he stood there while she beat on Micah.

The little man might have wanted to hit

back, but he didn't dare with Colby so close. One blow from his powerful arms might have knocked the girl out.

Finally, she stopped and said almost in a whisper, "You said you loved me. I thought you meant it. I thought you meant everything." Tears ran down her face as she gulped for air.

Micah didn't answer, but his prideful cockiness was gone. After a moment, he said in a tired voice, "I thought you understood we were just having a good time. That was all."

Madie nodded. "You're not building me a house, are you? You're not going to marry me."

"I already got a wife. You'll find someone better than the likes of me. You're just a kid."

"You said you loved me." She gulped out each word.

He hardened, obviously tired of listening to her whining. "You were more than willing that first night. It wouldn't have mattered what I said. Street trash like you know how to get a man to promise things he don't even mean. You may be young, but I could tell what you was the minute you smiled at me. I happened to be the first, that's all. The first of a very long line."

Colby swung before he thought. In one blow the man went down, hitting the ground so hard that dust billowed up around him.

Madie stared down at the only person who'd ever said he loved her. He'd lied.

"Get me out of here, would you, Colby?" she asked as she turned away from Micah. "I never want to see him or this place again."

Colby stared down at Micah, daring the man to stand and fight. When he didn't, Colby offered his arm to Madie. "All right, Madeline, we leave. There is nothing here that even needs to be remembered."

She managed to lift her chin and he nodded, thinking she might just have grown a little taller.

They walked out of the train yard and along the wide main street. Neither said a word until they were almost back to Andrew's town house. The morning was sunny, but neither of them felt the warmth.

"Can we tell the others we didn't find Micah?" She finally broke the silence. "I don't want them to know how dumb I was."

"It's not your fault. He was twice your

age. He should have known better." Colby swore under his breath, thinking he should have made the coward stand so he could hit him again. "As far as I'm concerned we didn't find the man you were looking for."

She shook her head. "I don't want to talk about it ever again."

"Then we'll say we couldn't find the man you knew. In my opinion, that would be the truth." Colby wished he hadn't heard what Micah had said. He'd always thought that women who lifted their skirts, as Micah put it, were ladies of the night. Madie wasn't one of those women; she was still a girl. She worked hard and cared about people. She treated Levi and his brother as if they were hers. "Forget all about him. He was wrong about you," Colby said. "You go on like this morning never happened."

She nodded. "That's what I'm going to do, only I don't never want anything to do with another man for as long as I live."

"We're not all like that," he said. "You'll see when you're older."

For once she didn't try to remind him that she was grown; she just looked at him and said, "I think it hurts too much to get older."

They walked the last few houses in silence. Beth was the only one home, so Madie told her about how Micah must have moved on. Colby couldn't bring himself to say anything. He paced the empty rooms of the house. For a time he thought of going back to the train yard and waiting for the short man to start home. Halfway there, he could easily pull him aside and beat him up.

Only Colby didn't have all his strength back yet, and he might be the one who ended up being beat up. Even if he won the fight and Micah was broken, it would only mean he couldn't work, and his wife and children would probably suffer.

Colby teetered between avenging Madie and maybe causing extra sorrow for some woman he didn't know. He finally decided that doing nothing was his only option. He had worries of his own.

After lunch he walked the few blocks to the telegraph office and sent his pa a note. The old man would be furious that he hadn't come straight home. He'd taught Colby how to run a ranch, how to work cattle, even how to handle himself in a fight, but he'd never taught him how to be kind. As he walked back from the telegraph office, he resolved he didn't want to be like his pa.

No one, including him, meant anything to the old man. When his mother left one night, all his father did was burn everything in the house that belonged to her and make Colby swear he'd never speak of her again. He'd kept his promise, but at night, when all was dark and quiet, he'd think of her, remember what she'd been like. He'd remember how his pa never talked to her or touched her or even seemed to notice she was around. He never said hello when he walked in the house, or good-bye when he left to work. Maybe she couldn't stand being invisible any longer and she had to run.

Colby walked back into Andrew's house and saw the two women at the makeshift table shelling peas. "Hello," he said, then cleared his throat. "I'm back."

"Good." Beth motioned him toward the empty stool. "Have a seat. I'll pour you some coffee and you can keep us company."

Colby hung his hat on the peg near the door. "I can get my own coffee, but thanks for the offer." His attempt not to be like his old man would start right now. He'd talk to folks. He'd even keep the ladies company, whatever that meant.

At first, he couldn't think of much to say as he sat at the table. The women were talking of how it wouldn't cost much to fix Andrew's place up. Colby listened.

When they finally changed the subject to horses, Colby joined in but noticed Madie didn't have much to say. The only topic of conversation they all jumped on was Andrew. He'd left the house dressed in a black suit and tie, and all three agreed he looked far better in his western clothes.

The day aged and Colby felt himself getting more and more restless. Finally, he guessed his telegram had had plenty of time to travel the lines to the small town near his ranch. The operator would have to ride two miles out of town to his pa, and then his pa would have to hitch up a team and drive to town, before he could send an answer.

Colby took the two boys with him and went back to the telegraph office, hoping there would be news waiting but realizing he might have to make more than one trip before his pa's answer came.

Levi talked most of the way, and they slowed him down some by stopping to look in every store window. They barely made it to the office before it closed.

"No answer from your father," the operator said, "but if you'll leave an address I'll run it over if it comes in late."

Colby wasn't sure what to say. "Two streets south, second town house on the left."

The operator jotted it down. "I think I know where that is. About a block down is a whole row of new houses going in."

"Right." Colby had never lived anywhere that might have a real address. When he left the telegraph office, he took the boys by the construction. It was exciting watching men building more than one house at a time.

The boys loved watching, but all the way home Colby thought that maybe his pa had been in the field and the runner had left the telegram on the door. Or maybe he was out hunting or down by the smokehouse slaughtering a hog. There were a dozen reasons his pa hadn't had time to answer, but one kept sticking in his mind.

What if his pa was out back burning his clothes?

CHAPTER 12

ANDREW SEARCHED EVERY BAR IN HELL'S HALF Acre looking for Levi and Leonard's father.

No one seemed to have heard of him, but everyone tried to sell him a drink or a night of fun.

He'd known it was a long shot, but he had to give it his best try. Gamblers tended to move on to the next town, but if Hawthorne had been here for a while, someone might know which way he went next. Every town in Texas that claimed three buildings seemed to have a saloon, and in every saloon a gambler would be waiting to take a little of a cowboy's money.

It didn't help matters that Levi mentioned that his father made them all remember that they were Hawthornes now, not Smiths. He'd told his son that he picked his name because it sounded like the man wearing it would belong on a stage. Levi's father swore everyone who heard it would remember Theodore B. Hawthorne, and he might as well use it for his gambling career also.

This whole state seemed awash in nicknames and shortened handles, Andrew reflected. Some cowhands were called by where they came from or how tall they were. For all he knew the boys' father could be going by Ted Brown or Jay Wilson by now.

In the haze of blowing dust, Andrew walked back toward the little town house he now called home. He'd talked to so many sleazy drunks and gamblers today, he felt like he needed a bath. He wondered how such good people like the Mc-Murrays could thrive in a place where the good guys seemed so outnumbered. Until he'd met Beth, he was beginning to think there was no such thing as the "code of the West" that so many dime novelists

wrote about. The state was poor in everything but cattle, and trouble seemed to
ride the wind. Beth might be living in a
world of her own making, but she loved
her family and she cared about other people. That kind of goodness had to have
been bred into her.

He grinned. If he were counting her
gifts, he'd have to add that she kissed like
most men dream their whole life of being
kissed. Just brushing her lips made him
forget to breathe. He knew his Hannah
was dead. He'd mourned her a long time.
Maybe it took someone like Beth to remind
him he was still alive.

Because, like it or not, he **was** still alive.

When he turned the corner, Andrew saw
two men standing a few houses down from
his place staring up at his windows. It was
dark enough that they could probably see
people moving around inside. They weren't
walking, or even talking, they were just
watching.

When Andrew drew closer, with his head
low into his upturned collar, they both
melted into the shadows. He crossed
the street, not wanting to get too close.
The streetlights offered circles of light

surrounded by a blackness so deep it would be hard to see where the road stopped and the narrow boardwalks began. But this was his territory and he knew it well.

He found his front door unlocked and hurried in, throwing the bolt immediately. Who were those men watching for?

Taking a deep breath, he forced worry from his features so he wouldn't frighten the boys. He was home. From the laughter around him, he knew they were safe.

When he turned around, Andrew couldn't believe the changes in the place. A huge crate had been turned on its side to serve as a table in the kitchen area. Stools made from barrels were now chairs. Candles were lit on top of a tablecloth as if they were having a fancy meal.

"It's about time you're home, dear," Beth said in her best almost-wife voice. "We're all ready to eat."

He smiled, loving the pretend game. Loving the idea that he might have someone to come home to again, if only for a few days.

Crossing the room, he politely kissed her cheek. Beth smelled of cinnamon. For a moment he wished they had the house to themselves. He hungered to kiss her again, softly this time, tenderly, as if there were a possibility they might become lovers.

He didn't want one night of passion and need, but a slow burn that had to be stoked like a long winter fire, building to white-hot and smoldering low even when they were a room apart, but always, always burning.

The sudden realization of how much he wanted her shook him. She wasn't the kind of woman to take pieces of a man's love. She'd want it all. She deserved it all, and he was a man who could never love that way again.

He was only telling himself a story . . . as though he could weave fiction into the real world and live there.

The boys thundered down from the attic, reminding him to stop daydreaming and deal with reality.

They were full of questions, but he had few answers. He'd met a man who remembered their father from Dallas but said he hadn't seen him in Fort Worth. Andrew said he'd also talked with a boardinghouse owner who said he thought he remembered the name but couldn't put a face to it. He said he thought a man named Hawthorne had rented a bedroom for a week or so three months back.

Andrew didn't add that the owner mentioned the man had left with a painted-up lady who said she was a singer at one of the gaming houses in the polished part of town.

"Did you ask if the man was dark-headed?" Levi asked. "Maybe he had a mustache. My father likes to wear a mustache when the weather turns cold, or a beard cut short."

"I asked," Andrew promised. "The man said he couldn't remember anything except for the name."

By the time Andrew described everywhere he'd looked, Levi hung his head in disappointment. Leonard had stopped listening and decided to watch the food being brought to the table instead. Regular meals were too new not to be exciting.

Everyone except Colby gathered round the table. Andrew took off his jacket and didn't miss Beth's frown. For a moment he thought she might consider him too informal, but surely shirtsleeves were all right for supper on a crate.

"You don't like these clothes, do you?" He found it hard to believe that the style he'd worn and thought looked very proper all his life was somehow offensive to her.

"There's nothing wrong with them. I don't like suspenders," she whispered so the others wouldn't hear. "The clothes don't seem you. I feel like you're wearing someone else's clothes. You look like a banker or a city lawyer. Was there something wrong with the clothes I bought you in Dallas?"

He frowned, thinking he should dig his dirty outdoor clothes from his saddlebags and wear them. That might make her happy. The shirt and jeans she'd bought him were far too informal for his liking and the belt not nearly as comfortable as his suspenders. "I've been a banker or at least a teller, and one year in Chicago I worked with a lawyer for a while."

Somehow he wasn't measuring up to Beth's image of him, which was very frustrating, since they'd met at a train robbery when he'd been wearing black. "I'm not a rancher, Beth. I know nothing of cattle. I don't carry a gun, and even if I did, I'm only a fair shot. I can ride, but not half as well as you do. My fingers have ink stains, not calluses from hard work." He didn't give her time to say anything before he added, "I guess in your eyes, I'm a total failure as a man."

"Not completely—there are a few things I've discovered you're good at—but we simply must talk about the clothes."

"I doubt that discussion will ever happen," he answered, wondering what kind of fool would allow a woman to pick out his clothing.

The others gathered around the table, talking of all they'd done to his house. He might not be willing to change one piece of clothing, but he wouldn't have minded at all if they'd painted the house red if it brought them joy.

There were obvious improvements. She'd put out little things that a woman would think made the house look like a home. But there was nothing expensive . . . nothing that he wouldn't leave behind when he moved on. He offered his thanks and she nodded, accepting the compliment.

"Where's our cowboy?" Andrew asked as he stood waiting until Beth scooted onto the stool. "Is he already on his way back to the ranch?" They'd been in Fort Worth a full day. It was probably time that one or two of his migrant flock flew away.

Beth and Madie both shook their heads. "He didn't hear back from his pa today," Beth said. "I told him I'd loan him the money for a ticket home, but he said no. I think he fears his father will be mad because he's late, and he wants to know he'll be welcome when he gets there."

"So where is he?" Andrew knew from the silence that followed that anything they said would be a guess.

"Out walking, I think," Beth tried. "He checked at the telegraph office and came back to tell us there would be no answer today, and then he walked out the door. If we were at the ranch, my papa would say he was riding the wind, which is what Mc-Murrays seem to do when they need to clear their minds and think."

"Maybe he's tired of our food and went out for a meal," Madie chimed in. "We had men stop by the café all the time who wanted to eat someone else's cooking for a change. One man stopped by almost every day on the way home from work for a piece of pie. He told me if it wasn't for the pie first he'd never be able to face his wife's cooking."

"Colby's not tired of your cooking," Andrew answered. "I can almost see him fattening up on your biscuits." He wanted to ask about Madie's man, but since she'd stopped talking about him, he decided to leave it alone.

Andrew was surprised at how much he was learning by what the women were not saying. They talked around subjects, never filling him in on anything important. Madie had cut both the boys' hair, but Leonard wouldn't stay still, so his was shorter on one side. Beth had rigged up a line out back and planned to wash tomorrow.

When the dishes were done, Andrew pulled down an old book of stories he'd written one summer in North Carolina. He pulled a stool close to the fire and the boys spread out on a blanket as he began to read aloud.

Levi and Leonard seemed to love hearing about a group of children who ran the streets of a sleepy town solving mysteries for a dime. "The Case of the Stolen Garden." "The Mystery of the Disappearing Boathouse." "Crime on Cemetery Road."

When he finished the third story, he looked up to find that not only the boys, but Beth and Madie were listening.

"One more," Levi begged.

"Tomorrow night. I promise. It's bedtime now." Andrew couldn't hide his grin. He'd never read his stories aloud. In truth, he'd never much thought about people enjoying them; he only thought of someday selling them.

Everyone, including Beth, protested, wanting him to continue reading, but he held firm. While Beth banked the fire in the stove, Madie took the boys upstairs.

The past two days the house had seemed alive, and right now it was settling, grumbling, shifting into sleep. . . .

He wanted to write his thoughts down, but first he had one more thing to do before turning in.

Andrew waited until he knew the children wouldn't hear him leave. He crossed to the back door, pulling on his coat as he went.

"I think I'll go for a walk. Maybe I'll find

Colby." When he saw the concern on Beth's face, he added, "It seems odd that he'd miss a meal, but then I don't know the boy well. If he went out in this town looking for trouble, I've no doubt he'll find it. The country is his territory, but the streets are mine." He could see by her eyes that she'd been worried too. "If I find him, I'll watch over him."

"Why not go out the front door?"

Andrew didn't want to alarm her, but he wanted her prepared. "I noticed two men watching the house when I came in. If I go out the back they won't know I've left. I'd like to get closer to them and find out why they're near as well as check on Colby. Stay here and keep the doors locked until I return, would you, dear?"

She nodded, and he was gone before she asked more questions.

He circled two blocks over before doubling back in the shadows. Over the months he'd often walked at night and knew these quiet streets well. A kind of off-key orchestra seemed to always play this time of night. A dog barking, a couple fighting, the sound of horses moving along the dirt-packed streets. A church bell chiming as if greeting the whistle of a train. All were the sounds Andrew knew from towns he'd crossed through. None were quite his home, but all were familiar.

He enjoyed being in the country, but the smells and noises of towns pumped in his blood. One more reason he'd never belong with Beth. As if he needed another reason.

The two men were still in the same spot. One was smoking, the other leaning against the building. Both looked tired and ready to leave. They were watching his house, not invading. He had a feeling they wouldn't be too friendly if he walked up and asked why.

After a few minutes, Andrew disappeared between two houses and crossed to a back street. If Colby Dixon was looking for a drink, he might pick one of the quiet little hotel coffee shops a few blocks over. Surely he was smart enough not to go alone all the way to Hell's Half Acre after dark, and he wasn't dressed to blend in at the hotel restaurants.

Most of the little hotel bars and coffee shops were closed already, but on the third block he checked Andrew found

Colby sitting at the counter of a place that served a late supper and beer to merchants and travelers alike.

Andrew simply sat down beside the kid as if he'd happened by.

"I'm not drunk," Colby said when he looked up. "So you've no business thinking you have to come after me. I've been my own man for three months on the trail and I can manage without a caretaker."

"I was passing and thought I could use some silence after being in the house with two little boys and two women who never stop talking. I come here often, but if you're going to rattle, I'll be moving on to a quieter place." He motioned for the waiter. "A pint of ale tonight, Cliff, if you please."

Andrew had no idea what the waiter's name was, but he guessed the man would play along, and he did.

"Evening, sir. We got an ale in today from England. It's a wee bit more expensive than the one you usually drink, but I think you'll like it." The waiter winked as he slid the glass down the bar.

Andrew didn't know what good—or bad—ale tasted like, but he took a sip. "Perfect," he managed with a smile.

For a few minutes Colby sat staring at his beer while Andrew drank his first, and probably his last, pint of ale.

"Want to tell me what's eating you?"

"No," Colby said. "You a preacher waiting to hear my confession?"

"No."

"Well, you look like one."

Andrew was finally starting to take offense at everyone's hatred of his clothes. Colby probably didn't change his shirt more than once a week on the trail and didn't bathe but once a month, yet the kid felt the need to complain about a fine black suit Andrew had bought in Chicago.

He chose to let it slide. If he was going to get mad at people making comments, Colby would have to stand at the back of the line. "I thought about being a preacher once." This time Andrew was telling the truth. "I spent a cold winter in Maine reading the Bible and thinking of how to say things that sounded like I was quoting the Almighty."

Colby finally looked up. "How'd it work out?"

"It didn't. To do any good at preaching, you've got to talk to sinners, and I learned real fast that sinners aren't always willing to listen. The third man I tried to get to change his wicked ways threatened to help me move along to meeting my maker."

Colby smiled.

Andrew shook his head. "It wasn't funny. After I insisted on preaching and he put a few dents in my head with a bar stool, I had no doubt he was serious. I learned two things in one day. Never try to preach in a saloon, and never cuss in a church. Both are career killers."

The young cowboy relaxed with a short laugh and took another sip of his beer.

Andrew did the same with his ale. Something was eating away at the kid, but he was too young to push it aside and too old to complain about it.

They walked home talking about Levi and his brother and wondering what would happen to them if they didn't find their father.

Andrew told Colby about the men watching the street. "Any chance they're waiting for you?"

Colby shook his head. "I can't think of any reason they would be, unless they're kin to the thugs back in Dallas and want to take their turn at trying to beat me to death. All I got on me is a few dollars and an almost-new pair of boots."

"I noticed them. Nice boots, but probably not worth the risk of being tried for murder."

Colby agreed. "My pa handed them to me the day before I left on the cattle drive. He told me to wear them 'cause he didn't want me coming home crippled up from wearing holes in my old boots."

He pulled his pant leg up to show the top of the boot marked with a Double D brand tooling. "Pa said they were handmade and would last twice as long as any others I'd ever had. He even made me swear I'd be wearing them when I came back." Colby shrugged. "It was like it was more important that they come home than I did. Which wouldn't surprise me. That's kind of how the old man thinks. People don't mean much to him, never have."

"You feel like that? You the same as your old man?"

Colby shook his head. "Sometimes I wish I didn't care about folks. It'd be easier, but I can't seem to stop. I'm worried about the boys, not knowing if finding their father is a good or a bad idea. I worry about Madie getting her feelings hurt. Hell, I even worry about your wife."

"Why my wife?"

"She's a brave lady, that's a fact, but she's afraid of something. Can't you see it? She goes around locking the doors and windows. She wears her Colt even when she's cooking. You may have seen the men watching the house, but she senses danger. She knows trouble's coming."

Andrew didn't argue. She'd said almost the same thing to him. He remembered the way Lamont LaCroix had glared at her, like she belonged to him.

"What should I do to help her?" He couldn't believe he was asking for advice from a cowboy who couldn't even talk to women.

"Hold on to her tight, I guess, and let her know that you'll stand with her. Levi told me of the man who came with the sheriff to take her away. If he didn't believe she was your wife, he might come back for her."

They turned into the alley behind the town houses. "I'll keep watch of those men from upstairs," Colby whispered. "I've got so much thinking to do I wouldn't sleep anyway. They looked like rough types, not the kind of men a senator would send."

Andrew was tempted to add that they were more like the kind an outlaw would send. If Chesty Peterson knew he was alive, he might come to the conclusion that Andrew had something to do with the trouble the night of the robbery. Only Chesty was in jail, at least for now. He'd heard the outlaw brag around the campfire that no jail would ever hold him, but Sheriff Harris didn't seem like the kind of man who'd accidentally leave the cell open.

Knocking lightly on the back door, Andrew was relieved when Beth opened it. He didn't miss the rifle in her left hand as he passed her. She'd been on guard while he'd been gone.

As he bolted the back door, he heard Colby apologize for missing supper and for making her worry.

She handed him a plate she'd kept warm for him, and he vanished up the stairs.

Andrew watched her as she turned around toward him. For a moment they stared at each other.

He knew she wouldn't stay here in the house with him for long. As soon as the little boys were settled she'd head back to her ranch. But maybe the kid was right. Maybe he did need to make her feel safe. The only problem was he had no idea how.

"Thanks for bringing him back." Beth set her rifle on the table. "I could smell the beer on his breath."

"He wasn't looking for trouble. Just went somewhere to think. He's all right, you know. From the few things he said about his pa, I got the feeling life isn't easy back home, but the funny thing is, he told me he worries about you."

"Me? I can take care of myself." She didn't sound sure of herself. "My sister Rose and her husband, Duncan, come to Fort Worth so often they keep an apartment. They always visit with Killian O'Toole and his wife." She gripped the handle of her Colt as if for security. "If something happens and we get separated, look for me there. O'Toole's a judge so he shouldn't be too hard to find."

"I've read about him in the paper." Andrew wished he could tell her that nothing was going to happen, but he couldn't lie.

Maybe for the first time in her life she didn't feel safe, and somehow he felt like he'd let her down. "Beth, look at me. I'm here now. If trouble comes, I'm not running. We'll protect the boys and Madie. Whoever those men are looking for, they'll have to face us first."

"What if it's me they want? I don't think we fooled Lamont, not for long anyway. He's hit a run of bad luck lately, and I think he thought marrying me would turn everything around. Now he may be blaming me for his trouble."

Andrew shrugged. "If he's after someone, he'll come after me, not you. He loves you."

She shook her head. "I don't think any man has ever loved me. Several said they did after meeting me, but it wasn't true— not after such a short time. It wasn't me they were in love with. Lamont wanted me, and probably my family, to help him in politics. That's all. He doesn't love anyone but himself."

When she moved to the window and looked out, he joined her, pressing close to her back, and gently pulled her away from the light shining in. "Do you think you and Madie might rig up some curtains to-morrow?"

"Of course." When he didn't try to kiss her, she asked, "The two men are still out watching, aren't they?"

He brushed her shoulder lightly. "I'm not sure. Colby and I couldn't see them in the shadows, but that doesn't mean they're not out there."

They fell silent as they watched the street. She was so close he could feel her breathe. Andrew wondered, if he strapped on a gun, would she feel safer? She'd lived around heroes all her life, and he knew he couldn't hope to measure up. She'd told the boys stories of how her father, her uncles, her cousins were all legends in Texas. No wonder no man who asked for her hand in marriage could win.

Lamont crossed his mind. He was tall, and probably most women found him handsome. He was powerful and enough years older than she was to be able to know how to win her heart. Only he too had failed. She'd built him up in her mind over the years and the real man didn't measure up. Probably no man ever could.

Beth McMurray was like one of those

beautiful china dolls to be forever left on the shelf to look at, but not touch.

Andrew realized he felt sorry for her with her grand family and her wealth. Right now, she was alone, and maybe for the first time.

He moved his hand over her back, stroking her tenderly. "How about I tell you a story?"

She smiled. "All right, but a true story, Andrew. A story about you. I've rattled on about my family for days, but I know little about you."

She leaned against the side of the window and he remained so close he would have touched her if he'd taken a deep breath. "I only have one true story worth the telling. I once fell in love with a quiet little woman named Hannah. She was afraid of everything: mice, the sound of a train, storms. But I loved her from the moment I saw her. I think we knew we'd be together from the first. I don't remember asking her to marry me; we both knew we would and, with no family, we didn't bother with an engagement. We married and rented a flat above a bakery. She laughed about growing fat from the smells.

"My friends said she wasn't pretty, but she was to me. I was always afraid of holding her too tight because she might break. We worked together at a bank and walked home holding hands. In warm weather we'd buy wine and cheese and eat it in the park for supper. On cold nights we'd sit at a little café and talk until the owner closed the place. I wasn't writing much then, but I told her my stories."

He closed his eyes, letting the memories flood over him. They were fading, bit by bit, but still almost too painful to remember. "As it turned out," he finally said, "I didn't hold her tight enough because she died after we'd been married a year."

"I'm sorry," Beth whispered.

"Don't be. It was a long time ago. I'm telling you the story because I'm lucky. I had a kind of all-consuming love for a time. A love so deep that it left a hole in my heart that can't heal. I don't ever want to feel that loss again, but I want you to understand that I wouldn't trade having that one love for all the pain that followed. The memory that I was once truly loved keeps me going. It's enough for this lifetime."

She looked up at him. "I didn't love Lamont like that. In fact, I didn't love him at all."

"I know, but you need to keep looking, Beth. Maybe one of those guys who tells you he loves you at first sight might be telling the truth."

She shook her head. "No, like you, it's a game I no longer want to play. This make-believe marriage is all I want to handle."

He looked down at her and felt so sorry for her. Maybe what she feared wasn't outside waiting to come in, but inside her.

CHAPTER 13

"COLBY? COLBY, ARE YOU ASLEEP?"

Colby Dixon turned from where he'd been watching the street to the shadow of the girl at his doorway. "No, Madeline, I'm still awake. Is something wrong?"

"Could I sit with you awhile? I can't seem to stop crying."

"I guess it would be all right if we leave the door open. I can't sleep either."

The plump girl with an old ragged quilt wrapped around her shoulders sat down on his bedroll. He leaned back against the wall and crossed his legs out in front of him. He guessed that a woman was not supposed to come into a man's bedroom, but since there was no bed and she was more girl than woman, it wouldn't matter. Besides, over the past week he'd gotten used to her being around.

He didn't have long to wait before she broke the silence. "I worry about Micah and what to do since he don't want me. You being older and all, I thought you might give me some words of wisdom."

He patted her hand awkwardly and thought he was all out of any words of wisdom. If he'd had any he'd have used them on himself. Last year he couldn't wait to leave home for an adventure, and now all he wanted was to go back. He'd even reached the point where he didn't care how much his pa yelled at him.

Finally he realized she was waiting for some kind of answer. "It's all right, Madeline. Don't give Micah another thought. Don't waste your tears on a no-good like him. Someday, when you're older, you'll find a good man to be **your** man. You wait and see if I'm not right. Micah wasn't man enough for a girl like you, and you were too young to know it. Ain't no crime in being dumb when you're young. I'm just now growing out of that stage myself. Course, some folks never get over being stupid, and I'm guessing Micah may be one of them." He smiled, proud of himself for sounding wise.

"I know what you mean. He lied to me and I fell for it." She gulped down a sob. "He lied to me from the first day I met him. He said he wasn't married and that I was the prettiest girl he'd ever seen. He claimed he loved me." She sniffed and added with a little cry, "When we went for a walk all alone by the river, he said he wanted to get closer. He said it wouldn't hurt, but what he did to me did hurt. It hurt bad and I bled a little."

Colby was glad it was dark, because he could feel the heat burning his face. She shouldn't be talking about such things. He was almost three years older than she was. He should give her some good advice, but she was talking about something he knew nothing about. What happened between a man and a woman couldn't be as simple as what happened between a bull and a cow, but he had no idea where all the differences lay.

Colby patted her hand some more, hoping that would help. He thought of telling her that if it always hurt women he guessed they wouldn't go running after men, but then she might ask questions and the girl had no bridle on her runaway mouth.

"I didn't even like the way he kissed, all slobbery and all, but I'd never been kissed, so maybe that's the way to do it." She straightened out the bedroll as if she could straighten out her life as easily.

"I don't think a kiss is supposed to be slobbery. I think it should be something both enjoy." He thought of a February snowstorm when he'd been twelve. It came in so fast the teacher said all the kids would have to spend the night. When the wind knocked a window out in the schoolhouse, they'd all bedded down in the half dugout behind the school that had been built in the early days and was now used for storage.

The younger kids slept downstairs around a crumbling old rock fireplace. Most of the wood was damp and the fire's smells blended with the earthy odor of the old homestead. The older kids climbed to the shallow loft formed by the pitch of the sod roof. It was above ground by three or four feet so not nearly as warm, but no one minded; they were all having an adventure.

Boys on the left, girls on the right, the teacher had called up. After she went to sleep, Colby remembered they all huddled together and played games while firelight shadows danced on the uneven ceiling.

He'd kissed every girl in his class that night, and one even told him he was the best kisser of all the boys.

When Madie kicked him, Colby realized he hadn't been listening to her. "What?" he asked.

"I said, have you ever kissed anyone?"

"Of course."

"Well, would you kiss me?"

"No. You're just a kid. It wouldn't be right."

"I'm not a kid. I—"

"I don't want to have that discussion again, Madeline. I'm almost eighteen and it wouldn't be right for me to kiss a girl of fifteen. There's a code of what's right and, to tell you the truth, I thought about going back to that train yard and shooting Micah for breaking it. Men don't kiss little girls."

She looked frustrated a moment before

she settled on crying again. "Some men think girls are grown at thirteen. My mother was thirteen when my father married her and brought her to Texas."

"How'd that turn out?"

"She hates him. The day he kicked me out she threatened to kill him, but he said they had too many kids and needed to start clearing the nest."

"And you were the oldest?"

She nodded. "When I have a kid I ain't never turning him or her out. I'm keeping them until they want to leave, and then I'm giving them new clothes and new shoes to walk away in."

"You and my pa have a lot in common. Sometimes I think I'll be fifty and still doing every chore he tells me to do. Me and the mule seem to have the same ranking on the ranch."

"I think my mom didn't want me to go because I was doing all the washing and cooking around the place while she was expecting, and it seemed to me she was always expecting."

He went back to patting her hand. In her cotton nightgown and her hair in pigtails, she looked young, but he couldn't help but notice she already had her chest rounded out. Micah hadn't had much going for him in looks or charm, and he'd talked her into bed. Colby didn't want to think about what would happen if she was on her own again.

Maybe he could talk to Beth and they could find her a good job here in town. Or maybe Beth could take her back to Whispering Mountain to work. He thought of asking his pa if they could hire a cook. Lord knew they needed one. But the old man would never spend the money. Every time they had a good year, he bought more land or cattle. When a bad year came along, they ate beans and didn't buy anything.

While she cried and held his hand, Colby thought about what it would be like to eat fresh biscuits every morning and have a clean shirt now and then. They'd had a woman come by the ranch now and then to do laundry, but his father had yelled so much, she'd finally stopped driving over.

"He didn't love me at all," Madie mumbled as she cried. "Not even from the first. I was just something he used."

"It's over, Madeline; no use in going on

about him," Colby finally said after half an hour.

Madie shook her head. "It ain't over. My belly's swelling."

Colby moved his hand to her middle and touched her. What he'd thought was too many biscuits was obviously the rounded swell of a child. "You're going to have a baby?"

She nodded and started crying again. "I know the signs. That's why I had to leave Dallas and find Micah."

"You going to tell him about the baby?"

She shook her head. "If he didn't want me, he won't want the baby."

"How far along are you?"

"About halfway. My ma always said she felt a butterfly flutter inside when she was halfway. I felt it the other day and again this morning."

Colby leaned back against the wall. **Hell**, he thought, now he felt like crying. He was always thinking how tough he had it with a pa who made him work every waking hour, and was probably not speaking to him for spending a few extra days getting back from the drive, but compared to her, he was standing on trouble's shallow end.

CHAPTER 14

BETH HAD FALLEN ASLEEP ON ANDREW'S SHOULDER when the knock at the door sounded at dawn. For a moment, she moved closer against the warmth of him, but then she realized her time for dreaming was over. Reality had come to call.

She'd spent the night in his study. They'd talked for hours, neither one wanting to face the night alone. They'd become friends, the kind of friends she'd probably never be with a man again. She'd teased him and laughed at his funny stories, and he'd touched her with an ease no man ever had. She'd grown comfortable holding his hand and feeling his fingers brush over her hair.

The second pounding came, harder, faster. Andrew stood, pulling her with him. "Go, light the lamps in the kitchen. I'll answer the door." He raked his hand through his brown hair and buttoned his vest, trying to look like he hadn't slept in his clothes.

When he looked down at her, he smiled and touched her cheek. "You might want to straighten your hair." He hesitated, as if not wanting this one moment to end. "I made a mess of it playing with your curls last night."

She ran to the kitchen, tossed a few logs on the coals and hoped they'd catch, lit the lamps, and picked up her rifle. There was no time to think about her hair.

Crossing to the door, Beth saw two men on the porch, both big, dressed in leather for travel, and fully armed. Raising the weapon, she waited. If they stormed past Andrew she'd take the first one over the threshold. This might only be her make-believe home and her make-believe family, but she'd defend it.

A movement at the top of the stairs drew her gaze. Colby sat with his Colt in hand.

For the first time since she'd heard the knock, Beth breathed. She touched her finger to her lips, warning the cowboy to stay silent.

"I hate to call on you this early," the thin stranger's voice bellowed in with the wind, "but the telegraph operator told me you might have a young man by the name of Colby Dixon staying here. He left this address if a telegram came in for him."

Andrew didn't move or open the door wider. "He's done nothing wrong, Ranger."

The tall man shifted. "I'm Slim Bates, a ranger based out of Waco. I need to talk to Dixon if he's here. And you're right, to my knowledge he has done nothing wrong, Mr. McLaughlin, right?"

"Right." Andrew still didn't move.

"I've read a few of the articles you've written for the Austin paper. Right good at telling things like they are out here. You should come by the ranger office; we'd bend your ear with a few more stories."

"Thanks for the offer." Andrew remained cold and solid in front of his entryway.

The ranger shifted. "I'm not here to bring trouble to your door, Mr. McLaughlin. I got a telegram from the marshal south of here, and he asked me to pass on a message to the boy."

Beth took a step forward and lowered her rifle. "Slim?"

The hardened ranger looked around Andrew and grinned. "Well, if it ain't little Bethie McMurray."

All his business was forgotten. The ranger shoved his way around Andrew and lifted Beth off the floor in a full hug. "You sure are a sight to see, little darling. Does Duncan know you're in town? I heard that ornery cousin of yours might be in this part of Texas." Slim glanced at Andrew. "He told me you was getting married, but he didn't mention to who. I never figured you for hitching up with a writer." He said the last word as if Andrew might be a lower life form she'd captured in the woods.

Beth giggled and winked at Andrew's frown.

Slim set her down and slapped Andrew on the shoulder. "Congratulations for tying a rope around the prettiest girl in the state." He shrugged when Andrew stared at him. "Of course, I knew when I turned her down 'cause I'm twice her age that she'd find someone else, but I knew it would take

her a while, being up in years like she is."
He laughed at his own joke even though
no one else bought into it. "It's a fine mess;
all the McMurray girls are married. I guess
I'll have to wait around for the next genera-
tion. By then maybe I'll have slowed down
long enough to let one of them catch me."

Beth remembered how her papa used
to say Bates's jokes were so bad they ran
him out of three states before he settled
in Texas. Slim rode with her uncle back in
the war, and he'd stopped by the ranch
for a meal. Like most of the rangers, he
thought he was part of the family at Whispering Mountain.

"Have you seen Duncan and Rose?"
Homesickness hit her all at once. If her
cousin and sister were in town, they'd
straighten everything out. Much as she
hated herself, she suddenly wanted someone else to solve her problem as they always had; she wanted to see them.

While Slim explained that he hadn't
seen a soul in two weeks, Beth noticed
Andrew motion in the other ranger still
standing outside. "Might as well join the
family reunion," he said.

The young ranger looked ill at ease. "I'm

probably the only one in the state who
doesn't know the McMurrays. I'm new.
Just got my badge last week and the cap-
tain told me to ride along with Bates till I
learn my way."

Andrew shook his hand. "I'm new to the
McMurray legends too. I married one of
them by accident, not knowing."

Beth found her manners. "Oh, Slim, I'd
like you to formally meet my—"

"Husband," Andrew finished the sentence. "And if you'll come in for coffee, I'll
go wake Colby."

He cut Beth a cold look as he turned
toward the stairs. She might trust these two
men, but Andrew wasn't so sure. He was
being ridiculous, she thought, but he
was also right. Lamont LaCroix was a
powerful man. Powerful enough to buy a
ranger, maybe? She might trust Slim Bates
with her life, but Andrew obviously wasn't
willing to do so.

"I'll make some coffee." She set the gun
down by the stairs. "Come on in, gentlemen, and have a cup while you wait."

Slim walked past the cluttered study
with books and papers stacked everywhere. "Nice sitting room you got there.

Reminds me of your papa's study. I swear if Teagan buys one more book, that room will tilt the ranch house."

She remembered Slim had never been long on tact. Like most, he tended to say whatever crossed his brain, whether it was a thought or a rambling.

She said smoothly, "That's where he writes."

"Oh," Slim answered, without much interest, and moved into the kitchen. "I've never known a writer for real. I don't read much except the paper now and then, and it's usually a month old before I get time."

Madie tromped down the stairs wearing her new apron, but still half asleep.

Slim and the young ranger stood when she walked in, making her blush. When Beth introduced her, she said Madie was a friend, nothing more. The girl managed a greeting, then slipped into the kitchen to start breakfast.

Slim barely noticed; he was too busy telling Beth about Duncan's latest capture of a bank-robbing gang. "The man's a legend same as his father, Travis. Duncan rode in alone and brought six men out, all tied to their saddles."

Beth smiled. Her uncle had adopted Duncan when he'd been found in a raiding party's camp years ago. He'd been only about four, but he was so wild that she and her sisters used to complain about him hourly. They called him Duck because he followed her uncle everywhere. No one in the family doubted for a minute that he'd study law and become a ranger.

Duck grew up spending his summers at Whispering Mountain and pestering his cousins. Beth and her sisters all loved him dearly even though they thought him half wolf. Like her and her sisters, Duncan was a McMurray by heart and not blood. None of the family thought he'd ever marry, but Duncan loved Beth's sister, Rose. He had loved her since they were children and often said his mind couldn't settle until he knew where Rose was.

Even though Duncan was a ranger and Rose a nest builder, somehow they'd managed to fit together. Like all McMurrays, they might leave, but eventually they'd come back to the mountain to settle.

After she served the coffee, Beth excused herself and ran up the stairs. Colby and Andrew were talking by the window.

They both looked her way and Andrew said, "I told him he didn't have to go down unless he wanted to. These rangers seem friendly, but I'm not letting them take him back to Dallas."

"I know Slim Bates. If he'd come to arrest you, he wouldn't be drinking coffee downstairs. He's not sent from Dallas but from south of here, near where your ranch is. I doubt he knows anything about what happened in Dallas."

Colby nodded and strapped on his gun belt. "I'll be ready this time anyway. No man's forcing my arm into a bag with a snake again."

They followed him down the stairs, but Andrew didn't look at her. She took his hand and he held on until they reached the rangers, but it wasn't a caring touch, only one for show.

Slim introduced himself to Colby and asked if he could speak to the boy alone in the study.

Colby nodded and the two of them left. Beth tried to talk to the other ranger, but he didn't seem to answer in more than one word. His longest sentence was, "My name's Stanford, miss."

Andrew paced in the hallway and Madie banged pots in the kitchen. All waited and worried.

Breakfast was ready by the time Slim returned, but no one sat down to eat.

Colby kept his head low as he stood at the doorway. "I have to go with the ranger," he said. "My pa's been killed. We're guessing he died two weeks ago, but they didn't find him for a week." His voice shook slightly, but Colby needed to finish. "The ranger seems to think the men who beat me up could have been hired by the same man who had my pa killed. He's buying up the small places around ours. I know my pa, he wouldn't sell."

Everyone started asking questions at once, but Slim didn't have many answers. All he knew was Colby's father had written the marshal asking for help about six weeks ago. He claimed threats had been made. When the marshal got to his land, they found Dixon dead. One shot in the head at close range. The house had been torn apart.

Andrew said what they were all thinking. "The night you were beat up, they were looking for something. When they didn't find it, they figured it would help their plan if you were dying. But why draw out your death?"

"I won't find out unless I go back," Colby said.

"But it could be dangerous. These men went to a great deal of trouble to try to get what they wanted." Beth wished there were a dozen rangers riding back with him. "You don't know what they're after, but you do know they want you dead."

"You might be safer here," Andrew suggested. "You know you're welcome to stay with me."

Slim shook his head. "They found him in Dallas, and my guess is they'd find him here. If the devil's gunning for you, son, you might as well turn and face him." He looked at Beth. "We'll be with him, Bethie. We'll watch over him."

The young ranger stood. "I'll go saddle a horse for you, Mr. Dixon."

Colby turned to go upstairs to collect his things. "Nobody ever called me Mr. Dixon. That's what they called my pa."

"You own land now, son. A lot of land from what I hear. I imagine most folks will call you that from now on." Slim frowned, feeling sorry for the boy who'd had to step into the boots of a man so quickly. "I'll help you have the deed changed over to your name."

Colby looked back. "I don't even know where it is."

"Don't worry, your pa put it somewhere safe. We'll check the bank first. I've done this before. If your pa's place was one of the Mexican land grants, it'll need to be passed on to you all legal-like."

Colby moved on up the stairs, obviously not caring about paperwork.

Beth expected Slim to say his good-byes, but the old ranger sat down at the table and helped himself to another cup of coffee. She and Andrew had no choice but to join him.

"Something else on your mind, Slim?" she asked.

Slim looked at Andrew. "There's two men watching your place, McLaughlin. I seen them when I rode over. Not cow-hands. Probably railroad workers; their overalls are stained with oil."

"I know. I saw them last night." Andrew

lowered his voice as the little boys stumbled down the stairs and took their seats at the table.

Slim barely noticed the kids. "Got any idea who they are or what they want?"

"Nope. If they followed us from Dallas, they're trouble, but I don't even know how they found us."

Slim tried to muffle a few swear words with a cough. "Well, I can tell you that. You folks left a trail wide enough for a blind man to follow. When we left Dallas, half the folks we passed remembered seeing a woman with two hurt men in the wagon." He turned to Beth. "You must have talked to everyone you passed on the road. That's not a good idea when you're running away. The sheriff told me you two were leaving because some fool thought he was married to you, Bethie, and planned to correct this mistake you made." Slim pointed a thumb at Andrew as if he were a horse bought in the dark.

"Engaged. I was never married to Lamont LaCroix, and I will never be in the future," Beth corrected. "He thought I accidentally married the wrong man after the train wreck."

Slim lifted his eyebrow. "Did you, Bethie? Marry the wrong man?"

"No," she answered honestly, and almost added that she'd only pretended to.

"And all the kids just jumped in the wagon, I guess," Slim calmly said as he waved his hand from Madie to the boys.

"That's right," Andrew answered, drawing the ranger's fire. "Madie wanted to come meet her fellow. The little boys think their father is here in Fort Worth, and Colby figured someone would finish the job of killing him if he didn't leave. Did he tell you that the man who beat him held him down and slid his arm into a bag with a rattler?"

"Nope, but that does sound like someone wanted his death to look like an accident."

"They almost got away with it," Beth said. "The doc kept him drugged up. He hadn't had the chance to tell anyone, and the sheriff said he wasn't conscious when he brought him to the little hospital."

"What about you, Mr. McLaughlin? You running to or from something?" When he didn't answer, Slim added, "A man who has married a pretty young bride usually wants to be alone with her, not haul a wagonload of folks home with him. Plus, by the look of it, you slept on that couch in your study and not upstairs with your bride. Seems a little on the strange side for a newlywed."

Beth knew Slim was guessing, maybe digging for something. Andrew wasn't helping by remaining silent as if he were guilty.

"We were in a train wreck the night we married," she whispered to the ranger. "My husband was hurt. That's why he was in the hospital with Colby." She hesitated the right amount of time to show embarrassment and added, "He isn't able to continue with the honeymoon."

Slim's eyes widened. "I'm sorry to have pried, sir. You have my deepest sympathy. You both do. I saw the wound healing on your head, but I never thought about you being hurt other places."

Beth straightened as if trying her best to be brave. "I can wait for as long as he takes to heal. The doctor says we can't rush these things." She glanced down at Andrew's lap.

Slim stood, suddenly in a hurry to leave the couple alone with their problem. "I'd better go help the pup with the horses. We'll be waiting out front when Colby is ready." He gave Beth a quick hug and was gone. When a ranger couldn't solve a problem, he rode away.

Beth turned to Andrew. He couldn't have looked any madder if smoke were coming out of his ears.

"I had to say something," she said defensively. "You were just sitting here."

"You told him I'm impotent."

"Well, what does it matter if my make-believe husband has make-believe injuries that keep him from making make-believe love?"

He moved closer. "If I ever make love to you, wife, it won't be make-believe and you'll know it. You saw the way Slim looked at me. If word gets out, every man in this town will pity me. I'll be the butt of whispered jokes. Poor McLaughlin, married to the prettiest girl in Texas and he can't sleep with her."

"I slept with you last night." She remembered waking against his shoulder.

"That is not what I'm talking about, and you know it."

"Lucky for me I don't know what you

mean. You should be grateful I told Slim that story, or my father and uncles would be riding hard right now to get to you so they could take turns killing you."

Andrew moved away from Beth as Madie walked through the little dining area on her way upstairs. "Yeah," he whispered. "I'm real lucky."

Andrew glared at his wife until Madie's footsteps moved upstairs. "We'll finish this discussion later, Bethie."

"Aren't you going to thank me for getting Slim off your back?"

"No," Andrew said, and walked to the hallway to get his coat.

CHAPTER 15

COLBY WAS STRAPPING HIS BEDROLL UP WHEN Madie walked into his room.

"I brought you some biscuits for the ride. I don't know how far away your ranch is, but these should last you a few days."

"Thanks. It's three days of hard riding and I've no doubt the rangers will move fast. The longer it takes, the colder the trail of the men who killed my pa will be." His voice grew hard. "I can't wait to get back and find out who did this."

"I don't want you to go. You've been a real friend to me in a world where I've had far too few. I've never talked with anyone the way I talk to you."

"Me either." He stood and moved close. "I'm older than you and I want you to promise me something, Madeline."

"You only call me that when you're being very serious."

"Well, I'm being serious now. I want you to stay with Andrew and Beth. If they move, leave word with the rangers where you've gone. Promise me you'll stay with them."

"What if they don't want me to stay? What if they don't stay together? They don't seem too happy with each other right now."

"Promise," he said softly.

"Why?" She looked up at him, tears floating in her eyes.

"Because I'm coming back to check on you when I get my pa buried and his killers behind bars. It may take me some time, but I swear I'm coming back and making sure you're safe."

"You'd really do that?"

"I will, and you'd better be here or with the McLaughlins. I don't want you going off with the first man who comes along and tells you you're pretty. Don't lift your skirt for no one. Do you understand?"

She stared at him and whispered, "No. I'm not sure I do, Colby."

He leaned closer and kissed her, pressing his lips against hers. When he stepped away, he added, "Now that should make things clearer between us. Don't go thinking I want to be your man or some fool thing like that. I care about you and want to make sure you and the baby are all right in this world. So you mind what I tell you."

He picked up his things. "You stay out of trouble, Madeline, and try to be a little more grown up when I get back."

"I'll work on it," she promised. "Could you kiss me again before you go? I liked that kiss."

"All right, but only one more. You're too young to be kissed often."

"I'm fully grown—"

"I don't want to talk about it, Madeline." He kissed her again, softer this time, and they both smiled when he finished.

She didn't follow him down the stairs and he didn't look back. They'd said all they planned to say. He was coming back and she was waiting.

CHAPTER 16

ANDREW TALKED TO SLIM AS COLBY SAID HIS goodbyes to the boys. He knelt on one knee so he could look Levi in the eye. "I want you to keep this twenty-dollar gold piece for me. If the women or one of you need anything, you spend it, but I'll want an accounting for whatever you buy when I get back. Do you understand?"

Levi nodded.

Sounding very much like their older brother, he added, "You mind the adults, but remember, you're your own man. You got to take responsibility for whatever you do."

Levi looked like he was taking an oath. "Yes, sir," he said, and poked his brother, who only nodded.

When Colby stood, Andrew thought he saw a tear in his eye, but they both turned their attention to the rangers.

Slim Bates swung atop his horse and said he'd pass by the office and tell a few rangers to check on the men hanging around the corner. As of now they weren't doing anything wrong, but that didn't mean they weren't thinking about it.

As the tough old ranger talked, Andrew fought the urge to pull out a pencil and write down the way he said things. He was the walking, talking, real deal. A man who'd fought his way through life. In the early days of Texas these men were the law. They lived with danger as a sidekick, riding straight into fire, never backing down, and all for "forty and found."

He made a mental note. Forty and found. Forty dollars a month and what food they found along the trail. Not much pay, but what a life. He might never be able to live that kind of life, but Andrew would love to write about it.

When he watched Beth give the old

ranger a hug, he realized these were the kind of men she'd been around growing up. No wonder no man measured up. An ordinary man like him wouldn't have a chance. She played her part as his wife well, though, in front of everyone. She took his arm and stood close to him as she waved good-bye.

Andrew accepted Colby's handshake. They both promised to keep in touch. In the years he'd been traveling, Andrew found that very few people actually did. He had a few friends he wrote now and then. In fact, he'd written one while camping and hadn't mailed the letter. It must still be in his journal, stuffed among his dirty clothes. A week ago the letter hadn't covered a full page; now, he'd be paying extra postage if he caught the friend up on his life.

As Andrew walked into his study, determined to clean out his bags, he found Madie waiting for him. She looked like she'd been crying. The girl was an emotional merry-go-round. If you didn't like her mood of the moment, wait, and she'd circle around to another one.

"Something wrong?" he asked, feeling

like the two words had become his greeting to everyone in the house lately. "You all right, Madie?"

The girl scrubbed her face and straightened. "Mr. McLaughlin, I was wondering if I could stay on with you and the missus. I can cook and clean. I'd work for my food and board; you wouldn't have to pay me." Her voice held an edge of panic. "I'd help with the boys too, till you find their father."

"You didn't find your man, Micah, did you?" He hadn't had time to talk with her or Colby about what had happened yesterday morning, but he knew it had been bad news from the looks on both their faces.

"I found him, but he didn't want me. I ain't got nowhere else to go, so I was hoping you'd let me stay on for a while."

He'd never hired any help, but glancing around at his mess of a study, he could see that he could use some. He paid for his laundry and ate most of his meals out. If that changed, it might save him enough money to buy food for the family he now seemed to have. They wouldn't be here long, so his bank account could probably handle the costs.

"Stay with us, Madie." Andrew saw Beth in the doorway nodding. "I know you'll help out where you can and it will be greatly appreciated, but stay as a part of our family. If you need anything, tell Beth, and she'll charge it to the account at the store."

Madie beamed. "Really?"

"Really. We couldn't do without you. We may not be here long, but while we're here, you're one of the family."

The girl started crying and ran out of the room. Crying happy, crying sad, the girl was circling again.

Beth walked into the study as he resumed searching for his saddlebags. "That was a nice thing you did. I was thinking that when I leave, I'll take her with me if she wants to come along. I'm sure I could find her a job in Anderson Glen near our ranch. It's just a small town, but folks watch over one another there."

Andrew had no idea what that would be like. He'd always lived places where he didn't usually know his neighbors' names. He could never remember a time when he felt "watched after."

"You planning to end our make-believe marriage soon, are you, wife?" He fought to keep the question casual. He didn't want her to realize how much it had meant having her here, even for a few days.

"Yes," she said as she poked at his type-writer. "I'll leave as soon as the boys find their father and I think of a story to tell my family about how I traded husbands during a train wreck." She hit one of the keys on the machine. When the ugly ma-chine trembled as if it might fall apart, she stepped back and glared at it as if it were something evil.

Before he said something stupid, he changed the subject. "If I'm going to have four more mouths to feed, I'd better get or-ganized and get back to work.

To his surprise, she said, "Want some help in here?"

He almost forgave her for telling Slim he was incapable of doing his husbandly duty. "I'd love some. Do you know how to use this new Remington model typewriter?" He knew she didn't, but wondered if she'd admit it.

"Sure," she lied, as he knew she would. "What is it?"

"It's the new Sholes and Glidden type-writer. I paid a hundred and twenty-five dollars for it last year in Chicago. It can type words faster than I can write them down."

She frowned. "I doubt it, the letters aren't even in order."

"Trust me, in no time you learn where the letters are. All I have to do to get stories out is to type them on this machine and mail them to an editor. Seems simple, but the steps never seem to fall in order. I'm always getting halfway through one project when another comes along."

"Show me how to use this machine and I'll help you."

"All right, but I warn you, I waste three or four sheets of paper starting over before I get one page right." He tossed his saddlebags down and began explaining a machine he was sure was possessed of devils. About the time he got it running smoothly and thought he'd get tons of work done, the thing jammed.

Thirty minutes later she was slowly pecking out letters. She wasn't going half the speed he typed, but she rarely made a mistake. When she did, she got so mad at herself he couldn't help but laugh.

They took turns typing. He corrected his

handwritten stories while she typed, and she corrected his polished copy while he typed.

Three hours later they were talking over an old story Beth had found about the ghost of a cat who lived in a boarding-house filled with aging gamblers. "You have to send this in," she begged. "People would love reading this to their children."

"I don't know." He didn't think it was polished enough. Nothing he wrote was ever polished enough.

"I write them, spend hours making improvements. Sometimes I even type up one or two, and then I never take the time to send them off. Every time I move to a new place it seems I have one more crate of journals and stories to ship along. I figure if I keep this up until I'm fifty I can move to Maine and have a house where all the furniture is made of boxed-up writing, and then I'll spend my old age reading them all."

"I could help you with the mailing too. Tell me the places and I'll pack them up and get Madie to run them over to the post office."

"Sounds like a plan, but I should warn

you most of the stories come back. Most of my luck in making money has been the short articles about the local life out west for newspapers back east. But don't think you have to help me; I'll manage fine."

She stood and placed her fists on her hips. "I've never been much help to anyone, Andrew. I'm the baby. The one everyone always spoiled and helped. Even when I was old enough to have chores, my sisters always stepped in to help me finish them. Just this once, I'd like to really be of some use to someone, if only for a few days." She surveyed the messy office. "And you are about as helpless a man as I'll be lucky enough to find."

He bowed slightly. "Happy to be of service. You got yourself a job, my dear. Now, get back to work."

Leaning forward, she kissed his cheek, then whirled around to the desk.

It was almost two when they finally stopped for lunch. Madie had cooked a soup and left it to warm. While they ate, she told them about going to meet Micah at the train yard. "He wasn't building me a house. He already had a wife." She teared up again. "I was a fool. He looked so short and old and mean standing next to Colby."

"We've all been there, falling in love with the wrong person." Beth took her hand. "I'm almost ten years older than you and I've had the same problem. I thought I was in love with a man who felt the same way I did about everything, but he didn't. I'm glad I didn't marry him."

"So am I." Madie grinned. "What changed your mind? Meeting Mr. McLaughlin, I'm guessing." She leaned closer and whispered, "He's quite handsome, you know, even if he does dress funny."

Beth smiled at Andrew, knowing that he'd heard and was acting like he hadn't. "Exactly," she whispered back. "When I met Andrew I was swept off my feet."

He stood and took her hand. "We've got to get back to work, wife." If they stayed visiting much longer, Beth would let it slip that they weren't really married.

"I should remind you that I believe women should have the vote in not only elections, but in everything."

He frowned. "How do you vote today about going back to work?"

"I vote yes."

"Good, it's unanimous. We go back. At this rate I may see part of my study floor within hours." They walked together back to his little study.

As he had all morning, he fought the urge to touch her. Having her so near was a sweet kind of torture.

While Beth and Andrew worked in the study, Madie took the boys with her to the mercantile to buy material for curtains so she could spend the afternoon sewing. The little town house was a great place for the boys to play, but by midafternoon they'd talked Beth into letting them go a block down the street, where a whole new row of houses were being built.

Andrew heard Beth make them promise to sit across the street to watch. "When the workmen quit, you two run home. That means it's suppertime."

Both boys shouted and took off running, and Madie yelled her thank-you for no longer having them underfoot.

Andrew couldn't remember a time since Hannah had been alive that he'd felt so happy. Most of his days passed with no laughs or tears worth remembering. With everyone in his house now, he felt like

PROMISE ME TEXAS 245

he'd somehow sat down in the middle of a circus. The boys' laughter filled the rooms, and Madie liked to hum as she worked. Beth challenged him and bullied him, complaining about his clothes and admiring his writing. When she smiled at him, the whole day got a little brighter.

He didn't know if the two men watching the house simply got tired, or if the rangers talked to them, but the corner was clear when he peered out. He went up to Colby's room and checked now and then, but he didn't see any sign of them all day.

When he called a stop to their work in the study, Beth went to help with supper and Andrew pulled on his coat.

"Going out, husband?" Beth asked. "Tired of my cooking already?"

"I need to check on one last place the boys' father might have gone, and I don't dare wait any later." He leaned and kissed her cheek. "The men watching the house are gone, but I think I'll leave out the back door to be safe."

Beth nodded, already busy organizing everything she'd need to cook. Just as she had in his study, she had an order to everything she touched.

"Lock the door behind me."

She didn't answer.

He waited on the outside for a minute, then opened the door again and ordered, "I said lock the door behind me."

A second later the door almost hit his face, and he heard the lock click into place.

He grinned. His make-believe wife sure didn't like to be bossed around. He was surprised she wasn't with that hero of hers, Susan B. Anthony, fighting for women's rights. Any man brave enough to really marry Beth McMurray better be willing to let her stand as his equal or she'd probably shoot him with that Colt she kept strapped around her waist and make herself a widow.

As he walked, Andrew thought of how much he'd enjoyed having Beth nearby all day. He tended to get distracted, drifting from one project to another, leaving a trail of half-completed chores. She was a woman on a mission, wanting everything completed. He knew that every ounce of joy he experienced at having her around would draw an equal measure of loneliness when she left, so he'd better enjoy every moment.

The streets seemed to grow darker as he crossed through the town. Smells changed from dinners cooking to rotting food, and trash blew in the road where leaves had before. He was stepping into the worst part of town. He'd heard that now and then a gambler or drunk died in the street and was left to rot. Andrew had no doubt that was true. There were fancy saloons with dancing girls on bright stages, but underneath, there was an ugliness all the drinks and loud laughter couldn't hide. Life slithered here, and most men who stayed too long couldn't walk straight.

Turning down a narrow alley, he hurried to the only door along a long brick wall. A faded sign over the door printed out the word DOCTOR. Scratched below it with what must have been a Bowie knife was DR. OSCAR LAERTES.

Andrew pounded on the door. After what seemed like a long time, a white-haired man with a patch over his left eye opened the door. "Where you hurt?" he asked.

"I'm not. I came to ask you a few questions."

The door started to close.

"I can pay," Andrew rushed to add.

The door opened again. "All right, but I charge by the minute." The old man shuffled through a storage room and into a surprisingly clean doctor's office. The equipment was old, the leather worn across his desk chair, but none of the odors from the streets hung in the air. "Only reason I'm taking the time to talk is it don't usually get busy this early and I'd like a minute to smoke."

"You're Dr. Laertes?"

The old man sat down and pulled out a pipe. "That's me, or at least it was before I got run out of Austin. They claimed I drank too much to be trusted, but the drunks and thieves around this place don't seem to care."

Laertes took his time lighting his pipe as if it were the most important thing he'd do all night. "You already owe me a dollar, mister; maybe you should ask your questions."

"I'm looking for a man who goes by the name T. B. Hawthorne. He's a gambler who might have passed through here a few months ago."

Dr. Laertes thought for a minute, obviously running up the time he charged for.

Finally, he said, "What was his full name, or did his parents just give him initials?"

Andrew shrugged. "I doubt his parents had anything to do with the name he carried. His son told me the full name was Theodore Benjamin Hawthorne. I'm not sure it was his real name."

The old doc smiled. "Maybe his mother got pregnant in a bookstore." He scratched his head. "I think I remember such a high-flying name. Odd fellow, fancied himself an actor. It's been my experience that once a man works on the stage you can never quite shake acting out of him no matter how hard you try."

"Did you treat him?"

"No." Laertes began rummaging through a stack of papers. "I think I played keno with him one night and signed his death certificate the next. To tell you the truth, I was heavy into drink both nights." He pulled out one paper and straightened, then poured himself a drink and held up a glass to Andrew.

Andrew shook his head and waited while the doctor stared at the paper in his hand.

"Yeah, this is it. He died in an accident

about three months ago." The doc squinted at the paper, pulling it almost to his nose. "Accidentally got caught cheating."

"Do you remember anything else?"

He thought for a moment and added, "Seems like I heard there were five men at the table with him that night. Sheriff said he found four bullet holes in Hawthorne, so one of the men must have missed. Rather than charge an innocent man, the sheriff told me to rule the death an accident, so I did. Fellow was so shot up I wouldn't have recognized him if it hadn't been for his fancy clothes. I remembered them from the night before. Velvet cuffs three inches wide, silver threads in his vest."

"Do you know if he left anything behind?"

"I wouldn't know. He was dealing over at the Blue Pony. I heard someone say the woman who owns the place was sweet on him. She might could tell you. I kept his pocket watch to pay for the burial. His bloody clothes had dried to him by the time his box was delivered, so we buried him in what he was wearing. The watch was all I found on him, so he couldn't have been much of a cheat."

"Thanks, Doc, you've been a great help.

What do I owe you for the time and the watch? I'd like to take it back to his little boys."

"Three for my time and five for the watch."

Andrew knew there would be no use arguing. Laertes had named his price.

As he walked out of the alley, he tried to think of the story he'd tell Levi and his brother. Accidental death would hurt less than knowing their father was shot for cheating, and he could tell them that their father had said he wanted his sons to have the watch. It wasn't much of a lie.

The owner of the Blue Pony wasn't much help. She said she couldn't really remember the details, only that Hawthorne was always getting into trouble. He liked to lie, pretend he was someone else. She claimed he knew every scam in the book, and she wasn't surprised they found him full of bullets. If she'd grieved for Hawthorne, it hadn't been for long.

To Andrew's surprise, she asked him questions. When he said he had met two little boys who were looking for their father, the tough old girl softened but still didn't add much information.

When Andrew finally made it back

home, it was Madie who let him in the back door. Beth had already gone up to bed, she told him. He noticed the girl was sewing by the fire, but he wasn't in the mood to talk.

Something bothered Andrew about the saloon woman's story. She'd been too quick to rattle off what she knew, almost as if she'd rehearsed it as a line in a play.

Crossing to his study, he closed the door and stumbled over the saddlebags he'd been looking for all afternoon. The dirty laundry could wait. Shoving the bags between two bookshelves, he sat down at his now-organized desk and began to write about the doctor.

As real people often did in his life, the doc became a character in a story.

An hour passed, then another and another. When he wrote, time lost all meaning. This was where he lived, where he felt. The brief trips into the real world were interesting, like hunting trips finding information, but it was here where he belonged.

The typewriter on the other side of his desk was silent now. It had rattled all afternoon, and Andrew guessed the new invention had turned out more pages today than it had in the year he'd owned it. But tonight he needed his pen to fight his way through a story about a drunk, almost-blind doctor who sold his time by the minute.

Finally, when the words began to blur across the page, he stood and crossed to the gray couch that was too small for him. He dropped down, not caring that his feet hung off the end. He fell asleep before the dust settled around him.

Sometime after dawn Andrew felt a blanket float over him and then the door closed softly. He rolled over without even looking at the clock and wondered if the shadow in his study was real or one of the many ghosts who drifted through from time to time.

CHAPTER 17

Bᴇᴛʜ sᴛʀᴇᴛᴄʜᴇᴅ ᴀᴄʀᴏss ᴍᴏʀɴɪɴɢ sᴜɴsʜɪɴᴇ to hang the last of the curtains upstairs as the front door popped against the hallway wall.

Climbing down from the stool, she ran for the stairs to tell the boys to be quiet. Andrew must have worked all night, and he needed to at least sleep the morning away. Everyone she'd ever known woke and slept with the sun, but not this strange man who called himself a writer as if it were a real job.

"Miss!" Levi gulped out. He leaned over,

bracing his hands on his knees as he tried hard to breathe. "Miss, come quick."

Beth grabbed her coat and followed him out. "What's happened? What's wrong?"

"It's Madie." Levi ran ahead of her as if trying to make her go faster. "She's in trouble. I tried to help, but they knocked me away, so I ran for you. Leonard was hitting them with a stick trying to make them back away when I left."

Beth lifted her skirts and ran full out like she hadn't run in years. The minute she turned the corner she saw the problem.

Two young men had Madie pinned against a corner of a half-built house on the new street. Leonard was lying on his back amid a pile of lumber, all twisted as if he'd been tossed there. The thugs were too busy bothering Madie to have even noticed Beth coming.

Beth's first instinct was to run to the boy, but she knew she had to deal with the men first or more might be hurt.

"I ain't going with you. I ain't." Madie's eyes were wide with fear.

"Oh, come on, girl. Micah said you wouldn't mind taking a walk with us. We could go down by the river where no one would see. We're not going to hurt you. We'll even bring you right back here when we're finished."

"No." She had a thin board in her hand. Every time one of the men reached for her, she swung. "Go away."

Beth widened her stance like she'd seen her papa do when facing trouble and took a deep breath. "Stop right there," she ordered. "Leave that girl alone."

Both men turned around and laughed. They were big boys whose brains obviously hadn't kept up with their bodies.

"Go away, lady. This is none of your business," the older of the two said. He couldn't have been out of his teens, but there was a hardness about him. "We're just talking to the girl. A fellow we work with told us to pay her a call if we came by here. Said she knew how to be friendly."

The younger one, who probably wasn't shaving yet, had the sense to look embarrassed. "We're not doing nothing. Honest, lady. We just want to take this girl for a walk."

"I said leave her alone." Beth wasn't about to go away.

The older one had turned from rude to mad. "Mind your own damn business. What are you going to do, call out for the sheriff because we want to take her for a walk?"

Beth had heard enough. She opened her coat and pulled out the Colt she always kept by her side. "Go away, now."

Now she had both boys' attention. The younger one started to back away, but the older one advanced a few feet. "She's not going to shoot us, Doug. I've dealt with women before, and they don't have the guts to shoot. Not an unarmed man like me. Right, lady?"

When Beth didn't move, he added, "Maybe she's mad because we didn't ask her for a walk. She's real pretty, but too old for my liking. It's the ones her age"—he pointed with his thumb to Madie—"that's so sweet. They squeal and cry, but in the end you know they want it. I've had me a few about her age and it was real nice."

"Leave," Beth repeated, "or I'll fire."

He took another step closer. "You're not going to do that lady, 'cause if you do we might hurt the girl. As it is, if you leave and take these little boys with you, I give you my word we'll bring the girl back in an hour." He wiggled his eyebrows. "She'll have been well used and ready to come home. From the looks of her, she ain't nothing but a housekeeper to the likes of you. Nothing for you to worry about."

He took one more step toward Beth and reached out as if to knock the gun from her hand.

Beth lowered the weapon and fired. His yell and the one round echoed off the walls of the buildings as if they were in a canyon.

Madie pushed past the other man and ran toward Beth, crying and trying to hold her torn dress together.

Folks came running from every direction. Carpenters from three houses down, store owners, mothers from the other houses. Shots in other parts of town might not draw much attention, but this was a quiet street.

The injured thug yelled that this crazy lady shot his toe off, but the first man on the scene, a barber from half a block down, ignored him as he knelt beside Leonard. Someone else in the crowd cursed at the two men and told the one bleeding to stop yelling or he swore he'd blow another toe off. One stout woman said she knew these two were up to no good from the minute she saw them. Several others agreed.

Beth holstered her gun and moved to Leonard. "How is he?" she asked, as if someone wasn't hopping around four feet away screaming that he was going to die.

"He took a blow. Looks like from a fist." The barber raised Leonard up as the boy revived. "He'll have a shiner, it looks like. Can you see me, son? Is the world looking clear or cloudy?"

Levi pushed between Beth and the barber. "Can you see me, Leo? Can you see me?"

The littler boy nodded and reached for his brother. He wasn't that much bigger than Leonard, but Levi half carried him while Madie tried to help.

Beth walked away with people whispering about her.

She saw the barber stand, his big hands in fists. "Either of you boys want to file a complaint against her? If you do, I'm guessing you'll both spend the night in jail 'cause I saw her hugging on a Texas Ranger yesterday morning. If you know what's good for you, you'll go home and count the toes you have left. Texas Rangers don't think much of men who hurt women, and we all know what you were planning for the girl. I'm guessing a ranger will aim a little higher than she did."

All Beth wanted to do was to get back to the house. She had a sobbing Madie and a little boy whose eye was swollen almost closed.

Andrew rushed to meet them at the door when he saw them. Without a word he picked up Leo and carried him to his study. "What happened?" he asked as he pushed the boy's curls away from his face.

Levi, as always, did all the talking. "You should have seen your wife. Some bad men were bothering Madie and she stormed down the street like an Apache warrior and stood right up to them. When they wouldn't listen, she shot one's toe right off."

Andrew looked up at Beth. "Is that the way it happened?"

"Pretty much. If you can get a cold rag on his eye, I need to go up and see about Madie. She's had quite a fright."

Andrew nodded and Beth ran up the stairs.

She found Madie standing at the wash-stand in her petticoats. As she cried, she scrubbed at her arms.

"Madeline?" Beth said softly, not wanting to startle her.

"I can't seem to get clean." She kept scrubbing. "I can still feel their hands on me. They said they wanted a good feel of me, but one held me while the other tried to get his dirty hands under my dress."

Beth moved closer, seeing that the skin on her arms was almost rubbed raw. "Madie, you're not dirty. Those are bruises on your arms."

"I'm dirty," she sobbed. "They told me I was dirty. They said I was nothing but a little tramp, and once a woman is a tramp she won't ever be nothing else. The one you shot told me that they was taking me somewhere I could scream all I wanted to and it wouldn't matter 'cause they was going to have a feel of me whether I like it or not." She gulped down sobs. "They said that's how men treat tramps, and since I was one I might as well get used to it."

"No, you're not a tramp. No one can tell you what you are. You get to decide what and who you are all by yourself." Beth looked down where the water had run over the front of the girl's petticoat. There was no doubt that Madie was pregnant. Beth had lived through many pregnancies with her mother, her aunts, and even her sister Em.

When she looked up, Madie met her stare. To the girl's credit, she didn't deny anything. "You going to kick me out, miss? The folks at the café said they would if I ever got in a family way. I hid it from them for as long as I could. That's why I jumped on your wagon. I had to get to Micah before they kicked me out without any money."

"What did Micah say?"

"Nothing. He don't know. He didn't want me, so I don't think he'd want my baby."

"Is it Micah's baby?"

"No. It's mine. Only mine. Nobody else's."

Beth picked up a towel and wrapped it around the girl, then closed her into a hug. As if she were still a child, Beth rocked Madie back and forth. "You're staying right here with us, honey. Don't you worry. We'll think of something together. I don't know what, but you are not going through this alone."

"I ain't giving it up. My momma gave me up. She didn't even say a word later when my pa walked me out of the house. She turned her back, like I'd never been a part of her life. I ain't never doing that."

"All right," Beth agreed. "Now you get dried off and put on your other dress. After we eat lunch, I'll go down to the store and buy material for a new dress that will allow room for that baby to grow. While I'm at it, I'll buy you some underthings that are looser."

"I can pay, miss, I got some money."

Beth shook her head. "We'll charge it to my husband."

She left the girl to dress and went back downstairs. Andrew had both boys curled up on the couch while he sat in his chair, leaning back as he read them another one of his stories. Something softened in her heart at the sight. He was a good man. Maybe not brave. Maybe not a fighter. But a good man.

He glanced up at her without pausing in his story, and she had a feeling she'd be in his next story. Probably packing a pistol and smoking a cigar.

When both boys were asleep, he set the book down. "Why didn't you wake me?"

"I didn't have time to think; besides,

those two were no more frightening than snakes in the garden."

As the afternoon aged, the house settled into a quiet sanctuary. Andrew worked in his study. Beth and Madie sewed, and the boys played with a game Beth had picked up when she'd bought the material.

When the children were finally asleep, Beth collected all the work Andrew had polished and moved to the table near the kitchen to put it in boxes to mail.

"It won't sell." He startled her from the doorway. "Not one in ten does."

"It won't sell sitting in your study, that's for sure."

He was silent for a while, watching her. Then he said, "You were brave today, Beth. Beautiful and brave. You'd be an easy woman to fall in love with." When she looked up, he added, "But don't worry, I'm not. I promise. I never will."

"Why, because you know I'll shoot you?"

He looked like he was thinking about it. "No, that's not it. Maybe it's because you're bossy and spoiled, always wanting it your way." When she didn't respond, he added, "Oh, and you've got a temper that would set fire to snow. You lie at the drop of a hat. Correction, a hat doesn't even have to drop before you lie." He frowned. "Give me a minute and I'll think of a few more."

"I don't lie." She stood and moved toward him.

"Right, **wife.**"

She was within a few feet of him. "Despite my faults, I could make you fall in love with me."

"Not a chance."

She rocked on her heels, wondering if she should play this game, but what did it matter? She'd be going home in a few days and she'd never see him again. "You up for kissing me good night?"

"You asking?" He folded his arms.

"I am." She took one more step toward him.

"Take off your gun belt first."

She opened her mouth to argue, then changed her mind. She unbuckled the belt that had been custom made for her and laid it across the packages to be mailed. When she turned around, she saw the warmth in his brown eyes and knew he'd been waiting, as she had, for the chance to kiss again.

He didn't move. She knew she'd have to go to him. Her make-believe husband would never advance, and somehow knowing that he didn't want her enough to charge gave her a challenge she couldn't resist.

He lowered his arms and she moved against him. When he didn't lean down, she stood on her toes and touched her mouth to his.

As she knew he would, he took over from there. His kiss was tender and new-born until his hands began to move over her body, pulling her close.

When she was relaxed and happy in his arms, he slowly pulled away. "How about we talk about this some more tonight?"

"What's your plan?"

"I'm going to take my time getting to know you when there is no chance of being interrupted, but right now, I need to know what happened to Madie."

She told him the facts, including the pregnancy. When she finished, he reached for his coat.

"Don't wait up for me," he said, and closed the door before she could ask where he was going.

CHAPTER 18

IT WAS ALMOST MIDNIGHT WHEN ANDREW RE-turned home. Beth looked furious when he walked in the door whistling, as if he hadn't frightened her to death.

"About time you got back," she said, obviously trying to keep her voice calm.

He looked up, shoving his windblown hair out of his eyes so he could study her. "You worried about me?"

"Of course I was worried. I didn't want you to go off and get yourself killed; then I'd have to look for a new make-believe husband." She whirled, turning her back to him. "I sound like a harpy and I don't mean to. Of course, you are free to go wherever you like. You told me when we got here that you like to walk and think at night. I should have listened."

He moved toward her. "You were worried about me. I only went over to the train yard to have a little talk with the boys who bothered Madie. I don't think they'll be coming back."

"You talked to them?" She turned back, more surprised than angry now.

He smiled again. "I didn't have a gun to shoot their toes off. So I had to talk."

Beth paced back and forth across the hallway. "Those were rough guys, Andrew. They could have hurt you. Real life isn't like stories in books. People get killed. You could have been hurt. They could have tossed you on the tracks to be run over. You could have—"

"I wasn't." He stopped her, then reached for her with his gloved hand. "How about a kiss?"

She jerked away. "No. I can't talk to you right now. Good night, Andrew."

She was gone before he could say another word. Andrew stood in the middle of the hallway, wondering what he'd done to make her so angry. **Another reason never to get involved with women**, he thought. They made no sense.

He walked to the kitchen, slowly pulling the glove off his bleeding hand. As he'd expected when he'd cornered the two boys who hurt Madie, they insisted on fighting him, bragging that they'd beat him so badly not even his pretty, noisy little wife would recognize him.

He'd left them both in the dirt without ever taking a solid blow to his body. One of the blessings of traveling from school to school every few years was that he'd learned to fight. Correction, not just fight, but box. The first thing the bullies always wanted to do was beat up the new kid. Between school in his early years and the streets later, he'd collected quite an education.

The first few years after he'd lost Hannah he'd even fought for money several times, then drank all his winnings away. Bar fighting was different than boxing, but he'd learned that, with practice, he was a natural. If he could size up the kind of fighter he was up against, he could use the man's size, or speed, or cockiness against him.

Only tonight he hadn't simply fought with reason, he'd been angry. He'd wanted to make sure the boys never bothered Madie again. He'd hit them harder than needed to win and not only bruised but bloodied his fist.

He heard footsteps and quickly dropped a cloth over his bloody hand before Beth came into sight.

"I forgot my sewing basket," she said, then stopped as if frozen in place.

He covered his left hand over his right, but it was too late; she'd already seen the blood in the sink.

"You're bleeding!"

"It's nothing. I scraped my knuckles."

She rushed to his side and started mothering him, as he'd guessed she would. All the time she worked, she lectured him about how he shouldn't go out after dark and how he was lucky he only scraped a wall. What if he'd been jumped or pulled into the alley and murdered for the coins in his pocket?

Andrew only smiled. He kind of liked the

idea that she saw herself as his guardian angel. He thought about telling her that he'd already tried to kill himself by drinking and fighting. Neither worked, so he settled for traveling, living alone, finding his friends in the pages of his stories. He'd been pulled into dark alleys in Paris and Boston, and he'd been the only one to walk back out.

When she followed him to his bed in the study, he asked, "You still mad at me, wife?"

"Yes. A husband should tell his wife where he's going when he leaves. How would you feel if I just walked out one night?"

"I'd follow you," he answered, and then realized that wasn't what she wanted to hear.

She helped him pull off his coat and jacket, made sure the bandage she'd tied wasn't bleeding through, and told him to go to bed.

"No good-night kiss?" he asked, suddenly finding himself in a good mood.

Before she could answer, he cupped the back of her head and pulled her close enough to brush his lips over hers.

For a second, she tried to pull away, and he thought he'd angered her even more, but then she came forward so fast he wasn't sure if she wanted a kiss or to attack. Maybe a little of both.

She kissed him on the mouth, a fast attack more than an endearment, then pulled away.

"No," he whispered. "Not like that. Never like that. Never angry."

His mouth claimed hers in a gentle kiss.

She didn't move or kiss him back.

"If you're going to kiss me, Beth, kiss me the right way or not at all." His unbandaged hand moved into her ginger-colored hair as he waited. "Maybe you're like me, wife. Maybe you were meant to be kissed very few times in this lifetime, so we should make each one count."

She nodded, circled her arms around him, and pressed her lips against his.

Finally he'd said the right words. She was kissing him the way he liked, with passion and hunger. **A loving kiss without love**, he thought.

Exactly what he wanted.

Exactly what he could handle.

Her body leaned into him and he realized he had no way to fight against all the feeling firing through his body. The last thought he had before giving way to passion was that if this was the last time she ever kissed him, he wanted it to be a moment neither one would ever forget.

CHAPTER 19

COLBY DIXON RODE OUT WITH THE RANGERS AT a pace few men could have kept up with, but he was used to long hours in the saddle.

The first night he shared his biscuits with the rangers over beans and coffee, but he kept one back, wrapped away in the cotton napkin. He told himself he'd eat it the next day, but he couldn't. Just knowing it was packed in his gear reminded him that Madie was back in Fort Worth waiting.

Maybe not for him, he decided, but waiting. He knew he should have his mind on the trouble ahead, but all he could think about was how he liked kissing her. She was still a child—well, maybe not a child, but she wasn't really a full woman. He was just being kind. Giving her advice and watching over her. That was all. The kiss meant nothing.

But he still didn't eat the biscuit.

At night, much as he tried to keep thoughts of her away, Colby remembered how she'd looked in her nightgown and how nicely her breasts were rounded. More a woman than a girl in that way, he thought, then silently called himself every name he could think of for even having looked at her so closely.

Who was he fooling? He wasn't kind like she said he was. He'd been raised by a pa who never used the word **kind** except maybe when he shot an animal to put it out of its misery. If Madie ever found out how cold he was, she probably wouldn't even speak to him. She didn't understand. Cowboys had to be hard to survive. But still, he couldn't get her off his mind.

If Colby didn't stop thinking of the girl's breasts, someone maybe should shoot him and put him out of his misery. That would be the **kind** thing to do. A man, a grown man like him, had more important things to think about.

The two rangers probably wouldn't understand. All they talked about were horses, and trouble on the border, and how next year they were going to take a few days off, but everyone knew neither would. The younger ranger was new at the job, too much in a hurry to make himself a legend among men who were considered the best lawmen in the country. Slim Bates might be older, but he needed the life of a ranger the way some men need opium.

On the second night, Slim shot a few rabbits and the eating was good. Since they were out in the middle of nowhere, Slim elected to pull out a bottle of whiskey and pass it around. Colby took two swallows, then felt like someone had chicken-fried his brain. Before the third round he acted like he'd fallen asleep.

The two rangers kept passing the bottle and talking. Now and then they mentioned a pretty girl they'd met, but none of their stories were good enough to make Colby want to rejoin the conversation. He drifted off, thinking he wouldn't talk about Madie. It wouldn't be right. She wasn't his gal.

On the third day, about sunset, they reached the town a few miles from his ranch. The rangers wanted to check in with the marshal. Even though the rangers were involved, this was still his case to solve.

Marshal Butler was locking up his office when they rode in. He said he had news and invited them to join him for dinner at the hotel.

Colby had come into town every month for years with his father, but he'd never eaten at the hotel, or anywhere else. His pa would have considered it a waste of money. The little restaurant was nice, with a cloth on the table and napkins. All the frills reminded him of how Mrs. McLaughlin had set their table. It might have only been a crate, but she'd bought a tablecloth and napkins for the last meal of the day and called it dinner instead of supper.

The marshal said he'd order drinks while they washed up out back. Colby wanted to hear the news about the men who killed his father, but he was starving too, so he

figured he could wait a few minutes longer.

"What're you drinking, Mr. Dixon?" the
marshal asked.

"Coffee," Colby answered, thinking it so
strange to hear grown men call him mister.
He'd held his own during the drives, but he
was just one of the guys taking his turn
riding drag with everyone else. He doubted
anyone on the trail knew that about a
third of the herd belonged to his old man.
He'd sent home good money for the cows
and kept his wages to himself. He wasn't
sure what he wanted to do with the money,
but for the first time in his life he felt like it
belonged to him alone and wasn't part of
the ranch funds.

Now the ranch was his. He didn't think
he was rich. Land didn't always equal
money, but he knew his old man kept
some cash at the bank. The thought crossed
his mind that he could sell everything, take
the money, and head out to make his life
anything he wanted. This dry country
was too hot in the summer and too cold
in the winter, and the wind never stopped
blowing. There had to be a better place to
live.

It crossed Colby's mind that he could travel like Andrew seemed to do, or buy a house in town where he could eat in fancy restaurants like he was doing now.

Only one fact stood in his way. All he knew was ranching. All he knew was the land. Where else would he ever feel at home?

Once they sat down near the windows, Colby drank his coffee and listened. The marshal asked the rangers a few questions about Fort Worth before he finally got around to talking about what needed to be said.

"I've done some checking, Mr. Dixon, and your father had everything made out to you about six months back. The bank account is yours; all holdings at the cattle company are in your name. No one, not even the men who killed your pa, can get to it. Over the years all the land your father bought around here was registered in your name."

Colby sat very still. His pa had never said a word. He'd always thought of everything as belonging to the old man. Sometimes, he'd been afraid the old guy would sell and not give him a penny. All along, everything they'd scraped up the money to buy had already belonged to him.

"I think your father knew trouble might be coming concerning the original home-stead." The marshal stopped long enough to order four steaks. "There's been some rumors that a few government land offices have been corrupted. If he'd filed the pa-perwork for you to own the land-grant part of your ranch, the biggest part, the paperwork might have ended up being tampered with. We've had a few com-plaints."

"My great-grandpa went all the way to Mexico to get that grant." Colby knew the story well. It had been his only bedtime story. "He even had to sign an oath that he was Catholic before the government of Mexico, which owned Texas at the time, would let him have the land. In 1830, when my grandpa fought for Texas indepen-dence, the state honored every grant."

"I know, son, I'm not arguing with you. It's just that we need the original grant. Otherwise you might get swindled out of the ranch by false paperwork and slick lawyers. Now think hard. Where would your father have put the paper to know that it would be safe until he could get it delivered to Austin and signed by a judge?"

"The bank?" Colby guessed.

Butler shook his head. "Banker told me he asked your pa and he said he'd put it where he knew it would never be stolen."

Colby shook his head. "He kept extra cash in a loose brick next to the fireplace. My mom had an old family Bible she had a few loose papers pressed into. I never saw my pa touch it, but it might be somewhere he'd put the grant."

The marshal nodded. "We'll look there first thing in the morning. Meantime, don't sign anything. I've heard tell of men swindling owners out of their land at times like this by getting them drunk or coming in when they're sick."

"I won't sign," Colby said. "I wouldn't even sign the paperwork for the doctor back in Dallas. He claimed he wouldn't treat me if I didn't. My arm was hurting so bad from the snakebite I didn't want to move it."

Slim leaned forward as the waitress delivered four plates of steak and beans. "That might have been why they were keeping you alive. They figured the bite would heal and you'd be so out of it, you'd sign anything, even the deed to your ranch."

All four men dug into the food. Finally, the marshal stopped to take a drink and said, "I'll contact Dallas, but first we got to find that deed." Everyone agreed and continued eating. "If it's gone, then we know your pa was murdered for it."

The marshal asked the girl who refilled their drinks if she had rooms for his three friends. "No sense going out to your ranch in the dark," he said as the girl nodded.

Colby agreed and when the rangers asked for a bath to be delivered, he did the same. He didn't want them to know how green he was, so he didn't ask about the price of the room or the bath.

After they finished pie, Colby went up to his room while the others kept swapping stories. The hotel room was fancier than anything he'd ever seen, with rugs on the floor and a lock on the door.

Colby took a real bath in a hip tub by the fireplace, then lay on his bed nude as a bedbug. Being raised by his father, he'd never had a nightshirt, but he thought that someday, if he ever married, he should buy one. He'd heard Beth telling the boys when she bought them nightshirts that women don't like seeing too much of the male body. So he'd slept in his clothes on his bedroll, same as Andrew did down in his study.

He decided if he ever did get this all straightened out, the first thing he'd buy would be a real bathtub and three or four changes of clothes. That would be more than he'd ever need, but it would be nice to wear clean clothes every day like Mr. McLaughlin did. They had good water on the ranch. Enough to bathe every Saturday night if he wanted to.

Colby smiled. In no time at all he'd be a real gentleman.

Just before he fell asleep he thought of Madie and how hard she worked around the town house. She'd have his place all cleaned up and proper in no time if she came to visit.

Not that she'd ever come to his place. The run-down way it looked would never attract a woman or even an almost-grown girl. She'd probably throw a fit if she knew they hung their clothes out every month to dry on the fence and took baths in the creek.

He thought of the biscuit still in his gear. While he was out buying the tub and clothes, he figured he'd buy some napkins and a tablecloth and maybe even a funny little teapot just in case Madeline did ever come to call. Then she could have her tea just like Mrs. McLaughlin did every afternoon.

The next morning when they rode up on his place, it looked worse than he remembered. Far worse. Whoever had killed his father had pulled most of the furniture out of the house and ripped it to pieces. Broken chairs, shredded straw mattresses beyond repair, and pieces of broken dishes that must have been used for target practice.

Colby stepped over the mess and moved inside. The stove had been pulled away from its rock stand. His mother's simple half cabinet she'd brought with her when she married was smashed into a hundred pieces, every pane of glass broken. Boards were ripped from the floor and walls. The fireplace brick, his pa's crude safe place, was open with all the money gone.

The marshal brushed his hand in where

the stone had been removed. "How much you think your father kept in here?"

"A few hundred, I guess, maybe more. He'd stash the money from a sale of a pig or calf and use it to buy our monthly supplies. He didn't believe in carrying credit at the stores in town if he didn't have to, and we rarely went in to pick up supplies in time to catch the bank open."

They walked out to the barn. It looked like whoever had killed his pa had taken all the horses along with a wagonload of other livestock. Only the chickens were left to run free. Probably too much trouble to chase.

"The stock might be easier to track. Men herding cattle and horses can't move as fast. The wagon's tracks could lead us to who did this. Can you give me a description of what he had here?"

"We butchered most of the pigs for winter, so only six half-grown pigs, a black milk cow, and four horses were around the barn this time of year. What cattle we didn't sell in the last drive are on the land. It would have taken days for good cowhands to round them up, and they were the wildest of our herd."

Slim walked around the barn, reading the scene like some men read a book. "And these men are not good hands, I'd bet. They make their money stealing and killing. I'm guessing they were hired to bully the old man into giving them the deed. When he refused, they thought they'd kill him and search the house. When that turned up nothing, they took the stock for their trouble. It wasn't part of the job they were hired to do."

The marshal nodded. "If they're moving with stock, maybe trying to sell some along the way, they'll be easy to follow. First they'll drive the wagon and stock far enough away so that no one will recognize your horses. That leaves out the farms and ranches within forty miles. After that, I'm guessing they'll stop at the first place they come to and try to make a little money."

Slim untied his horse from the fence. "If you want to stay here, Colby, we'll circle around to the ranches and see if anyone saw men with your stock passing by. With luck, in a few hours, we'll have a direction to head. In the meantime you might want to pay your respects to your pa. Maybe hammer him up a cross on the grave yonder."

Colby nodded. "Thanks, Slim, I'd like to do just that." He knew Slim's calling him Colby wasn't a loss of respect, but a sign of friendship.

While they rode out, Colby began picking up pieces of what had been his old life. Within an hour he had a huge fire burning in the yard with all the things from the house. In the loft of the barn he found his mother's old sewing machine and a crib that must have been his. The outlaws hadn't bothered to climb the ladder. On the treadle of the old machine lay the family Bible.

Colby took it with him as he walked up to where some of the neighbors had buried his pa. He nailed together a cross using broken boards that had once been a fence around the family plot, then pushed it into the ground at the top of the grave.

While he watched the fire burning, he thought of how his childhood was in the fire. When he walked away today, he'd be a man. He opened the Bible and saw his name at the end of the line of Dixons. He guessed there was something he could say over his father's grave, but all he could think to do was read the family names out loud. Births. Marriages. Deaths. The few papers he found tucked between the pages were only recipes his mother must have saved and one letter telling her that her sister had died.

Colby couldn't help but wonder if she was still alive or if she ever thought of him. She'd left when he was too young to hold on to even one clear memory of her.

He knew he should say more over his father's grave, but his thoughts were only about how he planned to be a better man. He didn't want to live his life working every day on the land without ever saying a kind word to anyone, even his son.

When he looked at the old house he could almost see a woman standing in the door waving to him. A woman like Madie, he thought, with her belly rounded with a kid. He'd like that.

Maybe, if she did what he told her to and waited for him, he'd go back and ask her to come here. After all, she was already halfway to one child, so it wouldn't take them long to start a family. Once she grew up, she'd make a good wife, and he'd always be considerate of her. He'd tell her how he liked her cooking and he'd hold the door for her and help her down from the wagon like Andrew did for his wife.

When the young ranger rode in, Colby stood cussing himself for daydreaming. Madie wouldn't wait for him. He didn't want her here anyway. She wasn't even a woman, much less his woman. She'd probably run off with the first cowhand who drifted by. He wanted a pretty woman who didn't cry at the drop of a hat and who knew how to kiss, among other things.

"We've got a direction," Butler yelled as Colby ran toward his horse. "And we've got some hard riding to do to catch up."

Every dream was forgotten as Colby rode northwest. All he had time to do was think about catching the men who'd raided the ranch. He told himself he didn't want to kill them, not unless he had to. All he wanted to do was see them behind bars. Something about starting his life as a man with a killing didn't seem right.

Colby smiled to himself. He was going to have a life . . . a real life, if he didn't get himself killed riding with the rangers.

CHAPTER 20

BETH FELL INTO A PATTERN THE NEXT FEW DAYS. She worked with Madie on sewing and housekeeping in the mornings, then helped Andrew in his study in the afternoons until Levi and Leonard came home from school.

Andrew had thought it foolish to send them to school for the short time they'd be here, but Beth insisted that it would be good for them since Andrew wasn't certain the man buried as T. B. Hawthorne was really their father. If he had to search more, then the boys needed to be kept busy.

She decided that if the doctor said Hawthorne was identified by his vest because his face was all shot up, maybe there had been a mix-up. Andrew pointed out that her theory belonged more in a novel than in real life, but he agreed to keep asking questions. A fake death might explain why the woman at the Blue Pony hadn't been upset to talk about Hawthorne's death.

Laughing, Beth reminded him they weren't exactly living in real life either, but, in truth, she found a kind of peace with him. An almost-life. After Lamont, she'd sworn to never marry; this might be her only taste of what it would have been like. The sounds, the daily chores, the companionship, and, of course, the kids.

Only none of it was real, except maybe his kisses. In the quiet times during each day, she remembered Andrew's kisses. They were like a long-held secret that grew sweeter with time. In the middle of everything, she'd stop and remember.

The children kept her busy. Madie, though she considered herself a full-grown woman, loved to play games with the boys and fold papers Andrew had tossed until they had all kinds of hats and tents scattered along the steps.

Since the day the thugs had tried to

attack Madie, everyone in the neighbor-
hood took an interest in their little family.
The boys walked to school with the other
children in the town houses, and Madie
often talked to the women on either side of
them while she did the wash out back or
swept the front porch. If Beth liked being a
part of this make-believe family, Madie
loved it.

Beth was friendly, but she stayed inside while Madie told her new friends that
she lived with this wonderful couple who
were so much in love they even worked
together.

Which couldn't have been further from
the truth. Andrew never mentioned love.
Since the night he'd hurt his hand, he hadn't
made an attempt to kiss Beth. Now and
then, when he was leaning over her shoulder as they both read something he'd just
written, he'd touch her hair but nothing
more.

It was like he'd shown too much of himself that night and now forced a polite distance between them. When he wasn't
working, he was reading or going for long
walks. In the evenings, when they were in
the same room, he usually had his head

buried in a book or one of the dozen papers he'd brought home after his walk.

For the first time since she'd been away at school in her teens, Beth was homesick. She missed being able to watch the sunrise every morning with her papa and having morning coffee with her mother after everyone else had left. She missed riding across the ranch and the dinner parties with guests and family crowded around the table.

On the fourth day she was in Fort Worth, she'd sent her momma and papa a short note saying that she was fine and happy and would be home soon. If Ranger Slim Bates had dropped by Whispering Mountain, they already knew she wasn't married to Lamont. Beth reasoned it was doubtful the old ranger would have had time. He was with Colby trying to solve a murder. He had far more important things to do than stop off for dinner and a chat.

Three days after she'd sent the note, when she hadn't received a reply, she guessed they weren't worried about her, but that didn't keep her from missing them. Her younger brothers were away at school, and this time of year her uncles and aunts seldom visited even though the train now made the trip in a day.

The big ranch house would be as quiet as it always was after Christmas. Winter would keep them inside more. Her mother and the housekeeper would set out the looms and begin to weave. Her papa would pace and complain. Her mother always said Teagan McMurray was like a caged bear when he was forced indoors. She'd claimed only two things would settle him down. Books were one, Beth thought, but she wasn't sure her mother ever said what the second one was.

"I've three more articles." Andrew interrupted Beth's thoughts of home.

She turned and reached for them but then didn't turn back to the typewriter. He stood straight, almost formal in front of her in his wool suit and white shirt. He looked more like he belonged in New York or Boston than in Texas. She couldn't help but wonder if this man fit anywhere. He'd said once that he called no place home for long.

"Something wrong?" he asked. "I know you like the stories better, but the articles usually sell. The **Austin Statesman** has been buying a few a month since I got here." He moved his head, pushing his brown hair away from his eyes.

"You remind me of a shaggy dog." She laughed.

He raised an eyebrow. "You're mad at me, right?"

"No, that's not it. I think shaggy dogs are adorable. I just wonder how much longer."

"How much longer what?"

She looked at him, almost feeling sorry for him. They both knew this was only a fantasy they played, but he did his part so fully she sometimes thought he believed they were really married with a family. "You do know, dear, that this marriage isn't real?"

He smiled. "I write fiction, Beth, I don't live it, but this marriage you've invented is both a kind of heaven and hell." He brushed her jaw with one finger. "If I thought this were real, I'd be in your bed and not on this blasted couch every night."

She turned away blushing, the frank-ness of his statement shocking her. "No, you wouldn't. You're still in love with your wife."

Beth regretted the words as soon as

they were out. He'd been kind to her. He'd put up with them invading his house. She had no right to pry.

She expected him to walk away, as he often did when he didn't want to talk, but instead, he knelt on one knee so that his face was even with hers. "You're wrong. When she died she took all the love I'll ever have away with her. I live with her memories and sometimes I think I live with her ghost, but I'm not still in love with her. If I were, I'd have died of starvation years ago."

She brushed his jawline lightly. "What do you feel for me, Andrew?"

"Need," he answered. "And you deserve a man who can feel so much more than just need. I sometimes think if I stand too close to you I'll drown in wanting you, but I'll ask nothing more. I can only handle a make-believe wife right now. I don't think I could survive a make-believe lover."

Before she could think of how to answer him, he stood and walked away, grabbing his coat by the door. As he usually did, he closed the door softly and disappeared into the streets.

Beth sat in the silent house, envying

him for having experienced such a deep love. His sadness hung between them like a lace curtain woven with iron threads. She could almost see what life would be like with him, but she couldn't break through.

Beth admired him for not offering less to her than all, but part of her wanted to scream that she'd accept any terms if he'd just stay near. He was a good man, a talented man who made people think and feel, but he was broken inside, and she had no idea how to fix him.

He didn't come home for supper. After Madie and the boys went to bed, she worked in his study awhile, hoping he'd come back and they could talk. It worried her that he was out walking the night, or in some saloon listening to drunks tell stories about the early days of the Republic. She couldn't help but wonder if he traveled for his stories or because he never wanted to get close to anyone.

But he'd kissed her. He'd kissed her like no one had ever kissed her. Had that been the real Andrew? Or had it merely been him pretending to feel?

Long after she'd gone to bed, she heard

him come in, but she didn't go downstairs. What would be the point? He'd made it plain that he was just playing a part and the few times he'd pulled her close had been a mistake he didn't plan to repeat.

The next morning he was asleep in his study, an open book by his side. From the number of papers crumpled around the desk, he must have worked all night. She covered him with a quilt and closed the door.

Before noon she sent another telegram to her family saying she'd be coming home soon. It had been over a week; if Lamont had been tracking her, he would have found her by now. She knew she was hiding, running away from her troubles, and that wasn't like her. She was a McMurray, built of stronger stuff. She would handle her problems. Her family would understand; after all, it wasn't like she hadn't turned down a dozen men before. She'd just turned down Lamont at the last minute.

Her papa hadn't liked Lamont. Of course, that shouldn't be considered in any decision she made. He hated every man who looked at one of his girls. To his way of thinking, none were good enough.

As Beth typed one of Andrew's stories

at the dining room crate off the kitchen, she realized her biggest problem wasn't Lamont, but the lie she'd told to get away from him. Her aunt and uncle lived in Washington, D.C., part of each year. Her aunt's father had been a powerful senator in his day. They were bound to hear about her broken engagement to Lamont and her rushed marriage. Plus, she'd told Slim Bates and he'd tell every ranger from here to El Paso. With each day that passed, the lie spread.

She stopped typing and put her chin on her palm. First, how could she get rid of a pretend husband without telling everyone that she'd lied? Second, why did part of her want to keep Andrew so badly? It had to be more than the way he kissed. The memory of his last kiss returned so strongly, she could almost feel it on her lips.

"What you dreaming about, Bethie?" Andrew startled her.

She looked up to find him leaning against the door frame, his hair a mess from sleeping and his eyes shaded in exhaustion. She almost felt sorry for him, but he did look downright adorable when he wasn't frowning.

"Stop scaring me."

"Sorry. I'll try to tromp more around the place." He pulled his handkerchief from his pocket and reached out to wipe the ink off first her finger, then her cheek. "So, what had you so deep in thought that you can't type? I think it was the silence that woke me."

"I have this idea for a plot to a story, but I can't figure out how it will end."

"All right, tell me about it. I've worried that with your imagination, if you hung around me long enough you'd want to write. So let me help you. Most folks after getting to know me figure out that if I can do this for a living, they should be able to do it too. So I'm not surprised you're plotting."

He moved across to the side of the room that was their kitchen and poured himself a cup of coffee from a pot that had sat on the warm stove since breakfast. After one swallow his eyes were wide open. He took a seat on the stool across from her and waited.

"Since you asked." She might as well get his help. "My story is about this spoiled, self-centered woman who feared she'd never marry, so she agreed to get engaged to a powerful man half a continent away. As the months went by he told her he felt just the way she did about women being equal to men and how they should get the vote. He said he also wanted a large family, but he wouldn't mind if his wife took up causes now and then. He even swore he'd take her to hear lectures in Washington and plays and concerts, which of course, made her fall in love with him. Then he told her he needed her by his side to do great things that would make the world a better place."

Andrew forced down another swallow of coffee. "You need to move your story along, dear. It's got a slow start."

"Oh, of course. So this powerful man claimed he couldn't live without the spoiled woman and asked her to meet him alone and run away to marry. He said they'd travel and see the country on a honeymoon. She, being a fool, agreed."

Beth closed her eyes. Even telling the facts made her hate herself for being so easy to manipulate.

"Go on," Andrew encouraged. "You forget to mention she was also beautiful and foolhardy."

"Oh yes, that too. Only if she hadn't

been, she wouldn't have discovered the truth in time. The night before they were to be married, she saw him without him knowing she was there to watch. She saw the man beneath the skin and knew he was a monster."

"Now the story's getting good," Andrew said, letting her hear a twinge of humor in his tone.

"Then one stormy night a train wreck happened, and she had a chance to swap a wounded train robber for the powerful man. It seemed like a good idea at the time. All the spoiled woman was thinking about was getting away from the monster. Only now . . ."

"Only now?" he echoed.

"She doesn't know how to get back home. Her lies have washed away the path. If she just leaves, she'll have no answers for her family when they ask about her husband. If she tells them she divorced the stranger she married, it will hurt them all. She can't tell them she made him up; too many people have seen the kind robber who claimed to marry her." Beth twisted the ring Andrew had put on her finger in the hospital. It had convinced the sheriff that they were really married, but now it seemed only a reminder of her lie.

Beth didn't look at him as she continued. "So, either she's got a husband she can't explain to her family, or she'll have to think of a new lie to cover all those she's already told. Something like that. Help me see the ending. You're the writer."

Andrew shook his head. "There are only two endings, dear. The make-believe husband has to die, or you have to take him back to your family to prove he's real. Either way, they'll accept you and believe you as long as whichever ending is true."

"You'd come back with me and play the part a little longer?" She hadn't thought of that as a possibility, but it might work. "You wouldn't have to stay long, and when you left, we could make up some reason. You'd write me letters for a while explaining that you were working, researching new places, hearing new stories, and when the letters stopped, we'd just wonder where you were."

He shook his head. "If I did that, you'd be left with everyone thinking you were married. Your chances of finding someone else and having a family of your own would be zero. I couldn't do that to you, Beth, not even if you were my imaginary wife."

Beth leaned back against the table. "That's it, then. The only way this story will end is if I shoot you." When he opened his mouth to argue, she hurried on. "Oh, don't worry. I'd claim I thought you were an intruder. They'd never send me to jail. In fact, I'd even wear black and visit your grave every year."

She liked this ending. It sounded so tragic, so sad. "Then, after I buried you, of course, I could go home as a widow. There are a great many men out there who wouldn't mind marrying a widow if I decided on that. Or, I can see myself continuing to wear black and becoming an independent woman. I've always looked good in black. As a widow I could set up a house in some big town and go to lectures and plays all by myself."

"And would you think of me fondly?"

She stood and moved close, circling his neck. "Of course I would." Without hesitation, she bent and kissed him. Not a light, playful kiss, but exactly the kiss she'd been wanting.

He pulled her onto his lap and returned

the kiss as one of his hands moved along her hip.

Before she could get too far lost in pleasure, someone pounded on the door.

Andrew stood slowly, moving his hand over her body as if apologizing for leaving. He motioned for her to move back into the kitchen, then walked to the door.

The pounding came again before he could turn the knob. Beth watched from the shadows as Andrew widened his stance and prepared to face whoever stood on the other side. He didn't look afraid, only cautious as he pulled the door.

Sunshine spilled in. All she could see was a huge shadow blocking out half the light.

"You Andrew McLaughlin?" a voice boomed.

"I am." Andrew didn't budge.

"Then I'm here to see my daughter." The giant pushed his way in and, to his credit, Andrew had the sense to step aside.

"Papa?" Beth whispered, and ran toward him. "Oh, Papa!"

Teagan McMurray lifted her high as if she were still his little girl, then pulled her into a bear hug. She had been only a toddler when she'd met him, but she'd known, just as her mother and sisters had, that this man was their safe harbor and he always would be. He was gray around the temples now and had more wrinkles, but he was still solid as an oak.

When he set her back on her feet, she asked, "How did you find me? How did you know I was here? Oh, Papa, I'm so glad to see you."

Teagan took off his hat and slapped it against his leg to dust it off. "I was north of here delivering some horses when your mother telegraphed me and told me I'd better stop and check on her baby before I started home." He grinned. "And you know I always do what she says."

Beth laughed. Her father was stubborn as granite with everyone but his Jessie. Beth swore that if her mother told him to walk to the moon, he'd be halfway there before dawn.

"But how did you know where I was?"

"We knew your telegrams came from Fort Worth. I bribed the man at the office to tell me who'd been sending messages to Whispering Mountain and he said, Mrs. Andrew McLaughlin. From there it was relatively easy. I just walked the blocks asking someone on each street if they knew where the McLaughlins lived. Fort Worth's not that big a town and I guessed I could mark off a few neighborhoods. When I got to this street, everyone I passed pointed me to this door."

Her papa finally took the time to look around. "Why are you and the senator staying here with the McLaughlins? I thought you'd be on your travels, not stopping off to visit folks."

Beth took a deep breath. "I didn't marry Lamont. I'll explain later about what a fraud he was, but first, Papa, I should tell you that I'm not **staying** with Mr. and Mrs. McLaughlin, I **am** Mrs. McLaughlin." She pointed at Andrew, who was still holding the door like a hotel doorman. "Papa, this is Andrew."

She couldn't tell if he was angry or confused. On her papa, the expression was about the same.

After a long silence, he turned and offered his hand to Andrew. "I'm Teagan McMurray," he said without smiling, then added, "If you hurt my daughter, I'll bury you."

Beth tried to laugh, but it came out more like a hiccup. "He says that to all the sons-in-law. Come on in, Papa, and I'll make you a pot of coffee. You might as well stop growling at my new husband."

Teagan glared at Andrew, then walked back out the front door. "I'll water my horse first and be right back. I need a while to chew on what you just told me. I was finally getting used to the fact that I'd have to put up with Lamont and now you switched husbands on me."

She and Andrew stood in the doorway, watching him walk his horse over to the nearest livery. He was a big man who fit with the land and didn't seem to belong in a town.

"Is it too late for you to kill me?" Andrew whispered. "If I get a vote, I'm leaning in that direction after meeting your papa."

She put her arm around him and held tightly, fearing he might yet run. "I'm afraid we'll have to go with plan A. From now on we'd better be married as far as he knows. My papa isn't a man who'd take well to being made a fool of."

"I kind of had that feeling. He wears two Colts," Andrew whispered, "and carries a rifle."

She smiled. "Maybe he needs them. He's got three sons-in-law. And right now you're his least favorite."

They stood in the doorway watching the street until Teagan returned with his saddle over one shoulder as if it weighed nothing. Wind kicked up dust and clouds darkened the morning as he headed straight toward them.

"Great," Andrew whispered as he watched Teagan pull his saddlebags and rifle off the saddle he left on the steps. Then Beth's father turned like a man facing trouble and headed straight toward him.

"He's not staying, is he?" Andrew managed.

She offered, "I'll ask him."

Andrew had the look of a man who'd heard bullets flying and was just waiting for them to hit.

"Storm's coming," Teagan said as he passed Andrew.

"I have no doubt," Andrew answered without looking at the sky.

CHAPTER 21

An hour later, Andrew sat across from his almost-father-in-law and tried to think of something to say. The man had the conversational skills of a broom and smelled of trail dust and horses.

Strangely enough, he was exactly as Beth had described him in her stories of the ranch. Bigger than life. A boy who had to become a man before he was twelve and had to fight to keep his land. A man strong enough to face any crisis head-on.

Andrew wished he could tell Teagan McMurray how much he respected him.

Teagan had thought of nothing but his family and the ranch until twenty-three years ago, when a little widow showed up at Elmo Anderson's trading post with three tiny girls. He'd taken Jessie and her daughters in as his own, and Andrew had no doubt that he loved them dearly.

Teagan was a breathing legend.

Beth told her Papa about meeting Andrew on the train and how he saved her life when the wreck happened. She said that she felt it was her duty to care for him at the hospital and couldn't help falling in love with him.

She described how Lamont had acted and mentioned a few of the cruel things he'd said about women. "I couldn't marry him, Papa. I just couldn't after I saw what he was."

"Of course not," Teagan agreed. "If I ever run into him again, I may just pound some sense into the man."

"Exactly what I thought," Andrew said, trying his best to jump into the conversation.

Teagan McMurray looked like he couldn't have been more surprised if the coffeepot had talked.

Andrew figured he'd stay out of the conversation.

When the boys and Madie came in, Teagan tipped his hat politely to Madie and shook hands with Levi and Leonard, taking great care to learn their names and ages.

"I got two brothers," he said to Levi. "It's good if brothers stick together. I'm sorry to hear about your father being missing, but we'll help you find him. He'll be proud of the way you two took care of each other when he gets back."

Andrew was surprised how he talked to them as if they were older, and the boys responded by straightening.

Beth's father knelt to one knee and put his hand on Levi's shoulder as he asked, "While Mr. McLaughlin is waiting for your father to pick up one of the messages he's been leaving around town, how would you two like to visit my ranch? We got a whole wing of rooms we're not using, and I'll cut you out a few gentle horses to ride."

The boys were too stunned to say anything.

Teagan addressed Madie next. "My daughter says you are between homes,

Miss Madeline. Is there a chance you'd join us and maybe help me with these little fellows? You're welcome to visit as well."

Madie glanced at Beth. "Does he mean it?"

"My papa never says anything he doesn't mean."

The girl turned back to Teagan. "When do we leave? I promised I'd leave word at the ranger station for Colby if we moved on. He traveled with us from Dallas, and he's coming back to check on me."

"We could leave tomorrow, I'd think. Take the night train as far as Anderson Glen. I'll telegram them to have wagons ready. We could be at Whispering Mountain in forty-eight hours." He looked at Andrew, and his face hardened. "I know there were circumstances to be considered, but you shouldn't have married my daughter without asking me first and looking in her mother's eyes so she'd know you meant to take care of our baby girl."

"I agree." What else could Andrew say? He was still thinking about Teagan's promise to bury him. He considered bringing up the fact that Beth certainly wasn't a baby but a full-grown woman. Only he feared

Teagan might ask him questions as to how he knew.

"Then we leave tomorrow evening. I have some business in Dallas to attend to, but I'll be back in time if I take the train." He stood. "Bethie, make the arrangements and close this house. You all will be staying with us at the ranch till spring."

Andrew stood silently watching as the big man walked out the door without bothering to close it. Part of him felt as if he'd just met his first bear, and he saw no point in arguing with the grizzly.

"If I could get that man down on paper, I'd have the perfect character to represent Texas."

"Good luck," Beth said. "My papa is not an easy man to figure out."

He put his arm around her, wondering how all the women in Teagan's life survived. "What do we do? Surely he's joking about us moving to a ranch until spring."

"He's not joking," she answered. "I suggest we pack. By the way, he likes you."

"Really, how could you tell?"

"You're still breathing." She didn't even smile, just seemed to be stating a fact.

Andrew stood in the center of the room

and watched as everyone around him went into action like an ant army hearing thunder. "I can't leave," he finally said. He saw himself as a man who always drifted with the wind, but this was too much.

"Of course you can." Beth brushed his elbow as she circled around him giving orders. "I know you voted for being shot earlier, but it looks like we were forced into the other idea. You'll have to play my husband a little longer, I'm afraid. If you back out now, I'm not going to be the one to explain how we've been living together for two weeks without really being married."

"Well, I'm sure not going to tell him." Andrew didn't want to think about what Teagan would do.

"Then you'd best pack," Beth whispered as Levi circled through the kitchen.

Andrew shook his head. "Until spring," he whispered, as if it were a death sentence.

A few minutes later, Beth bumped him as she passed with a box of kitchen supplies. When he didn't move, she looked up into his face, and he had no doubt that she saw his fear.

"Andrew, honestly, here in the middle of

everything is where you plan to make your stand? When you jumped from the train you didn't hesitate to save me. When you faced Lamont and the sheriff and lied, you stared them down even though you were too weak to stand from loss of blood. You walked the streets unarmed. But now, when all I ask is that you come back to my home, you look as if a firing squad stands beyond the door."

She set her box down and stood in front of him with her fists on her hips. "Andrew, what is it?"

"I don't think I can do this, Beth. Maybe we can come up with another plan. I've liked having you and Madie and the boys here, but a house full of people on a ranch, I don't know. I won't get to walk the streets at night and think. I couldn't write with all the people around. I couldn't work." He closed his eyes and added, "All I know is work. I don't know people."

"Just pretend they're characters in your stories. Believe me, a few of them would fit right in." She didn't laugh at her joke, and he saw how worried she was.

"I don't know."

"Consider this trip research. I'll even set

you up a study in one of the empty bedrooms." Her hand moved down his arm.
"You'll be able to work there. You'll see. I'll
make sure you have your time and a place.
It won't be for long, a few months, that's all."

His tired eyes closed and, when they
opened, reason had won over panic. "All
right. I go to a ranch, unknown territory to
me, and stay with a wife who's not mine
and children who don't belong to me and
people who have threatened to kill me.
Sounds like the only reasonable thing to
do."

She patted his cheek. "When you put it
that way, how could you resist? I'll pack
your study and arrange for everything to
be freighted. You go have your mail for-
warded to Anderson Glen in care of Whispering Mountain Ranch. I'll pack up the
house and it will be here waiting for you
when you get back."

He grabbed his hat and coat and walked
out looking like a man who'd been hit with
a cast-iron skillet. She wanted to go home,
he must understand that. She needed her
family, but how cruel was it to ask him to
come along with her? He hadn't started
this marriage thing, she had.

He liked living alone. He probably wanted it that way. She guessed he needed his solitude. If he went with her he'd have to play her husband, when he'd just finished telling her that he couldn't handle even being a make-believe lover.

She was asking too much. He should just tell her that the game she played ended here.

Gulping down a sob, she realized maybe he had tried but she hadn't listened. Most of the men she knew would have stomped and stormed, but Andrew had given in, not because he wasn't strong enough to fight, but because he knew it was important to her.

Beth didn't want to admit that he was broken somehow when it came to love. No matter how hard she tried, she couldn't make him love her, and that was a first for her. This one man could be attracted to her, even want her, but he never said the word **love.** Maybe he was telling the truth when he said he had nothing left to give.

Maybe he'd also lied to her about where he lived. It seemed to her that Andrew lived in books and merely survived in real life.

He hadn't wanted to let her down, so he hadn't argued. Beth fought back tears. She was forcing him into the real world and she had no idea how to stop. She only hoped he cared enough to go along with her lies.

CHAPTER 22

A WEEK HAD PASSED SINCE COLBY DIXON LEFT Fort Worth with the rangers, and they were no closer to catching the outlaws who'd raided his ranch than they had been the first day.

Slim Bates thought the men had sold the stock fast and then turned toward the border. The young ranger had the theory that the outlaws must have been close, maybe even seen Colby come back home, but since Colby rode in with a marshal and rangers, they gave up on their plan to get the deed. His ranch was good-sized, but not worth a shootout with the law.

After three days on the trail, Marshal Butler gave up talking altogether and started complaining. He was ready to call off the search, but he wouldn't turn his horse around before the others agreed.

On the fourth day, they found two dead men on display at a mission fifty miles from Colby's ranch. Apparently, they'd tried to rob a stage and only collected lead for their trouble. Among their belongings was a coin purse that Colby said looked like his pa's. The undertaker had set the bodies out in front of the mission hoping someone would identify them. With the cold weather they'd barely started to smell.

The marshal put his hand on Colby's shoulder. "Go home, son, get your affairs in order. You've got a ranch to run. The trail is cold. I'll do my best to see if I can find out the names of the two dead men. From there we may be able to get a lead on who they rode with, but it doesn't look promising."

Slim reluctantly agreed. "If there is a third man out there still alive, he'll brag to someone some night when he's drunk and the rangers will hear about it. I'll circle by your place one day with good news."

Colby didn't want to stop looking, but he saw their reasoning. He needed to be home.

He turned his horse toward home, already thinking of all that needed to be done at the ranch. When he got time, he'd write Madie and the others, telling them everything that had happened. He didn't know if he'd aged since he'd seen them, or if he was simply so tired he felt old.

Maybe, if he thought of it, he'd mention that Madie could write him back, if she wanted to.

CHAPTER 23

DARK WINTER CLOUDS BILLOWED FROM BEHIND the mountain as the sun set on the Mc-Murray ranch. Andrew decided for a bachelor who'd spent the past seven years of his life living totally alone, he'd somehow skipped dying and fallen into hell. He had a wife he couldn't touch, kids who weren't his, and a father-in-law who he was sure was still plotting to kill him.

As they pulled up to the bridge, Beth took his hand. "This is it, Andrew. This is Whispering Mountain."

He didn't miss the pride in her voice. "Should we wake the kids?" Madie and the boys were stretched out in the wagon, sound asleep after staying up all night on the train. It hadn't been an easy journey, with Madie throwing up twice and Leonard spilling his supper.

His beautiful almost-wife shook her hair free of pins. "No, let them sleep until we reach the house." With her hair tumbling she looked younger and so beautiful that she took his breath away.

He drove across a wooden bridge that he'd been told had been burned twice over the years to keep strangers out. Not exactly a good sign for him.

The mountain sat behind the huge ranch house as if on guard. It crossed Andrew's mind that the spirits of the McMurrays' Apache ancestors might still be watching over future generations. Spirits in the wind, maybe.

Or, maybe not. He hadn't had any sleep in two days, so maybe his imagination had started dancing with hallucinations.

"The first McMurray to come to Texas was named Andrew also," Beth said. "Teagan's father was Irish and still in his teens when he met Autumn at a mission. He'd studied to be a teacher and had inherited a little money in Ireland. Since he had no family left, he headed for Texas. She was Apache, and they fell in love as he taught her to read. Autumn's father told my grandfather about this land bordered on three sides by water, and they settled here. In the beginning all they had was a few fine horses he'd brought and a dozen ponies her father gave them as a wedding present."

Andrew studied the quarter mile to the main house as he listened. With luck they'd make it in before the storm broke. He watched a cowboy near the barn climb on his horse and ride out to meet their wagon. A one-man welcoming committee, or someone sent to warn him?

Beth might feel a sense of coming home, but all Andrew felt was an uneasiness whirling around him, colder than the wind.

When the rider drew close, he circled and came up beside Beth. "Welcome back, Bethie," he said with a tip of his hat. "Your mom told me to ride out and let you know that you've got parlor company."

Beth introduced the hand to Andrew as Jake, then asked, "Any idea who?"

"Yep, he told us all he was Senator Lamont LaCroix. Said it loud as if ordering everyone to remember his handle. When your papa got here about an hour ago on horseback, the senator asked to talk to him in private. Your father closed the parlor doors, but I figure they'll be out by the time you get to the porch."

Andrew studied Beth. To her credit, she showed no emotion. She obviously never thought LaCroix would be on the ranch or she never would have come home.

"Thanks for letting us know." She smiled at Jake. "I was hoping we'd get in without having to deal with company today. It's been a long trip."

Jake winked at Andrew. "You're a lucky man, sir."

"Yes, I am." Andrew tried to sound believable, but the last person, next to Chesty Peterson, that he wanted to see was Beth's ex-fiancé. Both men wanted to kill him, but the outlaw wouldn't want to talk first.

When the messenger rode off, Beth whispered, "When my mother says, 'we've got parlor company,' that's not good. Friends come into the kitchen for coffee. People doing business usually go into my papa's study, but if she puts them in the parlor to wait, that puts us all on our toes. What do you think he wants?"

"Same as everyone else," Andrew said simply. "He wants to kill me."

She looked frustrated. "Oh, I know that, but he's after more, otherwise he wouldn't have come to the ranch."

"It seems quite enough to me." Andrew grinned. "I spent a year wishing I were dead once. Tried everything: drinking, fighting, starving. Nothing worked. Who knew it would have been so easy if I'd just come out west and met you? Hardly a day goes by that I'm not reminded that I'm counting my remaining days in single digits."

"You regret saving me from that wreck?"

"No. Funny thing about almost dying— when you realize you're still breathing, you feel fully alive." He meant his words and wished he had time to tell her the hundred ways she'd made him remember to breathe lately. But there was no time now. They had another problem to face first.

"You'll stand with me on this lie?"

"Of course," he answered. "For better or worse, for richer or poorer. Till death us do part."

He could feel her watching him as she whispered, "I'm sorry. I never thought it would go this far. I thought Lamont would leave after I told him I was your wife. You'd get better and I'd say good-bye at dawn and ride away."

Andrew didn't answer. They were close enough to the house to see Lamont watching from what must be the parlor window. Thunder seemed to vibrate the ground as Andrew climbed from the wagon and lifted Beth down.

He'd grown used to the easy ways he touched her. Nothing too personal, just the way a man touches his woman in public. Only there were no private touches to balance out his hunger for more. He enjoyed talking to her; she had a strong mind. He liked working with her—she'd helped him greatly—but he missed really touching her. The need ached in him, washing over him when he least expected it.

For a moment, he held her a little longer, a little closer than needed, and, to his surprise, she didn't seem to mind at all.

A small woman with gray hair ran from the porch and hugged Beth as if she hadn't seen her in years. "My baby," she cried. "I'm so glad you're home."

Beth laughed, but he didn't miss the tears in her eyes. "Now, Momma, you know I'm full-grown. I want you to meet my husband."

Jessie McMurray stared at Andrew as if she thought he'd stolen her child, but all Andrew saw was her beauty. Beth might have gotten her stubborn streak from her papa, but she got her looks from her mother.

"Nice to meet you, Mrs. McMurray. I'm very sorry I didn't get the chance to meet you before we married."

Beth looped her arm in his. "I couldn't let go of him from the minute I met him. It's my fault I didn't bring him home first, but I thought of myself as married to him from the moment we met."

Jessie nodded. "I felt the same way about your papa." She started up the steps. "Now, come on into the kitchen. I know you didn't stop for supper. Teagan asked me to have something ready for you when he rode in earlier. You know your papa, he's not coming in on a wagon if he can ride a horse and be home in half the time."

Beth didn't follow her mother but backed toward the wagon. "Did Papa tell you we brought guests?" She helped Leonard down just as huge drops of half-frozen rain began to tumble from the sky. Levi scrambled out just behind his brother, then stepped in front as if guarding.

"No, he didn't, but get those kids in here before they get wet. I'll meet them while I'm putting food on the table." She smiled at Andrew. "Bethie knows I always make extra. I'll just add a little water to the gravy and we'll have plenty."

If LaCroix hadn't been staring out the window, Andrew might have felt right at home.

Jessie motioned everyone along the wide porch and around to the kitchen door, as if she'd forgotten there was a front door to the house.

Andrew seemed the only one to notice Lamont staring from behind the thin lace curtain. He thought he saw the outline of Teagan standing back near the parlor doors with his arms folded. If Andrew were guessing, he'd say Lamont wouldn't be joining them for dinner.

As they ate the best food he could ever

remember having, Beth told her mother all about what had happened from the time she left home. Except, of course, she left out the part about them not being really married or in love.

He liked watching her in her own surroundings. There was an ease about the way she moved, getting up to refill his coffee before he even thought to ask, touching his shoulder as if it were something she'd grown accustomed to doing, answering for him now and then when her mother asked a question.

Finally, when the boys and Madie had gone off with the cook to pick their rooms, Andrew found time to ask about the man in the parlor.

Jessie McMurray frowned. "Teagan's keeping him company. People who come unannounced often have to wait awhile in the parlor."

Beth laughed. "Papa never talks to anyone more than a few minutes, so I doubt Lamont feels like he has company."

"I know," Jessie answered, "but since he's been here, all Lamont does is talk. I think if we left a pair of bull ears in the parlor, he'd keep talking."

"How long has he been here?" Beth asked.

"Two days. When he arrived I didn't know you'd married someone else. He told me he'd come here to wait for you. Since your papa wasn't home, I didn't think it would be proper to let him stay in the house, so I had him set up in the bunkhouse."

When she paused, Beth finished her mother's sentence. "And now the cow-hands are complaining."

Jessie nodded. "There's a pot going on which man will knock him out first. He told them all about how he planned to run for one of the seats from Texas, and one of the men said he was thinking Texas should secede again." She giggled behind her hand. "Once he got around to telling them you didn't marry him, I think the men de-cided they'd had enough of his talk. He came over here for breakfast, but I left him with the cook."

Andrew fought to keep from laughing. Most of the time he thought he did little right to please Beth, but all he had to do was stand next to Lamont and he won out. Teagan would probably let him live now that he saw what Beth's other choice had been. An out-of-work writer looked far more prosperous than an out-of-work senator, and the writer would be quieter.

Teagan stomped into the kitchen, and Andrew stood. "Evening, sir," he said.

Teagan waved him back into his seat and poured himself a cup of coffee while Jessie served him up a slice of pie. "I told your ex-fiancé to call it a night, Bethie. You've been traveling all day and don't need to face him. He claims he wants to plead his case, but I think he just wants to talk us all to death."

"I don't need to face him again ever, Papa." She stood up to her father.

"He seems to think you do."

She jumped from her chair and paced. "That man has no business coming here. I told him I was married and that should be enough. If he doesn't—"

"Andrew!" Teagan shouted over her tantrum. "Get a handle on your wife before she wakes up the milk cow in the barn."

"Me?" Andrew said almost calmly. "I've had her for two weeks; you've known her all her life. Why don't you calm her down? You're the one who spoiled her until she thinks she always gets her way." He stared at Teagan. "And, you're the one who has got her all upset."

Teagan opened his mouth, obviously to swear, then thought better of it when his wife cleared her throat.

"Bethie," Jessie said as she pulled out a chair for her daughter, "we've faced this problem many times before. You smile at some man and he starts hanging around thinking you'll marry him. Half the men in the state have made fools of themselves trying to catch your eye."

"Only this time I'm married, Momma. I've done nothing to encourage Lamont. When I saw the kind of man he was, I knew I could never marry him."

"I know, dear; just like all the rest, he didn't measure up."

Teagan had calmed and was now staring at Andrew. "Why'd she marry you, McLaughlin? She finds fault in every man who looks her direction. What's so special about you?"

Andrew decided to go for honesty. "Hell if I know."

Teagan raised an eyebrow. "That makes two of us, but she must have seen something. Maybe you'll show better in daylight."

Beth's father looked him up and down, and Andrew waited for the insult about his clothes.

Jessie stepped between the two men. "We can talk about this in the morning. I planned on putting the newlyweds in Duncan and Rose's new little cabin by the stream, but we'll never get a wagon down there tonight with this rain, and we'll have ice and snow by morning. So, if you don't mind sleeping in the new wing, Beth, Papa and I will take the extra bedroom in the old wing and watch over the children you brought."

Teagan didn't look happy at having to move out of his room. "Bethie's room is all done up in pink with her doll collection on one wall. You have a problem with that, McLaughlin?"

"None at all," Andrew answered.

"I didn't figure you would, considering the way you're dressed and all."

Jessie patted Teagan on the chest as if he were a wild animal. "Come along, dear, you can pick on the new son-in-law in the morning."

Andrew listened to the middle-aged couple moving down the hallway to what he guessed was the older part of the house. He wondered if he'd ever understand someone as well as they did each other. Beth must have been raised around this kind of love and acceptance; he didn't even know how to react to it.

When he heard a door slam somewhere far away, he turned to his almost-wife. "Where am I sleeping tonight?"

"With me," she answered. "I'm not going to explain to both my momma and papa why my new husband isn't in my room." Heading up the back stairs off the kitchen, she added, "With Lamont so close, I'm not sure either one of us would be safe alone. I wouldn't put it past him to murder us in our bed."

"Good point," he said as he followed her. Exhaustion had long ago taken over his brain, but he felt his body trying to react to the possibility of sleeping in the same room with her. The image of her in a white nightgown, still wearing her gun belt, flashed through his thoughts, and he sobered to the fact that they weren't married and never would be.

He grabbed the traveling cases, noticing she'd brought along his saddlebags still stuffed with dirty clothes. He followed her up to what she'd called the new part of the house even though it was probably twenty years since it had been built.

Teagan hadn't lied. Her room was pink, with lace and frills everywhere. A fine collection of dolls filled one wall. Some were old and tattered as if much loved by a child. Others were made of porcelain and looked like they'd never been touched.

"When my sisters married and traveled, they always brought a doll home for me," Beth said. "It reminded me that they never quite thought I was grown. No matter what, I guess I'll always play the part of the baby in the family."

Andrew set his case carefully down on the pillows of the windowsill. "You're not a baby to me. You never have been, Beth. All I see when I look at you is a woman, strong and confident."

"Thanks."

He grinned. "I do think it's cute that they still call you Bethie."

"Remind me to argue that point in the morning. I'm so tired I could sleep standing up." She began unbuttoning her jacket. "You mind turning around while I slip into my gown, and then I'll turn around while you put on your nightshirt?"

"I didn't bring one," he answered. "I've been sleeping in my clothes since I met you and didn't think that would change just because we moved location." He watched her slip out of her traveling skirt. "Have things changed?"

He pulled off his jacket and shoes without taking his gaze off her as she stripped down to her camisole and drawers.

"No." She slid under the covers. "Just pretend you're downstairs on your couch and we'll both wake up alive in the morning."

He got her point. He blew out the lamp and moved beneath the covers, his undershirt and trousers still on. "Fine by me, Bethie. You mind if I kiss you good night in the morning?"

"No." She already sounded more asleep than awake.

Two nights without sleep took their toll as he drifted off. Andrew had one passing thought that maybe he should worry about what they were doing sleeping in the same bed, but he'd worry about it tomorrow.

CHAPTER 24

THE STILLNESS OF THE PLACE WOKE HIM AT dawn. He heard nothing. No trains. No town clock chiming out the hour. No movement on the streets or voices outside shouting. Nothing. The air in the room seemed frozen in place, but beneath the covers he felt warm.

Andrew slowly turned his head and saw Beth curled up against his side. She must have been there all night. Her hair half covered her face. He thought she looked younger than twenty-four. Almost the girl everyone would call Bethie. She was the most beautiful creature he'd ever been close to, but he knew better than to mention it.

Without giving it much thought, he moved a few inches and kissed the tip of her nose.

She didn't budge.

He tried again, this time brushing her cheek. "Wake up, sleepyhead," he whispered.

She waved him away with her fingers.

Leaning closer, he touched her lips with his and she finally came awake.

Sleepy eyes blinked at him, then relaxed. "What time is it?"

"Dawn," he answered.

"Was that my good-night kiss you forgot?"

"No," he answered. "This is."

For a while neither thought or reasoned. They just reacted to the nearness of the other. The shadowy room, the covers piled atop them, the lock he'd turned on the door, all helped them escape into a world of the simple pleasure of feeling. He'd longed for her, wanted her, but somehow all the talk and reasoning got in the way. This morning there seemed nothing but the two of them cuddling beneath the covers as if hidden away from the world.

When he finally broke the kiss, his arms were around her, holding her close. "I want this one thing to be real between us. No pretending. I can put up with all the lies, but this I need to be genuine between us."

Still-sleepy green eyes watched him, as if she were allowing her mind to finally start working and, for a moment, was angry that he'd pulled her from a beautiful dream they'd both been having.

"What do you mean?" She shoved her hair back and rested her hand on his chest. "I'm real, Andrew. I'm not some character in your stories."

He brushed his finger over her. "I know that, dear, but this game we're playing of being married isn't honest. The attraction I feel for you is. At some point we need to pause and remember what is authentic."

"This attraction you feel will pass. All men who fall in love with me get over it once they know me better. One man who offered me a ring offered it to another an hour after I turned him down. Love has shallow roots."

He laughed. "I'm not in love with you. I've told you before that it's impossible, but that doesn't seem to stop me from wanting to kiss you, or touch you, or—"

"I get the point."

"No, you don't, Beth. I don't want you to play at liking me. Don't touch me or brush my arm, or kiss me unless it's real to you. Don't play that game with me when we're alone, or in public. We can pretend, for safety's sake, to be married, but I don't want the other unless you mean it. Don't flirt with me. Don't tempt me."

"I've never—"

"Of course you have, dear. I think you must have learned it around fifteen. How to attract a man. How to flirt oh-so subtly so you can deny it even to yourself. You've played the game so well, for so long, you may not even be aware you're playing it, but I think you like the chase even though you plan to never be caught. When the man falls and declares his love, or makes a pass, you run. Maybe the shallow love isn't **his** offering, but **yours**."

Andrew expected her to slap him or argue, but in her intelligent green eyes he saw her thinking his claim through.

"I'm not asking you to change; just don't play the game with me. I'm not chasing you, so you can relax. If you touch me, do it because you want to. Kiss me because you want the kiss. Make love to me only when the need is too great in you to stop."

She turned her back to him.

He lay staring at the ceiling, waiting for her to yell at him or at the very least kick him out. What did it matter if she was real with him? He was only going to be around for a few months. Why couldn't he just enjoy whatever they had while it lasted? The memory would be real even if her feelings weren't.

"I'm not like that," she finally whispered.

"What?"

"I said I'm not like what you think I am. I don't flirt and try to break hearts. It just seems to happen."

He scrubbed his face. Maybe she was right. Beautiful women like her were simply cursed. "All right. Maybe you're not, but promise me you'll be genuine with me. I have enough imaginary friends already."

"I promise." She faced him. "Andrew?"

He waited, then finally said, "Yes?"

"You're different than any man I've ever

talked to. You make me think. You make me want to be more than I settle for being. Can we start over and be friends?"

"What kind of friends?"

"Friends who kiss good night even if it's morning."

"I think I'd like that."

Just as his lips settled over hers, a tap sounded on the door and both jumped.

"Beth, are you awake?"

"Yes, Momma, we're awake."

"Good. Your papa would like you both to come down to the parlor. It seems the cowhands packed Mr. LaCroix off last night after he gave them a lecture on the law while downing half a bottle of whiskey. He woke up in one of the barn wagons pointed toward town. He insists on talking to you before he'll leave."

"We'll be right down," Andrew answered, climbing from the bed and pulling Beth along with him.

Whispering against her ear, he added, "Before we can settle into being kissing friends, we've got to straighten out this mess of being married."

"We can't just tell Papa," she whispered

back. "He'd kill you for sleeping here if he knew the truth. We've got to—"

Her mother's voice sounded from the hallway. "I'll have coffee ready for you both when you pass through the kitchen."

As Jessie's footsteps tapped lightly down the hallway, they both looked for their clothes.

Andrew looked back at her and whispered, "You look adorable in your undergarments, Bethie."

She looked down and noticed her camisole had come untied at the top and the valley between her breasts was showing. As she tied the ribbons back, she said, "How did that happen?"

He couldn't take his eyes off her and said a bit too fast, "I wouldn't know."

She looked up and saw his raised eyebrow. Without thought, she swung, connecting with his shoulder, and he flew with the punch as if being knocked back into bed by the power of her blow.

When he didn't stop staring, she added, "By the way, husband, if you ever untie my ribbons again, there will be another swing and this time it will be a **real** hit."

He laughed as he rolled to the other side of the bed. "It was well worth the price of admission." Picking up his shirt and shoes, he was gone before she had time to swing again.

"Stay out," she yelled, then laughed.

Half stumbling as he tried to dress and walk at the same time, he made it down the stairs that opened into the kitchen. When he finally pulled his shirt from his head, he saw two big men in their forties who could only be Teagan McMurray's brothers. One was dark with brown eyes and black hair. The other slightly smaller with brown hair and dressed in Indian moccasins that came to his knees.

At the moment both men were trying to choke themselves to keep from laughing out loud.

Andrew glared at them. "Oh, go ahead. Laugh at me."

Both men roared.

Andrew had time to accept a cup of coffee from Jessie before they settled. The big one with the black hair and the dark eyes of his Apache blood stood and offered his hand. "Travis McMurray, Mr. McLaughlin, and this is my little brother,

Tobin." His smile was genuine. "I'm guessing you're the man who married our niece, Bethie. Tell me, son, did you talk to her before the wedding or were you just swept away by her beauty and didn't bother noticing that she's one headstrong woman?"

"I was unconscious," Andrew answered honestly.

Both men laughed, but neither questioned his answer.

"That explains it," Tobin offered when he could catch enough air to talk.

Travis shook his head. "She does have a way of running full speed into trouble, but I've never seen her drag a man along with her. She must really like you to bring you into this mess." He crossed to refill his own coffee, then offered Andrew a seat. "We traveled most of the night to get here in time to help. I don't want you, or my brother Teagan, doing anything illegal."

"What mess?" Andrew had heard enough of Beth's two uncles to know they were good men. Travis was a respected judge in Austin, and Tobin split his time between raising horses in Texas and managing a ranch in Maryland.

The two men looked at each other, but

it was Travis who spoke again. "Don't you know? Lamont LaCroix has told half the state that he's coming to kill you. Claims you kidnapped his bride. He wants her back and doesn't believe you two are married. He told the Dallas paper that he would rescue her and marry her after he killed you. If you bullied some preacher into making her your wife, he says he'll still kill you and marry the widow. Half the saloons around have a bet going as to who will survive."

"Oh, that killing." Andrew waved the problem away. "I know all about Lamont's threats. As for him marrying her after I'm gone, he might want to rethink that plan. Being married to your niece isn't as easy as some folks think it might be."

Both the uncles laughed again, and Andrew decided he liked them. They knew their Bethie well enough not to be surprised that she'd kicked him out of the bedroom, and they hadn't let a death threat from a windbag worry them.

Travis took a drink of his coffee. "If I know LaCroix, he's making all this racket to get his name in the papers. I doubt anyone will accept that he was wronged, left at the altar, so to speak, but Texans tend to admire men who are willing to fight for what they believe even when they know they're wrong."

"How do you know I didn't kidnap her?" Andrew stared at them both.

"Because, first, if Bethie was off this land, she was armed. Second, if you were a fighter you would have knocked that bedroom door down when she kicked you out. But what did you do? You came down here to wait out the storm." Travis nodded once when Andrew didn't argue. "You're a man of logic, not a fighter. Teagan saw it when he met you in Fort Worth. He went to find Lamont and straighten him out, but the senator had already left Dallas after spilling all his troubles to the newspaper. The article must have hit the day you left Fort Worth for here."

Andrew followed the story. "And Lamont was already here, hoping to win the family over to his side."

Tobin finally said something. "He was here, but not convincing anyone. Jessie's shy. She wouldn't talk to him, and Teagan was gone."

Travis agreed with his brother. "I don't

think Lamont thought you'd come here. He probably had this grand hunt across Texas planned. He'd be out trying to save Beth, talking to every newspaper along the way. He figured you'd run and hide, giving him lots of time to build a name for himself."

"It's a dumb plan," Andrew said. "The guy didn't deserve Beth, but then neither do I." Andrew hoped the uncles didn't realize how completely he'd meant his last words. Most men would think themselves blessed to be married to a woman so beautiful, and he had to admit there was nothing more enjoyable than watching her in her undergarments, but being make-believe married to her was torture. Hell, just being around her made him feel like Moses waiting for the next plague to strike.

"So, what do we do now? Just let Lamont kill me? Might as well, because I'm not running or hiding."

"We could do that, or you and Beth could divorce. That way Beth could turn him down to his face like she should have done in the first place."

"It was a little more complicated than that." Andrew remembered the night in the hospital. Crazy as it would sound to the uncles, she'd taken the only choice she could by claiming he was her husband. Lamont had already convinced the sheriff that she'd lost her mind in the train wreck.

Travis leaned closer and said in a low voice, "I heard from a ranger who talked to Slim Bates, and he said Bates told him that you can't do your duty as a husband because of an accident. If that's so, an annulment would be the only practical choice. You'd be free of your responsibilities and she'd be free to marry Lamont if, as he claims, she wants him back."

Andrew closed his eyes thinking he should jump up, run to the bridge, dive in the river, and put himself out of his misery. Maybe twenty feet underwater he wouldn't have to try to explain his wife's lies.

CHAPTER 25

BETH WALKED SLOWLY DOWN THE STAIRS TO-ward the ranch house kitchen. She could hear her uncles laughing and wondered if they were picking on Andrew. He knew nothing about how tough they were. Andrew was a quiet man, a gentle man. Sometimes when her uncles got together they shook the house with their discussions.

Only this time, when she reached the kitchen, the men were all laughing, including Andrew.

Uncle Travis saw her first. "Mrs. McLaughlin," he bellowed, silencing the other two.

Andrew stood and met her at the bottom

of the stairs. "I've just met your uncles. They're fascinating." He'd kept his voice low, but she had no doubt they both heard Andrew's comment.

Travis stepped closer. "Your new husband was telling us about his adventures in Hell's Half Acre."

Beth shook her head. "He's making it all up, stretching the truth."

Travis tilted his head. "I'm a lawyer, Bethie, and a former Texas Ranger. Your Uncle Tobin lives half the year in Washington. Don't you think we'd know a lie if we heard one?"

Beth had no idea if he was kidding, so she turned back to Andrew. "Momma told us to hurry into the parlor. Apparently Papa has Lamont trapped in there again."

Uncle Travis stepped out of her way and waved them on. "If you're still alive after the talk, Andrew, come on in for breakfast. I've got a few stories about the early days of the Acre you might like to hear."

Andrew nodded as she pulled him along. He knew she didn't want to face Lamont again any more than he did, but there seemed no way to avoid it. They might as well get it over with.

When she stopped in front of the parlor doors, Andrew reached around and opened them for her. Then he took her hand in his and whispered, "I'm right here. We stand together. What could go wrong with both your father and me in the room with one man?"

Beth glared at him. "Everything," she whispered as she passed her almost-husband and moved into the room her mother called the parlor.

Her papa sat in one chair, a book in his hand.

Lamont stood by the fireplace and, for a moment, she was relieved to see that he appeared simply bored. Then he raised his gaze and met her stare. Hatred crossed over his face like poison spreading through veins.

Teagan stood. "Bethie, I told the man he could have his say before he left. You'll allow him that and he'll ask for no more."

She nodded. No matter how much she wanted to run, she knew her papa was being fair, which was more than Lamont deserved.

He glared at her as if he didn't see or hear anyone else in the room. On the train that night he'd been boastful and in command; here he seemed less sure of himself, maybe even a bit frightened.

She took a seat in a chair a few feet from her father and noticed that Andrew moved to stand next to her, resting his hand lightly on her shoulder. The room was quiet and warm from the fireplace, but all she felt was Lamont's hatred.

"You ruined my life, Beth," he began, as if he had prepared a speech. "You destroyed my plans and gave no reason. You stole my chances at a career in politics."

She took a breath. She could deal with this. The meeting wasn't going to be as bad as she feared it might be. "I didn't do anything to you, Lamont, except decide not to marry you. You're not the man you portrayed in your letters, and I'm thankful, for both our sakes, that I found it out before we married."

"I demand to know why you would think such a thing." His tone sharpened. His voice grew hard. "I think I have that right. I'd prepared for a wedding in Dallas, but when I see you, you're married to him." Lamont pointed to Andrew in disgust.

She started to say that he didn't have

any rights, but she wanted this meeting over as soon as possible. "I don't love you, Lamont. I don't think I ever loved you, it was more the ideal of you. That night, before the wreck, I rode in the back of your passenger car. You were drinking and bragging to a group of army officers. You called me 'that McMurray woman.' You said you'd allow me one, maybe two children. You bragged that you'd keep me in line because women are like children, they sometimes need a strong hand."

To her left she saw Teagan start to rise and knew if she said more her papa would toss the man out. "Any love I had for you died then. Killed by your words and nothing else."

"Don't lie to me, Beth. You already had another man. You just led me along so you could embarrass me. Add another broken heart to your long list that you can brag about." Lamont finally turned to Andrew. "Then, for no reason, you married a nobody, Beth. A man who owns no property or business. He probably can't even keep you in shoes, much less in the manner you should be kept. Hell, he probably doesn't even vote."

Andrew didn't seem to take offense at the insults.

"I don't want to be kept, Lamont. I never did. I want to contribute, to be of use."

Lamont snorted. "You're a beauty thing, aren't you? Good for nothing but show, and now, just to spite me, you've married a man who dresses like a wrinkled, out-of-work undertaker."

Andrew's hands molded into fists, but he still didn't say anything.

"He's more man than you'll ever be. He's good and kind and funny." She looked at Andrew, and for a moment their eyes held. "And I love him," she said, more to her almost-husband than to Lamont.

Even wrinkled with uncombed hair and several days of stubble, he looked wonderful to her.

"He's a thief," Lamont shouted. "And no one steals what is mine." He pulled a small derringer from his vest pocket and waved it like a banner.

Everyone moved in the half heartbeat before the gun fired. Andrew stepped in front of Beth. Teagan lunged, shoving Lamont sideways. Beth screamed and tumbled back into the chair. The room spun with yells and curses and arms and legs flying.

Teagan flattened the senator, knocking the breath from the man, then pounded on his still body as if not ready to stop fighting. Her gray-haired papa was a warrior, once more protecting his own.

It's over, Beth thought, as the violence and noise settled around them like dust. She felt her tight muscles begin to relax. The nightmare that had begun on a midnight train was over. No more running. No more lies. Her papa would toss Lamont off the ranch so fast he'd think he flew, and her world would be safe again.

Suddenly the little parlor was filled with her mother and uncles moving furniture around, asking questions, issuing threats to an oblivious senator. Lamont moaned once, and Teagan's fist patted his jaw, sending the man back to sleep.

"Are you hurt?" Travis yelled at Teagan, who was still on top of their guest.

"No. How about you, Bethie?" Teagan rose from an unconscious Lamont. "I thought the bullet went wild, but did it clip you?"

Jessie was kneeling in front of her

daughter, already moving her hands along Beth's arms.

"I'm fine. He didn't hit me." She fought to control her anger. "He tried to kill me. Oh, Momma, he tried to kill me. If Andrew hadn't stepped in front of me, I might be dead."

She moved into her mother's arms as fear shook her.

Andrew still stood beside her, silent, unmoving, his hand pressed against his wrinkled trousers. "It's over," she whispered as she reached for his hand.

Warm blood trickled between their fingers. She looked down and saw crimson spreading across his leg and onto the rug.

"Andrew?" She looked up.

He let go of her hand and stared down at his leg. "I fear, dear, that I may have been shot."

His eyes closed as he crumpled to the floor.

CHAPTER 26

EVERYONE MOVED AT ONCE AROUND THE SMALL parlor, which was designed for women's teas and not gunfights. The uncles lifted Andrew and moved him slowly down the hallway to the study.

Jessie ran ahead of them to clear the desk. She yelled at the housekeeper and Madie standing on the stairs to bring towels and sheets, then put water on to boil.

Beth followed the others, her heart pounding so wildly she feared it might break her chest. Andrew was hurt because of her. He'd acted, as he had before, to save her. This was all her fault.

"I'll go get the wagon." Teagan lifted Lamont's head and let it drop with a thud on the floor. "As soon as we check the wound and tie it off tight, we should be on our way to Sage's hospital in town."

"No," Tobin said. "I'll ride to get her. One horse, going through the back way, will be twice as fast as traveling overland in the wagon. I'll have her back here in no time."

Travis looked at Tobin. "Bring Drum back. We'll need the sheriff to haul Lamont off."

Everyone circled around Andrew. When Beth raised his head, she cried softly. He looked so pale. He was losing blood again.

Travis lit the fire in the fireplace as Madie rushed in with a mountain of towels, blankets, and bandages. The girl took one look at the blood dripping off Andrew and started crying. Her yelling brought Andrew back, and Beth fought the need to hug him.

He smiled weakly and took a breath, as if allowing himself a few seconds to come into his right mind. "It's all right, Madie. I'm not dying. I've only been shot." Andrew looked at Beth. "Everyone calm down, including you, wife."

Teagan cleared his throat, as if hinting that he might not allow any man to talk to his daughter so, but Jessie touched his arm, silently telling him to back away.

Beth almost laughed. She would have bet that the McMurrays couldn't have cared at all about her new husband, but she'd have been wrong. They liked him enough to worry.

"Lie back," Jessie ordered Andrew. "I'll take a look at the leg. The least I can do is have it cleaned when Sage gets here."

"Sage?" Andrew managed.

Beth answered, "My aunt. She's a doctor in town. Do you have any problem with a woman doctor?"

"None." Andrew gritted his teeth. "It hurts like hell."

While Andrew leaned his head back, silently taking the pain, Teagan slid his knife into the hole in his trousers and cut them open with one slash.

Andrew leaned on his elbows, suddenly having something besides the pain to worry about. "You cut my pants?"

"You weren't saving them, were you, son?" Teagan looked confused, then glanced at Beth. "I hope Tobin hurries up with Sage. Your husband's talking out of his head."

Beth moved beside Andrew before her father stripped any more clothes off. "It's all right, Andrew." She patted his arm. "You're going to be fine."

He looked at her as if she'd joined the crazy gang in the room trying to kill him. "I know I'm going to be all right." He said the words slowly, as if hoping she'd hear him. "Could you get me my journal? I don't want to miss getting any of this down. I've never been shot before."

"He's gone loco," Teagan said. "We need to get some whiskey down him."

"No," Beth demanded. "If he wants his journal, I'll get it for him."

Her papa shook his head. "Why would a man want such a thing at this time? Whiskey, even a gun, I could understand, but a journal?"

Beth ran down the hallway, across the kitchen, and up the back stairs. In panic she rummaged through both their cases, trying to remember where she'd stuffed his journal. He'd filled one on the train and stepped off at a quick stop to grab another one. Now she couldn't find it.

When she'd gone through everything twice, she ran back downstairs and found his saddlebags. Pulling out dirty clothes, she remembered stuffing it in the side, thinking it would be safe there until they made it to the ranch.

With the cook watching her as if she thought the entire household had gone mad, Beth ran back to the study.

When she returned, her mother had cleaned the wound and wrapped it tightly to keep the bleeding down. Her papa had stuffed enough logs in the fireplace to keep the house warm for days, and Andrew lay back on the desk, now covered with a sheet. Uncle Travis was missing.

"Andrew," she whispered, and was relieved when he opened his eyes.

The pain was there in his brown eyes, but he hadn't made a sound.

"I brought you the journal." She laid it on the table and offered her hand. "Can I help you sit up?"

He locked his fingers around her forearm and as he sat up slowly, she pulled, careful not to move the leg. "The bullet went in about halfway between my hip and knee." He seemed to be forcing words out.

"If you'll help me get to the chair, I could elevate it and still be able to write."

Everyone in the room watched as Beth helped him move the few feet to the chair by the fire. Apparently they saw no need to coddle an insane man by offering help.

When he was settled with the journal across his lap, Beth turned to this family of fighters she loved so dearly. "Andrew is a writer. He wants to get what he's feeling on paper."

Her papa frowned. "A writer? I thought he was unemployed. Don't tell me he makes a living writing those articles for the paper he told me about."

Beth didn't want to say no, or worse, lie, so she added, "He also writes stories."

Uncle Travis yelled from the parlor before anyone could comment. In all the excitement no one had noticed Lamont. The man must have revived during the excitement and run from the room the minute everyone moved to the study. He was nowhere to be found.

Uncle Travis was shouting orders as if he still commanded a company of rangers. "Search the house!" He pointed at Madie and the two little boys sitting on the main stairs watching. "Tell one of the men to saddle fresh horses!" Beth jumped, knowing her order. "We'll need a few days' supplies. If he's made it past the bridge, we'll have to track him. If he can ride—"

"He can ride," Beth finished. "He wrote me once that on a fast horse not a man alive can catch him."

Uncle Travis frowned. "My guess is he's on a McMurray horse by now, but he's wrong. I'll catch him."

Teagan and his brother grabbed their hats and coats. Her papa took the time to lean into the study and say to Andrew, "Don't die before we get back, son. I want to talk to you about what you write. Damn! I've always wanted to meet a writer, and now, when I've finally got one right here bleeding in my house, I got to go chase the worthless bum who shot him."

Beth and her mother laughed, and the house settled. There was nothing to do but wait now. The few inches of snow that had settled over the land during the night would make Lamont easy to track; unfortunately, it would also slow Sage's progress.

Madie brought them breakfast, but no one in the study ate.

The boys came in, but when Andrew refused to let them see the bullet hole they lost interest and went to the kitchen.

Beth sat across from him and watched her make-believe husband. He was hurting, probably more than he would admit, but he kept writing. Her mother offered him several things to drink, but he kept shaking his head. When Beth changed the bandage, the blood had soaked through the layers of cotton.

"You're bleeding again," she said as she knelt beside him to wash the wound gently. "It's lucky you found a wife who doesn't faint at the sight of blood."

He looked up from his journal and brushed his hand over her head. "Lucky." He winked at her.

"Bleeding is a good sign, I've heard," Jessie interrupted. "It means the wound is cleaning itself. Less chance of infection, maybe. I'll go set everything out that Sage might need when she gets here and make more coffee. It's going to be a long morning." The little lady smiled down at him. "Will you be all right while I'm gone?"

"I'll watch over him," Beth said as she draped a blanket over his legs.

Looking up, she watched her mother take the bandages out of the room and added, "Don't you dare die on me before we get you doctored properly."

"I don't think I have enough blood left to argue." He tried to act like he was joking when she gave him a worried look.

"You shouldn't have stepped in the way. You wouldn't have been shot."

"But you might have." He tried to make his words light. "There seems to be something in me that doesn't want you to die."

She leaned forward and brushed the hair away from his forehead, feeling the warmth beneath her touch. "Maybe you have a death wish and you figure your best chance for dying a hero is to stand near me."

He shook his head. "I'm not a hero, Beth. Or at least I never thought I was until I met you."

"Are you in much pain?" she asked.

"No. It's settled into a dull ache. I want to finish this article before the doctor has to cut the bullet out. I'm afraid I'll lose my train of thought once I start screaming."

"What can I do?"

He studied her. "Don't listen if I scream,

and if I pass out, make sure you're the last face I see. I don't want to float through unconsciousness without you by my side."

She leaned forward and kissed him. "There is something very lovable about you, Andrew."

"That stray-puppy look I have?"

"It's a shaggy-puppy look, and no, that is not all that makes you lovable."

He winked. "Just don't leave me here with your crazy relatives. Your father would kill me if I died before he had a chance to talk to me. Your mother seems to think scrubbing a wound is part of nursing, and I'm not sure, but I think your Uncle Travis is just here for what he thinks is fun. He looked his happiest during the shooting."

Before she could argue that her family was perfectly sane, Madie rushed into the room. "The priest is here, Mrs. McLaughlin."

Beth started to ask a question, but a man in a priest's robe stepped up behind Madie. He wasn't tall or built for strength, but he was handsome in his way. She'd guess him in his thirties. He had dark hair and eyes that twinkled with laughter.

"Top of the morning to you." He stepped into the room, waving hands that looked like he should be directing an orchestra. "I'm Father Benjamin. The men on the road told me there had been a shooting here. They were in a hurry and gave no details, so I feel called to come to offer my prayers for the afflicted." His intelligent gaze studied the room as if searching for someone who was absent. "The young lady who let me in said it was a Mr. Andrew McLaughlin who had been injured. I presume you are he, so I'll humbly offer my services." He made a small bow.

"That's kind of you, Father, but I'm not dying." Andrew studied the priest carefully, but Beth could see nothing amiss.

"We're all dying, son. Some of us faster than others. I myself have dreamed of my headstone so many times I swear I've seen it."

Andrew closed his journal. "Beth, dear, would you get the priest some coffee? While you're gone, I'd like to ask him to take my confession."

Beth stood, feeling confused and a little frightened. What if Andrew knew something she didn't? He could be hurt worse than she thought. "Yes, of course," she managed as she stood and moved to the door.

"And close the door for a few minutes, will you, love?"

"Yes," she said, and followed his orders.

In the hallway, she took a deep breath and fought back fear.

CHAPTER 27

ANDREW WATCHED THE PRIEST MOVE FORWARD, removing his thin white stole from his coat pocket and looping it around his neck. One of Andrew's stepfathers had been Catholic, and he'd attended mass regularly when home that year. Something about this priest didn't ring true, but no one else seemed to notice.

"Would you like last rites, my son, as well?" Father Benjamin opened his hands as if releasing doves to heaven. "I know you think it a simple wound, but there are sometimes complications. It is best, before you go into troubled waters, that your bags are packed and you are ready to meet your maker. Death claims us all."

Andrew lifted the poker from beside the fire and said simply, "You'll see your maker before I do, Father, if you don't tell me right now who you really are."

The boots of polished leather, dusty, but not worn, gave the priest away.

When he saw the priest hesitate, Andrew added in a deadly whisper, "I might not be able to hit you with this poker, Father, but the Colt under this blanket will strike its mark before you can reach the door."

The priest froze and, for a blink, Andrew feared he might have read the signs wrong. Could the man before him really be a priest?

The man lowered his head. "How did you know? I thought I played my part well."

"You did, but rural priests rarely bow in greeting. And your boots were your final tell. Broken in, but not worn out. Gambler's boots, I'm guessing."

The man sat down on the chair across from him. "I didn't have enough time to steal the whole costume, and an actor should never go on stage half prepared."

Sensing no danger, Andrew lowered the poker. "Again, who are you?"

"I'm Benjamin Smith, Levi and Leonard's father. When you were looking for me I was going by the name Theodore B. Hawthorne. The 'B.' real was a part of my name, but that was all. By the time I investigated and found out you were for real, you'd moved everyone here. If one of the neighbors hadn't remembered your wife's maiden name was McMurray, I'd have lost the trail. As it was, everyone in Texas knows the McMurrays own Whispering Mountain."

"You've come to get your boys?"

"No. I came to make sure they're in good hands. I have to move on and get set up somewhere first before I take them on to raise. I pray you'll keep them for a few more days, a month at the most."

"All right, I'll keep them." Andrew figured if he said no, the boys would be hanging out at the back of saloons. "But don't tell the others. Visit with your sons alone and tell them not to mention that you've been here."

Benjamin smiled. "My sons and I have played the stranger role before. We have a code in place. Many a time we've played a scam where we didn't know one another."

"You have?" Andrew was interested both in the man and in his story.

"Sure, the boys would go in looking for a handout at a restaurant and I'd walk in acting like I didn't know them. I'd offer to buy their food and several others would offer to help. Then I'd suggest taking up a collection to help the lads get along on their way to their poor mother down the train track." Benjamin winked. "We'd collect enough money for fares and enough food to last us days."

Andrew opened his journal as Benjamin continued. "But that's not the life I want for them. As soon as I go respectable, I want them with me. Levi doesn't mind the traveling so much, but it's hard on Leonard. He talked when we had a home, but once we started moving, I don't think he's said a word."

"You're right. Not even the teacher back in Fort Worth could get him to talk." Andrew lowered his voice. "Why'd you fake your death?"

"Oh, you know about that." He looked

embarrassed. "It proved to be expensive. I was working regular last fall, making good money and putting some away. I got in a wee bit of trouble and a lady friend of mine said there was talk of killing me. By chance one night, another gambler took my table and was killed for cheating. It was simple really to put my vest on him; we already had the same build and hair color. Add a near-blind doctor and the die was cast.

"I thought I'd disappear, reinvent myself, and start over. I was just about ready to step out with my new name and look when you showed up at the saloon asking questions. About that time the lady decided being my friend was more trouble than it was worth. She kicked me out, nameless and homeless, so to speak. If I hadn't stolen these clothes, I would also have been naked. And, sir, it was all your fault."

"My fault?"

"Yes. After she talked to you, she went looking for me and found me quoting Shakespeare in another's bed. I chose to exit the stage."

"She kicked you out the day I asked about you." Andrew finished the story.

"Without a dime. If I hadn't found the priest's robes in an old costume box at her place, I couldn't have followed you and my boys. Strange thing, no one gives a down-on-his-luck gambler a ride, but multitudes of folks welcome a man of the cloth. Most even try to feed me."

"Then play that role here, Benjamin. Visit with your boys. Stay out of the way, and let me know before you leave." Andrew hated telling the man to continue to lie, but he wanted to give Benjamin a chance to be with his sons. He didn't seem an entirely bad sort, more lost in life. Andrew had been there and saw no need to judge.

"Fair enough." Benjamin watched Andrew. "If I didn't know better, sir, I'd think you were also playing a role. I mean you no insult."

"I'll take none." He couldn't help but like the con artist. Andrew had learned a long time ago that most people are acting in the play of their lives. If they could only sit in the audience and watch, they might not have near the drama on stage.

When Beth opened the door, the priest was finishing his prayers.

She smiled at Father Benjamin, handed him a cup of coffee, and asked if he'd consider joining the others for breakfast in the kitchen.

"Only if I'm not in the way, Mrs. McLaughlin," Benjamin answered, his hands steepled in front of him.

"Oh, you won't bother me. We have two little boys eating in there now. Maybe you could keep them out from underfoot while the doctor is here. Madie has offered to be a runner if we need anything, and the cook will have her hands full getting lunch ready for all the crowd."

"I'm glad to help." He bowed slightly and backed out of the room. "Bless the bond that ties you two together, my children."

Andrew couldn't hide his grin.

Beth relaxed in her chair across from him. "What a nice man. We're not Catholic, but I still feel blessed to have a priest beneath our roof."

"May good things come of it," Andrew answered, wondering how he could hint that they might want to count the silverware before Father Benjamin left.

CHAPTER 28

COLBY DIXON WALKED IN AT SUNSET AND LIT the first lamp, hardly recognizing his own house. The warm glow across his new furniture made him happy. He'd spent the first day back cleaning up the old place and the second day ordering furniture from a catalog. Most of it had to come all the way from Austin, and, thanks to the trains, it only took a few days. Good solid furniture a man could be proud of, but it looked plain in his plain house.

He had known from the first that he'd need help if he planned to get the house finished before spring roundup started.

So, unlike his father, he rode into town and hired three carpenters. They came out the next morning loaded down with lumber and paint. All three were family men and thankful for winter work.

They called him Mr. Dixon, though he'd said it wasn't necessary. Even when they finally used his first name, there was respect. He felt it. He didn't think he deserved the honor, but he bore the responsibility of it. He wanted to be a fair boss and work harder than any man he hired. The trail boss on the cattle drive had taught him that.

Day by day the place changed. One man built a wide porch while another put in a new stove and redid the fireplace. The third painted and repaired walls and flooring.

One Friday, when he drove them back to town and paid them from money he'd drawn from the bank, they all thanked him, saying the pay would help them make it through the winter.

Colby thought of all the money his dad had squirreled away while the ranch fell apart. "If you've got the time, I could use help with the corral fences, and the barn needs a new roof."

All three promised to be out Monday morning ready to work.

Colby waved and headed to the hotel for a meal. This time he took a bath first and dressed in new clothes he'd bought. He knew the sensible thing to do was to ride home—even in the dark he wasn't likely to get lost—but somehow the hotel with its china and tablecloth made him feel like he was back at McLaughlin's place with friends around him.

As he took his bath, he remembered the conversation he'd had with Andrew in the bar one evening and the last one he'd had with Madie before he left.

When he dressed he promised himself he'd have more, with them, or maybe someday with his own family. The new clothes were quality work clothes but nothing fancy. He'd thought of buying new boots, but the ones his pa had bought him just before he left for the cattle drive looked to be still in good shape. As he examined them for any holes, he remembered how his pa said he'd better be wearing them when he came home.

A seam along the top of the boot had pulled free, just far enough for him to slip his finger between the broken stitches. A sliver of white shone through between the pieces of leather.

Colby tugged, thinking his pa had paid too much for boots padded with paper. But as he tugged, he realized the folded paper had been hidden inside on purpose.

In the lamplight of his hotel room, he unfolded the note and smiled. His pa had sent the deed to the ranch with him, trusting that he'd bring it home. No one would ever take his land away.

"Thanks, Pa," he whispered, realizing he was staring at proof that his father had loved him.

When he went down to the restaurant, everyone greeted him, but his mind was on the paper in his pocket. He'd go to the bank tomorrow and put it in the safe.

He ate alone, but the girl serving food stopped by whenever she wasn't busy.

She was pretty, but far too thin for his liking. When she hinted that she'd be off work soon and hated walking home after dark, Colby acted like he didn't hear her. The town was so small anyone could pretty well see every house, so she'd be safe enough.

He turned in early and started a list of

what he'd need to order the next morning if he planned to build on another bedroom along with a washroom to the back of the house. One of the carpenters had drawn up a plan on the back of a paper bag.

Colby figured he'd need a real bed in both bedrooms in case of company, and nightstands like the one in the hotel. A comfortable chair for him to sit in and read by the fire would be nice, and maybe he'd frame in a bookshelf. Maybe this trip to the store, he would remember dishes. He'd been eating his meals out of the pot he cooked in.

He fell asleep trying to remember all the stuff Mrs. McLaughlin had bought for Andrew's house. She'd made it look nice.

Madie crossed his tired mind. He worried about her having a baby so young. Worried that no one was making sure she ate right and got plenty of sleep. He woke several times during the night trying to decide between writing her another letter and riding back to Fort Worth to talk to her. He had no doubt she'd need some more of his advice.

CHAPTER 29

ANDREW WOKE TO THE FIRST SUNNY MORNING in three days. It had been cloudy when he'd been shot, and the snow seemed to hang around with the pain. Dr. Sage Roak, Teagan's sister, had cut the bullet out that first morning and, as Beth had promised, she'd been the last person he saw before he passed out.

He didn't remember much of the day after that, or the next. It seemed people moved him from first the study, then the parlor. The study desk was hard and the little bed in the parlor was too short, but Andrew barely noticed.

All were worried about Teagan and Travis. They knew they would find LaCroix, but Sage and Jessie worried because the senator was sneaky. Beth said she was more worried that Lamont might have lost his mind. Andrew tried to assure them that it would take a few days to catch him, then maybe more to get him to a town. He also suggested that the McMurray men would refuse to turn him over to any small-town sheriff. They'd take him all the way to Austin.

Everyone agreed, but his reasoning didn't seem to stop their worry.

By the third day he felt well enough to complain. Tobin surprisingly seemed to understand that Andrew was tired of being the center of attention. He and Sage's husband, the sheriff of Anderson Glen, loaded Andrew in the wagon and took him down to a little cabin Sage and Drum had often used before they had the twins.

It was small, with a potbellied stove in the center, but the solitude fit him. The stream outside his window almost made him believe he was hearing traffic, and the birds in the evergreens and cottonwoods sounded like noisy neighbors.

For the first few hours Madie and Beth were like bees buzzing around the place, bringing in a wagonload of what they thought he needed. Beth circled by, always checking on him, mothering him as they unloaded all they'd shipped from Fort Worth.

By the fourth day he was able to hobble around on a cane and begin writing again. Beth stayed with him the first few nights in the cabin, sleeping in a hammock she strung in one corner. She made trips to the main house every day. Madie and the boys came out to visit and Sage stopped by, but for the most part, he was comfortable and alone.

He found he liked walking the path beside the stream. There were no people or stores to look at, but he laughed at rabbits and squirrels. Horses came in for a drink on the other side of the stream, and he often heard other animals who never stepped out of the darkness at night.

As he watched Beth cooking breakfast on the fifth day since he'd been shot, he finally thought of something to say that didn't relate to his recovery. "I'm surprised you packed the typewriter. It's too heavy to be hauled around. You do know that when your father suggested we stay until spring, I had no intention of taking him up on the offer."

"I guessed your intentions, but you don't know my father. I figured you might need it." She glanced over at the corner, where she'd made his office complete with a desk, bookshelves, and two chairs. "When you're ready, we can get back to mailing out material so you won't miss work. Someone from the ranch usually takes the mail in once a week. When Sage came out yesterday, she brought a letter for Madie from Colby. It was in care of you, but someone had scratched out the address in Fort Worth and put in Whispering Mountain. So if any of those envelopes come back from the publishing houses or magazines, they'll eventually make it here."

"What did Colby say?"

"At first, we all waited for Madie to tell us. Finally, she admitted she couldn't read and asked me if I'd read the letter to her. Colby wrote that the rangers didn't find his father's killer, but they were thinking that with a ranger presence on his ranch now and then, whoever wanted the land won't try again."

She leaned on the edge of Andrew's chair, close but not touching. "Colby's back at his ranch and told her he was making improvements. After that he mostly wrote a list of things she was not supposed to do. I found it a little insulting, but Madie didn't seem to mind."

Andrew smiled. "He worries about her. They formed a friendship while they were together."

"I think it may be stronger than that," she agreed. "I see what a sweet girl she is. She watches everything I do and tries to imitate me like I'm her hero. She's so kind to the boys. I'll not put up with Colby hurting her feelings."

"I don't think you'll have to worry about that. Colby's turning into a fine man. I should have told you before that you were right to go back into that hospital and bring him out. He'd be dead by now if you hadn't."

Sitting near him, Beth seemed to want to continue visiting, and he realized what a foul mood he must have been in since the bullet hit his leg. He was surprised she hadn't started just dropping his food off at the door.

He turned his chair to face hers, almost close enough to brush knees. "Tell me what else is happening back at the house? Any word from your father?"

She shook her head, then changed the subject. "You'll be happy to know Father Benjamin has offered to teach Madie to read, and he's been doing the boys' lessons with them every morning."

"I'm surprised he's still here. Doesn't he have a mission to get back to?" Andrew thought Benjamin's game dangerous. One slip and the McMurrays would know the truth, and they wouldn't be too happy about the lie.

He closed his eyes, knowing the one he and Beth told was far worse.

Beth didn't seem to notice his worries. "No, lucky for us, Father Benjamin is between assignments."

Andrew decided to simply add, "Yeah, lucky for us." No telling what the con man was stealing.

Silence stretched between them. Since the shooting, they'd seen a great deal of each other, but somehow they'd become strangers. He missed her touch, her kiss. He'd fallen asleep every night with the memory of how she'd looked that morning in her room. Her camisole had been opened and the thin cotton she wore did nothing to hide the curve of her body.

"I worry about you," she finally said as her fingers brushed over his leg. "If you start back to work, go slow. That leg needs time to heal."

"The work will keep my mind off it." He wanted more on his mind than a wound. He longed to talk to her. Not about the shooting or their make-believe marriage. Not about anything that was really important. He fought the urge to capture her hand in his, but he'd feel like a fool saying simply that he needed her near.

"Can I get you something before I leave?" she asked as she stood and stepped back into her role as nurse.

He fought to stay still. "Some writing paper would be nice. I'd like to send Colby a note."

She smiled at him, that sweet smile he was starting to hate. That smile that said he was hurt and she was nursing him back. "I thought I might go help with the quilting today while you take a nap. I'll return with supper before dark."

"Fine," he answered, turning away.

"Want to go in with me? Sage and Drummond are staying the night. They brought their twins. Their boys are a little older than Levi, but they became friends over milk and cookies. The house seems alive with the sound of children running and laughing."

"No. I'll stay here."

She circled around the room to leave but ended up right back in front of him. "What's the matter, Andrew? What do you want?"

"I want you to sleep with me tonight. In the same bed, like we did the night before the shooting." His need for her had formed words before he thought.

"But—"

"You won't hurt my leg. I'm not bored, looking for something to do. I simply miss the nearness of you."

"All right. I'm tired of hiding the hammock away every morning." She turned and went back to loading up laundry to take back to the main house.

He felt even more miserable for asking. Maybe she felt grateful to him for saving her life and thought she'd be nice to him. He didn't want that. The need to hold her was an ache greater than the one in his leg, but he didn't see the longing returned in her eyes. He needed her, but only if she wanted him in the same way.

After she left, he paced, forcing his leg to move, working the muscles until they burned. It was almost dark when she returned.

As she set the food on the little table, he tried to keep his voice calm. "Beth, I've been thinking. I was out of my head asking you to sleep with me. I don't know what came over me. Maybe you should sleep at the main house tonight. I'll be all right here alone." He wanted her to stop mothering him, and the only way he could think to make that happen was to cut the cord clean.

"But—"

"Get a good night's sleep and come back with breakfast. We'll begin work again. I could use your help with the typing, if you're still willing."

She watched him, but she didn't argue.

"All right. If that is what you want, Andrew. Momma says arguing with a wounded man is like poking a bear."

"I'm not arguing. I just want to be left alone." He couldn't let this need he had for her open his heart. The injury had finally knocked some sense into him. This cabin would save his sanity while they were here on Whispering Mountain. He could work and be alone. She would be safe with her family. In a month he would leave, making a show of promising to be back soon. Having her near at night would be worse than a drunk watching over a full bottle of whiskey.

Reason told him one fact. If the wreck had never happened, a woman like her would never be with a man like him.

Beth gathered up her things. As she stuffed her bag, she pulled out a worn leather pouch. "Oh, I almost forgot, the housekeeper found this among your dirty clothes."

Andrew raised his eyebrow as he took the pouch bound with string. It looked familiar, but he knew it wasn't his. Turning it over in his hands, he thought of where he'd seen it before. A campfire the night before Peterson's men climbed on the train. They'd been talking about the robbery, and Chesty said something about as soon as they had money for a stake they'd all be going hunting for treasure.

"I've got the map." Peterson had laughed, showing a few missing teeth. "Won it in a poker game in East Texas," he'd bragged. "All we have to do is climb down in the Palo Duro Canyon, follow this map, and dig out as much gold as we can carry. There will be no more trains to rob; I'll be so rich we can buy our own. Every man here will get a pocket full of gold."

Andrew looked at Beth as the memory of that night faded. "This belonged to Chesty Peterson. I saw it the night before the gang planned to rob your train. How did you get it?"

"I didn't. It was in your saddlebags. Except for the night I bought your horse I've never crossed paths with Chesty." She looked like she was flipping through memories in her mind. "I saw him checking the saddle when he walked the horse out. He must have slipped it in then. Maybe he thought passing it on with the horse was safer than getting caught with it in his pocket."

Andrew slowly unfolded the oiled leather around what looked like a very old map.

"What does it mean?"

"It means if Peterson gets out, he'll be headed our way. He might not bother to come after me, but he'll come after the map."

Beth's face paled.

"It's all right." He pulled her close. "He's in jail, on his way to prison for life, and he has no idea where we are."

She stood starched stiff.

"Don't worry," he tried again.

"Papa sent a telegram this morning saying they were escorting Lamont to Austin for a hearing. They caught up to him fifty miles from here trying to board a train. At the end of the note Papa added, **Outlaw Chesty Peterson escaped. Rangers mounting a manhunt.**"

"And you didn't tell me?" Andrew didn't know whether to be angry or frightened.

"I didn't think it mattered. He'll never find us, and if the rangers are after him there won't be anywhere in Texas he can hide."

"If Colby's letter found us, an outlaw can find us." He held her against him. Now wasn't the time to step away from her. It wouldn't take much for Chesty to figure out that Beth was with him, thanks to all the news about her and Lamont. If he knew Beth was the one who bought the horse, he could read a paper and see that she'd married Andrew McLaughlin, the same Andrew McLaughlin who'd seen his map. The only man who didn't die with the other outlaws. The stranger they'd taken in who rode a pinto with white stockings. Lamont had probably told the papers Beth's last name. Peterson might go to Dallas or Fort Worth first, but eventually, he'd be riding toward Whispering Mountain.

"Go back to the house and tell Sheriff Roak that I want to see him." Andrew wasn't sure he liked Sage's husband, but he'd been the sheriff for years. Andrew had no doubt he was an honest man who loved his family, but from time to time he looked at Andrew as if he were wondering what crimes he'd committed. Something about the sheriff made Andrew feel like he should start confessing.

"We'll be safe here," Beth whispered. For the first time, she didn't sound like she believed her own words.

He watched her go, knowing that she'd be safer without him around. If only he could ride, he would be wise to disappear, but wisdom seemed to have deserted him the moment he saw Beth on the train looking worried and frightened. He'd had to save her, just as he had to stay and keep her safe now, even if the only way might be to stand between her and a bullet.

The dinner she'd brought was forgotten as he watched the sunset. Winter had turned everything into shades of brown except for the evergreens along the creek. The air was crisp tonight, hinting of another storm, but he'd never seen the moon so big. The place was hauntingly beautiful with the black of the mountain behind the house and the sound of the creek rushing between rocky shores. He could understand why all the McMurrays fought for this place. A slice of heaven.

Sheriff Drum Roak was within twenty feet of him before he heard the man. Even then Andrew had the feeling he'd made a sound on purpose to announce his presence.

"Evening, Sheriff." Andrew tried to swallow his surprise.

"Evening, Mr. McLaughlin. Heard you wanted to talk to me."

Andrew nodded as the tall, lean man walked toward him. He wore his gun low like a gunfighter, and like many of the men born to this life he seemed more legend than real. A man built of rawhide and guts. He didn't seem to fit with the tiny doctor, but Andrew had seen them together and they lived for each other's smile.

Andrew said the first thing that came to mind. "I figured you'd ride over."

"I grew up running across this land. When I was a kid I used to swim the river and walk to the house just to see what the McMurrays were up to. Except for once, they never caught me, and the night Teagan did I thought he might kill me."

"The way I heard it, you almost killed him."

Sheriff Roak was close enough that Andrew saw him fight down a grin. "I tried, but I was just a kid. He tied me up in the barn to wait for the sheriff, and the McMurray women tried to feed me to death. I fell in love with Sage the minute I saw her."

"Did you two marry young?"

Roak shook his head. "No, I had to chase her for a while; then she shot me and I gave in." He laughed. "I'll tell you the whole story someday if you have the time. Who knows, I hear you're a writer, you might even write it down."

"I'd like that." Andrew limped into the kitchen with his cane. "Beth brought over enough supper for an army. Will you join me?"

He shook his head. "I've already had some of Jessie's cooking, but I'll have pie and coffee. No sense in walking back to the house before the kids are asleep. Four boys in the house does more than double the noise."

Andrew offered him a chair, realizing that this was Roak's house. "Thanks for letting me recover here at your place."

"You're welcome. We don't get a chance to use the cabin much anymore. Sage likes to be in town in case someone needs her, and nothing's changed with me. I like to be where Sage is." He poured them both coffee while Andrew lowered into a chair.

When Andrew didn't say anything, Roak leaned closer. "What's on your mind?"

With total honesty and leaving out no details, Andrew told Drum about meeting the Peterson gang. Of traveling with them. Of trying to stop his friend from climbing on the train. Of saving Beth, and how she pulled off the bandanna that tied him to the gang and probably saved him from going to jail.

Roak asked a few questions, but for the most part he just listened. Andrew told him what he'd heard about Beth buying his horse from an outlaw in the middle of a gunfight, but he left out the mess they'd faced with Lamont LaCroix later that night.

When the sheriff refilled their coffee, Andrew reached across the table and handed Roak the pouch. "All we can figure out is that Peterson must have stuffed this into my saddlebags. It's a map to what Chesty called the Gold of the Palo Duro. He claimed a cave in the canyon held more gold than the entire gang could spend in a lifetime. That was the reason for the train robbery. He said it would give them enough money to buy all they needed to mine a claim and bring it out. Land's cheap up in the panhandle, and his idea was to homestead a small farm off the rim so he looked like a rancher. No one would suspect."

Drum looked at the map, but he didn't seem overly interested. "I've heard tales of that gold all my life. Part of Coronado's search for El Dorado, the city of gold. They say it's cursed because every man who goes in search of it never returns." The sheriff smiled. "But you know, McLaughlin, it would make an interesting story for a novel."

Andrew shook his head. "I don't care about the gold, or the story. All I'm worried about is Peterson hunting me down to find the map. When he sold Beth the horse he might have guessed she was buying the pinto for me. The only lead he has about where I am is through her, and we left a trail Slim Bates said a blind man could have followed. It wouldn't take much for him to find out we went to Fort Worth. We stabled our horses in a public livery. Hell, I even left a forwarding address."

The sheriff leaned back. "I'm not going to arrest you for the robbery. I wouldn't even if you weren't married to my wife's niece. You're either the greatest storyteller I've ever met, or you are the worst outlaw this side of the Mississippi. I'll bet my badge you weren't even wearing a gun that night you jumped on the train."

Andrew didn't bother to answer. Roak had probably figured out that much, and far more, about him already.

The sheriff continued, "Near as I can tell, half the folks you've met since you've been in Texas have a reason to kill you. Peterson and his new gang—he'll have one by now—are coming for you." He held up one finger. "My guess is he'll have no trouble taking the map from your dead hand. Then there's LaCroix, who tried to shoot you." He held up two fingers. "Now add my brother-in-law, Teagan, who will finish the job if he thinks you hauled his baby girl into this mess." He lifted three fingers and looked at the count. "You're a dead man, partner."

"I know." Andrew didn't appreciate the summary of his life these past few weeks. "Any chance you could arrest me and lock me up? Maybe if I sit in jail I'll stop rubbing folks the wrong way."

Roak shook his head. "If Peterson can break out of jail, he'll have no trouble break-ing back in to murder you. Beth's right, you two are safest here. I'll talk to Tobin and make sure he puts a couple men on guard duty at the bridge. He still rides the perimeter at night, and I heard him say he's not leaving until Teagan gets back. We've got a few old Texas Rangers working here and they'll probably be happy to hang around the headquarters watching over the place. They may be past their prime, but they'll know trouble riding in when they see it."

Andrew felt better just getting the problem out. He relaxed and decided to eat one of the dinners Beth had brought. Roak ate the other one.

Halfway through his second supper, the sheriff asked, "How'd you have time to court and marry Beth in all this mess?"

"I don't know," Andrew answered. "It seemed like I got hurt and passed out. The next thing I remember, I woke up married."

"Yeah, it kind of happens that way. I figured she'd be back from the big house by now."

"She's not sleeping here tonight." Andrew had been thinking about how to handle the question. "I told her to sleep over there. She'll be safer."

Roak frowned but didn't comment. He finished off his second slice of pie and left, saying he'd keep in touch. Andrew walked him to the door and watched him disappear silently into the night.

Then, with his head full of stories, he turned back to his desk and began to write. There was nothing he could do to make things better in the real world; he might as well work on a story.

CHAPTER 30

ON A COLD WINTER MORNING A WOMAN NAMED Maryanne Wells welcomed Colby Dixon into the trading post. She had on a white, starched apron like Madie and Mrs. McLaughlin had worn, so he knew he was speaking to a lady.

She helped him order all he'd need to make his place look like a home. She might have been considered too chatty, but she had three unmarried daughters, so she needed to keep a record of every single man in the county.

A few months ago Colby had been simply a kid, but now that he owned a ranch she said he'd be perfect for Pamela, her youngest daughter. She might be twenty-six, but she looked younger and still had all her teeth.

He picked out dishes as fast as he could. He'd seen all three of Maryanne's daughters and thought them fair to pretty, but if they talked as much as their mother, he'd go nuts alone with one for days on end. At twenty-six, when she did start losing those teeth, the youngest could move into fair to ugly real fast. If he married her, he'd be stuck with a wife eight years older, a chatty mother-in-law, and two old maid sisters-in-law to support.

On the ride home he figured he'd go south the next time he needed supplies. It would take him a few more hours, but the other trading post owner didn't even have a wife, much less daughters.

That night, when he looked at the inside of his place, he knew something was still missing. It just looked like pieces of furniture spread around, a few supplies on the shelves, a few pieces of material tossed over benches. It didn't quite look like a home.

In the few weeks he'd been home, Colby

and his three carpenters had made the place look grand. They'd even rebuilt the little fence around the family grave, but it didn't matter. Colby still didn't feel like this was where he wanted to be.

Before, when his pa was ordering him around, he hated his life and dreamed of getting away. He'd thought the cattle drives might be the answer, but they were mostly long days of hard work, just like on his father's ranch.

When the house didn't make him content, he turned to the ranch, building fences and corrals to be used in the spring. Clearing a field for planting a crop. Stringing wire along his property line. Putting up windmills where streams ran shallow in the summer months. The days were hard. He worked from before sunup to full dark. At night, when he finally hit the bed, all he thought of was what needed doing, not what he'd already done.

Right before he fell asleep, he sometimes remembered how it had felt to kiss Madie. He told himself he'd just kissed her to teach her how a kiss should be. He told himself he was a fool, and alone in his house no one argued with him.

He tried to make his life better. He hired a woman to come out from town one morning a week to clean house and do laundry. He rode into town a few times to eat and bought bread and canned goods that his pa would have thought were unnecessary. Nothing made him happy.

He missed the few days he'd spent with the McLaughlins in Fort Worth. He missed there always being people around to talk to and three meals a day that were edible. He missed playing cards with the boys and talking with Madie. Colby felt like he'd had one small slice of what life was supposed to be, and now he'd be hungry for it forever.

As the first hint of spring came, Colby Dixon was seriously considering running away from home.

He wrote another letter to Madie, even though she hadn't answered his first two.

CHAPTER 31

ANDREW FINALLY FELL ASLEEP A LITTLE AFTER dawn. An hour later someone pounded on his cabin door.

Grabbing his cane for a weapon, Andrew limped to the door of his cabin. It had taken him three days after she started sleeping at the main house to convince Beth that she didn't need to come over until after noon. He had no idea who was bothering him before the sun was fully up.

Pulling the door open with swear words already crossing his lips, Andrew came face-to-face with Father Benjamin. "Hell," he mumbled at the con man.

Benjamin crossed himself and pushed Andrew aside. "What a way to greet a man of the cloth." He acted insulted.

"You're not a man of the cloth." Andrew scratched his head. "If I remember right, you're a dead gambler."

Benjamin shrugged. "Few of us are what we seem." He raised an eyebrow as if daring Andrew to throw the first stone.

Andrew didn't take the bait. Benjamin might suspect something wasn't as it seemed, or he might just be guessing. "If you brought breakfast, come on in. Now that I'm awake, I'm hungry. I thought I made it plain to all that I like to work at night and sleep late in the morning, but apparently you didn't get the message."

"Be that as it may, Mr. McLaughlin, I'm here on an errand of mercy. Your wife informs me you're living out here like a bear in a cave, so I've come to make sure you take a bath."

"Like hell!"

Benjamin frowned. "Find a bigger vocabulary, sir, and she is right, you smell of an odor most foul."

Andrew wasn't surprised by his assessment or that Beth had mentioned the smell to him. She hadn't come within five feet of him in days. Since he'd made her sleep in the main house, she'd been cold as a stranger. She would bring out his food and tidy up, and then she'd ask if she could help him with his work. When he grumbled, she'd leave. She hadn't been close enough to smell him.

He told himself it was for the best. He wasn't really a part of her life, just the ghost of a make-believe husband still hanging around. If Peterson did come to kill him, Andrew didn't want Beth near, but that didn't keep him from missing her even if she was walking through his life daily. He missed the good-night kisses and her light touches.

"I've brought a tub, soap, and pots for boiling water." Benjamin glared at Andrew. "Mrs. McLaughlin suggested a weapon, in case you fight, but I'll have you know, sir, I am adept in the ancient art of karate developed in the Ryukyu Kingdom. Don't make the mistake of underestimating me." He smiled and added to his résumé, "I also played a butler once in a stage production, so I know what to do to help with a gentleman's bathing."

The little man stood straight as if he

thought he could threaten Andrew. "You're going to take a bath, sir. The only question is, will you be conscious or unconscious?"

Andrew didn't have the energy to fight. He'd been wishing for a good bath for almost a week. Dried blood was stuck to his skin and his beard itched as if it had fleas. "Let's get this over with."

Benjamin rubbed his hands together in a frantic kind of way and went to work.

Andrew managed to strip while the pretend priest heated water. The small wound where the bullet had entered was scabbed over, and he figured it would take a washing. The hot water might help his muscles relax.

When he slid into the hot tub, the water felt great. Even the strong soap that burned his nose and scrubbed off a layer of skin smelled wonderful to a man sick of smelling himself.

Benjamin, to his credit, seemed to know what he was doing. He covered the tub with a towel to keep the steam in and repeatedly poured more hot water when needed. By the time the water was at the top of the tub, Andrew had relaxed.

As he washed his hair, he said, "I hope you brought me some clothes."

Benjamin laughed. "I had quite a discussion with your bride. She seemed to think you needed western clothes, but I insisted that clothes make a proper gentleman, and you, Mr. McLaughlin, are a gentleman. She finally agreed and I brought your black suit and starched white shirt with a proper collar. Since someone sliced your other tailored pair of trousers, Mrs. McMurray insisted on ordering you another suit, but it will take a few weeks."

"Thanks." Andrew dunked his head. When he came up spitting soap, he added, "But I think I'll wear the western style she sent over yesterday and save the suit for when I leave. Maybe it's time for a change, and the clothes she brought fit with this life."

The little man didn't miss a beat. "Very good, sir." He played the part of a man's valet for an hour, cutting Andrew's hair, assisting with the shaving, and even polishing the boots Beth had sent.

"You look like a new man." Benjamin stood back when his job was finished. "I've done wonders."

"I do feel better," Andrew answered as he poured two cups of coffee and motioned his guest to take a seat. "Thanks for the help. I almost feel back to normal, whatever that is in my life."

Andrew sat across from Benjamin and opened the small basket of muffins he'd been smelling for an hour. He took one and pitched one to Benjamin. "Now, when do you plan on telling the McMurrays you're not a priest? You can't play this role much longer. You're bound to trip yourself up eventually."

"Never," he answered with a loud sigh. "I couldn't let them down. They're all so kind." He blew on his coffee. "But I'm not taking advantage of their hospitality. I've taken on the task of teaching Madie to read and write, and I have morning lessons with the boys."

"They're your boys," Andrew pointed out.

"I never forget that fact. I only regret that I didn't spend more time with them before now. Their mother was a hard woman to live with. I left her after Levi was born but returned for another try. That was when Leonard came along. I started wandering after his birth. It's in my blood, but I tried to be a husband. I sent money when I had it but didn't really know the boys until she died. I kept them with me for a while as I moved around. When that didn't work I left them with relatives." He stopped, almost in tears. "That didn't work out."

"I heard," Andrew admitted. The uncle must have been terrible to them if they were willing to run off.

"Now that I've seen my sons again, I swear to you, this time I'll do right by them. I'll find a job and make a life that includes them."

"Once you get out of the robes?" Benjamin didn't seem to be in any hurry to give up regular meals, and the longer he stayed the harder it might be to leave the boys.

"Of course, the robes will go as soon as I'm out of sight." The little man folded his arms and leaned back in his chair. "I think there is a possibility my calling could be teaching. After all, it's much like acting. You stand in front of an audience and project. I never had formal training, but growing up in a traveling medical wagon, I spent my days reading the classics. The people traveling with us always had things to teach me: world history, math, card tricks. I've always thought I had better training than most colleges offer."

The little man smiled. "You should see how fast I'm teaching Madie to read. We work at least three times a day, and she's flying through the lessons."

Andrew almost felt sorry for Benjamin. He wondered how many men hid behind one mask or another. In truth, Benjamin's lie didn't seem any worse than his own. "Get a real job, and I'll bring the boys to you. No one here will have to know you're playing a role."

"You'd really do that for me?" The man stilled, as if waiting for the catch.

Andrew nodded. "As long as you promise not to steal anything from the McMurrays."

He looked offended. "I may be many things, sir, but a thief is not one of them."

As he walked out, Andrew couldn't help but wonder if the man was telling the truth or simply playing another role. Maybe it didn't matter. After all, since he'd met Beth even he didn't seem to be able to tell the difference.

Before he could settle in to write, his

almost-bride bumped her way into the cabin with a huge box.

She smiled at him. "You look very handsome, husband."

He stood, not reaching for his cane for the first time since he'd been shot. "Thank you, darling. What do you have there?"

"Mail." She dumped the box in the middle of the bed.

Week-old newspapers from New York and Washington tumbled out, as well as a few books he'd ordered months ago. Among all the boxes and rolled papers were envelopes. Big brown ones. Small white ones. Andrew dove into the pile, feeling like it was Christmas morning.

She caught his excitement. "What can I do to help?"

"Start opening," he said. "I've missed news of the world so badly."

As he pulled open the first newspaper, she slit the end of an envelope and shook a single piece of paper out. A bank note tumbled out.

He was too busy reading the headlines to pay her much attention until she whispered, "Money. One hundred dollars. In payment for your first story in the Ghost Cat of Bailey Boardinghouse series."

"Really?"

"Really." She squealed and hugged him, then quickly pulled away to open another letter.

The newspapers were forgotten as they opened everything. Some asked for more details on a story; a few said, **Not at this time, but send more**; but most held money orders or bank notes. When Beth stood and spread the payments out on the table, she said simply, "You're rich. There must be a thousand dollars here."

"Thanks to you," he said. "I never send out more than a few at a time. This . . . this is enough to buy a house."

"No. You wrote them, Andrew. I just got them ready to mail. It was a small part." She smiled, obviously pleased with herself. "I think we should get back to work today. You've been writing for days; it's time I started typing out the pages. Where is that beast? I'm ready to face him and type away."

He touched her hair, thinking how he'd missed the simple act. Pulling her against him in a gentle hug, he whispered, "We make a good team."

She slipped her arms around his neck and kissed his cheek. "We do, and I've missed you. Is the bear who lives in this cabin gone?"

He didn't even act like he didn't understand what she meant. They'd been together all week, but not like this, not touching. "He's gone and not coming back. I needed time to heal and think." He leaned down until his forehead pressed against hers. "I've missed being this close. Forgive me for being so hard to put up with."

"There is nothing to forgive."

He couldn't fight the need for her any longer. He lowered his mouth and kissed her like he'd never kissed another. The warmth of her body moving against him washed away all reason. Being with her couldn't be as bad as being without her. It couldn't. The gods wouldn't play that cruel a trick.

For a long while he held her, thinking of nothing but how dearly he'd missed the feel of her.

Finally, she gently shoved him away. "I'll make you lunch, and then we'll work."

He nodded, hoping he could pull his

thoughts together enough to form sentences. When he moved to his desk, he heard her humming.

The morning passed into afternoon with her always near. When he watched her work at the typewriter she called **the beast**, he stood close, letting his hand move into her hair. The feel of her ginger curls, now unbound, warmed him from inside out. Their days together were numbered and he didn't want to waste any more time.

When she walked near his desk to ask a question, she'd lean into his shoulder as she stood beside his chair. They were communicating again with far more than words. There would be time, oceans of time, to be lonely when they parted, but right here, right now, he wanted to remember one slice of happiness.

As he worked, he forged every detail of the day into his memory. The cool breeze from the open door. The stove popping away almost as regularly as the ticking of a clock. The sounds she made, humming when she was thinking, scolding herself when she made a mistake. Touching him lightly when she passed as if checking to make sure he was real.

When the sun ran a long stream of light across the cabin floor, she stood and stretched her back. "I'd better stop and go pick up dinner or it will be dark before I get back to the house tonight."

"Stay with me." He looked over his shoulder.

"For dinner?"

"Yes, and for the night." He watched her carefully, realizing he'd said almost the same words before changing his mind and sending her away. "I don't want to let you go. Not tonight." He almost added, **Not ever**, but those two words would shatter the last wall he'd built to keep everyone away.

Even if he were fool enough to fall in love again, she wouldn't have him as a real husband. He had nothing to offer. But it was time for him to fully play this game she'd invented; then the memories would be real even if the marriage wasn't.

She moved beside him, her hand resting on his shoulder. "I'll come for dinner," she said. "I'm not sure either of us could handle more."

He nodded. "We'll start with dinner."

CHAPTER 32

BETH DROVE THE WAGON BACK TO THE MAIN house, trying to sort out her feelings. Andrew had asked her to be real with him, not to pretend, and all day she had been. She really wanted him, but she wanted love from him as well. A marriage built on need would never work, but if he offered, she'd be willing to turn their pretend marriage into a real one.

If he'd just say he loved her once. If . . .

She'd heard the word **love** used too many times to believe it had much purpose. He'd said the loss of another love would kill him. She'd never loved anyone like that. To her, a man who'd loved too deeply and a woman who'd never loved seemed a poor match.

But when she lost him, would she forever wish she'd at least persuaded him to try? Maybe she was as spoiled as the family thought she was, but she didn't want him just to have him to herself. She wanted Andrew because he needed her, and he was too dumb to know that she'd be good for him. In an odd way, being needed felt like being loved even if he wouldn't say the words.

A tear dripped down her cheek. "What will I do," she whispered to Whispering Mountain as it loomed before her, "when Andrew is no longer in my life?" A part of her believed the lie she told everyone in Dallas after the train wreck. She'd said it was love at first sight. A part of her wanted to believe it still. She knew, when she lost him, she'd grieve, for her mind couldn't seem to convince her heart that she was only pretending.

As she neared the house, Beth noticed a horse that didn't belong to the McMurrays tied up at the end of the porch. Her first reaction was to reach for the rifle beneath her wagon bench. Only reason told her no one could have crossed the bridge without a warning shot being fired, so the guest must be friend, not foe.

Maybe her father was back from Austin. They'd been waiting for news about what had happened when they caught up with the senator. He could have taken the train, borrowed a mount at the station, and come home to tell them all about it.

Beth jumped from the wagon. Even if Lamont claimed self-defense, which wasn't likely since Andrew wasn't armed, he'd get some jail time. Prison wasn't exactly what he was used to, and a Texas prison would be a lower level of hell for a man who thought he deserved only the best.

As she ran up the steps she realized this all might be over in a few moments. All. The good and the bad.

She slowed. All but Andrew. That wasn't over, not now, maybe not ever.

When she walked into the parlor, a lean cowboy stood by the window. He wore the chaps of a seasoned rancher, bloodied and scratched, and the Mexican spurs of a wrangler.

For a moment she didn't recognize him. He'd gained weight and hardened in the month since he'd ridden away with Ranger Slim Bates.

"Colby?" Beth whispered.

He turned grinning. "Mrs. McLaughlin."

When he started to offer his hand, Beth pushed it aside and hugged him. "Oh, Colby, we've been so worried about you. How are things? Did you find the men who killed your pa? How are you surviving out on the ranch alone? You look like you've been eating regular."

Colby laughed. "You'll have to slow down a little, ma'am. I know I've been gone awhile but I'm not fast enough to catch up all at once."

Beth took his arm. "Fair enough. Have you eaten? We'll start there." She pulled him along to the kitchen. "The boys and Madie will be so happy to see you. They talk about you all the time. Madie's read your letters so many times they're falling apart."

Colby stopped walking. "I've been riding hard, ma'am; I was wondering if I could wash up first. I saw a stand at the side of the house."

"Of course, but use the mudroom. I'll tell the others you're here and we'll all meet in the kitchen. You can wash up while I put something on the table." She pointed him toward the back of the house. "My family rode into Anderson's Glen for a town hall meeting, so it'll just be us for supper."

He smiled. "Like it was at the house in Fort Worth?"

She pulled him along. "Except for Andrew. He's recovering over in a cabin by the stream, but he'll come in for breakfast tomorrow if he knows you're here."

"I need to talk to him soon." Colby lowered his voice. "Sheriff Harris out of Dallas stopped by my place and told me Chesty Peterson told one of the other prisoners that when he broke out he was going to hunt McLaughlin down."

"Andrew already knows that, but don't worry, he's safe here. We had another little problem with Senator LaCroix, but I'll let Andrew tell you all about that. You're welcome to stay for as long as you like."

"Thanks, but I'll be heading back day after tomorrow. It does feel like home with all of you here."

She knew what he was thinking. For a few days they'd been their own kind of mixed-up family.

Colby disappeared into the mudroom as Beth asked the cook to set a few more places at the table. She ran upstairs and told Madie and the boys that they'd be having company for dinner, then asked Father Benjamin to go fetch Andrew. She'd surprise Colby, and Andrew would come knowing he was here.

Twenty minutes later, Beth was putting stew and cornbread on the table when Madie walked in, all smiles. She'd combed her hair and put on one of the new aprons she'd made.

Colby had been sitting, waiting, but he almost knocked his chair over when he stood and watched Madie. The warmth in his eyes surprised Beth.

"Hello, girl, how you been?" he said.

"Fine," she answered. "I read your letters."

"You didn't write me back, so I came fearing there was something wrong."

"No." She stared at the floor. "I'm working as fast as I can to learn to write so I can answer you."

Beth didn't miss the way Colby's shoulders relaxed. "I'm glad to hear that. You eating regular here, Madeline? With the baby coming I don't want to think about you missing many meals."

She nodded. "It's nice here, Colby, real nice. I help out where I can, and I'm learning all kinds of things a lady should know."

"That's good." He shifted, as if not knowing what else to say.

"A priest who is visiting is teaching me to read, and the cook is showing me all kinds of recipes that I've never baked."

"That's good."

"Father Benjamin mostly works with the boys on lessons, but I sit in after the chores are done and you wouldn't believe all I've learned about history."

"That's good."

Beth motioned them both to sit down. Surely he hadn't ridden a hundred miles just to ask a few questions and answer Madie with the same two words.

"I can quilt now, and Mrs. McLaughlin's mom is teaching me to use a loom," Madie said, as if someone had poked her reminding her that it was her turn to talk.

"That's good," Colby said again, obviously stuck in the conversation.

Beth drew a long breath when the boys and Andrew stormed the big kitchen. Suddenly, everyone was hugging and yelling. While she put the rest of the food out, she caught Andrew's stare. This wasn't the dinner either of them had planned, but it was all right.

Everyone talked and laughed and ate. Colby couldn't seem to stop smiling. He'd obviously missed them all. Madie was quiet mostly, almost shy.

Beth insisted Colby stay with them when he asked if he could camp out on the ranch.

While Madie showed him to the only empty room in the old wing, the boys rushed out, saying they'd take care of his horse. All planned to meet back in the parlor to listen to one of Andrew's stories, just as they'd done in Fort Worth.

Beth suddenly found herself alone with Andrew in the empty kitchen.

"Where's the cook?" he asked as he stood.

"She usually goes to bed as soon as supper is served. It's always kind of been a rule that the family cleans up the kitchen at night."

"I'll help," he offered, and picked up a few bowls. "It's good to have the boy home."

He sounded as if they were really married and Colby belonged to them. "He's more a man than he was when he left." She followed him to the counter, where two tubs waited, one with soapy water, one with clean.

Andrew nodded. "He's been through a lot lately."

They talked quietly, aware that there were others in the house. Father Benjamin was just beyond the back door, waiting for the boys to return from the barn. She told him what Colby had said about Peterson, but Andrew didn't seem too worried. The second warning never seemed to sound as threatening as the first.

"We had a good day working together." Andrew slid his hand lightly around her shoulders. "After no sleep last night, I'm about ready to turn in, dear. How about you?"

"After you read, I'll drive you back."

"And then?"

"And then we'll see," she answered as

the boys came in and pulled him toward the parlor.

They all gathered around and listened to Andrew's new story. The boys laughed and hung on every word, and Father Benjamin clapped when he finished, proclaiming Andrew a fine writer.

Andrew closed his journal and said simply, "Take me home, wife."

Before Beth could answer, the priest stood. "I'll drive you both home, my children. It's chilly, but the boys can come along and watch the night sky. Tomorrow we begin a study of the planets."

She didn't miss the tightening of Andrew's arm around her shoulder. He'd never seemed very friendly around the dear little priest. "That's not necessary, Father. I don't mind taking him." She didn't add that she planned to return to the main house after a good-night kiss or two.

For once Andrew smiled at the man. "That would be grand if you'd take us, Father. Thank you for offering. I wouldn't want to leave the team outside all night."

Beth could hardly explain to a priest why she had not planned to sleep with her husband, and she couldn't tell Andrew that the afternoon of flirting had been nice, but she felt they'd gone quite far enough with their playing for one day.

When the father turned to grab his long coat, she jabbed Andrew in the ribs, then straightened and said sweetly, "We'd best say good night to Colby and Madie, dear."

"Of course, dear," he added, then gripped her hard as if he had no intention of letting her go.

To their surprise, the two young people had vanished.

CHAPTER 33

COLBY FOLLOWED MADIE UP THE FRONT STAIRS to a hallway with three doors. All through dinner when he'd talked to everyone else at the table, he'd been thinking of what to say to her, and now that they were alone for a minute, he couldn't think of a word.

She was prettier than he remembered, with a sweet round face that a man could get used to looking at. She'd also followed his advice and was growing, learning to read and write. In no time he'd be able to keep up with her in letters, and that made him proud.

"The first room is where Father Benjamin

sleeps. He kind of dropped by and decided to stay for a while. He says he's here to **feed the souls,** but I'm not sure what he means."

Madie moved down the hallway. "This room belongs to the boys. They play mostly downstairs in the dining room. That's where we set up the school. Father Benjamin knows all about history and plays. If the boys get all their lessons done, he reads a few acts of William Shakespeare after lunch, and everyone in the house stops to listen. He could have been an actor if God hadn't called him."

Colby couldn't think of anything to ask. He'd never met a priest, but he guessed it was some kind of rule that everyone had to like them even if you weren't Catholic. "I'd like to stay around long enough to hear him read."

She stopped at the third door and faced him. "I'd like that too."

Before he could say anything, she opened the last door and added, "This will be your room."

He followed her into the plain little room.

"It's nothing fancy, but it's clean. I made

the doily on the nightstand yesterday and thought it might dress the place up a little for you."

He touched the bit of crochet made from a thin string. "It does." He hesitated and added, "You mind if I take it home with me when I leave?"

She grinned. "I'd like that."

Colby set his saddlebags down on the room's only chair and faced her. He didn't know how much time he'd have alone with her, and he didn't plan on making a fool of himself with an audience. "Madeline, I rode here to check on you. I catch myself worrying about you from time to time." He cleared his throat. "No, that ain't right. I worry about you pretty much all the time."

"I'm all right, Colby. I swear I've been doing everything you told me to do."

"Good." He could feel the minutes they had alone ticking away. "I thought you might need some more advice."

She nodded.

He let out a breath. "Then I'm glad I came. What is it you have a problem with?"

She lowered her head, and he knew she must be uncomfortable. Hell, he was so nervous he could probably run down the stairs and around the big house and be back before she noticed he'd gone.

"Now don't be shy, girl. I won't be here long, so you need to tell me what's on your mind."

She nodded but didn't look at him.

He tried not to sound so bossy. "It's all right, Madie. I'm here. I'll help you with whatever's bothering you."

She finally looked at him. "Would you kiss me again first?"

He frowned. "I guess it would be all right. But don't go thinking I showed up here just to kiss you."

"I won't, Colby."

He took a step toward her and lifted her chin. Then, very carefully, like he might hurt her, he lowered his lips to hers and kissed her.

For a moment, it was nice, just nice, and then she leaned closer and put her hands on his shoulders as if she might need steadying, and he let the kiss continue.

When she moved a bit closer, he kissed her as he'd thought of kissing her.

She pressed her chest to his and the

feel of her against him almost buckled his knees, but he didn't break the kiss. She'd asked for a kiss, and he didn't want to be impolite and not give her a real one.

When they heard footsteps thundering up the stairs, she finally pulled away. Her cheeks were red and her eyes sparkled.

"Thank you, Colby," she whispered. "That was real nice."

"You're welcome." He smiled, letting his hand slide along the side of her rib cage. "But don't go asking for another. A girl your age and certainly one in your condition shouldn't be thinking of such things."

"I'll remember that, Colby." She looked so innocent until she added, "I'll be thinking of it tonight out on the back porch while I look at the stars after the house has settled."

He wasn't sure if she'd just offered him an invitation to join her, but he knew he wouldn't be looking at any stars with her tonight. It wouldn't be proper. When he had time he'd explain to her why.

It crossed his mind that since she was five or six months pregnant, she probably knew why. He remembered all she'd told him about Micah taking her down to the river so they could be alone and how she cried when he didn't listen to her when she told him to stop. She'd said he hurt her, and Micah's saying he loved her didn't make the hurt go away.

As the boys ran into the room, Colby made himself relax, even though he was thinking of going back to Fort Worth and beating up Micah.

An hour later, when they were clustered around the kitchen table playing poker with matches, the priest joined them. He warned them about the evils of cards, then shuffled and said he'd play dealer.

Colby watched Madie as she sat across the table, laughing and talking. He loved the way she helped the boys with their cards; sometimes, he suspected her of folding her own to help them win.

When they finally called it a night, Colby followed the boys upstairs, leaving Madie to go up the stairs off the kitchen where her bedroom was located. He'd thought he'd have a minute to say good night, maybe even touch her hand, but he hadn't dared with the priest watching.

Standing in his room alone, he smiled. Though he'd ridden all day, he hadn't wanted the evening to end. It was fun to have someone to talk to after supper. When he went back to his ranch, he'd miss that most of all.

He walked over to the window and looked out onto the sleeping ranch. Even the stars looked brighter than he remembered.

It crossed his mind that Madie might be on the back porch right now looking at the same stars. Maybe he should go down and tell her to come inside. It was too cold for her to be outside this time of night.

If he did go down, the girl would probably ask for another kiss, and he didn't have time for that sort of thing. He was eighteen last week, a full grown man now, and had a ranch to worry about. She must be close to sixteen by now, and she seemed to have matured some since Fort Worth, but she was a long way from being grown. She'd probably need his advice for a few more years at least.

She'd never gotten around to telling him what she needed his help deciding. She'd asked for the kiss first and then there had been no time.

Colby picked up his hat for no reason

and decided he'd better go down. After all, she might truly need his advice, and the kiss had distracted her as much as it had him. The least he could do before he slept was hear her out. Maybe if her problem was a big one, he'd tell her he'd have to think on it awhile and let her know come morning.

Walking down the stairs slowly, he made sure not to wake the boys. That wouldn't be right. He'd just step out on the porch, ask to hear her problem, then give her guidance and head back upstairs. No one would miss him for a few minutes and he would have set the poor girl's mind to rest.

Halfway across the kitchen, a low voice froze his progress. "Forget something?" the priest asked.

Colby turned. Father Benjamin was sitting in the shadows, looking like he was finishing the last of his coffee.

Colby wasn't used to lying, but he might as well give it a try. "No, just thought I'd say good night to Mrs. McLaughlin if she was still up."

"She stayed down at the cabin with her husband. I told them I'd drive over after dawn and get them for breakfast. You can say good morning and good night at the same time."

"Sounds like a good idea." Colby turned around, thinking he'd have to wait until morning to talk to Madie.

"Good night, son," the father said. "I think I'll sit here for a while. It's a full-time job keeping married folks in bed with each other and the unmarried ones apart, but I guess we all have our load to carry."

Colby had no idea what he was talking about. He wasn't planning on climbing into bed with Madie. First, she was still just a girl, and, second, she was pregnant. But darn the priest for mentioning such a thing, because now he was thinking what it might be like to have her beside him in the new bed he'd bought.

As he crossed the big room that had no purpose as far as he could tell except that it connected almost every other room in the house, Colby saw a flash of plaid hanging above a low-burning fireplace. On top of the tartan rested what looked like Apache beads.

A blending of two worlds, he thought. He'd heard stories that the McMurrays were part Apache, and this confirmed it.

Looking down into the dying fire, he caught a slight movement to his left. "Madie?"

She froze. "I couldn't go outside. I would have had to pass the priest, so I slipped down the hall and came in here."

He laughed softly. "Me too. He'd make a great palace guard in one of those stories Mr. McLaughlin used to read us."

Before she could move into the light, he stepped into the darkness with her. "We'd better not talk or he might hear us."

"All right. What should we do?"

"If you've no objection," Colby said as he placed one hand on her waist, "I was wondering if I could touch you and see if the baby's grown. I've never touched a woman who is carrying a child."

She took his hand and placed it on her middle. "I feel him moving inside me."

Colby took a few minutes to relax enough to touch her, and then he felt where the baby rounded her. "You don't mind this?"

"No. You have a gentle touch."

His voice shook slightly. "I've never been told that before. Does it hurt? The skin feels tight. Are you sure you'll stretch enough to carry the baby a few more months?"

"I think so. The doctor from town told me everything was coming along as it should. I'll simply get bigger and bigger until the baby comes out. You ever see a birthing?"

"No," he admitted. He slid his hand up to just below her breasts. "You're bigger here too."

She didn't make a sound as his hand edged slowly up, lifting her full breast slightly. He liked the feel of her, well rounded and warm. Definitely all woman.

"You all right?" he whispered against her hair. "I'll stop if you don't want me to touch you. I'd even understand, Madie. We would still be friends."

"No," she said, but he could feel her shaking. "Don't stop." She leaned against the wall. "All I could think about tonight was that maybe we'd have a moment to be this close. I like being close to you, Colby."

He kissed her cheek and then leaned back. "I want to remember the feel of you," he said as his hand closed over her. "I'd never hurt you, Madie, you know that."

"I know." She smiled up at him. "Do you think you could touch me and kiss me at the same time?"

He placed his hand on her waist. "You sure?" he asked one more time.

She laughed. "I'm sure, Colby. I'm real sure."

He pressed his mouth over hers as his hand trailed across her tummy, then higher to her breasts. When she made a little sound, he pulled her to him and moved his hands down her back all the way to her nicely rounded hips.

She fit against him, her breath shallow as he molded her close. To his way of thinking, she fit just right.

With his last ounce of sanity, he whispered, "This is something a man does to his wife."

"Do you want to marry me, Colby?"

He knew this was one of those questions he should think about, but he had a feeling the answer wouldn't change. "I do when you're full-grown." Pulling away far enough to see her eyes, he added, "I always wanted to marry a pretty woman, and you're about as pretty as they come. You're kind too, Madie, I can see that. And good tempered."

She took his hand in hers. "I'm full-grown, Colby. I swear I am. You touching me feels right, but I'd understand if you didn't want to marry someone who is already pregnant."

"If we married, I wouldn't sleep with you until after the baby comes, and when it's born, it'll be mine as far as everybody knows. I won't have anyone talking about you." He brushed light kisses over her cheek. "I'd love the baby like he was my blood."

"I believe you, Colby, but you have to promise me, if we married, that you'd kiss me every night. I've always thought that having someone to kiss at night would be nice."

He tightened his grip around her fingers. "I won't take orders, Madeline, we best get that straight from the start."

She lifted her cheek and brushed it against his jaw. "Of course," she said as he kissed her.

"Good. Now we have that straight, I think I could kiss you once more tonight, but don't expect such foolishness every night. I'll have a lot more on my mind once we're married than kissing my wife."

He kissed her again and again, lost in the pleasure of her.

Once when he stopped for a breath, she whispered **more** and he realized she was not going to be an easy woman to ration, and he wasn't even sure he wanted to try.

CHAPTER 34

Andrew held Beth's hand as he stood at the door to the cabin and waved good-bye to Benjamin. He had little use for the man, but tonight he said, "Nice of the father to bring us home."

From what he'd gathered and guessed, the boys' father had spent his life pretending, either on stage or in some kind of scam he might play. Only this evening, the man had done him a favor. Beth was here in the cabin for the night, and he was steady enough on his feet to chase her.

As the wagon disappeared, Beth jabbed

him hard in the ribs. "Did you put the priest up to this?" she teased.

"Me? No. It was all his idea." Since the day he'd pushed her away and told her to sleep at the main house, he'd regretted it. Logic had convinced him she'd be safer there. He'd had no idea how lonely being without her would be. "We've spent many a night together, dear. I'm sure we can survive another." This playlike marriage was about to end, and he wanted to pile up as many memories as possible.

To his surprise, she smiled that knowing smile women have when they see into the future.

"How about we just enjoy being together tonight?" He told himself that would be enough—well, maybe together with a few good-night kisses.

"I think I'd like that. What do we do first?"

"A walk in the moonlight. I've discovered a path in those trees."

Before he finished speaking, she tugged back on her knit hat. Without a word they walked along the stream by the cabin. The air was still and cold as if all the world had paused just for them. When they finally talked, it was in whispers, as if neither wanted to disturb the air. He told her of growing up among strangers in private schools, first in New England and later in Europe. She told him of her childhood here, and he would have traded for her memories in a second if he could have.

She talked of her family, mentioning her sister's husband. Her uncle Travis had found him as a little boy tied up like a dog in a raiders' camp. He'd taken him in and they'd called him Duck. As he grew, he'd changed into Duncan but he never knew his past. When finally he got a letter with information, he never opened it. By then, his past didn't matter, only his future did.

Andrew stared down at her. "You think it could be that way with us?"

She shook her head. "I think it **is** that way with us. You're the man I've always looked for. The one man who sees me."

When they returned to the cabin, he built up the fire while she moved about the kitchen. He lit the lantern and began to read her the story he was working on about a little boy who thought he was the marshal of his family farm. He investigated an egg theft and rounded up outlaws who disguised themselves as pigs.

Beth laughed as she listened, drawing closer to him until her hand rested on his shoulder.

He almost lost his place in the story as she pressed her hip against his arm. The nearness of her felt so good. When he set the story aside, he pulled her down into his lap.

For a moment he just stared at her, and then he had to act. Without asking or talking it over, he kissed her deeply and completely, pulling her into the heaven he'd been longing for all day.

When she ended the kiss and stood, he didn't try to stop her. Making love to her was something he didn't want to talk her into.

"Andrew," she said as she stood just out of his reach, "I need to see your wound."

He brushed his leg where she'd been sitting. "You didn't hurt it, Bethie. It's healed. Don't worry about me."

"I need to see where the bullet went in." The stubborn streak he knew so well was back.

He stood, tugged off his boots, and unbuckled his trousers. Both pairs of his cotton long johns had been cut above the wound those first few days so Sage could doctor it. Since he had no others, Andrew was still wearing them, though all the blood had been washed away in the laundry. "When I get to town I'll buy some more underwear." Right now he was thankful for even the cut pair as he dropped his pants.

"I could—" she began.

"No. That's one thing a man would rather buy for himself. Don't you dare tell your mother to pick me up some—or worse, let that old man, Elmo, at the trading post choose my clothing."

She knelt before him and brushed her fingers over the small scab halfway between his hip and knee.

Her touch almost buckled his legs. It was so familiar, and he knew without asking that she'd brushed his leg many times in those first few hours after Sage had cut the bullet out. The doctor had given him something to help him sleep, but still he'd felt Beth's touch.

As he stood silent, she moved her hand over the tight muscle of his leg as if making sure he was well. Slowly, she traveled higher than he thought was necessary to simply check the wound, but he wasn't about to complain.

She leaned close as her fingers brushed along his leg in a gentle caress. "You're scared because of me."

"It doesn't matter, Beth," he whispered, thinking her touch was branding him far deeper than any scar.

She stood and unbuttoned his shirt. As she spread it open, her fingers touched the scar at his throat. He forgot to breathe as she kissed his throat. "I'm so sorry," she whispered against his skin still wet from her kiss.

He snapped like dry wood struck by lightning and pulled her mouth to his. She might be worrying about scrapes and cuts on his body; didn't she know that she had healed his heart?

At first she held back, not pulling away, but not completely relaxing. His hand molded over her as his mouth showed her how dearly he needed her. When she finally melted against him, out of breath and liquid in his arms, he lifted her, taking her with him into the shadows.

Moving the few feet to his bed, he laid

her atop the pile of boxes and newspapers. "Now it's my turn to check you for scars."

"I don't have any." She laughed as she shoved the mail aside and tried to scramble off the bed.

"I'll have to make sure." He tugged her back and began unbuttoning her blouse.

She leaned back, letting him have his way without protest. "Oh, all right, but you won't find any."

He kissed his way down her throat. "I need you so much," he said, forgetting everything but her nearness.

"I know. I haven't been able to sleep without you." She began unbuttoning the rest of his shirt and pushing it from his shoulders. "I need to feel you near me."

When he moved closer, she whispered, "Against me. Touching me. Loving me."

He kissed along her body as he undressed her and gave her what she wanted. Returning to her lips, he asked as he kissed her mouth, teasing it open, "You won't shoot me if I pull the ribbons free tonight? It's time we stopped playing, Beth, and started feeling."

She didn't answer, but lay back, her eyes

closed, as he pulled open the ribbons of her camisole one by one.

The sight of her took his breath away. She was so beautiful and she was waiting for him to love her. It seemed there had been no great storm of passion that consumed them, but a gentle rain that brought them together. She was here, in his bed, wanting him as much as he wanted her. All the reasons no longer mattered. This night would be only him and her. This night they'd make a memory that would hold true all their lives.

He moved his fingers over her, loving the way he made her feel almost as dearly as he loved touching her. When he looked in her eyes, he saw passion and need and . . . love. He also saw Beth, his Beth, the strong woman she was, the one woman he'd dreamed of touching like this.

Even as he kissed his way over every part of her, he knew she was giving him not just the gift of her body but of her love. She'd said she loved him once. She might never say it again, but once was enough.

He spread his hand wide and moved it slowly down from her throat, feeling across her soft breasts, sliding across her flat stomach and lower into the warmth between her legs.

"What do you want from me?" he whispered against her cheek. He was on the edge of insanity and needed her to say the words before he fell completely off.

"I want you to love me," she answered in a soft cry. "I want it to be real between us."

She wanted to be loved, and if he couldn't say the words, he'd do his best to show her how he felt. He claimed her mouth, catching her moans in a deep kiss as his hand began to please her. She crossed over into passion with him, hungry for more, but he didn't break the kiss, not until he moved above her. Then he held her gaze, wild with hunger and need as he entered her.

She cried out softly in pain, but he didn't stop and she didn't turn away. In the firelight shadows he watched her newborn obsession rise. Other times, they would make love in darkness with eyes closed, but this time, this first time, he wanted to see into her soul as they mated.

His chest lowered against her breasts

and she shook with pleasure, then whispered his name as he felt her body relax. Only then did he find his own pleasure. As the world rocked, he held her so tightly he feared he might have hurt her.

When finally he was able to speak, he whispered, "Are you all right?"

She rolled against him. "I don't think I've ever been better."

They laughed and teased and caressed as the night aged. Andrew had never felt so complete.

Finally, she took his hand and wrapped it between her breasts. "Good night, my love," she mumbled, already asleep.

He closed his eyes, drifting with all the feeling. As he fell asleep, Beth filled his dreams just as she filled his reality.

Sometime deep into the night, he felt her patting him and left one dream for another. Beth in his bed.

"That was wonderful." She sat up, pulling the covers with her. "Does it always feel so good?"

"No. I think we'll get better with practice." Even in the shadows she was so beautiful he had trouble thinking. "Shouldn't we be asleep?"

"No, I woke up and had questions, so, since you're the only one who can answer them, I had to wake you up too."

He smiled. Still spoiled rotten; at least she hadn't changed. "All right, ask away."

"So, it really gets better?" She didn't sound like she believed him.

Andrew leaned close and molded the sheet over one of her breasts.

"How soon can we practice again, Andrew?" She pushed his hand away.

"Practice what?" he said as he slipped his fingers beneath the sheet and captured her breast. He knew she would be tender, but the slight ache would be sweet with memory, so he molded her flesh and felt her breathing quicken.

"That's a good start, Andrew. A very good start."

"Beth." He loved the way her velvet curves brushed against him, begging him for more. "People don't talk about this. Not before and certainly not afterward."

"Why not?" she asked. "I loved it when your mouth covered my breast the same time you—"

He ended the discussion with a kiss. A long, deep kiss, that she was more than ready for. Her hunger for more both surprised and delighted him.

When he finally kissed his way across her cheek to her ear, he whispered, "If you'll stop talking we could start practicing again."

She shook her head and pulled away. Without a word, she wrapped a quilt around her and crossed the room. When she returned with her brush, she sat on the end of the bed and brushed away the tangles in her hair.

The sight of her reflected in firelight almost stopped his heart. As she raised her arms, the quilt dropped to just below her breasts. "I'll come to you when I'm ready," she finally said, "but I'll tell you the truth first."

He waited, feeling the need for her building again, twice as strong as before. At this rate, she'd kill him, for he wasn't sure he'd ever get enough of this woman.

"Andrew," she said, pulling the blanket higher, "I love you. Not the kind of love people talk about after meeting, but the forever kind. I know you don't want to love me, but I can't help loving you. I'll not try to stop you when you go, but whether you are with me or not, I'll not stop loving you."

He felt like his heart lodged in his throat and he couldn't say a word. He watched as she stood, dropped the quilt, and moved beneath the covers. Curling against him, she drifted off to sleep as if her confession had totally relaxed her.

He brushed her hair away from her face and wrapped it around his hand. For a while, he let his mind float backward in time to the months he'd been with Hannah. She'd been shy and needy for attention, but never passion. For the first time, he saw her clearly. She hadn't loved him as completely as he'd loved her. There had been times she'd agreed to sex, but he wasn't sure she'd liked it and she'd never spoken of it. They'd both wanted to be a family, but she'd only said she loved him when he'd asked. She'd never just declared it as a proclamation, asking nothing in return.

Beth had been open, even letting him watch her body as she combed her hair. He'd enjoyed mating. Even now, in sleep, she cuddled against him as if waiting for him to catch up with her and do it again. In all the mix of stories she'd told, first to save him and then to save herself, he'd learned her and he knew that this one time she hadn't lied. She truly loved him.

He brushed his hand over her warm body as he kissed her throat. "Wake up, dear, it's time to make love again."

She stretched, pushing her breasts against his chest. "Wake me up with your hands on me, Andrew."

And he did.

CHAPTER 35

THE NEXT MORNING ANDREW OPENED ONE EYE and saw Beth rushing about fully clothed, unfortunately, and making coffee.

"Wife." He said the word as if it were an endearment. "We're going to have to cure you of this infernal habit of waking up early. Come back to bed."

She laughed and came to him, carrying a cup of steaming coffee. "We promised we'd have breakfast with the kids, so you have to get up."

"No, come back to bed."

She smiled. "I'd like to. Last night was wonderful, Andrew." Setting the coffee on the table, she perched on the edge of the bed. "The first time was all new and I was half afraid I'd do something wrong; the second time was slow and I felt like I was floating; but the third time . . . The way you did that thing with your—"

He grabbed her arm and pulled her to him. After a quick kiss, he said, "Are you always going to talk about it? Beth, people just do it, they don't talk about it. I don't think it's proper conversation over breakfast."

"Why not? I think it would be fun to write a book about making love. Of course I've got a lot to learn first, so I'll have to practice and I'll have to use a pen name. My papa would kill me."

He cupped the back of her head and kissed her again. She might be headstrong, but she was adorable, and her talking about what they'd done filled his mind. He'd never made love so completely, and one night's taste of her body would never be enough.

When she giggled, he pulled away and raised an eyebrow. "You're teasing me about the book?"

"Of course. How else will I get you to

kiss me so early? Have you ever noticed you always kiss me when you want to shut me up?"

He reached to kiss her again.

She moved away before he could make his brain work. His woman was teasing him. No one ever teased him. Not lovingly. Not for fun.

"You're sleeping with me tonight, and I plan to make you pay by torturing you with the promise of a morning mating, then moving out of reach."

Her sweet innocent smile was back. "Sounds like fun. I'll make a note to allow time for that next time, but right now you have to get dressed."

They were still laughing as they walked toward the main house hand-in-hand. All he wanted to do was spend the day in bed, but she had other plans, and Beth wasn't a woman easily talked into changing her mind.

"Are you sure your leg is strong enough for this walk? It's almost a mile to the house."

He gripped her hand as he shortened his step to match hers. "I've been walking a little more each day. In truth, I think the bath helped more than anything, but I'm not moving back to the main house. While I'm here, I'll stay at the cabin."

He looked at her. "And you'll be staying with me at night."

She was silent. An ocean of unsaid words floated between them. They might talk about their mating, but they'd never talked of a future. He knew it was too late to walk away with his heart, but how would she react if he told her he wanted what they had to be real? She'd said she loved him, but she hadn't asked for love in return.

He held her hand tighter, wishing everything could stay exactly like it was now. Only he knew it couldn't. The world never stopped spinning and changing. There was so much he had to say to her, but he wanted it to be the right time, the right place.

As they walked in the crisp morning air, she told him about the horses raised on their ranch. Andrew only half-listened. Everything between them had changed last night in the little cabin. They'd changed. He'd stopped fighting his need for her, and she'd told him she loved him. The feelings were too raw to talk about. For now, it seemed all right to pretend there was only today.

Colby and the boys rushed out to greet them, Levi talking as fast as he could and Leonard smiling. Colby had already taken them riding at dawn, and Levi claimed he rode faster than the wind.

Andrew didn't miss the way Colby stared at Madie when she stepped onto the porch. She smiled at him.

"Mr. McLaughlin," Colby said, pulling off his hat as they entered the house, "I was wondering if I could have a word with you two before we go in with the others."

"Can this wait until after breakfast?" Andrew asked.

"No, sir," the cowboy answered.

Andrew nodded and crossed to the study with Beth beside him. "We must have trouble if it has to be talked about before we eat."

"No, sir," Colby answered, but he had the look of a man about to be shot.

Andrew studied him. "Just say what you need to say, Colby. You know we're on your side whatever happens."

Colby made an effort to stand still. He

cleared his throat twice and started. "Since you're the closest thing Madeline has to parents, I thought I'd ask you if I could marry her. We talked about my place last night, and she said she wouldn't mind living out on a ranch. I'd have to teach her to ride and shoot, but she says she's willing to learn."

Beth shook her head and moved forward to protest, but Andrew spoke first. "Are you sure you could provide for her?"

"I can. I got a nice house on my land, and I'm planning to run three hundred head come spring. There's a spot for a garden behind the house, and my grandma planted apple trees down by the stream. She and the baby wouldn't want for anything."

"Have you asked her?"

"No, not directly, but I mentioned it." Colby looked nervous. "I thought I'd talk to you first. Then, I'd tell her to pack."

Andrew swore he could feel the heat firing from Beth.

"You'll do no such thing," Beth snapped. "You'll ask her, right and proper, and if she says no, you'll walk away without saying a word to hurt her feelings."

Colby looked at Andrew and asked, "That's how it's done? I don't see no need of it. She'll marry me if I tell her to."

Andrew had no idea how it was done. He and Hannah just spent an evening talking and went to the courthouse the next day. She moved her things in that night.

He cleared his throat. "That's how a man does it, Colby. It's her decision, not yours. If she says no, you walk away."

Colby didn't look happy. "Then call her in now and I'll ask. I don't want to do any more planning if she's not smart enough to say yes."

Since Beth looked like she might hit Colby at any moment, Andrew asked her to go get Madie. While she was gone, he talked to the kid. Andrew felt like he knew little more than Colby about women, but Colby knew nothing.

Madie seemed frightened when she stepped into the study. "What's wrong?" she questioned. "Breakfast is ready."

"It will wait," Colby said. "I have something I want to ask you in front of witnesses."

Madie straightened, but her eyes showed her fright.

Colby awkwardly took her hand. "Madeline, will you marry me and come live with me?"

"All right," she said. "But I've been thinking about what you said last night and, if you won't sleep with me until after the baby comes, I want to stay here until then."

"But—"

She raised her head. "Mrs. McLaughlin said I was to speak my mind when I came in here. I love you, Colby, but I want a real wedding in a church with a white dress. I want a hope chest to bring with me that's full of all the things I've made, so your house will be my house too."

Colby frowned, glanced at Andrew, and then made up his mind. "All right. You stay here until the baby's born and you're recovered. It will be easier on you having other women around, but we marry now. I have to leave at dawn tomorrow and I'll know you're my wife before I go."

"But why?" Madie asked. "The wedding can wait a few months."

"No," Colby answered. "I need to know that you belong to me. I need a wife and you need me." He looked at Andrew as if remembering what he'd been told. "We'll make a good life together, you and me. I'll be kind to you."

"Do you love me, Colby?"

The cowboy blushed. "How could I not, Madie? I should tell you it wasn't something I planned, but when I left you in Fort Worth, you refused to leave my head. I need to be on my ranch, but I needed to see you more. The only peace I'll get in this life is if I have you with me."

Madie agreed. "Then we go to town today. You can find a preacher and ask if we can borrow the church. I'll buy a dress from the store."

Beth straightened like a soldier hearing the battle call. She'd planned parties for years; a wedding wouldn't be that different. "The McMurrays keep a little house next to the church in town. You can dress there while we make all the plans."

Andrew shook his head. "We can't leave the ranch. This is the one place we know we're safe. Beth, this doesn't make sense."

"It's the only thing that makes sense." Beth moved away from him. "We'll take guards. It will only be for a few hours, and

Madie will have the wedding she wants. You don't understand how important it is for a woman."

He looked over at Madie and Colby. They were both kids, probably having no idea how hard their lives would be, but as they looked at each other, he saw all he needed to see. They belonged together.

"All right. I'll talk to Tobin. We'll go in early and make sure everything is safe. All of you can drive in under guard later. Two hours in town. No more." Andrew reasoned that the only threat was Peterson, and he wasn't likely to pull anything in the middle of town. Besides, Peterson just wanted the map, and maybe Andrew dead. He wasn't after anyone else. "Two hours," he repeated, as if he thought they could pull off a wedding in that amount of time.

"Yes, dear," she said as she kissed his cheek and vanished to find her mother.

Six hours later Andrew stood next to Colby in the little chapel and watched Madie walk down the aisle in a white dress with bluebonnets embroidered on the hem. It was a size too big for her in the shoulders, but it fit around her waist.

Father Benjamin sang a song in French

that he said was a love song. With his beard now two inches long, he really was starting to look like a priest.

The young preacher, whom they'd found still moving into the parsonage, nervously performed what was obviously his first wedding. The boys and Tobin sat in the first row along with Beth and her mother. A line of old Texas Rangers who'd retired to Whispering Mountain sat in the back acting as guards.

When all the **I do**'s were said, they moved to the little house and had a late lunch. Madie cried with joy at each one of the gifts Jessie McMurray had bought and put a different person's name on.

Colby couldn't seem to stop smiling. Andrew heard him tell Madie that they were now a family, and before long he'd have to build onto the house to hold all the kids.

She kissed his cheek. "Promise me you'll never toss the oldest one out because we have too many."

"I promise," he said. "With each one I'll count it a blessing."

Andrew wasn't sure he'd ever given much thought to having children, but he doubted he'd ever be brave enough to tell a woman who seemed to get in a family way as easily as Madie did that he'd welcome as many as possible.

Beth moved beneath his arm. "It was a nice wedding even if we did have to put it together in a few hours."

"Do you ever wish you had a wedding, Beth?"

"No, I guess I'll stick to my plan to never marry once you leave me. I'll wait for a while, claiming you'll be back, and then I might wear black and tell everyone you died. After a year, I'll move into town, a respectable widow. There will be no wedding for me."

Suddenly the plan they'd talked about seemed terribly sad. He wanted to tell her that maybe there was a new plan if she'd consider keeping him on at the job of husband. But now wasn't the time or the place.

He tried to keep the mood light. "If I die in this plan of yours, do I have to show up in a box? I can manage to play a pretend husband, but I'm not so sure about a pretend corpse."

She shrugged. "I'll tell everyone you died at sea."

"You've got it all figured out, don't you, wife? What if I spoil your plan and stay around for a while? I wouldn't mind repeating last night a few thousand times."

She shook her head as her thoughts tumbled into words. "No. If you stayed, you'd have to marry me for real, and I'd never marry a man who wouldn't say he loved me."

Andrew closed his eyes. "Don't tease me, Beth; we promised we would never lie to each other. Not about this. You must know how deeply I care for you."

"I'm not teasing. I'm stating a fact. Because of last night I know what paradise I'm giving up, but if you can't love me, then you have to leave me."

Other people circled around them and he had no time to say more. He wanted to tell her how much she meant to him, but not like this. Not in a room full of people. Not because she'd driven him to it.

They were silent on the way home. Beth sat at his side and joined all the others in conversation. He could feel the warmth of her leg pressed against his. He could see her frosty breath in the cold air, but she seemed a million miles away.

When they reached the main house, she climbed out with the others, and he knew he'd be sleeping alone tonight. She was stubborn, headstrong, spoiled, and about to drive him mad.

"Beth," he shouted as she reached the door. "Could you bring me that journal I left in the parlor?"

"Of course."

Andrew stood waiting, feeling more alone than he had in his entire life. He wanted to tell her he loved her somewhere romantic, not in front of her house because she'd forced him to make a choice. How could she not know how he felt about her after last night? How could she be so stubborn?

When she came back, he tossed the journal into the wagon and grabbed one of the bedrolls always left under the seat. "Walk with me," he ordered, more than asked.

She hesitated, stuffing something in her pocket to buy time. But Father Benjamin stepped out to watch them and she must have decided not to make a scene.

"Where are we going?" she whispered as soon as they were away from the house.

"We're going to climb the mountain and sleep on the summit."

"But it'll be dark in a few hours, and I've told you what happens up there. The dreams my family have had there have not always been good."

"I don't care. We'll build a fire and sleep there. Then, in the morning, we'll know where this is heading between me and you."

"But your leg?"

"I'll make the climb fine. What I will not be able to do is sleep alone without you. Stay with me one more night, Beth. One more night on the summit and we'll know our future."

She shook her head, but he kept pulling her to the path leading up the mountain.

When they reached the lookout point where the McMurrays always climbed to survey their land, both were out of breath.

Andrew stopped to rest. He turned her hand loose as they sat on the huge rocks. If she broke and ran back down now, he didn't have the energy to chase her.

"This won't work, Andrew." She finally gulped out words between breaths. "I'm not a true McMurray. I told you my mother married Teagan McMurray when I was a baby. I won't have the dream."

He almost told her he didn't believe in the legend anyway, but he'd started this crazy quest and he planned to finish it. "We're not climbing off this mountain until sunrise. I've got things to say to you and I'll say them before we climb down."

She looked at him at that moment as if she hated him, but she didn't say a word. She stood and started the climb. Now there was no trail to follow and only one direction to go . . . up.

His leg burned, but he didn't slow. Sometimes she waited for him to catch up. Sometimes he pulled her along, but they didn't stop until they reached the flat summit.

Without talking, they gathered enough firewood to last the night. While he built the fire, she spread out the bedroll and sat down, hugging her knees for warmth. The sun sank, setting the western horizon on fire, and then darkness settled in around them.

"I don't suppose you brought any food?" she asked.

"Nope. I'd take that piece of cake you

offered me after the wedding. It would taste real good about now."

"I'd go for a glass of wine and some of the cheese. My mom always makes the best little sandwiches for gatherings. I should have put them in my pockets just in case my crazy husband wanted to go for a walk later."

He smiled, hoping she was teasing him again. She was right. He'd gone completely mad since he'd met her.

"It was a nice wedding," Andrew said, just to break the silence. "I'm glad Colby got a room at the hotel. Madie looked tired. He said he'd bring her back here tomorrow before he headed to his place."

She cuddled a little closer to him. "Colby tried to leave money for Madie's keep, saying that she was his responsibility now. I finally took the money, thinking I'd give it to her to buy what she'd need for the baby. By the time Colby gets back, she'll have a wagonload to move."

Andrew sat beside Beth on the bedroll and offered his arm as her backrest. "They're so young. You think they have a chance? They hardly know each other."

"As much as anyone." She giggled. "Better than I knew you when we married."

"You didn't know me at all. You thought I was a train robber." He knew they weren't talking about what needed to be said between them, but he thought it best to give them both time to relax.

As the night aged, they talked about their adventure, and he saw all the color she'd brought to his world. Piece by piece he figured out just how much she'd changed his life. In the dark, when he couldn't see her beauty at all, he still couldn't turn away.

When the wind whipped up, they cuddled into the bedroll and fell asleep listening to the other breathe.

"Beth." He whispered what he'd been wanting to say. "I don't have to dream tonight. I already know I'm in love with you. I think I always have been from the moment I saw you on the train. If it's fatal, then I die. If it's not, I'll live the rest of my days by your side."

She didn't answer, but he smiled. He'd said the words he thought he'd never be able to say again. When he repeated them in the morning, it wouldn't be so hard.

CHAPTER 36

BETH WOKE AS THE SUN SPARKLED ALONG THE treetops. Andrew was against her side, his arm folded over her, warming her, protecting her. She thought of the one page she'd torn from his journal last night. One line he'd written on the back page as if hiding his feelings away. **If beauty had a voice it would whisper Beth.**

His words warmed her heart. The one line had been the reason she'd climbed the mountain with Andrew. He might not tell her how he felt, but he'd written it.

The sun reminded her it was late. She'd slept later than she could ever remember sleeping, and, even on the ground, she'd slept solid in his arms.

She tried to remember what she'd dreamed, but it was too late, she couldn't catch it.

They'd wasted their time. She'd ruined her best dress climbing the mountain. Her mother was probably worried sick about her and all for nothing. She'd have no dream to take down from the mountain.

As she listened to Andrew snoring softly, she thought of all the lies she'd told and wondered if one more would matter. Maybe if she told Andrew that she'd dreamed of a big wedding with him as the groom, he'd decide that it would be all right for them to marry. Or maybe if she told him she'd dreamed of them with gray hair, rocking on a porch together, he'd stop worrying about her dying on him.

Slowly, she realized that at some point the lies had to stop. He'd put up with them all, but he'd never lied to her and she couldn't lie to him. She'd told him she loved him and meant it. He was the kindest man she'd ever met. She couldn't lie to him, not even to keep him.

When she tossed more wood on the

fire, he opened one eye. "Up early again, I see."

"I didn't dream," she pouted, "or at least I don't remember it, and now there is no coffee or breakfast."

"It's good to see you didn't lose your spoiled ways. I thought a night sleeping on the ground might change you and I'd have to take a new woman back down." He winked at her. "By the way, I did dream."

Before he could say more, her papa's voice came bellowing out from the trees. "Step back, Bethie, while I shoot that lying, no-account of a man with you."

Beth turned in time to see Teagan McMurray storm out of the trees with the priest and both of his brothers trailing behind him. They looked like a hunting party and she was standing between them and the prey.

"On second thought," he yelled, "I think I'll kill him slow with my bare hands. The priest told me he dragged you up here against your will, so you can watch."

Beth stood and faced the papa she'd loved since her first memories. "Don't you dare kill my husband, Papa."

Andrew had the good sense to look

frightened, but to his credit, he didn't run. He stood his ground beside her.

Teagan slowed and his brothers closed rank. Both her uncles were frowning, looking like they planned to watch Teagan beat Andrew to death as long as it was a fair fight. It didn't seem to matter that Teagan outweighed Andrew by fifty pounds and had lived his life outdoors. The man who wrote children's stories seemed like fair game to them.

"Back away, Mr. McMurray," Andrew said almost calmly. "How about telling us what you're so upset about?"

Teagan didn't look like he planned to explain anything, but he asked, "Are you or are you not married to my daughter, because if you're not—"

"Save the threats. I get the picture." Andrew stepped in front of Beth. "Who told you I wasn't married to her?"

Travis, always the lawyer, jumped in. "The boy, Levi, told Father Benjamin that he heard you two talking about a make-believe marriage back when you were living together in Fort Worth."

Teagan butted in. "The priest told me that you two slept together night before last"—he glanced at the bedroll—"and obviously last night. No one sleeps with a woman he's not married to, right?"

Beth didn't miss that both her uncles looked away.

"Right!" Her papa answered his own question. "So, I'm asking one more time, while you still have teeth, are you married to my daughter?"

"No," Andrew answered. "But I would be if she'd have me. I'd marry her anytime, anywhere."

For a moment her strong father looked confused, then angry. He turned to her. "You won't marry him, Beth? Why'd you bring him home and tell us you already were?"

"I will marry him, Papa. I promise I will. Things just happened so fast and we thought we'd just pretend to be married, but I fell in love with him and then he had to think about it and then we decided to sleep on it."

"I do not want to hear about that part." Teagan glared at them both. "Let me get this straight. You want to marry her." He pointed to Andrew. "And you want to marry him." He pointed at his daughter. "You've got the rings and you've already had the honeymoon. Appears all we need is a preacher."

"Or a priest," Uncle Travis chimed in with a smile. He almost lifted Father Benjamin off the ground as he moved the man from behind Teagan to stand in front of everyone.

"Not Father Benjamin." Andrew shook his head.

"Why not?" Teagan slapped his future son-in-law on the shoulder so hard Andrew stumbled forward. "We can fix this problem right now before your mother finds out about it, Bethie. It would break her heart if she thought you two weren't hitched. She tells me she loves having a writer in the family, and you know for a fact that if my Jessie wants something I'm going to damn well make it happen, so marry the man."

Beth nodded, but saw Andrew glare at the priest.

Father Benjamin was nudged forward by both the uncles.

"Go ahead," Teagan said removing his hat. "I figure this is about as near to heaven as any church."

"Dearly beloved, we are gathered here today to join—"

"Isn't the service supposed to be in Latin?" Andrew asked, still looking like he was thinking of killing the priest.

"It is, my son, but I thought I'd translate as I went along. Now where was I? Dearly beloved, we are gathered—"

"Wait," Andrew interrupted again. "Beth, don't you want a wedding in a church like we saw yesterday with your papa to walk you down the aisle? A white dress? Wedding cake? All the trimmings?"

"No, thank you, dear. This will do just fine."

Teagan locked Andrew's arm in an iron grip. "Stop interrupting the priest or you won't remember the ceremony."

"I've already been to that service," Andrew mumbled.

Teagan shook him like a rag doll. When he stopped, he mumbled to his future son-in-law, "Pay attention."

With all watching, Andrew leaned forward almost politely in a bow, caught Teagan by the leg, and flipped the big man into the dirt. Then, before Beth's uncles could come to the rescue, Andrew barred

Teagan's arms at his sides with the rifle and clamped his hand on Teagan's throat.

"I'll marry your daughter, sir, but not by force. If you want to be conscious to give the bride away, you might think twice before trying to bully me into doing anything."

Teagan struggled but couldn't move.

No one in the history of his life had ever knocked Teagan off his feet. All the McMurrays including Beth stood frozen, waiting to see what he would do.

Nothing. Her big powerful papa did nothing.

Andrew released Teagan's throat and offered his hand.

Teagan took it. "Where did you learn to fight like that?"

"The streets of Berlin," Andrew answered. "I'll show you the move once I'm in the family, and, Mr. McMurray, let me say that I'm honored to have a great man like you as a father-in-law."

Teagan never took compliments well. "The jury is still out on you, son, but it's good to know you can protect my baby girl."

"With my life, sir."

Teagan nodded. "I'd expect nothing

less." He dusted off as he told the priest to continue.

Beth expected him to be angry or even embarrassed, but, in the oddest way, her papa seemed proud.

The priest cleared his throat. "Take your places and we'll begin again. Dearly beloved, we are gathered here to join . . ."

She didn't remember all the words he said. All Beth remembered was that she was truly married on the summit of Whispering Mountain and no one, not even her father, had forced Andrew into anything.

CHAPTER 37

AN HOUR LATER WHEN THEY ALL CLIMBED DOWN from the mountain, no one, not even Teagan, mentioned what had happened.

They all ate a late breakfast in the dining room, now crowded and noisy.

Travis filled them in on what was happening in Austin. Lamont LaCroix had told a grand story about thinking he was saving his fiancée only to find out that she'd secretly married another. He did such a fine job of acting that the judge released him on his own recognizance until the trial.

"The bad news," Travis boomed over

the others, "is that we all have to go to La-
Croix's trial to testify. I asked for a few
days to ensure Andrew's full recovery, but
I'm afraid if we don't show up, the man will
get away with shooting one of us."

Beth couldn't hide her grin. Andrew had
become one of them.

As the family always did, they planned.
Jessie and Tobin would stay at the ranch
with the boys and Madie since none of
them were in the room during the shooting, so couldn't testify.

Everyone but Andrew seemed happy
that the little priest offered to stay with
them as well. Teagan, Travis, Andrew, and
Beth would take the train in two days. Travis said he'd send a wire to the judge to
set the trial so that they would be in Austin
for as short a time as possible.

Everything around her was the same,
but Beth felt different. She'd heard her
mother say once about a couple living together that marriage wasn't a game you
could play at. Maybe she was right. Something had settled in Beth. For better or
worse. In sickness and in health.

She looked at Andrew listening to everyone talk, taking it all in, probably already

thinking of how he'd get each feeling, each story, each emotion down on paper.

He'd married her. Not because he had to, but because he wanted to.

Finally, the subject turned to the newlyweds. Travis spoke first. "Bethie, now you're married, I'm guessing you'll want a house somewhere on the property. Em and Lewt took the hunting cabin way up in the north pasture, and Rose and Duncan are still having too much fun traveling to settle down." He looked at Andrew. "Drum and I talked when I stopped by the sheriff's office in town, and he says you can have the cabin for a while, but soon as the boys are grown, he wants it back."

"We could build them a house or let them have the little place in town," Jessie suggested.

Andrew finally spoke. "We'll be going back to Fort Worth. I have a place there."

Teagan nodded. "Strange place. A row of two-story homes built stuck together. He's so surrounded by houses he can't see the sunrise or the sunset."

Everyone at the table shook their heads, except Andrew and Beth. The thought of spending time alone in Andrew's funny house didn't seem such a bad idea to her.

As usual, Teagan offered his opinion. "We'll talk about it in the spring. By then Madie will be moving to her new home and the boys' father will probably be coming to pick them up. I told the rangers to put out a notice that we're looking for him."

Everyone seemed to agree. Beth looked at Andrew and shrugged as if to say she was sorry. Somehow their lives had been taken over by committee vote.

He reached for her hand. "It's all right. I can write here for the time being. I'll sleep anywhere as long as you're in my bed."

She knew he was still thinking that Chesty Peterson might be coming to get them, but with each day the chances seemed smaller.

When the talk turned to the outlaw, Andrew explained to everyone about the map and how Peterson might try to reach him, even in Austin.

Tobin suggested Andrew carry a gun, but the writer refused.

The priest asked to see the map. When Andrew pulled the pouch from his inside coat pocket, Father Benjamin spread it out on the table, studied it a minute, then seemed to lose interest.

As the morning aged, everyone scattered except Andrew. The McMurrays had work to do, the boys had lessons, and the women were all quilting on a huge frame set up in the great room that he'd thought had no purpose.

Beth watched her new husband wander into the study, looking over the shelves of books. He didn't belong on a ranch. She could almost feel his restlessness to walk the streets of a town. Half the time, when the family talked of ranching problems, she wasn't even sure he understood. Their adventures were outdoors, fighting the weather and taming the land, but his were in his mind. Slowly, as she watched him, she realized what a lonely career he'd chosen. He had his imagination, but no one to share the adventures he created in his thoughts.

"I'm going to pack up supplies. I thought I'd cook dinner at the cabin tonight," she said, feeling like what they had between them was suddenly newborn.

"It doesn't matter. I don't mind coming in."

She touched his arm. "Want to tell me about your dream now?"

He shook his head. "Later. I think I'll go back to the cabin and work awhile."

"I'll come with you."

"No. I'll go alone." He walked to the hallway and reached for his hat. "You stay here and visit with the women. I've read that quilting bees can be great fun."

"They are nice. We talk and laugh. I grew up taking my nap beneath quilting frames."

He turned and smiled at her as if seeing the little girl everyone called Bethie in the woman.

"When Colby brings Madie back, we'll stop for lunch and all give her advice. She's an old married lady now."

He watched her, and for the first time she saw the love in his eyes. It frightened her a little. Andrew was a man who loved deeply, and she couldn't help but wonder if she'd be able to return that kind of love.

Not caring who was watching, she walked up to him and kissed his mouth lightly.

Before she could think of anything to say, he was gone. When they'd been almost married he couldn't keep his hands off her; now he didn't even say good-bye. Only she had no doubt he'd be back before dark.

Madie would build her hope chest while

waiting for the baby. For years Beth had had hers packed full of all the things she'd made, but now that she was married, she didn't feel like she had a home to take them to. Andrew's place in Fort Worth wasn't a real home, and neither was the little cabin that belonged to her aunt and uncle.

What if he wanted to move to New York or Boston? She'd never lived anywhere but here. She hadn't seriously considered marrying Lamont until he'd said that they'd be living in Austin. In the back of her mind she knew they'd have to go to Washington, D.C., part of every year if he was elected a senator again, but that would just be a visit. Her home would be in Texas.

Beth sat at the study window and watched Andrew drive away in the wagon. He didn't even want her to cook supper, so she guessed asking him to talk about where they'd build a house was probably out of the question.

She'd married a man who had no roots. A stranger. And this time the marriage was for real.

CHAPTER 38

ANDREW FOUGHT TO KEEP FROM RACING BACK to the cabin. He needed to be alone. All the talk. All the people. He felt smothered. When he'd said yes to marrying Beth on the mountain, he'd thought he was marrying her, not a tribe.

Then, the impossible happened. His mood darkened even more when he looked up and saw Benjamin standing in the doorway of the cabin.

"What do you want?" Andrew snapped as he climbed from the wagon.

"Now don't get mad at me," the little man answered. "I'm not the one who got you in this mess. I only married you two to keep that father-in-law you admire from killing you."

"No, you didn't marry us. You're not a real priest, remember." Andrew pushed past him and stepped into the cold cabin.

"I know that and you know that, but everyone else thinks I'm the real thing, even your wife. I've played my part well."

"Yes you have, Benjamin." Andrew shoved logs into the old stove. "And if my father-in-law ever finds out, he'll shoot us both."

"What difference does it make if you jump the broom or just tell folks you're married? To my way of thinking, if you say you're married, you are. Do you really think every circuit preacher has the right to marry folks by law?" The priest made himself at home by putting on a pot of coffee to boil and pulling a day-old muffin from the tin by the stove. "I climbed that damn mountain to save your life, Andrew. You're lucky I was there."

"Priests shouldn't swear," he mumbled to himself, then raised his voice. "Why are you here, Benjamin? Haven't you made a big enough mess of things for one day? Go back and play priest at the main house."

"I'm here about the map, but first answer me one question. Are you married in your heart?"

"I don't deserve her," Andrew answered. "But I don't want to live without her." He raised his eyebrow. "However, I think I could get along without all the family and friends butting into our lives." He stormed halfway to the door and then turned. "In answer to your question, yes. I love her. She is my heart."

"Then nothing else matters. You're married. You were, I think, even before this morning. She's in your blood, Andrew, so you might as well get used to it and stop thinking of yourself as alone."

"You're lecturing me about marriage? Fleas have more staying power than you obviously have."

Benjamin waved his hands. "I know. I know. Consider me the bad example. If you care about her, don't wander in and out of her life. Be her life just as I think she wants to be yours."

Andrew closed his eyes. The actor was

right. He had to give it a try. He'd shut
people out long enough.

When he opened his eyes, he stared at
the little man. "You still here?"

Benjamin pouted. "I told you I came to
talk about the map."

"Right." Andrew patted the pouch still in
his pocket. "What about the map? You're
planning to steal it, right? Lift it, or kill me
and take it, then run off on a treasure hunt?"

"No," Benjamin said as he chewed on
half the muffin. "I drew it or at least one
just like it." When Andrew laughed, he
added, "A few years ago in Galveston a
group of us came up with a scheme to
make some quick money. We soaked paper in tea, aging it. We even burned the
edges a little and rubbed it in dirt to make
the folds seem worn. Then we drew maps.
No one knows much about the Palo Duro
Canyon, so we could pretty well do what
we wanted. I remember burying my make-
believe stash of gold in a cave halfway
between the bottom of the canyon and the
rim."

Andrew was hooked. He sat down across
from the little man. "Go on."

Benjamin smiled. "It was a game, really.

Six of us. The one who could get the most money for the map won. The Gold of the Palo Duro has been a legend for a hundred years. It wasn't that hard to convince people that the map was real. I sold mine to a gambler who, I heard, lost it in a card game."

"So," Andrew said, "Peterson may be looking for me, maybe even willing to kill me, for a map to nowhere?"

"That's about the size of it. What are you going to do?"

"I'm going to keep it close when I leave the ranch. If Peterson does show up, I plan to hand it over."

"If he's out of jail, he'll show up. I've spent my life following wild hunches and dreams. I figure the kind of man who'd rob trains would also kill for this map."

Andrew stood and poured them each a cup of coffee. "Why tell me this?"

"Because you've been honest with me. You kept your word about not telling anyone who I am. You offered to bring my boys to me. I guess I didn't like the thought of you risking your life over a map that's fake. Hand it over without hesitation. Outlaws usually don't ask twice."

"If Chesty ever shows up, I'll do that."

They talked for a while, and then Andrew let Benjamin take the wagon back to the house, knowing that Beth would be out to get him for dinner. He needed time to think about all that had happened and to write.

Just as he knew she would, Beth came to get him an hour before sunset. He'd been standing by the stream thinking of her when she drove up. He went to the side of the wagon but climbed up instead of helping her down.

"I missed you today." He wondered if it was proper to kiss one's wife every time he saw her.

"Did you get lots of writing done?"

"No, I mostly just thought." He fought down a smirk. "It takes a ton of goofing off to be a writer."

"Apparently." She laughed.

They talked of nothing: the day, the weather, the trip into Austin. Neither mentioned the wedding they'd had that morning or the future. She didn't ask him about the dream he'd had.

Everyone seemed tired at dinner. The conversation moved, but slowly like a quiet stream, no longer a rushing river.

After supper, Andrew sat on a blanket by the fire in the great room and read one of his stories to the boys. Madie, as always, drifted in with her sewing to listen, and tonight Benjamin joined them.

When Andrew finished his tale, he looked up and saw the rest of the family standing in the shadows of the room.

Teagan spoke first. "I'm glad I didn't kill you, Andrew."

Jessie patted his chest and translated, "He loved your story. We all did. Will you read another soon? Just think, we're hearing your stories before anyone else in the world does."

Andrew nodded, too touched to say a word.

Beth saved him by offering her hand. "Come along, dear, we need to be going so everyone can get to bed."

He didn't argue, only followed her out. On the ride home, he couldn't think of anything to say. He wanted to tell her his dream, but he wasn't sure it might not frighten her more than not knowing.

They walked into the cabin. He watched as she moved about, turning down the bed, brushing out her hair, slipping out of her nightgown. His wife, he thought; legal or not, they were married.

"You coming to bed, dear?" she asked, slipping beneath the covers as though she'd done so in front of him a hundred times.

"In a minute," he said, moving out onto the porch. The fact that he knew they weren't really married ate away at his gut. One lie. He shouldn't start a marriage, a real marriage, with one lie.

He couldn't tell her about Benjamin, he decided, but he could tell her one truth.

Walking back inside, he made up his mind.

He stood at the side of the bed and removed his clothes. When he moved in beside her, her bare body touched his.

"You're cold," she whispered, sounding half asleep.

He lifted her into his arms, pulling her from the covers. "Are you awake?"

"Yes, but we need to get back—"

"No. I need to make sure you're awake. Bethie McMurray, will you marry me? I'm crazy in love with you and I want to ask you. Beth, marry me."

She punched him on the shoulder. "You

fool, we **are** married, now put me back under the covers."

"I'll hear a yes first."

"Yes. I'll marry you."

He moved them beneath the quilts and held her close. "Good. Don't say I didn't ask you."

"All right, but I'm not telling our grandchildren about how and when you asked me."

He kissed her gently. "Just tell them one thing, wife. Tell them I loved you."

There were no more words between them, only a sweet passion that they both craved so dearly.

CHAPTER 39

BETH WASN'T SURPRISED WHEN ANDREW WORE his dress clothes to the trial. They'd talked a tailor into opening his shop the night their train got in so he could buy a suitcase full of clothes. While the sleepy tailor fitted him, Andrew explained that marriage seemed to be hard on a man's wardrobe.

Then he looked over and said to her, "When we're on the ranch, I'll wear western clothes, but in town, I wear the suits I've always worn."

She didn't argue. He looked a very proper gentleman, nothing like the outlaw who'd saved her in the train wreck, but still very much the man she loved. After three nights of lovemaking she'd decided she liked him best wearing nothing at all.

They testified separately while the other waited in the hallway outside the trial. Beth paced, wishing she could see what was happening when alone in the hallway, but she knew Andrew wrote. He always wrote. When he was upset. When he was happy. When he was worried.

Once he left his journal with her, she discovered the beginnings of a poem to her on the back page.

At the end of the day, they sat side by side and listened to the judge's verdict. Lamont LaCroix had refused to look at her or Andrew during the trial, and he didn't break his habit now. He stared straight at the judge as the sentence was announced.

"Three years in a Texas prison," the judge said simply, "or a lifetime of never stepping foot in Texas again."

"I'll be on the next train." Lamont let out a long breath. "I swear I'll never return."

"If you do, you'll serve all three years." The judge adjourned.

For a moment, everyone just stood still, and then Lamont turned and looked at

Andrew. "I can't believe she settled for you," LaCroix shouted, in hopes of embarrassing Andrew.

"Me either." Andrew shrugged. "But she did."

The senator walked out of the courtroom.

Teagan gathered up his hat and coat. "Can't believe the judge was so hard on him. Out of Texas for life."

Beth looked up at Andrew and saw his confusion. She couldn't help but laugh. Only a Texan would think that a horrible sentence to have to live with.

They walked back to the hotel, talking of things they wanted to pick up before heading back to Whispering Mountain. The boys needed new clothes. Madie could use a few things made for this time in her life.

Once at the hotel, Andrew had talked her into ordering a meal delivered from the restaurant below so they could enjoy the evening in peace. Her father and uncle had made plans to have dinner with a group of rangers, and she was looking forward to being alone with her husband.

She wasn't surprised after they ate that

he pulled on his coat and said he thought he'd walk awhile. She took the time to take a bath and put on a new nightgown she'd bought. Things were settling down and it was time for them to talk about their future.

As she curled up in the chair by the window, someone tapped on the door.

"Come in," she said, not looking up from her reading. "I'm finished with the tub."

A low voice answered, "I didn't come for the tub, pretty lady."

Beth looked up, recognizing the voice of the outlaw she'd heard one night a lifetime ago when she'd bought a pinto.

"Mr. Peterson." She forced down her fear, realizing her gun was still packed in her case.

"Mrs. McLaughlin. It's been a long time since I've seen you." He stepped into the room and closed the door. "It took me a while, but I figured out you married Andrew. I have some settling to do with him. Doesn't it seem strange to you that he was the only one of my men to survive the train wreck?"

"He was never one of your men. You're too smart to have thought that. An unarmed man doesn't join an outlaw gang."

A possibility formed in her mind. "You knew he was a writer and my guess is you were filling him full of stories."

Chesty Peterson laughed so hard that dust shook off him in a cloud. "You're not only pretty, but smart. Wouldn't want to leave that man of yours and come along with me? As soon as I get the map, I'll be a rich man. I could buy you the moon."

She shook her head. "Thanks for the offer, but I don't know what I'd do with the moon; besides, I'm crazy about Andrew. Always have been. Maybe he didn't die that night because he wasn't thinking of the robbery, he was busy saving my life."

"So you married him as a thank-you, pretty lady?"

"No, I had to really work at getting him to fall in love with me. I, as it happened, fell for him at first sight."

"Love at first sight, was it? That happened to me with my first wife," Chesty admitted, obviously enjoying the fact that he didn't frighten Beth. "I've always wished I'd had a little of the second sight that day. I finally got up enough nerve to run, but I wouldn't be surprised if she's not still looking for me."

Beth laughed just as Andrew pushed the door open.

Peterson stepped closer to her and pulled his gun. He looked tough enough to kill them both without blinking.

Beth had to do something fast, before Andrew was shot.

"Welcome back, dear. We have company."

Andrew moved a few steps inside and closed the door. "I can see that," he said. "Step away from my wife, Chesty. I'll give you what you came for, but don't hurt her."

Peterson looked offended. "I didn't come to hurt her. I came to kill you. I was just trying to talk her into marrying me while I waited for you to come back."

"He doesn't have the map," Beth said. "I do, and I'm not giving it to you."

Peterson kept his gun pointed straight at Andrew. "You're lying."

"No, I'm not. I pulled it from his pocket and hid it. You'll never find it. You'll never find the treasure unless you bargain with me."

Both men looked confused.

Peterson backed against the wall. "So

I'm bargaining with you again, pretty lady. Name your price."

"I want my husband alive. I'll give you the map if you'll leave without firing a shot."

"All right." Peterson didn't look like he trusted her, but he seemed to be playing along.

"Don't, Beth, he'll kill us both." Andrew stared at her as if he were thinking they would both be dead in a minute and he wanted her to be the last thing he saw.

"I've bargained with him before, Andrew, and found him a man of his word. Do I have your word, Mr. Peterson? You'll leave Andrew alive if I hand over the map?"

"You do." Peterson straightened.

Beth pulled the pouch from under the rug and handed it to him. "It was nice doing business with you."

Chesty smiled. "And with you, pretty lady. If you ever decide you want a new husband, you'll find me up in the panhandle digging out gold."

"I'll remember that." Beth walked past Andrew and opened the door for Peterson. "Good night, Mr. Peterson, and good luck."

When he was gone, Andrew grabbed

her by the shoulders. "Don't ever do that again, dear. I thought for a moment I'd lost you."

"You don't mind that I gave up the map to the Gold of the Palo Duro?"

He pulled her to him. "I've got all I want and need in this life. The map is nothing to me. Only, dear, you need to get dressed."

"But it's late. I'm already ready for bed."

"I've got a surprise waiting for you downstairs."

Beth pouted, but she changed into her clothes as Andrew watched, and then he took her hand and almost ran down the stairs.

There, in a little drawing room off the main lobby, the judge waited for them.

Before she could greet him, Andrew said, "Here she is, Judge. I want you to marry us right now."

"But . . ." She seriously considered the possibility that her dear husband might have snapped and begun living in fiction. "We're already married."

"Will you say the words again?" Andrew asked. "You haven't changed your mind?"

"No, dear." She played along. "Of course I'll marry you again."

As the judge read through the brief ceremony, he turned to her. "Do you promise to love and cherish him all the days of your life?"

"I do," she answered, loving the warm forever look in Andrew's eyes.

He took both her hands. "And I promise you'll be forever in my heart and we'll make our home forever in Texas."

Beth jumped into his arms. He'd given her all she ever wanted, a man who loved her and a home. At that moment she realized that she would have moved anywhere with him. He was her life and she was his heart.

As they walked back up the stairs, she whispered, "Andrew, you didn't have to promise that in front of the judge."

"Yes, I did. It was the only way I could make the dream I had when we slept on the summit come true."

"What did you dream?"

He held her close. "I dreamed that all our children were born in Texas."

EPILOGUE

THE LEAVES AROUND THE COLLEGE CAMPUS were changing from green to brilliant reds and yellow as Andrew walked beside Levi and Leonard. In the months he'd had them in his home, they'd grown and matured. A sadness had settled over them both when they'd said good-bye to their father almost six months ago, but he'd kept in touch with letters.

"You sure he's here?" Levi asked. "This isn't the kind of place my father would be."

"His last letter said he'd meet us here."

A thin man wearing a funny hat came

toward them. A gentleman with a flair about him.

Andrew smiled. "Professor Smith, I believe."

Both boys stared for a moment, then ran into the professor's waiting arms.

Benjamin looked like a man whose heart was exploding with joy. He winked at Andrew. "It took me a while, but with the right papers I'm now teaching here at the college. I have a cottage on campus that will suit the three of us."

"I'm glad," Andrew answered. "I'll miss them."

Benjamin held his sons. "I'll read them your stories. I see another collection is due to come out soon. What's it called?"

Andrew couldn't hide a hint of pride as he answered, "**Peterson's Gold.**"

As they turned to walk away, Andrew added, "Bethie told me to remind you to come for Christmas. She's already planning. Colby, Madie, and the baby will be at Whispering Mountain too."

Benjamin shook his head. "I don't know if the McMurrays would welcome me."

"Of course they will. I've already read them a story about a man who loved his sons so much he pretended to be a priest to get close to them. They think you're a grand hero."

"Papa," Leonard said. "Can we go home now?"

Benjamin took his sons' hands and nodded his thanks to Andrew. "Take care of Bethie."

"I will." Andrew turned and walked away, thinking he could just catch the midnight train and be back to her before dawn.